PRAISE FOR

Brontë's Mistress

"A convincingly multifaceted picture of Lydia, a smart, passionate woman who is caught between her own thwarted desires and the gears of society's conventions . . . Austin has written a stirring defense of the maligned Mrs. Robinson, and who can say if it isn't also the truth?"

—*THE CHRISTIAN SCIENCE MONITOR*

"A truly intoxicating combination of literary mystery and passionate love affair that will appeal not only to Brontë fans and scholars, but to historical fiction and romance lovers alike. Whether or not you were already familiar with Lydia Robinson prior to reading this novel, you are sure to be swept away by Austin's dazzling prose and creative imagining of the truth behind Branwell's spectacular downfall—and his mistress's role in it."

—*BOOKREPORTER*

"*Brontë's Mistress* is reminiscent of the novels of the Brontë sisters, but with a modern sentiment and enough subtlety that I needed to have it pointed out in the author's note. (Speaking of which: read the author's note. It was as fascinating as the rest of the novel.)"

—*SAN FRANCISCO BOOK REVIEW*

"Austin's passion for all things nineteenth-century England glows in this marvelous debut. She skillfully resurrects a slice of buried history, grounding *Brontë's Mistress* in actual characters and events. The irresistible details of the scandal and its dramatic aftermath, however, are wholly her own impressive creation."

—*SHELF AWARENESS*

"Austin [allows] Lydia to shed the title of 'mistress' to reveal a complex woman with a story of her own."

—*POPSUGAR*

"While *Brontë's Mistress* is an extremely satisfying read, Austin's greatest stroke of brilliance is her Author's Note. . . . In addition to a convincing story that gets us thinking about Lydia Robinson's behaviors and motivations in an era that surely repressed and constrained her, we are privy to the author's unique journey as she weighs fact and fiction and determines the balance."

—*BRONTË STUDIES: THE JOURNAL OF THE BRONTË SOCIETY*

"Finola Austin's riveting debut novel presents a deftly rendered, complex heroine swept up in the allure of forbidden passion—and the heartrending consequences when the romantic illusion shatters. Beautifully detailed and richly atmospheric, *Brontë's Mistress* portrays one of literature's most famous families from an intriguing new perspective."

—*JENNIFER CHIAVERINI, New York Times* bestselling author of *Resistance Women*

"A beautifully written, highly seductive debut in which Finola Austin delves into the life of a relatively unknown member of the Brontë family . . . Masterful storytelling which is sure to delight fans of the Brontës and of historical fiction. *Brontë's Mistress* comes highly recommended by this Yorkshire lass."

—*HAZEL GAYNOR, New York Times* bestselling author of *The Lighthouse Keeper's Daughter*

"*Brontë's Mistress* gives us a fascinating new perspective on one of literature's most famous families. Smart and sexy, this captivating novel is true to the romantic spirit of the Brontës themselves, with a modern feminist twist. A delicious treat for Brontë fans!"

—ELIZABETH BLACKWELL, author of *Red Mistress* and *On a Cold Dark Sea*

"Confident, convincing, and engrossing, and with a sure historical touch, *Brontë's Mistress* illuminates another dark corner in the Brontës' story."

—GILL HORNBY, author of *Miss Austen*

"A page-turning read full of passion and fire. The life stories of the famous Brontë siblings, Charlotte, Emily, Branwell, and Anne, have been chronicled in depth by countless biographers, and now and then in works of fiction. But an important aspect of Branwell Brontë's life—his life-altering, doomed love affair with the infamous Mrs. Robinson, an older woman whose son he was tutoring—has never been examined in such depth before, and makes a tantalizing read."

—SYRIE JAMES, author of *The Secret Diaries of Charlotte Brontë*

"Dark and moody, *Brontë's Mistress* unearths the secret love affair of Lydia Robinson and Branwell Brontë in all its shocking scandalousness. Anchored by meticulous research, Finola Austin has created a heart-tugging portrait of a passionate woman more akin to Emma Bovary than Jane Eyre, but equally trapped by the constraints of her era. Bittersweet and beautifully written."

—KRIS WALDHERR, author of *The Lost History of Dreams* and *Doomed Queens*

Brontë's Mistress

A Novel

FINOLA AUSTIN

ATRIA PAPERBACK

New York   London   Toronto   Sydney   New Delhi

ATRIA
PAPERBACK

An Imprint of Simon & Schuster, Inc.
1230 Avenue of the Americas
New York, NY 10020

First Atria Paperback edition June 2021

ATRIA PAPERBACK and colophon are trademarks of Simon & Schuster, Inc.

For information about special discounts for bulk purchases, please
contact Simon & Schuster Special Sales at 1-866-506-1949 or
business@simonandschuster.com.

The Simon & Schuster Speakers Bureau can bring authors to your live
event. For more information or to book an event, contact the Simon &
Schuster Speakers Bureau at 1-866-248-3049 or visit our website
at www.simonspeakers.com.

Manufactured in the United States of America

3   5   7   9   10   8   6   4   2

Library of Congress Cataloging-in-Publication Data is available on file.

ISBN 978-1-9821-3723-6
ISBN 978-1-9821-3724-3 (pbk)
ISBN 978-1-9821-3725-0 (ebook)

For the women who didn't write their novels

MYSTERY "BRONTË MANUSCRIPT" DISCOVERED AT YORKSHIRE SCHOOL

YORKSHIRE—Brontë scholars and fans are reeling today from the discovery of a manuscript purported to describe a long-suspected affair between Branwell Brontë, ill-fated brother of the famous Brontë sisters, and his employer's wife.

Steven Hill, janitor at Queen Ethelburga's Collegiate in Yorkshire, was cleaning a storage room in preparation for the new school year when he came across the document. "It was very yellow, very dusty," he told reporters who'd flocked to the quiet village of Little Ouseburn. "And the only name on the front was 'L. Robinson.' I was about to chuck it out with the rest of the rubbish when I flicked through it and noticed a word several times that stood out to me—'Brontë.'"

Queen Ethelburga's has long been proud of its Brontë heritage. The school is on the site of Thorp Green Hall, the house where Branwell worked along with his youngest sister, Anne, whose novels *Agnes Grey* and *The Tenant of Wildfell Hall* have won more modest fame, compared to Charlotte's *Jane Eyre* and Emily's *Wuthering Heights*. The students chose Charlotte Brontë's novel *Villette* as the inspiration for their end-of-year play last term, while one of the younger classes has been caring for four pet mice appropriately christened "Charlotte," "Branwell," "Emily," and "Anne."

"We're all very excited about the manuscript," a spokesperson for the school told reporters today. "Though we fear not all of its contents may be suitable for children."

Indeed, if the manuscript is genuine, it promises to put an end to nearly two centuries of speculation about the Brontë/Robinson affair—one of the most scandalous episodes in the literary family's brief but momentous lives. Mrs. Gaskell, fellow Victorian novelist and Charlotte's first biographer, described Lydia Robinson, the assumed authoress of the text, as a "profligate woman" who tempted Branwell "into the deep disgrace of deadly crime."

The school board must also be anticipating the potential financial windfall from any sale of the document. The Brontë Parsonage Museum in Haworth didn't even wait to confirm the manuscript's veracity before launching a crowdfunding campaign to secure this salacious piece of British history, while wealthy American collectors are said to already be circling this sleepy English village.

Generations of book lovers have delighted in the "madwoman in the attic" and the timeless love of Cathy and Heathcliff on the moors. Will Mrs. Robinson's newly discovered account prove that fact can be just as dramatic as fiction?

CHAPTER ONE

January 1843

ALREADY A WIDOW IN all but name. Fitting that I must, yet again, wear black.

Nobody had greeted me on my return, but Marshall at least had thought of me. She'd lit a feeble fire in my dressing room and laid out fresh mourning in the bedroom, spectral against the white sheets. I smoothed out a pleat, fingered a hole in the veil. Just a year since I'd last set these clothes aside, and now Death had returned—like an expected, if unwanted, visitor this time, not a violent thief in the night.

What a homecoming. No husband at the door, no children running down the drive.

I'd sat alone in the carriage, huddled under blankets, through hours of abject silence, with only the bleak Yorkshire countryside for company, but I didn't have the patience to ring for Marshall now. I tugged, laced, and hooked myself, racing against the cold. I had to contort to close the last fixture. My toe caught in the hem.

The landing outside my rooms was empty. The carpet's pattern assaulted my eyes, as if I'd been gone for weeks, not days. Home was always strange after an absence, like returning to the setting of a dream.

But it wasn't just that.

Thorp Green Hall was unusually still. Silence seeped through the house, except for the ticking of the grandfather clock that carried from the hall. Each home has its music, and ours? It was my eldest daughter banging doors; the younger girls bickering; Ned, my son, charging down the stairs; and the servants dropping pails and pans and plates with clatter upon clatter. But not today. Where was everyone?

I halted before the closed study door and gave a light rap, but my husband did not respond, much less emerge to greet me. Edmund would be in there, though. He was always hiding in there. I could picture him—taking off his glasses and squinting toward the window at the crunch of the carriage wheels on the gravel, shaking his head and returning to his account book when he realized it was only me.

I shouldn't have expected anything else. After all, I hadn't bid him good-bye on my departure, just turned on my heel and exited the room when he'd told me he wouldn't come with me to Yoxall.

"Your mother's death was hardly unexpected," he'd said with a shrug, and something about how she'd lived a good life.

He was right, of course. Or, at least, the world's opinion was closer to Edmund's than to mine. Mother had been old and ill. Her life had been happy and her children were many. Few thought it fit to weep, as I did, at her funeral.

But something had come over me after the service when the splintered crowd stood around her open grave, although I wasn't sure it was grief for Mother at all. The wind howled. The sleet smacked against us. My brothers flanked our fading father, their faces uniform as soldiers'. My sister was solemn, with her eyes downcast, as her husband thanked the vicar. But I had been angry, with an anger that leaked out in pathetic, rain-mingled tears and made me angrier still.

I didn't knock again but went instead to the schoolroom—to the children. I needed them, anyone, to embrace me, touch me, so I could feel alive.

I could not suppress my disappointment when I reached the threshold. "Oh, Miss Brontë," I said, my voice flat. "I didn't know you'd returned."

Our governess was alone. She'd been retrieving a book from below the Pembroke table but at my entrance, she stood to attention. "I arrived back yesterday, Mrs. Robinson," she said. "I hope you'll accept my condolences."

Was it the ill-fitting mourning dress, or was she even thinner than when I had seen her last? Her gown gaped at the cuffs and hung loose around her waist.

"And you mine," I said, avoiding her eye.

I'd taken to bed with a headache that day a few months ago when a letter had summoned Miss Brontë home to her dying aunt. I had meant to write to her, but somehow there had never been time, what with the house and Christmas. Or perhaps the empty words would not flow from my pen now that I'd been forced to endure so many.

"Where are my daughters?" I asked, anxious to end our tête-à-tête.

Miss Brontë gestured toward the clock on the mantel, half-obscured behind a volume of Rapin's *History of England*. It was five minutes past four. "We have just concluded today's lessons with an hour of arithmetic," she said, failing to answer my question.

I sighed and sat, slumping onto the low and book-strewn couch and staring into the last of the spluttering fire.

It had never appeared to bother Miss Brontë, the lack of common ground between us, but it stung me as yet another rejection. She had been little more than a child when she'd joined us nearly three years ago. Pale, mousy-haired, unable to meet my eye. I had thought she might look up to me. I could have acted as her patroness, bestowed on her my attention and all I could have taught her of the world. But time and again, she'd snubbed me, preferring the solitude of her books and sketching.

I'd persisted with my overtures until, one day, I'd come across a half-completed letter of hers, addressed to a sister, Charlotte. I shouldn't have opened it—wouldn't have if Miss Brontë hadn't evaded me until now. But I couldn't help myself when I saw the discarded page in the schoolroom, the impossibly regular handwriting broken off mid-word. In it she described me as "condescending" and "self-complacent," anxious only to render my daughters as "superficially attractive and showily accomplished" as I was. It was a vicious caricature but one I could not scold her for, since I should never have seen it. That's how I'd learned that our innocent Miss Brontë wasn't so innocent at all.

"So where are they?" I asked her again, more sharply.

"I believe the girls went to join Ned in the stables."

Those children had run riot for months during Miss Brontë's absence. The least she could do was teach them now that she was here.

"And why is my son and heir spending his days in the stables?" I asked, although young Ned, bless him, had always been too slight and simple a boy to deserve the title bestowed on him. He wouldn't be dressed properly. He'd catch a chill. The children might be fond of Miss Brontë, but she didn't watch them with a mother's care.

"I believe, madam—that is, I know—Mr. Brontë found him more attentive there," she answered, without flinching.

Mr. Brontë. Of course. I'd forgotten that her brother would be returning with her. He was to be Ned's new tutor, and so Edmund had managed everything.

As if on cue, a quick pitter-patter struck against the window and despite everything—my tiredness, my loneliness, my desire to join my mother in her grave—it pulled me to my feet. Miss Brontë and I stood as far apart as we could, looking through the checkered panes at the party gathered below.

There was Ned, without a coat. He was laughing, his waistcoat unbuttoned and his face grubby.

Beside him was Lydia, my eldest and namesake. She'd been running, which was unlike her. She'd bundled her dress and cape in her hands, revealing her boots and stockings, and her perfect ringlets had come unpinned, creating a bright halo around her face.

A few steps behind the others, my younger daughters, Bessy and Mary, giggled to each other.

And in the center of them all, his arm drawn back to fling another handful of gravel, was a man who couldn't have been more than five and twenty, with a smile that reached to the corners of his face and hair that rich almost-red Edmund's had been once.

He beamed back at Lydia before calling something unintelligible toward the schoolroom. His eyes were a deeper blue than Miss Brontë's, his whole being drawn in more vibrant ink.

But when his eyes slid to meet mine, when they moved on from his sister and from Lydia—that reflection of what I had once been—his smile melted away. His arm fell. The stones ran through his fingers like dust. It was as if I could hear them scatter, although the schoolroom was deathly silent.

Mr. Brontë mouthed an apology, his gaze subordinate. Lydia dropped her skirts and smoothed her hair. Even Ned buttoned one fastening of his waistcoat, although the sides were uneven and the result comical.

"I apologize on Branwell's—"

"You apologize for what, Miss Brontë?" I said, dragging her back from the window by her spindly arm. "You think I don't appreciate high spirits? Or care for my son's happiness?"

"I—"

"I fear to imagine what you say of me to others—strangers—when you think me such a dragon." I did not wait to hear her response, but left, slamming the door behind me.

As I passed the study, I paused, panting hard.

I could go in, throw myself into Edmund's arms, and cry, as I had to Mother when I was a girl. But when you are forty-three, you must not complain that the world is unfair, that your beauty is going to seed, and that those you love, or, worse, your love itself, is dead.

I did not go to Edmund, and alone in my rooms that night, I did not weep.

With my dark hair loose and my shoulders bare, I struggled not to shiver. I sat at my dressing table for a long time, staring into the glass and imagining the young tutor's eyes gleaming back at me through the gloom. *Branwell*, Miss Brontë had called him. What sort of a name was that?

There'd been a time when we'd all gather in the library or the ante-room after dinner. I would play the pianoforte. The girls would turn the pages. Sometimes they'd sing. And Edmund would quiz Ned, pointing to far-off climes on the spinning globe and asking him to name each port, kingdom, colony.

But we hadn't done that in a long time. Not since before.

Instead Edmund would retreat to his study while I played from memory to an empty room. And our daughters would stitch and sketch in the schoolroom, supervised by Miss Brontë, long after their brother had been sent to bed. The four of them probably spent their evenings complaining about me, but I couldn't know for sure.

Yet they were silent tonight when I ventured there for the first time in the three evenings since my return.

Miss Brontë was bending over a letter scribed in a minuscule hand.

Lydia lounged with her legs askew in a floral-covered chair by the fire.

"Good evening, Mama," Bessy and Mary chorused with the vestiges of childish affection from the window seat, where they'd been poring over a novel.

Lydia flicked her hand at me but continued to gaze toward the hearth.

"Could you excuse us, Miss Brontë?" I asked.

She nodded and plowed past me, face still buried in the letter. It was probably from "Charlotte." And Miss Brontë would reply to her, chronicling my family's private moments and making a mockery of our woes.

I surveyed my girls—seventeen, sixteen, fourteen. Hard to conceive of it when their younger sister would forever be two.

Time should have halted in the year since she'd been taken from us, but instead it had marched on regardless, with the regular pattern of meals, seasons, holidays. In the course of eleven short months, my three girls had blossomed before my eyes without me even noticing. But then I had survived too. I was the same, inch for inch, pound for pound, for all I felt I should have wasted away.

"How have you been?" I asked them stiffly. The words sounded ridiculous.

Lydia and Bessy exchanged a glance across the room at the strangeness of my question.

"I am well, Mama. We missed you when you were gone," said Mary, blinking at me through her pale lashes. Timid as she was, she'd always been the most affectionate, saying what she thought would be best received rather than speaking the truth.

I looked to the older two in turn. Lydia was blonde and beautiful even when yawning. Bessy was dark like me, but there the resemblance ended. Compared to the rest of us, she was a veritable hoyden—large and ruddy, like a fertile, oversized shepherdess. Beside them, Mary wasn't fair or dark enough to stand out. She had neither one type of beauty nor another.

"Well, *I* have been bored," said Lydia, swinging her legs to the floor. "But now here is something at last." She was waving a letter of her own, a short note in a large and looping cursive. The writer hadn't tried to conserve paper.

"Well?" I asked when her theatrical pause became unbearable.

"Can't you guess?" Lydia said, performing to all of us. Clearly Bessy and Mary weren't in on her secret either. "It is from Amelia. The Thompsons are to hold a dinner party at Kirby Hall, and we are all invited. Well, not you, Mary—you are too young and of no consequence.

I do hope Papa doesn't have us leave early as he did at the Christmas feast, when we missed the caroling. If he'd wanted to go to bed, he could have sent William Allison back with the carriage. What else is a coachman for? But then I've nothing to wear. Black doesn't suit me, and this dress is an inch too short. And—"

"Lydia." I spoke sternly enough that she fell silent. "Don't be unkind to Mary. And give me that."

Lydia looked at my outstretched hand. For a heartbeat, I wasn't sure she'd obey, but at last she surrendered the letter. As I read, she skipped away to scrutinize her reflection in the mirror above the fireplace, pouting at her high black collar.

"Are we to go?" asked Bessy, jumping up from the window seat. Unlike Lydia, she hadn't mastered the art of affected nonchalance.

Mary was staring at the discarded novel in her lap, feeling sorry for herself.

"No," I said.

Mary's chin jerked up. Her expression brightened.

"No?" repeated Lydia, spinning back to face me, all pretense of indifference forgotten.

"You may write to Miss Thompson thanking her, or rather her father, for the invitation. But we are in a period of mourning and won't be making social calls." I kept my voice level, trying to remember what I had been like at the age when selfishness was natural. My mother had merely been their grandmother. They'd hardly feel her loss the same.

"But—" Bessy started.

"I won't have discussion or arguments."

Lydia ignored me. "But, Mama!" she cried. "We haven't seen any gentlemen for months, except the Milner brothers—"

"Will Milner don't count!" said Bessy, rounding on her sister and turning even pinker than usual.

"Grammar, please." I sighed. Why pay a governess at all when Bessy still spoke like a groom?

For some reason, she'd found Lydia's comment objectionable and was listing everything that made the eldest Milner boy a poor gentleman and horseman—from his manners to his seat.

"And now we still shan't see any gentlemen at all," continued Lydia, shouting over her sister. "It isn't fair."

I folded the page smaller and smaller until I could no longer crease it down the middle, letting their voices wash over me.

"I suppose we'll have to content ourselves with Mr. Brontë," said Lydia, when Bessy paused for breath. "I'll pay calls to the Monk's House and have him read Byron to me."

"You'll do nothing of the sort," I snapped, trying to create one more bend in the paper.

So Mr. Brontë liked poetry.

The fold wouldn't stay. I flicked the page into the fire, where it flared for a second before crumbling.

"My letter!" cried Lydia, as if it had been precious. "How could you?"

"Oh, please!" I'd discarded it without thinking, but that hardly merited an apology. I couldn't deal with any more of Lydia's histrionics. "It's time we were all abed."

"Couldn't you stay with us a little longer, Mama?" whispered Mary from the corner.

Her sisters glared at her.

"Not tonight," I said. Yet I gestured for her to come to me.

She ran over and planted a fleeting, wet kiss on my cheek, as she had countless nights before.

Lydia and Bessy stood still, united in their act of small rebellion.

I UNDRESSED QUICKLY, WITHOUT Marshall's help, and discarded my petticoats like a second skin on my dressing room floor.

There was a romance in walking the corridors barefoot and dressed only in my nightgown, even though this was my house and I could wander where I wished. I tiptoed down the landing, dancing to avoid the floorboards that creaked, my body lighter without the swathes of fabric that weighed me down in the day.

"Edmund?" I opened his bedroom door just wide enough to peer in and shielded the candle I was carrying in case he was already asleep.

"Lydia?" my husband called out, the confusion that comes with being pulled back from the precipice of slumber evident in the haste and volume of his reply.

In the days since I'd returned from Yoxall Lodge, our communications had only been of the most perfunctory kind. Each morning Edmund had asked me what was for dinner from behind the *Times*. And each night I had lain in my bed, flat on my back and hands rigid by my sides, waiting for his tread outside my door.

But tonight, prompted perhaps by the warm relief of Mary's lips pressed against my face, I had softened and come to him.

"Is anything the matter?" he asked.

"The matter? No, not at all." I hurried in, shutting the door behind me.

Edmund half closed his eyes, shrinking from the light, but then clambered onto his elbows and propped himself up against the bolster behind him.

I set the candle on the mahogany washstand and twitched the hangings of the four-poster bed over a few inches, protecting him from the glare.

"I am very tired, Lydia. It has been a taxing day," Edmund said, stifling a yawn. But he moved over to accommodate me, lifting the sheets so I could slide under the heavy scarlet blankets, faded from years of use.

My legs were cold beneath my nightgown. He flinched when our limbs made contact, flinched and then tensed as I wrapped myself around him like a limpet and rested my head on his chest.

"You haven't asked me about Staffordshire," I said after a minute or two of enjoying the familiar waves of his breath, like an aged sailor who can now only find his legs at sea.

"What is there to ask?" he said. "It was difficult?"

I nodded as much as I could, held fast as I was against him. He didn't want me to move. He wanted only to sleep, exhausted by a day of— what? Account books and reading the sporting pages? I wanted to run a mile, release the horses from the stables, and gallop beside them, crying, *No more! No more needlework and smiling through stunted arpeggios for me.*

"Your father must know it's for the best," he said. "She had suffered—"

"And what if it were *your* mother?" I bit my tongue too late, knowing how he hated being interrupted.

"Lydia," Edmund warned. Eviction would follow if I continued in this strain.

Somehow it was even colder under the covers. The hairs along my legs stood up against the sheet.

"People rarely call me that now," I said, snuggling close against his hard, ungiving chest. "It is like I lost my name to our daughter."

Down here, I could pretend Edmund was the boy I had loved, a boy with chubby cheeks and a full head of hair, the boy I had won into wooing me, despite his shyness and that endearing stutter he'd had when conversing with the opposite sex.

How proudly I had sat, watching him give one of his first sermons, thinking, *That is my husband, the father of my sons,* whether the thought had crossed his mind yet or not. Less than three months later, he was mine.

"We must speak of the children," I said. My hand burrowed under his crisp nightshirt to play with the wisps of hair that led from his heart to his belly. "Lydia thinks I am a tyrant for refusing a dinner invitation from the Thompsons so soon after her grandmother's death."

"Lydia is bored," Edmund said. "We should send her away. To your sister, Mary, perhaps, or to Lady Scott at Great Barr Hall. The Scotts see more society than us."

"I doubt it," I said, stiffening. "My cousin Catherine is an invalid."

"But she is married to a baronet."

All these years later and that still stung. It was Valentine's Day 1815 in Bath, and I was my cousin Catherine's bridesmaid. I'd held the train of her dress as she married Edward Scott, heir to his father's baronetcy, a minor member of the nobility, but to me, the hero of a fairy tale.

He would have been mine had I only been older, I'd wept, wishing for a few more years on top of my fifteen. And now? Now I wished I could be Lydia Gisborne once more, uncrease the lines in my forehead, shrug off my worries and turn back the years as easily as I could wind back the clock on the mantelpiece.

"And then there's Ned," I said.

"Ned?"

"The new tutor, Mr. Brontë," I said. "Ned seems to like him."

My hand circled lower, scuttling spider-like across Edmund's paunch.

"Lydia, that tickles," he said, levering me off him as he sat up to blow out the candle. He rearranged the pillows and lay back, pulling my hand higher to rest on his chest.

This was it, then. Our conversation was at an end.

The darkness enveloped me. I imagined the trail of smoke snaking its way to the ceiling but couldn't even discern the shape of Edmund's chin. From the pattern of his breathing, I knew he was slipping away from me.

"Has Mr. Sewell said anything about him?" I asked, tapping Edmund like piano keys to bring him back to me.

"Hmm?"

"I wondered if Sewell had any complaints about his new companion."

Mr. Brontë wasn't sleeping in the Hall, but in the Monk's House, where our steward, Tom Sewell, lived. I'd insisted, for the girls' sake, that the young man's sleeping quarters be far away rather than in the main house. And that was probably just as well, since his brooding brow and love of poetry marked Mr. Brontë out as a romantic.

It's a strange little property, the Monk's House. It dates from the 1600s, Edmund would tell visitors. *Not nearly as old as the Hall, of course. It could have housed Henry the Eighth himself.* And his chest would swell with pride.

The cottage was too grand for servants, to my mind, if you wanted the staff to know their place. No wonder Tom Sewell's sister, our housekeeper, gave herself such airs. Miss Sewell was a flighty thing, too young to manage a household, and yet she thought herself mistress of two, whiling away evenings with her brother at the Monk's House. No doubt she'd be there even more frequently now there was an unmarried gentleman to toy with.

I hadn't even seen the new addition to the household since Mr. Brontë had hurled stones at the window. The schoolroom was the girls' domain, and Ned was taking his lessons at the Monk's House. The weather had proved too inclement for wandering outside or hunkering down in the stables.

"No, no complaints." Edmund's voice was just louder than a whisper.

To others, he was the stern father and the generous landowner, above all a man of morals and convictions. But to me, he was as vulnerable as a child, my partner through the years, my companion in the dark. Driven by an unexpected impulse, I kissed his neck, his cheek, his nose, like an explorer in the desert who has finally happened upon water.

He grunted.

"Edmund," I said, lips skirting across his collarbone, hand reaching through the thicket of hair between his legs.

"Lydia," he said, very much awake. He grabbed my hand and pushed it aside. "There'll be none of that." He turned onto his side, his face away from me, pitching up the sheets so a draft flew across my body.

I'd been a fool to attempt when it had been so long. That was a second cruelty—how our marriage had died along with our daughter. But I should have accepted it by now. Being with Edmund was like being in my own bed but lonelier. Having someone, but someone who did not want you, was worse than having nobody at all.

Edmund was asleep by the time I had conquered myself enough to excuse him. I wrapped my arm around him and he did not stir, brought my mouth close enough to his back to drink in his smell without risking a kiss.

All through the night, I stayed there on the brink of sleep, terrified to wake him, the cold playing across the goose bumps on my arm.

CHAPTER TWO

"Don't you wish to hear about Mary too? She has made admirable progress," Miss Brontë asked me, tucking a strand of hair behind her ear.

We were sitting in the bay of my dressing room window, looking out at the stew pond, which had frozen over in patches. A few more days of this cold, and Bessy would have her fondest wish: the children could go skating.

"There is little life in her. I fear she hasn't the older girls' character," I said, watching my breath steam up the triangular panes of glass and cursing the interminable winter.

"Mary lacks Lydia and Bessy's vitality, perhaps, madam," said Miss Brontë, measuring every word and plucking at a loose thread on her shawl. "But she shows determination, a quiet resolve. It is hard for her, I think, to follow in her older sisters' footsteps."

This was more forthcoming than I usually found Miss Brontë. For years I'd longed for her to voice the opinions she was so ready with in her correspondence. To while away my tedium, yes, but also so I'd know I wasn't the only woman in the house with a feeling heart and a fiery soul. But now it came to the rub, I wasn't sure I liked it.

"Oh?" I said, tracing an "L" in the condensation.

"She hasn't told me as much, but I feel it in her. I too am the youngest daughter—"

"Mary was not the youngest," I cut Miss Brontë off and stood. How could she forget so soon? She who, with Marshall, had taken shifts at my darling's bedside when I could no longer nurse her without rest.

"Of course not, Mrs. Robinson. I didn't mean—I also lost—"

"Enough," I said, choosing not to entertain her apologies.

There was judgment in her eyes. For her, my wealth, my grace, and my once handsome face spoke against me as surely as they had pled my case before all other courts. It was easy to paint herself as the victim— poor and young and plain—but life is rarely so simple.

Throughout the whole interview, I had steeled myself to ask her one question, yet now I could not bring myself to ask it. I walked to the polished wood table that served as my desk and flicked through condolence letters.

She started to leave, thinking she was dismissed.

"Miss Brontë?" I called after her.

"Mrs. Robinson?" she said, with something between a jump and a curtsy.

"Can you tell Mr. Brontë I wish to speak with him?"

A small crease appeared across her forehead, but she said, "Of course."

"Very good."

I sat, pretended to read, and listened for the rustle of her skirts and the familiar click of the door, but instead there was only her breath, always audible, irregular, and rattling, like a window only just holding out against the wind.

"You wish to see him now, Mrs. Robinson?" she asked, her emphasis on the "now."

"At Mr. Brontë's earliest convenience." I met her eye with as convincing a smile as I could muster. "Thank you, Miss Brontë."

She nodded and left.

Strange that Miss Brontë was so partial to Mary.

Your first child is a miracle. A man and you have met and married and made a person, with nostrils and eyelashes and toes. Every breath she takes seems to swell your heart. You didn't know what love was until today.

Your second, if another girl, is a disappointment. You feel the low, aching guilt of that as you gaze down on her. Crescent nails and downy hair. She is perfect in every way, except for the most important.

Still, no need to worry. You are young. You have years to mate and make a boy.

With the third, though, the tide turns—or it did with my poor Mary. Your husband's face falls when he hears the news from the midwife. You can hardly look when you place the baby in the third-hand cradle. Your body is in ruins, another year of your life has faded away, and there is still no son to set the world to rejoicing, no boy to grant the tenant farmers an unearned holiday.

Worse yet, when the heir comes at last, he is not *yours* at all, but everyone else's. You have made what you could never be. You have fulfilled your function and are useless, spent.

"Only think, Lydia, you need never have another baby," Mother had said, dandling Ned on her knee.

I had burned then with desire for another child. I had begged, and at last Edmund had given her to me. She would be the child who fixed us, who brought back the love that we had lost. My dearest, sweetest Georgiana. The child I had wanted in spite of reason, almost to defy logic, the daughter born only to love and be loved. And she was the only child taken from us, as if in confirmation of the world's perverse cruelty.

A tap at the door. Mr. Brontë. My insides contorted.

"Come in," I called, but I had spoken too quietly and was forced to repeat myself twice before he entered.

"Mrs. Robinson," Mr. Brontë said, bowing. He didn't even look at me. His eyes swept my dressing room, taking in the feminine trappings—chintz floral curtains, a few engravings, a deep pink rug one of my brothers had sworn was from India when he gave it to me—but also Edmund's gun case, which was positioned above the chimney glass and looked strangely out of place.

My life was laid out before him, in stacks of library books, letters tied with ribbons, half-finished pieces of embroidery. These were the baubles with which women must entertain themselves. Ours were pursuits, not passions, taken up in a quiet moment, and just as easily set aside. Everything was just so—neat and in its proper place. Was Mr. Brontë thinking how different the room was from Edmund's haphazard study?

"Thank you for coming, Mr. Brontë," I said. "Pray, take a seat."

I had risen at his entrance half unconsciously, and now, as he came toward me, I could see that he was shorter than I'd thought when I saw him from the window, not much taller than me.

His face, though, was full of character. Sharp jaw, imperial nose, and abundant chestnut hair, much darker and redder in color than his sister's and so curly it gave him the appearance of a child despite the beard that covered his chin.

Mr. Brontë cleared his throat as he waited for me to stop staring, hovering by the painted chair opposite me.

"I trust your first few weeks at Thorp Green have been comfortable, Mr. Brontë," I said, retaking my seat and fidgeting my hands below the table, hidden from him.

"Very comfortable, Mrs. Robinson. I owe you thanks for trusting Anne's recommendation," he said, flicking up the tails of his coat to sit.

Oh, yes. Miss Brontë was another "Anne." Like Marshall and our hapless housemaid, Ellis. Perhaps, for him, the name "Miss Brontë" conjured the other one, "Charlotte." And wasn't there a third sister too?

"All my husband's doing, I assure you," I said quickly. "Ned is only ten and might have stayed longer with the girls, I think. He would have learned enough Latin from your sister to prepare him for Cambridge, but what do I know of such things?"

He did not reply. His silence struck me as insulting rather than deferential.

Miss Brontë, too, had been quiet at our first interview, but she had quaked in anticipation. Her eyes had skated across the floor as if watching a mouse, and she'd answered me in monosyllables or with a tactless innocence about the ways of the world.

"Why did you leave your last employers, the Inghams, Miss Brontë?" I'd asked, smiling to try to reassure her.

"They were unkind to me," she'd answered.

Unkindness. I had been indifferent toward her, yes, once I'd discovered what she really thought of me, but at least she couldn't accuse me of that.

I tried once more to engage the brother, to play the lady of the manor, although the household had run just as smoothly during my absence at Yoxall Lodge, and now even this young man was more necessary to its operation than I was.

"You have met all my children, I think?" I ventured.

"Yes. Ned is a good-natured boy, and your daughters are charming." Mr. Brontë's face broke into a smile.

I swallowed my annoyance. "Yes, Mr. Brontë," I said, clasping my hands on the desk. "That is why I wished to speak with you."

The smile faded. He looked troubled. His eyes wandered from mine to my cheek to my hands, making me flush at his impertinence. He was taking me apart and putting me back together, puzzling me out. "Indeed?"

"My daughters, Mr. Brontë, they are young and—how was it you put it?—charming. Miss Robinson, Lydia, my eldest, in particular is considered something of a beauty." *As I was once*, I nearly added, but I couldn't risk being met by a look of disbelief or patronizing indulgence.

"Mrs. Robinson, I hope you don't think— I was commenting only on their sweet dispositions," Mr. Brontë said, leaning across the table, his palms upturned for emphasis, his words spilling over each other in his desire for me to understand.

I laughed.

I could accept, even boast, that Lydia was beautiful, with her gold ringlets and periwinkle-blue eyes, and it was true that she *could* be charming. But a sweet disposition? If only young men could see the girls who dominate their imaginations when the door is closed or the dance is done. All too often, I had suffered the sting of Lydia's slaps and stood in the tidal waves of her anger. And as for Bessy, my second daughter was ever gallivanting around the property, falling from horses, scraping her knees, and eating with the appetite of a boy. She would have been a stable lad if left to follow the cues of her own nature.

"This is not an admonishment, Mr. Brontë," I said, after leaving him to sweat for a moment. "I only wish to rely on you as a gentleman and a friend."

And then I did something extraordinary. Without making the decision to do so, I placed my hand on top of his.

Mr. Brontë looked down at my fingers but did not pull away. His hand was large and soft, his fingers stained with ink.

"Good." I drew back, surer now in my control. He had thought me one way and I had surprised him. "Lydia is young and impressionable," I continued, reveling now in the years I had on him, the years that made him closer in age to Lydia than to me. "And she sees little of the world here. Even the two villages—Great and Little Ouseburn—are at least half an hour's walk away. The advent of a young and handsome man might unsettle her."

The tutor's face reddened when I called him handsome. "Of course," he said, nodding. "I understand."

"I knew you would." I smiled wide and gracious, bringing my hands closer to my chest and circling my wrists, thrilling to see that his gaze followed the movement. "After all, you have a sister."

"I have three. I had five," he said, his tone different—sharp, raw. "But that was a long time ago."

The correction threw me. "Oh, yes," I said, with a nervous laugh.

Three years Miss Brontë had lived in my house, and now her

brother knew I had never discovered much about her family, though I'd often wondered what else she wrote of me to Charlotte. My father had had some connection to hers at Cambridge, and that had been enough of a reference to satisfy me. She'd rebuffed my early questions about her home with short answers until I'd given up asking. I hadn't even known she had a brother until Edmund, or rather, Edmund's mother, decided that Ned was now old enough to require a tutor.

"So you know what young ladies can be like. Fanciful," I said as lightly as I could, although I was imagining these other Brontë sisters, the ones who had died. In my mind they were twins, Georgiana's age, with her button nose but Mr. Brontë's curls. Their baby lips rested on their pillows when the coughing subsided and they at last found rest, but soon after, their perfect, pale skin would turn purple as they gasped for air.

"I wouldn't describe my sisters as fanciful, Mrs. Robinson. My sister Charlotte is the cleverest woman I know."

I don't know why—we had only just met—but this seemed like a rebuke. His words confirmed everything I'd feared, that this Charlotte Brontë was just like *our* Miss Brontë, thinking herself better than other women for having read a few more books.

I stood and stalked to the window, forcing Mr. Brontë to stand too. I imagined him dithering behind me, wishing I would touch him again, and resisted the urge to turn.

Outside, the steward Tom Sewell was berating our stable hand, Joey Dickinson, pointing at Patroclus's front left hoof, which the poor horse was raising and replacing on the ice-coated gravel in turn. Joey bowed his head in submission. I pictured the quiver of his smooth upper lip.

Was I clever? I'd never really considered it. Mother had praised me for being "beautiful," "neat," and "well mannered," but never "clever."

"Tell me more about her, about Charlotte." The words left my mouth before I had judged them prudent.

The old French clock, a wedding gift, ticked behind me. My corset creaked as I inhaled hard.

Joey led Patroclus back to the stable, burrowing his face in his sleeve for a second as if to wipe away a tear. Tom Sewell turned his attention to Ned, who had hopscotched into view, glad no doubt that Mr. Brontë had released him early from his studies.

The compulsion to turn was strong, but I held out, daydreaming that when Mr. Brontë next spoke, his breath would blow against my neck.

"Perhaps another time," he said, as far away as ever.

I glanced back, ready to do battle, but almost gasped at the intensity of his stare. No one had looked at me and really seen me for months—years, maybe—but this boy, his red-rimmed eyes, bore into my soul. I was afraid to know what he found there.

"Good day, Mr. Brontë," I whispered.

With a slight inclination of his head, he left me.

"I THOUGHT YOU WERE dying of boredom, Lydia," I said. "Desperate for something to do."

"I was. I am!" cried my eldest, tossing her bonnet on the schoolroom floor. "But this is worse than nothing. I won't go! It is beneath me. Why can't Miss Brontë go alone as she always does?"

"Miss Brontë, will you excuse us, please?" I asked, holding out my hand for Lydia's bonnet, which the governess had rescued from imminent destruction.

She gave it to me, bobbed, and left, silent as a shadow.

"Lydia, this behavior is uncalled for and unseemly," I tried again. "It is our duty to visit the poor, the sick—"

"*You* haven't been in months!" Lydia shot back at me, her eyes burning like a demon's, framed by her angelic curls.

Bessy let out a snort from the corner.

"I am going today," I said, as calmly as I could, as if to prove that Lydia had not inherited her petulant humor from me. "I cannot force you to join us, but only imagine what Mother—your grandmother—would have thought."

"Grandmama is dead!" Lydia shrieked. "And I wish our other one was too." She grabbed her bonnet from me and flew from the room.

I shut my eyes, calculating the likelihood of the onset of one of my headaches.

"*We're* ready, Mama," said Mary, slipping her arm through mine and bringing me back to myself.

"Good. Very good," I said.

Bessy rolled her eyes at her sister but walked over to me too.

The three of us trudged along Thorp Green Lane in silence. It was muddy underfoot from the last few days' rain, which had washed away the children's hopes of snow. At times it was difficult to navigate around the puddles that had gathered in the ditches, reflecting the canopy of gray clouds above, so my dress grew heavier with each step. And the basket of gifts I carried—old linens, freshly baked pies, jams from the pantry—weighed down the crook of my arm, cutting into my flesh.

But I had determined to do something other than wait. I ignored all this and Mary, who was wrinkling her nose at the stinging odor of manure. If Mr. Brontë was as pious as his sister, my Christian gesture was sure to impress him when he heard of our outing from Ned. Though I had a lingering suspicion that Miss Brontë went visiting so often less due to her Godliness than to her desire to escape our house and spend more time with the curate, Reverend Greenhow.

The Stripe Houses were a row of dirty, mismatched cottages, a few inhabited by the most destitute in the vicinity of the Ouseburns but the majority abandoned. The first was home to Mrs. Thirkill and Mrs. Tompkins, widowed sisters who were already half-deaf in their sixties. They nodded with hungry eyes at the gifts bestowed upon them and curtsied to the girls and me in turn, which was gratifying. All too often the poor give you only suspicious glances when you bring them aid.

We did not go into the next cottage. Beth Bradley stood at her threshold with a baby on her hip, a toddler clinging to her ankle, and an expression of exhaustion on her face. Benjamin, their eldest boy, had fallen ill, she told us, and Dr. Crosby said it might be the scarlet fever.

I ushered Bessy and Mary away from her and from the remaining Stripe Houses. Yet I glanced back at the upper windows of the two-story shack as we continued toward Little Ouseburn, almost hoping I would catch a glimpse of the sickroom, barer than Georgiana's but with the same unmistakable scent of vomit, iodine, and sweat.

The rain was starting up again, but it was only spotting. It wasn't hard enough to excuse us from the rest of our visits.

"My feet are wet," said Mary. She stood on one leg to show me the hole in the toe of her left boot.

"Honestly, Mary, you are growing as big as your sister," I said, gesturing at Bessy, who was stomping ahead of us through the puddles. "God knows what Miss Sewell is having Cook feed you."

When I was Lydia's age, they'd laced me so tight that my waist was eighteen inches. Mother had been proud of that, and so was I. I'd told Lydia once, and she hadn't eaten for days just so she could say the same. She'd succeeded but given up an hour after Marshall had encaged her in one of my corsets. She'd been defeated, pale and short of breath, screaming at us to "get this cursed thing off her."

But Bessy, for all her hair was dark like mine, might have been a different species from us. She was broader, taller, more athletic. It was hard to imagine the giant of a man who might consider her dainty.

"Whatever is the matter with Lydia today, Mary? Do you know?" I asked, transferring my basket to the other arm and lowering my voice so that her sister could not hear us.

Bessy and Lydia were so unlike each other. Yet what I said to one was always made known to the other, to the exclusion of Mary, who, at fourteen, they thought of as a baby.

"She is upset that no one has sent her a valentine," said Mary without a second's hesitation, looking up at me, unabashed, little traitor that she was.

A valentine? In the first years of our marriage, Edmund had left posies on my pillow, but today I hadn't even noted the date. I nearly smiled at the girls' naivety but then I remembered Mr. Brontë, the curve of his lip, the smile in his eyes and how he had called Lydia "charming."

"From whom was she expecting a valentine, Mary?" I asked, walking a little faster now that Bessy had disappeared around a bend in the hedgerow-lined lane.

"No one in particular, Mama. Although if she had her pick, she says she'd take Harry Thompson," said Mary, hopping along to keep her foot dry.

My shoulders relaxed. My pace slackened. The heir to Kirby Hall was double Lydia's age, and it was doubtful he even knew her name. Besides, Edmund had told me a profitable marriage was brewing between Harry Thompson and the daughter of some merchant's son turned baronet in Kent.

"She was upset, as Bessy was sent one by Will Milner," Mary continued, her eyes widening. "It didn't strike Lydia as fair, since she is the oldest and prettiest, but now, since Grandmama died and we all must avoid company, she sees no gentlemen at all, so when is she to have her chance? At church? Reverend Lascelles is so dull she says he'd kill any hope of romance. And she claims she'll be old and haggard before we're out of mourning, especially as our other grandmama will also die sometime, putting us back to the beginning. Oh, will I be pretty like Lydia, when I am seventeen? I know I shouldn't care so much, but I do. It is wicked, and yet I cannot help it." Childish confession tumbled out after childish confession. There was mud on Mary's cheek and a look of terrible sincerity in her eyes.

"There is no harm in praying for beauty, Mary," I said, reaching over to wipe away the dirt with my handkerchief, "although it should not be the first virtue you desire."

Maybe there was no need to teach Bessy better manners or limit her dinner portions when young Will Milner was so devoted to her. It was a strange thing for a youthful attachment born out of a shared love of horses to have survived into the boy's adulthood. It would have irked me too had I been Lydia. Her younger sister would have everything a girl could wish for—money, a husband only a few years older than her, and a property a short ride from ours. And Bessy hadn't even done anything to earn it, while Lydia wasted her coquetry on her bedroom looking glass or, perhaps, on Mr. Brontë.

"Why, there are Mama and Mary now," cried Bessy, as we rounded the corner. She was swinging on a wooden cow-gate beside the next house and conducting a shouted conversation with Eliza Walker.

Eliza was standing in the cottage doorframe, cowering from the thickening rain. She was daughter-in-law to George Walker, a rustic who'd been on his deathbed since I'd first come to Thorp Green Hall as mistress nearly twenty years earlier. The townspeople claimed he would soon be one hundred years old. Each day, Eliza made her thankless pilgrimage from Little Ouseburn, the smaller of the two villages, to tend to him since the obstinate old man refused to leave this rundown shack where he'd lived with his late wife for decades.

There was a flash of lightning, followed by a thunderclap in quick succession. The rain beat down so hard it rebounded from the ground. The three of us ran toward the house, seeking shelter before Eliza had worked up the courage to invite us in.

It took a few minutes to adjust to the dimness. The only room in the hovel was thick with peat smoke that clouded my eyes and coated the inside of my throat.

Mary, forgetting all her breeding, had dropped down to one knee to remove and examine her offending boot. Bessy stood at the door, watching the storm and delighting in the shocks of lightning and percussive thunder.

I didn't have the energy to chide either of them. At least they'd come. And they hadn't pointed out to me what a terrible failure this had been as Lydia would have, had she been of an age when I could have boxed her ears and dragged her along. What was I doing, traipsing round the countryside to impress a mere boy? Had I been so long alone that attention from any man could delight me?

Eliza untied my cloak and hung it over one of the two roughly hewn wooden chairs by the fire. In the other, her father-in-law slept, his breathing labored.

"We brought you . . ." I trailed off in embarrassment but passed her the soggy basket.

She curtsied in thanks and scurried off to unpack it.

I walked toward the fire to dry myself, but the heat was so fierce against my cheek that I had to hang back. It was a miracle that old George Walker hadn't been mummified in the years he'd sat there, waiting for death.

There was a stool beside his chair I hadn't made out before. I dragged it back from the fire and sat next to him. I gazed up at his face, took his ancient and withered hand in mine, and tried not to gag at the smell of feces and tooth decay. I should set an example to my daughters, although one of them was entranced by a worn shoe, another by the elements, my oldest would not come with me, and my youngest girl was dead.

"Mr. Walker," I said, shouting toward his ear. "We have come to visit you."

His hand stroked mine in response. I could have kissed him. There was someone in the world who thought me young and good, who took joy from my presence.

"You are in our prayers," I said, my confidence growing. "You and your family."

I could not make out her expression in the gloom, but Eliza was watching me.

George tried to speak but only a cough came out.

"Mary, fetch Mr. Walker some water," I said, but she gestured toward her unshod foot and Eliza had passed me a mug before I could call to Bessy.

"Here." I raised it to the old man's lips with the reverence of a vicar doling out the Communion wine.

He gulped down what he could, although at least half the water ran down his bearded chin, the droplets hanging like dew from the scraggly gray hairs.

"You do me such good, my child, thank you," he said, shutting his eyes from the effort of speaking.

My heart seemed to swell bigger.

"Your visits *always* do me so much good," he croaked. "Yours and the curate's. You are truly an angel, Miss Brontë."

I jerked away from him and dropped the cup to the floor.

Eliza turned to scrub the already clean table, unable to look at me.

"Mary, put that boot on now," I said, grabbing my still-dripping cloak and hauling her up. "We're leaving."

CHAPTER THREE

"A LEG OF MUTTON for dinner tonight, Lydia. Have Miss Sewell see to the extra settings," Edmund barked at me from behind his newspaper, as I stood to leave the breakfast table.

I sat down again, as happy to have something to speak about as I was curious to hear what was happening tonight.

I hadn't been able to bear the silence that had fallen over the room since I'd dispatched the children to their lessons, leaving me with only the portraits on the walls for company. Ned had skipped off to the Monk's House. Lydia and Bessy had grumbled their way upstairs. And Mary had sloped away, her head bent in chagrin, after I sent her to Marshall to see to the jam stain on her dress. A girl her age—she would be fifteen in just over a week—shouldn't be so clumsy.

"Is company expected?" I asked, leaning closer to Edmund. I replaced the lid on the silver butter dish when he did not emerge.

"The Reverend Brontë is coming to York," he said, his voice as tired at nine in the morning as it was late at night.

"He is coming to York? Or coming here?" I asked, my heart quickening.

What if Mr. Brontë was going and his father had come to take him away? Although why I should care if that was the case, after only a handful of conversations had occurred between us, I could not say.

"Yes," Edmund said, absentmindedly.

"Must you do that?" I asked.

The housemaid, Ellis, who'd appeared at the door to clear the last of the breakfast things, retreated, as if I'd chastised *her*.

"Do what?" Edmund sighed, folded the paper, and set it before him.

My face flushed, knowing that he thought me difficult.

"Make your answers ambiguous," I said, smiling to lighten the mood. "So Reverend Brontë is to dine with us tonight. Is he to bring his other daughters?"

Funny how the idea of clever Charlotte had taken such a hold of me. I longed to assess her intelligence for myself and examine her to see if she could provide the key to the mystery of the Brontë family. What sort of household could produce such different specimens as the dashing Mr. Brontë and docile Anne?

"No indeed," said Edmund. "His is not a social trip. Business brings him to York. And seeing as he has connections in the Church and is a John's man—"

"Business, what business?" I asked, cutting him off.

Edmund just wouldn't stop talking whenever he invoked the name of his beloved Cambridge college. Soon I'd be forced to endure reminiscences about rowing races and long-dead horses.

"He is to testify in a forgery case," he replied.

"Forgery?" I gasped.

Edmund's face crinkled at my overreaction. "Nothing to Reverend Brontë's discredit, Lydia. What has come over you?"

"Me? Nothing." I looked down at my lap and swept away a crumb.

"Are you unwell? Your nerves—" He trailed off. "Should I call for Dr. Crosby?"

Anger bristled in me, but I quenched it. With Edmund it was always "Call for Dr. Crosby." My reactions were never acceptable and were often the subject of discussion, dissection, and medication. When

I kept my feelings to myself, I was "unfeeling," but if I voiced them, I laid myself open to the worst of charges: that I was "hysterical."

"I am well, Edmund." I stood and ran my hands along my sides, taking reassurance from the hug of my corset beneath the silk. "The children should dine separately tonight," I added, imagining Lydia, her head thrown back in laughter, batting her eyelashes at the Brontë father and son in turn.

Edmund yawned. "As you think best."

DESSERT HAD BEEN SERVED, and the evening was drawing to a close. The time had come to make the conversation more personal. I surveyed my audience. The candlelight and shadows danced across their faces, obscuring the finer details of their features, but every one of them was turned toward me.

And why wouldn't they be? I had taken nearly three hours preparing for tonight, helped by Marshall, the nurse I couldn't bear to part with as the children aged and so made her my own untrained, unskilled lady's maid. She'd dragged a copper tub to the center of my dressing room and helped me bathe for the first time in weeks, making no remark as I dabbed perfume along my collarbone and massaged it into the blue rivulets at my wrists. I'd schooled her in how to fix my hair, using a spring plate from one of the London magazines that Lydia devoured, and she'd endured my commands without complaint, teasing my curls higher, and draping three perfect ringlets so they fell against the snowy skin of my partially exposed shoulder.

I'd been nervous when I emerged, but Edmund had kissed me on the cheek for the first time in a long time, his lips rough and dry. "Lydia, you are yourself again," he'd said, looping my hand through his arm. "I am a fortunate man to have you for a wife."

I'd proved him right. My performance thus far had been admirable, as the Reverend Brontë was the kind of man I knew how to handle— the kind of man who'd frequented my father's set. They shared not only the same Cambridge college but their religion—Evangelical, of course. It took only the smallest of encouraging interruptions and the occasional question from me to delight him. I nodded at his interpretations of Scripture, cooed in sympathy at his struggles with finding an appropriate curate, and, when an opening in the conversation presented itself, expressed my distaste on the subject of slavery and delight at manumission, another of my father's hobbyhorses.

"You must be proud to have such talented children, Reverend," I said now.

"I am, Mrs. Robinson," the Reverend Brontë replied, his face grave, but with a warmth in his unexpected Irish lilt. "It brings joy to a man like me to see his son and daughter valued in their positions, to know there is a place for them at their employer's table."

Mr. Brontë was watching me, or rather the path of my hand as I grasped the crystal stem and brought the wineglass to my lips.

Heat slid down my throat as I swallowed, kindling a fire deep inside me. Nothing could suppress my fevered joy tonight, not even Miss Brontë's silent accusations. *A place at my employer's table*, her eyes seemed to say. *Until my brother came, Mrs. Robinson never asked me to dine with the family—not once.*

I still could not have the Brontës join us at dinner every day. I'd first suggested the idea around a month ago as an antidote to Edmund's lack of male conversation, without thinking that the invitation must naturally extend to Miss Brontë too. Every few evenings, Edmund and I sat at opposite ends of our long mahogany table, the Brontës and Ned stationed along one side, the girls on the other. Mr. Brontë was always farthest from me, placed at my husband's elbow so that he could listen to Edmund elucidating his latest agricultural experiments.

But sometimes, maybe only once or twice a night, Mr. Brontë's gaze would slide to meet mine and we'd engage—I thought so, at least—in a shy and silent conversation. After dinner, we would all retire to the anteroom. Once the girls had finished bashing out their simple tunes or squabbling over cards and bagatelle, I'd take to the piano and sing and play—with skill, yes, but also with all the feeling I had in me. Maybe Mr. Brontë knew what each note contained, maybe he did not, but the possibility raised the temperature in the room and fizzed like a firefly through the air.

"My children, unlike yours, Mrs. Robinson, did not have a mother to guide them," the Reverend Brontë continued, shaking his head as the Irish do when they speak of death.

My smile became forced at the reminder that we were the parents at the table and Mr. Brontë one of his father's children.

"When my poor wife was taken from us—and Anne just an infant!—I reared them as I knew how, with the help of books and my late wife's sister. But in some ways, they were raised by the moors around Haworth, our home. It is another world out there. Just steps from our parsonage, you escape the town and the smoking chimneys. The house itself disappears from view. Instead, there are rolling hills and hidden waterfalls. Miles without fences and only the occasional rock to sit on, thick purple heather you trample underfoot or make your rustic daybed. Now that she's alone, with Charlotte teaching in Brussels and her other siblings here, my daughter Emily vanishes for hours and comes back with her eyes clouded over with bracken and burrs in her hair. You'd take her for a gypsy."

Emily—so this must be the third sister.

"In such a place it is unsurprising that my children grew up in worlds of their own imaginations," he went on. "As youngsters, they astounded me with their tales of far-off lands, their writings, and their art. Did you know they created books and magazines in miniature, as if scribed by fairy hands?"

I had not known this. But I'd seen the letters Miss Brontë sent and received, and how the cursive raced over the page in tightly coiled lines, as if the pages could hardly contain the writer's confidences.

"Father," Miss Brontë said, reaching out to touch his arm in a gesture that conveyed in equal parts her affection and her desire that he change the subject.

But I wanted him to keep talking, to speak specifically of Branwell and, most of all, of Charlotte. Alone, and in Brussels! I'd only ever been abroad on my honeymoon.

The Reverend patted Miss Brontë's hand. "My Anne needn't worry," he said, turning back to me. "I know few of my children's secrets. My daughters—Charlotte, Emily, and Anne—squirrel away as if preparing for winter and don't think to inform me of their plans. But when you trust your children, it warms your heart to see them conspire. Isn't that so, Mr. Robinson?"

I couldn't think of my children in the plural. They had inherited only the worst of each of us—Bessy and Ned Edmund's love of horses and hunting, Mary his avoidance of conflict, Lydia my vanity. And, worse, unlike these talented Brontës, they didn't possess an artistic bone among them. Only little Georgie had. She'd told fantastic stories that Edmund deemed lies and invited me, and only me, to watch her plays and join her at her reverent, imagined tea parties.

Edmund laughed. "There is little occasion for secrets here at Thorp Green Hall."

My stomach clenched. My heart held its own secrets. And Bessy's valentine was only the start. Soon my remaining girls would deceive me, resist me, leave me.

"No secrets," said Mr. Brontë, raising his glass, "unless it is the secret of how to manage such a happy household, which Mrs. Robinson holds close to her chest."

The men laughed.

Miss Brontë frowned at her brother as he refilled his wine without waiting for a servant.

I blushed, not at the compliment—they never bothered me—but at the admiring glance that accompanied Mr. Brontë's reference to my chest.

"To Mrs. Robinson!" he toasted.

The party drank.

Edmund beamed at me.

I smiled down at my plate.

There was a knock on the dining room door, and Marshall interrupted our festivities, bobbing awkwardly and looking in my direction.

"Excuse me." I rose.

The men did too as I hurried past them.

"Is anything the matter?" I asked her, once we were in the cool hallway.

"It is Master Ned, ma'am. I am so sorry to have come for you," Marshall said, her pockmarked face earnest and a little fearful. "But he woke up screaming and wouldn't be comforted."

"Thank you, Marshall. You were quite right. I'll go to him."

I ran up the stairs, longing to be back in the dining room but not having it in my heart to be angry, as I would have been had the summons been from one of the girls. I'd almost expected Lydia to stoop to dramatics to spoil my evening, but this was unlike Ned.

He'd drawn his blankets up to his throat and was shivering when I entered his room, although he had a bed warmer and a fair fire.

"Ned, darling," I said, taking his small damp body in my arms. "You are far too old for nightmares. You know they aren't real." I stroked his hair, imagining the scene two floors below, the meal drawing to its conclusion without me.

"It wasn't a nightmare," said Ned, burrowing his head against my breasts. I hoped his tears wouldn't stain my neckline.

"Then what is it?" I asked, pushing his forelock from his eyes.

He paused. "It's a secret—" he muttered.

"What kind of secret?"

If Lydia and Bessy had been tormenting him again, those girls wouldn't dine with us but would have only bread and butter, for a week.

"A secret about Mr. Brontë," Ned whispered. "I saw him, and he was different."

"Different? Different how?" I held him by both shoulders and looked square at his snot-covered face.

"I don't know. Different. Angry." He sniffed. "It was the other night, after supper. I went to the Monk's House—"

"You went to the Monk's House at nighttime, Ned?" I said, my voice a little sterner.

He looked down and nodded.

"Then no wonder Mr. Brontë was angry."

"But—"

"No 'buts,'" I said, running my hand down his cheek. "You mustn't leave the Hall by yourself and a boy your age mustn't cry so. What would your papa think?"

I stood to leave but felt a twinge of guilt at his woebegone expression. "There." I bestowed a kiss on his forehead. "Now sleep."

Marshall was waiting outside his room, so I instructed her to stay with him.

I padded down one flight of stairs and was just about to round the corner to descend the next when hushed voices emanated from the hall below.

I paused, registering the Reverend Brontë's low growl and the soft timbre of Miss Brontë's voice.

"The seclusion here is what Branwell needs," said the father. "The temptation is too much for him in Haworth, what with the Black Bull just around the corner from the parsonage. I hope he will prove worthy of the trust we have all placed in him. I don't want a repetition of what happened at the railway."

"I fear— I hardly know what exactly, but that my own position will be compromised," said Miss Brontë, her voice more animated than I had heard before. "Did you see how much wine he drank at dinner? Or how he looked at Mrs. Robinson? He's immoderate, reckless. I wish you would take him away. No good will come from this."

My heart expanded and contracted with each sentence she uttered, then overflowed with the most important revelation. He had looked at me. He had noticed me. I was no longer alone.

"Hush, daughter," Reverend Brontë said.

There was a pause. I imagined they were embracing and gave them a moment before I swept down the staircase and into sight.

"Dinner is over, then?" I asked them with a smile.

Father and daughter exchanged a worried glance.

"Mr. Robinson and my son are settling a geographical dispute by consulting an atlas in your library, Mrs. Robinson. When they are finished, I'm afraid I must be on my way," the Reverend Brontë said, with a short bow.

"You won't stay?" I reached out my hand so the Reverend would kiss it. It was difficult not to let my face fall.

There would be no music tonight, then. No more chances for me to watch Branwell and assess the truth of Miss Brontë's observation. At the beginning, in the early years of living at the Hall with Edmund, I couldn't wait for guests to depart at the end of the evening, leaving us, at last, to each other. But now—

"I'm afraid not," Reverend Brontë replied. "My presence is necessary early tomorrow in York. Please accept my deepest thanks for your hospitality and that of your husband."

"OH, I DOUBT ANYONE will even notice, and here I am fretting, Marshall. You shouldn't let me rattle on so," I said, turning from the mirror.

"I'm sure they'll mark how fine you're looking, madam, but they won't pay no attention to some gray crepe at your cuffs. At least I reckon not, ma'am."

Marshall was right. Nobody but me would care if my black was trimmed with gray, a promise of an easier tomorrow. Besides, it was a foolish thing to wear your grief, to veil yourself with what you felt inside.

I smiled up at her, leaning against Marshall's bony chest since the dressing stool had no back. She always knew just what to say, in situations when Edmund would not. Or no, he knew by now what it was that I wanted to hear, but withheld it almost from spite.

"Leave my hair." I grabbed her hand—large, chafed, red—a little too hard and then kissed it by way of apology. "It is early and the sun is shining at last. I'll take a walk and let it dry in the air. The exercise will do me good."

"You'll catch a chill, madam," she said, but she stepped aside to let me go, lifted a silver brush from the dressing table, and started to extract the hair, remnants of the youth and beauty I would never regain— long, silky, black.

I passed the housekeeper, Miss Sewell, on the landing. My throat tightened to think that she might note the lighter details in my dress and judge my grief light also. But she was scolding Ellis and didn't notice me sail by.

There was something delicious about the solitude of the Hall's grounds early in the morning, when the sun was out and the world alive to the promise of spring. I threw back my head to let the rays lick my face. The wind lifted my hair, dispersing the water that had weighed it down. A duck skipped from one spot on the fishpond to another with a confusion of wings, setting circle upon circle vibrating across the surface.

I imagined Edmund, deep in thought, strolling from his desk to the window and catching sight of me far below, his heart stirring in recognition of the girl I had been, sensitive to each tremor of nature's orchestra, subject to the seasons as much as the birds and the flowers and the trees.

"Your capacity for joy almost scares me," he'd said once, in the weeks before our wedding, when we, a betrothed couple, were at last allowed some time alone. "For mustn't it be matched by fathomless unhappiness? I have always been a quiet, steady man. No woman has moved my heart before. Until you."

I sat on the low stone wall that surrounded the pool, but not because I wanted to rest. It completed the picture—the woman in black gazing out across the troubled reflection of the sky, trailing her gloveless fingers in the water.

I drew back. It was cold. Winter was not ready for her abdication. I rubbed my hands together and glanced back at the house and then in the other direction, toward the outbuildings, to check if anyone had seen me indulging in my fantasy. I might not be as young as I was back then, but mightn't I still move him?

I was alone, but floating toward me on the wind was something unexpected—a sheet of paper. It circled nearer, yet evaded me when I reached for it. I jumped up and grasped it with my wet hand, leaving a constellation of dark blots along the right side.

March 30th 1843, Thorpe Green

I sit, this evening, far away,
From all I used to know,
And nought reminds my soul to-day
Of happy long ago.

"Thank you!" I was interrupted before I could read the rest—four more verses that snaked down the page in strong, dark, even handwriting. Mr. Brontë was striding toward me, his shirt hanging loose, his hair uncombed, and a bundle of manuscript pages and sketches clamped under one arm, while in his other hand he held a cane.

"Mr. Brontë," I said, flustered. I proffered the page, as if there were no scribblings in the world I wished to read less.

"Please excuse my appearance, Mrs. Robinson," Mr. Brontë said, equally embarrassed, not taking the poem, but switching his cane to the other hand and smoothing his hair. "A morning habit of mine— editing last night's feeble attempts at poetry. Forgive me."

It was ridiculous. Me, with wet hair, in a gown too frivolous for a housekeeper to see me in, constructing a tableau for an absent audience, and the unkempt tutor playing the eccentric poet. I laughed, and, while Mr. Brontë looked puzzled, I felt a new fragile bond forming between us.

"Are you really that unhappy here?" I asked him, as he sequestered the escaped paper amongst the others. "You might have told your father so."

He shrugged. "I am as happy here as I'd be anywhere else."

The bitterness of his reply shocked me. He was young, unfettered, and the darling of his father's eye. Could he have felt life's cruelties already? *I don't want a repetition of what happened at the railway.* That's what the Reverend Brontë had said. Whatever had brought him to this place, and to me, Mr. Brontë had the look of the man who wrestled with demons.

"And you, Mrs. Robinson?" he asked, the left side of his lip curling. "Are *you* happy?"

I struggled between my desperate want of company and a desire to put him in his place, but he went on before either side could win the battle.

"To lose your mother and your daughter in a year must be a lot to bear. Do you think of her often? I'm sorry, I do not know her name."

"Georgiana," I whispered. I'd missed saying it. "I do."

"And when you think of Georgiana, do you dream of some glorious day when she will be returned to you, when the dead will join the living throng, or do you see only the day that you lost her, when she was stolen from you, although she was innocent and you have always praised God and considered Him kind and just?" His rage bubbled below the surface, shooting up like sudden hot springs in the sea of his eyes.

"I cannot—that is to say, I dwell on it only rarely," I answered, not looking at him but somewhere beyond him, near the washhouse, turning over each word before speaking, inspecting its honesty.

Yesterday Ned had run into my dressing room, excited, his foolish fears of a few weeks before forgotten. "Do you know what Mr. Brontë says?" he'd asked, tugging at me. "He says that in Egypt, they weighed your heart against a feather to see if you were good enough for heaven."

I walked away from the house, where others would be stirring, sure that Mr. Brontë would follow me.

"When I come too close to it," I said, "to thinking of Georgiana, I mean, it seems to me that I am in danger of blinding myself by staring into the heart of the sun."

Ned's talk of an exotic afterlife must have given my thoughts an imaginative bent. I almost cringed at my sincerity but spoke on, my opinions on questions others had never asked me about crystallizing before me, my words tumbling out as if I were afraid I might lose them.

"Edmund and my father wouldn't like to hear me say so, but with others I have seen buried, I see nothing, nothing at all, beyond absence and darkness—the same darkness I know will one day swallow me, you, and everyone up."

We had passed the last of the outbuildings, the granary, and were now quite alone and out of sight. But which way to go? If we veered left, we'd end up back at the Monk's House, where Mr. Brontë slept. I made instead for the track that ran through a thick cluster of trees that the children called "the woods."

"Mr. Brontë, it is my deficit of feeling that alarms me, then," I continued. "My eyes stay dry, although when I was a child, they could have watered the world with my tears. But Georgiana's loss—it burns through me. So I busy myself with ordering Lydia's bonnets or correcting Bessy's manners, even though they don't care for me at all and didn't even when they were little. Not the way Georgie did when she threw her arms around my neck or called out for me in the night. Only I, not Marshall or your sister, could console her then."

I could not remember the last time I had spoken at such length, and panic rose inside me when he did not reply at once. But I shouldn't have feared. Mr. Brontë was a rebel as much as me, both of us the children of dour clergymen yet unsuited to a life of piety.

"It is not the same, of course," he said quietly. "But when I was a child—barely eight years old—two of my sisters died. Our mother had passed four years before. The girls left for school so happy, but first Maria and then Elizabeth came back to us, wasted, pale, and struggling to breathe."

"You were at home?" I asked.

Mr. Brontë nodded. "My father wished to educate me himself, relive his boyhood years, and keep an eye on me. And Anne was still in Haworth too, as the baby."

I stayed quiet so that he'd continue.

"Their deaths were weeks apart, yet the scenes have melded together in my mind. Blood on a pillow. My father weeping. A small coffin lashed by rain on its short journey to the church. How could I think God great after that?" He had drawn alongside me and was gazing at the path, beating back the encroaching greenery with his cane.

A few more weeks, and bluebells would cloak the woodland floor. Not as brilliant as at Yoxall, my first home, but stirring in me the same longing that spring had awakened in the final years of my girlhood, a yearning for activity, purpose, change. I had thought to hold them in my wedding posy, but my marriage had come in the dead of winter, when the woods around the Lodge were bare and stripped of their majesty.

"Maria was the best of us," he said, coming to a complete halt. "The most talented and the most tender. She corrected my father's proofs before many children can read. She taught Anne and me not just the words of the Lord's Prayer but the feeling behind them. Maria was just eleven when she left us and yet still it was like losing a second mother. In her absence, Charlotte took up the mantle as the eldest. She has ever fought to be as kind as Maria, and as good, though her nature is wilder, her anger is quicker, and her sense of injustice runs deep."

Charlotte again. Not only was this woman clever, but she'd conquered the faults that I could not, and quenched the fire within.

"You must think I am spoiled," I said. "To have suffered keen losses only now, when you and your sisters saw so much, so young."

Mr. Brontë caught my hand so abruptly that it stunted my breath. "I thought what you said about Georgiana very beautiful," he said, gripping me so hard that the skin buckled and my bones cracked.

Heat tingled in my cheeks, and I pulled away, walking ahead, without him playing advance guard. Stems caught at my skirts. The dew sketched a spider's web over the hem.

"I did not mean you to think it so," I told him, the words catching in my throat, for how could I know whether anything I said was true?

Maybe I had framed that speech only so he might think me just as clever, just as deep, as Charlotte.

"No. There is artistry, not artifice, in you," he said, half to himself. "You too are a poet. I feel it in you when you play and sing."

His compliment, if this was meant as one, made me laugh out loud. I was a lady, who dabbled in the activities on which I spent my time. Nobody had ever even pretended to take my music seriously. The weight on my chest lightened, the phantom pressure of his grip evaporated.

"And you are a fool, Mr. Brontë," I said, spinning round to face him. "Or maybe just very young."

"You may tell me these are one and the same, Mrs. Robinson, but I believe that some of us have souls that are ageless, timeless, and when two such souls meet—" He faltered and blushed. "Have you never felt that there is, or ought to be, something of you beyond you? And if you found that, well, the sheer force of it would wipe all other considerations aside, right every wrong?" He stepped closer, his face inches from mine. "Emily and I have spoken of it often. To resist that call would be as futile as wishing to delay the sun, sitting on the sand in hope of holding back the tide."

Red lips, imperfect, flushed, boyish skin, the light aroma of fresh sweat. The fact of his body forcing the knowledge of its existence upon mine, even if his bundle of papers acted as some security that he could not take me in his arms.

"I fear you have lost me, Mr. Brontë," I said, stiffening. "You and your nomadic sister, Emily, are too poetic for me."

I pushed past him to take the path to the Hall, dodging his protesting arm, and ran back with my skirts scrunched in both hands. Drinking in the air, I smiled with abandon, like a child skipping home from a day of play.

CHAPTER FOUR

EASTER. IT WAS A day when Reverend Lascelles subjected us all to a second lengthy sermon without the relief of the curate Greenhow's concise preaching, and the occasion of another dreaded ritual—late luncheon at Green Hammerton Hall, home to my mother-in-law.

I had pleaded for reprieve to no avail and remained stoic when my daughter Lydia came to me begging likewise.

"The servants appreciate the chance to visit their families," Edmund had admonished me as I'd hovered by the study door a few days previously. "And it means so much to Mother."

"We're going, Lydia," I'd snapped at my daughter when she'd interrupted my toilette that morning, as I was focusing on the gray strands streaking my black locks rather than on her fair head in the looking glass. "That's all there is to say."

Edmund, Lydia, Bessy, and I set off in the carriage a little after one, at least three of us wishing we could eat cold meats with Mary, Ned, and Miss Brontë. This party, due to the younger children's ages, was excused from today's feast. Would Mr. Brontë join them? I imagined mirth ringing out from him; Miss Brontë giving in to a rare smile; and Ned and Mary chuckling with glee.

The countryside was chill and damp, the milestones we passed along the short and jolting ride to Green Hammerton familiar—the fallen bridge, the barn where a farm laborer had hanged himself, the old oak.

My mother's words seemed to float to me across the years. *You'll never be good enough for that wretched woman, Lydia. Tie yourself to a man that attached to his mama and you might as well be marrying her.* But I wouldn't take the bait. Not today. How difficult could it be to play the obedient daughter-in-law? And, besides, the Reverend John Eade, who'd been married to Edmund's late sister, Jane, would be there too, and that was sure to be a distraction. Edmund had informed me he was visiting from County Durham.

We rounded the corner, and the house came into view. Large, it was in a darker brick than ours and covered in matted ivy, which obscured the windows and strangled the many chimney pots. There'd been little to recommend the place when Edmund's mother had taken the lease around the time Mary had been born, except, of course, its proximity to Thorp Green. I might have proven victorious in the battle ejecting her from my house, but her move here rang as clear as a bugle, letting me know the war was far from won.

Our coachman, William Allison, handed me down from the carriage. Even he looked far from his cheerful self. Perhaps he was imagining his wife and children eating their Easter dinner without him.

"So you've arrived at last, Edmund," our hostess squawked at us as soon as we joined her in the parlor, which smelled of decaying flowers and sherry.

She was an imposing woman, one who had always been more impressive than handsome.

"Lydia," (this addressed to me), "you're too pale and Bessy is getting fat."

I kissed the old lady's parched cheek and watched the girls do the same, viewing Bessy's figure with something between distaste and defensiveness. I chastised her for eating too much, it was true, but

Bessy was taller and more active than the rest of us. It was hardly fair to call her fat.

"You look wonderful, Grandmama," said Lydia, who gave out compliments only in hope of receiving them. "I wish I could wear lilac. I do miss color."

Her grandmother waved her aside. "Dear John is recovering from a dreadful cold, isn't that right, Reverend?"

I noticed John Eade for the first time. He was standing sentinel in the corner, by a tasseled lamp, and watching the proceedings with an expression as morose as if he'd been beside an open grave.

"A terrible cold, Mrs. Robinson," he confirmed, with a sniff. "Just terrible. I feared I'd be unable to visit at all. I didn't wish to subject any of you, and you especially, madam, to such a horror. But your last letter convinced me."

"Stuff and nonsense, John!" Mrs. Robinson threw the Reverend toward me and grasped Edmund's arm. "I am of good Metcalfe stock. It'll take more than a cold to kill *me*. Now, to luncheon."

I didn't wish to touch the clergyman's arm and so merely pinched his sleeve, leaning away from him and trying not to listen to his congested breathing. Lydia and Bessy linked arms and fell into step behind us. This was it, then, the dreaded dinner. We trailed, two by two, behind our hostess, like slaves going to the galleys.

YET IT WASN'T UNTIL the end of our meal, when I was struggling through the final forkfuls of a dry, week-old seed cake, that the expected onslaught came.

"John brought letters from my Mary's girls," Mrs. Elizabeth Robinson began, settling back in her chair—the only one with arms—for a round of interrogation, her favorite digestive.

"Indeed," I said, as this comment appeared to be directed toward me.

"Her Mary" was Edmund's other sister, the one who, despite her ob-

vious failing in not being Jane, was favored for the large brood of biddable girls and necessary son she'd borne to Charles Thorp, who had the
living in Ryton, not far from Aycliffe.

"Your cousins write so well, and with such penmanship, Lydia,
Bessy!" Edmund's mother continued, turning to my daughters. "And
show such care for their grandmama, despite the distance between us."
Here a pause, a sigh. "I thought—didn't I say so, John dear?—that I
would see you two, and your brother and sister, more often now that I
am your only grandmother. You might even walk here from Thorp
Green were you not so lazy."

I winced.

The Reverend Eade nodded with slow solemnity, closing his eyes
and resting his hands high on his domed belly. A dewdrop was hanging
from his left nostril.

"Hmm?" The old woman rounded on Bessy, who jumped in her
chair. "Have you stopped and thought, girl, what your life might be like
if I were gone as well?"

"No, Grandmama," said Bessy, tracing the floral pattern around the
edge of her bowl with the tip of her spoon.

"Duty. Didn't I say so, Reverend? A decided lack of duty is what de-
fines the younger generations. That is what Mary and Charles Thorp
have fought so hard against. Most young people care only for their parties and their gossip and their ringlets." She shot a glare at Lydia, whose
hand froze mid-twirl, a curl still wrapped tight around half her finger.
"Not like my Jane."

"We are all very happy your health is so strong, Mother," said Edmund, ignoring her oft-repeated invocation of his dead sister's name.
He took her right hand from where it lay on the table between them
and planted a kiss on the raised network of veins. His chin puckered,
wedged against one of her rings, a garish ruby that brought out the
blotches in her skin.

"And there is old Mrs. Thompson lying on her deathbed at Kirby
Hall." Edmund's mother had veered onto an entirely different topic:

our grand neighbors. She was gesturing so widely that she nearly smacked a servant in the face as the woman bent in to remove the remnants of a jelly. "Over ninety years she's lived, and for what? To be forgotten in her own home and ill treated by that brood of spinster granddaughters?"

"Oh no, Grandmama," said Lydia, her interest piqued at the mention of the Thompsons. I could practically see the wheels in her head turning as she plotted to bring the conversation around to Harry, the heir. "Miss Amelia, who, you know, is my most particular friend, says they treat old Mrs. Thompson royally. Mr. Harry Thompson even brought her—"

"Lydia, why do you let these girls interrupt their elders?" Mrs. Robinson blinked at me. "No expense has been spared on them. They've had gloves, hats, countless dresses, a governess."

This was a point of debate between us. She, who had petitioned for Ned to have a tutor, had told Edmund not once but several times that she couldn't see what I did all day if I let some other, less accomplished woman finish my headstrong daughters. And educating girls hardly merited such an expense.

"To hear them, you'd think they didn't have an ounce of breeding or cultivation between them. You should get rid of that woman," she concluded with a flourish.

"Of Miss Brontë?" exclaimed Bessy, dropping her spoon into her bowl with a clang that rang through me. "But we all care for her very much."

"Enough, Bessy," I said as mildly as I could. I gave her shin a sharp kick under the table and watched her eyes grow watery and accusing.

"Ned's new tutor, Mother, actually came to us by way of our governess. They are brother and sister." Edmund, ever the diplomat, dabbed at his beard with his napkin.

Old Mrs. Robinson smiled. "I see. The father is a clergyman, I think? How fitting that the son should be one too."

I dropped my chin so she wouldn't see me smile. How horrified she'd be to hear Mr. Brontë's views on God!

"Mr. Brontë isn't a clergyman," said Bessy, too foolish to keep out of the fray. "He used to be a painter and he wants to be a poet."

"A painter and a poet?" Our matriarch spoke the words slowly, sounding them out. "How eminently unsuitable. This is your doing, Lydia, I suppose?"

The good Reverend Eade stared up to heaven as if praying for our souls.

The smile dropped from my face. Blood rushed to my head. I wasn't so special. Others also knew of Mr. Brontë's poetry. It was as if the scene in the woods were playing out before me amongst the half-eaten dishes of custards and preserves, shaming me. The poem, Mr. Brontë's hand on mine, the words he'd spoken about souls, words I'd struggled to remember precisely since.

I opened my mouth to speak, but my throat, still coated with crumbs, was too dry.

"All my doing, Mother," said Edmund. "I assure you."

"Don't defend her, Edmund," Mrs. Robinson said. "This tutor is young, I suppose, girls?"

Lydia and Bessy nodded.

"Unmarried. Unordained. And you invite this man, this self-proclaimed poet, around your daughters? What were you thinking? There can only be one result."

"I—"

She waved my unvoiced protest aside. "These eccentricities, these flights of fancy, might have been charming in a bride, Lydia, but at your age, you should know better."

"Edmund, girls, we're leaving." I rose, steadying myself by grasping the table.

"Lydia, sit down," said Edmund, without an ounce of passion.

The Reverend coughed and sneezed at once, breaking the silence.

"Well, *I'm* leaving," I said.

My husband didn't repeat his objection.

I practically ran from the room and from the house, back toward the carriage.

William Allison was leaning against one of the old poplars, smoking. When he saw me, he stood up straight and clasped his pipe behind him as if to hide it. The plumes of smoke radiated around him before vanishing into the air.

"Is owt the matter, ma'am?" he asked, cautious, scared to address me, as if I were a small child mid-tantrum.

"Oh, William!" I cried. "I wish I were dead."

A shadow of panic passed over his face.

But I laughed one of those laughs that's on the edge of tears and held out my hand.

"Ma'am?" he said slowly.

"Your pipe, William."

I could tell he didn't want to, but he handed it to me.

There was a pleasing weight to it. The wood was smooth where William had circled his thumb, caressing the bowl for years. He was younger than me. Perhaps it had been his father's before.

I inhaled, closing my eyes as the smoke clouded my insides, then exhaled with the world still dark, although I could feel that Allison was still watching me.

"Thank you," I breathed, as the grounds of Green Hammerton Hall came back into focus—row after row of regimented and labeled rosebushes, with the dark shadow of the house behind.

Once I'd returned his pipe, Allison handed me into the carriage. As soon as he shut the door, I began to cry.

Two hours Edmund and the girls tarried while I waited there. And they all avoided my gaze when we finally wended our way back to the Hall through the shadowy dusk.

The night was drawing in, making the fields, us, and me, most of all, invisible. The unbearable monotony of my life pressed heavier on my chest as we rounded the corners before Thorp Green Hall. How funny it is that men and women struggle as they die, but few of us kick or scream as we are lowered alive into our tombs.

FOR THE FIRST TIME in recent memory, Lydia and Bessy trod the stairs to their bedrooms unbidden. When both doors had closed and the creaks of their floorboards above us stopped, Edmund and I walked into the drawing room.

"Go on. Tell me how I embarrassed you in front of your mother," I said, too weary to argue, wishing this Godforsaken day were over.

But he would not give me an escape.

"Mother can be blunt—difficult—but she was only trying to help, Lydia. She raised three children herself. And she raised us well." Edmund was not looking at me but at the chimney glass, which reflected his expression, tired and pained.

"Raised? Rather, tyrannized," I spat, the anger surging again inside me.

"Quiet," he said, pacing even farther away. "The servants and the children will hear us."

I imagined the girls stealing to their doors, Ned hiding beneath the covers, and Marshall at my dressing table, ready to take down my hair, pretend the day was uneventful, and guide me, like a frail and senile woman, to bed.

"You are all afraid of her," I said. "You, Charles and Mary Thorp, John Eade. You all do exactly as she says."

He did not answer.

"I daresay it was the shock of being free from that woman that killed Jane rather than her condition," I went on, taking a different tack and watching for any response from him. "She didn't know, at more than forty, what it was to be her own mistress."

Edmund stiffened, but that was the only change perceptible in him. I flailed about as if drowning, clutching at anyone, even if it meant dragging him down with me.

"How can you live with yourself?" I cried, even louder. "How can you think yourself a man, still clinging to your mother's petticoats?"

"Lydia." It had worked. Edmund said my name, turned, reached out his hand, and took a step toward me. But tonight I could not stop. My anger burst from me, like the sparks from the fireworks I had seen many years before one Guy Fawkes Night.

"I have had enough." My tears streamed now, undermining each word and underscoring my volatility. "I will not have her speak to me like that or hold the Thorps up as a paragon. She must not come to Scarborough this summer. I will not have her ruin my life in the last days of hers."

"Were we speaking of Scarborough?" Edmund raised his voice for the first time. He hated how, with me, one fight became all fights, forming and re-forming like different configurations of dancers at a ball.

Why was it that when I wanted love, I took anger as a worthy consolation?

"I need some air," I said, starting for the door. "Do not follow me." And although we had been married nearly twenty years and I knew he would take me at my word, somehow I still hoped that he'd ignore me.

I WALKED UNTIL I reached the Monk's House, which was shrouded in darkness. The Sewells, like most of the other servants, had not yet returned. Only one light burned in one of the upper rooms—Mr. Brontë's room.

Would he be preparing Ned's lessons or reading a letter from Charlotte or Emily? There was a chance he was tinkering with his poetry. Whatever the pattern of his solitary hours, he would set everything aside were I to come to him, were I to let him see me with my face red and tears in my eyes. And it wouldn't just be for manners' sake. He would understand.

But I couldn't go in, could I?

Just about visible through the gloom was the white statuette of the monk himself. The figure, hood worn so low it covered his face, had watched over the entrance to the Monk's Lodge for centuries from his niche above the door. One of his hands was raised, making the drapery of his robes uneven. I hadn't thought it before, but perhaps his hidden gesture was a warning or a threat, not a blessing.

The front door opened at my touch. I stepped inside.

It looked the same: narrow, uncarpeted, with low, dark beams and an uneven central staircase. The hallway was empty except for a stand, which held a broken umbrella and a pair of Tom Sewell's discarded boots.

I had not been in the Monk's House above a handful of times since the morning after our honeymoon. Edmund had led me by the hand from building to building and from room to room of my new home.

"You are mistress here, and here, and also here," he'd said. "The bells of Holy Trinity have been ringing out your arrival. They will fête you in the villages." He twirled me so hard I nearly fell, but then caught me just in time and pushed me up against the wall to kiss me.

I gave the place little notice then, for all it was a fine house, beautifully preserved and unmistakably English, with its sloping roofs and lattice windows. I'd cared only for the Hall. I would drape curtains fit for the stage in my dressing room just to see Mother gasp at the expense. I'd take inspiration from the Venetian frescoes I'd just seen for our dining room. I thought then they'd never fade from my memory. And I'd commission a great fountain to make a feature of the stew pond.

"It's allegorical," I would say with a wave of my hand, when my unmarried friends came to marvel at my good fortune. "Edmund, my husband, can explain the mythological subject."

But a month later, I was pregnant, sick to my stomach, and fretful when I slept. My grand schemes evaporated faster than Edmund's ardor and sounded as distant as Italy's opera houses. Soon I was unable to either sit or stand with ease, and the doctor prescribed rest. My own mother came to nurse me, and Edmund's mother extended the time she was to live with us, reclaiming her dominion over the household. She, just as domineering then as she'd been tonight, hung floral chintz curtains in my dressing room, in the very same material she now had in her own.

"Mr. Brontë?" I called from the bottom of the stairs, hanging on to the wooden banister, but afraid to venture any farther, get any closer.

He didn't answer.

I climbed the first step with my left foot, as always. The habit brought me some comfort, but a lump was rising in my throat.

The second. The house gave a great groan. It knew I was here.

This was foolish.

The third, taking two steps this time, regardless of the pattern.

I would go to him. And then?

I paused. Something had caught on my hand. A splinter.

He would understand if only I could find the words with which to confide in him.

I climbed again.

Other young men might think it improper, my coming here, but he would not care for such niceties. Our conversation in "the woods" had confirmed this. And what was it the Reverend Brontë had said? Mr. Brontë and his sisters were children raised by the moors.

I cupped my eyes with my hand to protect them from the light that streamed across the landing. His door was ajar.

Maybe when he saw me, he would take me in his arms, and I would have no choice but to melt into him. His kisses would be fevered like my bridegroom Edmund's, drinking deep of me, his hand guiding me by the waist, drawing me down.

"Mr. Brontë," I stuttered, rounding the door.

But it wasn't Mr. Brontë, or at least not the strong, willful, sure version of him I had conjured up.

The tutor was lying on a low and threadbare couch. His head was thrown back, his shirt open at the neck and stained with something yellow, and an empty bottle was discarded by his side.

"Mr. Brontë!" I repeated, catching onto the doorframe to support myself.

He was drunk.

Mr. Brontë raised his head, looking the wrong way, to the side, at first, before seeing me. "Lydia!" he cried, flinging his arms wide in welcome.

I froze. How dare he?

"Lydia Gisborne," he said, hissing out the "s."

Which of the servants had told him my maiden name?

"Join me!" he cried. He grabbed the bottle and offered it to me, upside down.

"Mr. Brontë, I'll ask you to address me only by my married name," I said, feeling myself turning as red as he was, ashamed that all it had taken was a petty argument with Edmund to send me running to him.

"Lydia, you are beautiful," Brontë said, attempting to rise but giving up when his legs did not cooperate. "I thought you'd be old, but you're not. Or at least not to me."

I didn't stay to hear more. I turned and closed the door, although Mr. Brontë was in no state to follow me. Taking my dress in my hand, I raced down the stairs, skidded across the hall, and nearly hurtled into the housekeeper, Miss Sewell, as she stepped through the front door.

She let out a yelp of surprise. "Mrs. Robinson?" she said, hesitating, as if distrusting her eyes.

I was frozen, like some statue of a fleeing nymph, my weight on my front foot, my free hand reaching for the knob.

"What was that, Liz?" Her brother appeared behind her but stopped in his tracks at the sight of me. "I hope nothing is the matter, madam," he said, removing his hat slowly, eyes exploring the darkness behind me.

His question brought me back to myself.

"The matter?" I dropped my skirts, brought my feet together, and pushed a strand of hair behind my ear that had been plastered to my face by nervous sweat. "No, yes—That is to say, nothing serious. Mr. Brontë has taken ill. A bad cold."

"Ill?" said Miss Sewell, her morbid curiosity awakened. "Should Tom ride out for the doctor? I'll bring him some sage and honey and take care of the boy."

"That won't be necessary, Miss Sewell," I told her. "I won't have Dr. Crosby called at every sneeze, or 'the boy'—who, might I remind you, is a man nearly as old as yourself—bothered when all he needs is a day's rest."

"As you think best, madam." She pursed her lips together and glanced at her brother.

"I just brought him some brandy to see him through the night," I continued, hoping I was not protesting too much. "He is not to be disturbed until tomorrow luncheon at least." I gave them each a sharp nod.

"Very good, madam," said Sewell, stepping to the side to make room for me to leave.

"*You* brought him brandy?" parroted his more suspicious sibling, her confusion returning.

"Is that worthy of commentary, Miss Sewell?" I asked.

"I only meant to say that was very kind of you, ma'am."

What else could she say? She lowered her head as I floated past her, wishing the pair a happy Easter.

Tonight, before the housekeeper returned to the Hall, they would discuss the lady of the house tending to the strange young tutor.

"I always knew she was a hypocrite," Miss Sewell would say, her viperish eyes flashing as she kissed her brother good night. "She's never let *me* have a man. How many years do you think she has on him?"

CHAPTER FIVE

SALT IN MY NOSE, sun in my eyes, and the wind whistling past my ears, loosening my hair and carving out sharp valleys in the sand. I had to fight against the thick folds of my dress to walk, as they flew back— black, billowing, warning of disaster as surely as the sails of Theseus's ship.

There was a time when summering in Scarborough had been an escape. And now? In the week since we'd arrived, it had proved as bad as home. Worse, for here Mr. Brontë was with us at much closer quarters, and my mother-in-law was next door rather than at the safe distance provided by Green Hammerton Hall.

"Mama!" Mary cried, ahead of me, dancing sideways to avoid an incoming wave.

I squinted to make out her newly freckled face.

"It is Ned and Mr. Brontë," she called. "I can see them."

I could not. I had always struggled with my sight but was too vain to use eyeglasses to correct it. What's more, with age, the sliver of world that was clear to me was narrowing. The foreground was now hazy too—the pages of my novels and the neat lines of my sister Mary's letters as much of a blur as the muddled blue of the horizon.

"Go to them," I told the daughter I'd named for *my* Mary, pausing to catch my breath. "And use your parasol. You will lose your complexion."

Mary ran up the beach, without heeding how she looked. The lace-trimmed parasol bobbed uselessly behind her, as she dodged stray children, invalids, and a man leading a donkey. The beast's head hung low. His gait was slow. I imagined staring into his tragic eyes.

"Pomfret cakes, madam, a halfpenny a bag." I waved a seller aside, and he trundled on with his cart.

There was a sad lack of people worth knowing here this year, for all that the South Bay beach was so crowded. None of the Thompsons had traveled from Kirby Hall, out of respect to the grandmother who had finally quit this world not long after my mother-in-law's predictions. And many of the other regulars had delayed their trips until August, although Edmund's mother had insisted on July.

Yet Lydia and Bessy had still found a pair of girls their own age and station to giggle with, who provided the double advantages of plain faces and a fashionable married sister to play chaperone. Ned kept at his lessons and spent hours in the Rotunda Museum talking geology with Mr. Brontë. Miss Brontë used her moments of freedom to play with Flossy, a black-and-white terrier the girls had given her a month or so ago, or to visit St. Mary's, the church in the old town, although on Sundays we attended services at Christ Church. And Edmund played escort to his mother, excusing me from sharing most of these duties.

So today I was alone, or as good as alone, with only Mary—the leftover child—who moped around, awkward to a fault as girls are when on the cusp of womanhood, although she seemed to have more energy today.

I couldn't fight against the wind any longer so strode away from the water and sat where the sand was soft, fine, and dry. I didn't bother to lay out my plaid but burrowed my hands deep and inspected how the light shone through the tiny crystals that gathered under my fingernails.

I didn't look after Mary, afraid of meeting Mr. Brontë's eyes as they walked toward me. I gazed instead at the Woods' Lodgings on the Cliff, our home here for the next month.

I had hardly spoken to Mr. Brontë since that night in the Monk's House three months ago, although I had studied the scene a thousand times, second-guessing my intentions, and his, and not knowing what I regretted more—going to his room, or the state I had found him in there.

For a week I'd been convinced that he would seek me out, apologize, and explain away what I had seen so that we could continue as before. Instead, he avoided speaking to me, or even looking at me, until I felt like a stranger at my own table. Miss Brontë and I both watched her brother raise his wineglass to his lips, again and again, as if competing over who could tally each sip.

"Edmund, darling," I'd said one night, raking my fingers across his scalp on a rare occasion when he let me touch him. "I wonder if Mr. and Miss Brontë have become a little *too* accustomed to joining us for dinner?"

"Oh?" he said. "I thought they amused you."

"Miss Brontë barely speaks, and Mr. Brontë may be losing his novelty," I quipped. "But of course if you want them there . . ." I trailed off.

Edmund moved my hand to the other side of his head. "No, no. Whatever makes you happy, Lydia. Tell Miss Sewell we'll dine with them once a fortnight."

A laugh—Lydia's most affected laugh—floated on the breeze. I couldn't help but swivel to the cluster of clouds moving along the beach toward me. I'd let the children set aside their mourning, and so the girls and their friends were a riot of colorful ribbons, as uncoordinated as a circus tent.

I scrambled to my feet and shook off the sand. Lydia was framed by those silly and uncomely girls, while Mr. Brontë was walking between Bessy and the married sister, Mrs. Whatever-she-was-called. And Ned and Mary were running this way, racing to arrive first.

"There is a play tonight!" yelled Ned, coming within shouting distance. "With sword fights and a hunchback!"

"You mustn't listen to Ned go on so. It is by Mr. Shakespeare," said Mary with authority, when they stood almost breathless in front of me. She appeared to have lost her parasol during her short absence. "And it's at the Theatre Royal."

"I see," I said, trying not to laugh at them.

"And Mrs. . . . Mrs. . . . Agnes's and Bella's sister has tickets and we must all go!" Ned ended on a flourish. "Oh, can we?"

I calculated. Edmund was accompanying his "dear Mama" to one of the Spa Saloon concerts tonight and, with the children and their keepers gone, I would be able to enjoy the Lodgings in solitude.

"Mr. Shakespeare, did you say, darlings?" I said, taking both children by the hands and walking them away from the others. "In that case, I have no objections."

"Oh, Marshall, I should have gone with them!" My desire to be alone forgotten, I paced the library, which was small and ill furnished compared to ours at home. I pressed my nose against the cold glass and struggled to see anything of the world beyond the window. The fabled view of the beach far below had faded.

"To the concert, madam?" Marshall said, still concentrating on the hem she was letting down on one of Mary's petticoats.

"No, no, to the theater." Wild horses couldn't have dragged me to spend time with Edmund's mother tonight.

I strode back and sat on the chaise beside Marshall, studying her expressionless face. She saw me, the real me, more than anyone else, yet wouldn't give up this playacting. She was the servant, and I was the mistress. We had our parts and, with them, our corresponding lines and silences.

"Is that right, ma'am?" she said, after a long pause. "Well, mightn't you have gone with them?"

"Yes, yes," I snapped. "But that isn't the point."

She didn't ask me to elucidate what the point was, but only because she knew that I would tell her anyway.

"Marshall?" I said, drawing so close to her that I blocked the light. She dropped her needlework into her lap and looked up at me.

"Not one of them was anxious that I join them. Not one of them. It was all the same, either way. And isn't that a slight? There was a time when I had invitations and friends, when parties weren't complete without me. But now it's 'Bring your daughters, Mrs. Robinson,' if anyone thinks to ask me anywhere at all. And not an ounce of gratitude from any of them, no respect for where they came from."

There was only sympathy in Marshall's eyes, although even to my own ears, my speech sounded petty. I laid my head on her shoulder and let her stroke my temple, feeling all the sorrier for myself that Ann Marshall was the only one who cared for me.

There was a knock at the door, and I sprang away from her, as if we were a young couple who'd been caught kissing.

"Come in," I called, expecting William Allison or maybe Bob Pottage, our gardener who'd also come with us to Scarborough in the guise of a groom.

But it was Mr. Brontë.

"Mrs. Robinson." Brontë addressed me for the first time in months and walked into the center of the room without waiting to be summoned closer. There was a confidence in his manner I hadn't seen recently, a directness in his stare that made me think there had been a crisis.

"The theater—? Is all well?" I asked, drawing my hand to my chest. My breathing was shallow.

"All is well. We were one too many for our tickets, and I volunteered to step aside."

I nodded, though my heart was still racing. "But why are you here?"

"I knew that Mr. Robinson—that you were also without company tonight. Both of you." He added the caveat, with a nod toward Marshall, pulling us back from the brink of impropriety.

She resumed her sewing, gaze downcast.

I had no reason to doubt her absolute loyalty. My struggle was with my emotions regarding Mr. Brontë. The disgust I had felt that night at the Monk's House fought against my joy that he had appeared and at that juncture when I had most longed for succor.

"I thought you might be in need of amusement," he said. "Are you?"

But that wasn't the question. The question was, *Can you forgive me? And, Can we be as we were?*

I swallowed my pride. Hadn't I wanted to be sought out above others? And to learn more of Mr. Brontë and his dangerous, different mind?

"I am," I whispered.

Mr. Brontë walked to the bookcase on the far wall and strained his arm to reach the upper shelf. I could see the muscles of his shoulder rippling, even through his shirt.

"I doubt they have much of a collection here," I said. I had to say something, or they'd both hear how my caged heart rattled against my ribs.

"I think we should have some Shakespeare of our own. Don't you, Mrs. Robinson?" he asked. He was already leafing through the pages, seeking out the play he had chosen.

What a refined and romantic form of entertainment! Was this how the Brontës spent their evenings, reading and debating great literature with each other? And Mr. Brontë thought me capable of this too.

"Marshall and I would be very grateful," I said.

My maid bent even lower, as if trying to blend in with the furniture.

"Go on," I whispered.

Mr. Brontë dragged an armchair from across the room to read by our solitary lamp. He sat, pushed back his curls, which had grown long enough to fall into his eyes, and positioned his feet so they were nearly touching mine.

"If music be the food of love, play on; / Give me excess of it, that, sur-feiting, / The appetite may sicken, and so die." He barely looked at the page, focusing instead on me.

I closed my eyes to avoid his gaze, picturing the characters, and let-ting his liquid words wash over me—rhythmic, warm, and inescapably earnest. My Illyria bore a striking resemblance to Scarborough, but the beaches there were clean and empty and the sea a dazzling turquoise, as still as a looking glass in the peace that followed the great storm.

At the end of the second scene, between Viola and the Captain, Mr. Brontë paused for breath.

Marshall poured the tea, which one of the local servants had brought in for us.

"I forget how visceral he is, how immediate," said Mr. Brontë, turn-ing back one of the almost translucent pages to study an earlier line. *"My desires, like fell and cruel hounds, / E'er since pursue me.* It is in-credible to be pulled into the humanity of it, leaping off the page al-though centuries have passed."

"You forget, I think, Mr. Brontë," I said, my lip curling slightly, "that the Duke knows nothing of love. He is suffering under an infatuation, a boyish delusion."

"What!" Mr. Brontë cried, with mock derision. "Who could question Orsino's choice before he met his match in Viola? Would you deny that Rosaline was fair just because Juliet was fairer? You are a harsh critic of men, Mrs. Robinson, to demand their first affections, as well as their deepest."

I opened my mouth to say something through my smile but my joy mingled with longing. The toe of his boot was now pressing against my slipper but I wanted him closer, and my hand in his yet again. Perhaps I could send Marshall away on some pretense, to bring sugar? But the door flew open, sending a vibration through the room that spilled tea from the cup I was holding into my saucer.

"Here she is, Edmund!" my mother-in-law cried. "Taking tea with the tutor."

"And Marshall," I protested, but my maid was already scuttling toward the side door.

"You didn't go to the theater?" Edmund asked, undoing his cravat to dab at the perspiration that had gathered on his forehead from the walk up to our buildings.

His mother, *damn her*, looked unaffected from the exertion.

"I took one of my headaches," I said, not trusting myself to glance in the direction of Mr. Brontë, who was standing to attention beside me, still holding the *Works*. "And Mr. Brontë was so good as to read to us. He was just leaving."

"Leaving, nonsense!" Elizabeth Robinson boomed, taking the spot that Marshall had just vacated and spreading out her skirts so wide that I was wedged against the scroll at the foot of the bench. "Read on, Mr. Brent. I am sure this will be most educational."

An expression of distaste passed over Mr. Brontë's face as she butchered his name, but he nodded and reopened the volume on a random page.

"*Go thy ways, Kate: / That man i' the world who shall report he has / A better wife, let him in nought be trusted, / For speaking false in that,*" he began to drone.

Old Mrs. Robinson stared at the tutor.

Edmund watched my reflection in the mirror above the mantel.

I nodded every now and then as if following the lines, although in truth, I no longer knew which play Mr. Brontë was reading from.

Whichever one it was, the drama was tedious and Mr. Brontë's tone monotonous. It was as if he too had lost the import of what he was reading, as if the four of us would be stuck here forever, waiting to discover who would be the first to break.

The sound of the children's raised and irritable voices was a relief. It was the sign I had been waiting for. I sprang to my feet and called them in from the hallway.

Miss Brontë looked tired, Lydia jubilant, Ned and Bessy illtempered, and Mary on the verge of tears.

"How was the play, my darlings?" I said, swooping in to kiss Ned's rosy cheek.

"Mary took ill and insisted that we leave before the end, which is such a bore!" complained Bessy. "I wanted to see Richmond run his sword through the king."

Ned mimed the action, invisible sword pointed at Miss Brontë's abdomen.

"You are unwell, Mary?" I asked.

I was more surprised at Lydia's even temper at being dragged away from an "occasion." Her color was so high that her face matched her fuchsia dress and a smile was playing on her lips.

"I—" Mary began.

"Of course she is unwell, Lydia," Edmund's mother said. She, the only one who remained sitting, had lounged back even more so I could hardly see her behind her stiff, voluminous skirts. "Late nights! Theatricals! Miss Brent shouldn't let the girls go on so, even if *you* are oblivious about how young ladies should be reared."

"I am sorry, madam," whispered Miss Brontë.

Her brother shot her a look of incredulity. "Brontë, Mrs. Robinson," he said to Edmund's mother, with a bow.

"I beg your pardon, sir?" she said, sitting up so that her head emerged once more.

"Our name is Brontë," he said. "Not Brent."

Everyone stared, waiting to see how Grandmama would react to such a challenge.

"Edmund!" she called, sticking out her hand. "Escort me to my rooms. I have had entertainment enough for this evening."

Edmund helped her up from the chaise and offered her his arm.

Mary tried to whisper something to me, but her words were inaudible. I brushed her aside.

"And you!" my mother-in-law shot at Miss Brontë. "Get those children to bed!"

Miss Brontë inclined her head.

"Good night, Mr. Brontë," I said, very deliberately, before Edmund and his mother were out of earshot, anxious that they hear him leave with the others, and still more scared of what I would do if he did not.

Mr. Brontë bowed and held the door for Lydia, as Ned and Bessy lined up to give me the expected kiss good night.

"Mama," hissed Mary. "I must speak with you."

"Mary," I protested, the desire to be alone again overwhelming me in a sudden flood. I would take the Shakespeare to bed. Maybe Mr. Brontë and I could discuss the play in the morning.

"Please, Mama."

The door clicked closed behind the tutor.

"Well, what is it?" I dragged Mr. Brontë's chair back to its original position and, when I turned back, was surprised to find Mary crying. "My love?" I pinched her chin and teased her face toward mine.

"Mama, I'm frightened," I made out between her sobs.

"Whatever is the matter?" I asked, my heart beating a little faster, thinking of Georgiana and how she'd said she was afraid to journey to heaven alone.

"I'm—I'm—" Her voice dropped even lower. "Between my legs. I'm bleeding."

I dropped her chin, laughed, and gave her shoulder a quick (I hoped comforting) squeeze.

Mary's expression fluctuated with confusion.

"Is that all?" I asked. "Mary, you are a goose. There is no need to be frightened. I thought the other girls would have told you? Or Miss Brontë? But no matter. I'll have Marshall bring you rags."

I walked over to pull the bell cord.

"I'm not dying?" Mary stuttered, clenching and unclenching her fist at her side.

"No, no," I said, beckoning over Marshall, who was hovering at the door. "But I'm far too tired to teach you anything tonight. Marshall here will see to the soaking of your things."

CHAPTER SIX

THE THEATRE ROYAL SMELLED of oil, tobacco, and sweat. The crowds trod on my dress as we fought our way through the foyer, and I was nearly winded climbing the stairs to the finer seats. But then we emerged into a galaxy of candles and gas lamps glinting off the gilt decorations and reflecting in each crystal of the great chandelier.

The musicians tuned their instruments, the atonal symphony making me cringe. The throng buzzed with a thousand questions and observations. Men and women of every station lived out their dramas in groups and pairs. But at the sound of a gong or flicker of the curtain, all that would no longer matter. We would enter another world, beckoned in by Mr. Samuel Roxby's summer company, a world where the line between villain and hero was clear, where misunderstandings were always reversed by the end, and where love and beauty never aged.

In the fortnight since Mr. Brontë had read to me, there had been something in the air, a shared mania that drew us all (except for Edmund and his mother) time and again to the theater. The children were too delighted to question my change of heart, and even Miss Brontë softened in light of this new, harmonious pastime. Together we'd quaked at the murderer, Eugene Aram; laughed at Bottom, transformed into an ass; reveled in the romance of *The Love Chase* and in its farce.

Mr. Brontë was always at my side, making comments only he would, about the poetry of the piece, as well as its substance. Miss Brontë would find morals in the scenes, largely drawn from the curate Greenhow's sermons, but only Mary and Ned would listen to her explanations. And Lydia, who grew more beautiful each day, would elbow her way to the front of our box and crane her neck over the side. She was oblivious to the admiring looks she drew from other patrons, her eyes were so fixed upon the stage, except when she turned to whisper a confidence to her co-conspirator, Bessy.

Tonight was the hottest night we'd had yet, and we were sweating through the fifth and final act of a history play by Mr. Bulwer-Lytton. I fanned myself so hard that my wrist ached. Ned slept, drooling into Miss Brontë's lap.

"Should we leave early to avoid the mob?" Mr. Brontë asked softly, his breath blowing a stray hair against my cheek.

Miss Brontë coughed.

"I will soldier through to the end," I said, seeing that Lydia showed no signs of fatigue and wishing I had her energy.

The last scenes were torturous, but I held my ground. If only I could lean against Mr. Brontë, see the rest of the show sideways from the vantage point of his shoulder, and trust him to steer me home.

At the final line, a sigh of collective relief rippled through the auditorium, followed by rapturous applause. The actors, oblivious to the true reason for this outpouring, took the cheers as their cue for an extended curtain call.

In the center was the people's favorite: Harry Beverley. At this distance, his features were indecipherable, but I imagined his face beaming with joy at the validation, with a blush deep enough to match his red cardinal's robe.

Now. I nodded at Mr. Brontë and gripped Lydia's milky-white upper arm, pulling her back.

"Ow!" She shoved my hand away and continued to applaud as a trio of actors dressed as manservants took their bows.

"We're leaving, Lydia," I said. "Bessy, Mary. Ned, wake up!"

Miss Brontë, ever fragile, was struggling to rouse the boy between her coughs, but her brother stepped in, guiding Ned out of the box. She stood, steadying herself by holding on to a chair.

"This way!" I told her, using my folded fan to gesture toward the exit. "We don't wish to be caught on the stairs."

We were.

Somebody must have whispered to Mr. Beverley that his improvised finale was becoming tiresome and dragged him into the wings. For as we reached the stairwell, the doors to the auditorium flew open and a flood of people streamed out, their voices raised even higher than before the enforced silence, dissecting the play or, more likely, debating their entertainment for the rest of the evening.

Heat.

Panic rising inside me when we were in the midst of the fray, surrounded by faces, yet losing the ones we knew, glancing back and shouting indistinguishable instructions at each other about which way to go and where we should meet.

Halfway.

Just breathe.

The chaos around us took on a different character. The crowd parted like the Red Sea, which was strange, as a moment before there'd been no space at all.

A man with a commanding voice was shouting, "Move aside, please. Move aside! A lady has fainted. Bring smelling salts and water."

I went up on my tiptoes but could see only the backs of men's heads and ladies' crumpled bonnets.

"Mama!" I looked down, and there was Ned, now very much awake. "It is Miss Brontë—she has fallen!"

Hand in hand, we fought our way to the clearing. There indeed was Miss Brontë, lying on the litter-strewn floor, with Lydia and Bessy crouched on either side of her.

She couldn't be ill. I'd have to find another governess and maybe, if she left, Mr. Brontë would leave us too. But, ah, she was fine and coming to. What a fuss over nothing.

"Step aside, madam. Step aside. This lady is unwell," said the man I'd heard policing the scene earlier.

"This lady is only our governess," I snapped at him, at the very second that Mr. Brontë emerged.

The tutor was apologizing to a larger lady he'd knocked into in his haste. Thank heaven he hadn't heard me.

The crowd was thinning now that the people could see Miss Brontë wasn't a striking damsel in distress and that her life was in no immediate danger. We were in the theater after all, and beauty and death always provided the best spectacles.

"Thank you, sir, for your assistance," I told our self-appointed director. "Would you be so kind as to fetch someone from the theater?"

He nodded and left, subdued.

"Anne?" Mr. Brontë bent over his sister.

"Branwell, I—I'll—" Miss Brontë collapsed into a coughing fit that sounded a little forced to my ear.

"Mr. Brontë." I touched his arm.

He spun toward me as if attracted to a magnet.

"Trust me to look after dear Miss Brontë." My hand lingered a second too long. His arm was warm, his bicep taut.

He went to protest.

"No, no. I insist," I said. "I wouldn't have anyone else see to her."

Miss Brontë's coughing was constant, upsetting my nerves even more than the earlier clapping and bravos.

"Can you walk with the children?" I asked her brother, sorry to be rid of him but reestablishing control. "Take them back to the Cliff? Here's Ned, the older girls, and— Where's Mary?"

"I'll find her." Bessy kissed Miss Brontë's forehead, stood, and hurried to the top of the next staircase.

Ned and Mr. Brontë followed her.

"Lydia," I said in a tone I hoped was warning.

My oldest daughter hadn't moved. She was still kneeling beside Miss Brontë and had a strange glint in her eye.

"Go with your sisters," I said.

"Oh no, Mama," she answered with a smile, her words ringing clear now that Miss Brontë's fit had subsided. "I insist. I wouldn't have anyone else see to dear Miss Brontë."

Was she *mocking* me?

I didn't have time to react to her insurrection. Three of the "manservants" were striding toward us, still wearing their tights.

"We hope you'll allow us to assist you, madam." One of them, a very handsome young man who must have been around Mr. Brontë's age, addressed me. "Mr. Beverley is anxious that the lady be made comfortable."

WE WERE USHERED THROUGH a disguised side door and led through a series of winding corridors, with uneven floorboards and greasy fingerprints along the walls. We must have looked a sorry procession—Lydia openmouthed to be "behind the curtain," me flinching at the proximity of the actors, the incapacitated Miss Brontë at the rear. Soon we were in some sort of office and face-to-face with the man of the moment himself.

Up close, you could see that Mr. Beverley was born to be an actor. His face was large, flexible, and expressive, with arched brows and almost womanly full lips. He must have been six feet tall and dominated in the low-ceilinged room as much as onstage, his rich voice booming out just as loudly.

"No trouble at all, miss, I assure you!" He talked over Miss Brontë, hitting her with the full force of his chivalry and kissing her gloved hand.

She fell back in the chair our medieval gallants had deposited her in and drew a glass of water to her lips, quivering.

The desk in front of her was covered with receipts, playbills, and all manner of props—a pistol, a handkerchief embroidered with strawberries, and Mr. Beverley's discarded skullcap. The room itself was cramped and windowless, with a pungent smell of gin.

"It is a pleasure, Mrs. Robinson, Miss Robinson, to meet you all," the actor continued.

Lydia and I pulled back our hands in unison as he veered toward us.

"And my boy. Where is my boy? Well, we both say so, don't we, my lad?"

The most handsome of the "manservants," who had come to Miss Brontë's rescue—the young man who had addressed me—had remained, unlike the others, and now stepped forward to join his father.

The likeness to Beverley was there, although the young man's features were more classical. His mother must have been a beauty. His face had an honest look about it despite his profession, but that wasn't enough to speak in his favor. We needed to extricate ourselves from this irregular situation and quickly, especially since Lydia had refused to leave with the others.

"Delighted, Mr. Beverley," my daughter said, holding out her hand and giggling as the son swept into a bow flamboyant enough to rival his father's curtain call.

"Not Beverley but Roxby," he said, hovering over her knuckles and flashing her a smile. "Henry Roxby."

A bastard? Shameless, intolerable. What would Edmund say if he could see the company our daughter was keeping?

My disgust must have been visible, for "old Harry," as the locals called him, hurried to correct my assumption.

"Beverley is my nom de guerre, Mrs. Robinson, and my son Henry Roxby *Junior*. And so, I suppose, we now meet again!" This time he succeeded in planting a kiss on my fingertips. "Not every visitor to the theater can say she has met the man behind the mask."

"No indeed," I said, wondering how many women had heard him use that line. I turned back to Miss Brontë. "You are quite well enough to travel, I trust?"

The governess's cough belied her nod of acquiescence.

"Oh, but Mama, I have so many questions!" cried Lydia, still simpering at the young Mr. Roxby. "An actor's life must be so romantic. Pray, tell us, are you often in London?"

But Henry Junior had no time to speak.

Instead, his father, our leading man, took off his cape with a flourish, and draped it over Lydia's shoulders as if he was conferring a great honor on her.

"Ah, London!" he rhapsodized, extending an arm toward the heavens or, rather, toward the stained yellow ceiling. "What can I tell you of London?"

Lydia took a step away from him but didn't remove the costume.

"Any visitor can't help but fall for her charms and yet, for natives, London is more than that. It is"—he paused for effect—"in the blood!"

"I thought you were born in Hull, Father," said young Roxby, eyes twinkling at my daughter.

She let out a peal of laughter.

"What's this?" a gruff voice called out from behind the door. "Harry, if you have a woman in my office again, I swear to God—"

The door opened, and a man a little younger than me, who bore marks of kinship with the others although he was at least a head shorter, entered the room.

"Oh." Nonplussed at our strange party, he stopped, taking in my fine clothes, Miss Brontë's blanched complexion, and Lydia's bizarre attire.

"These ladies are theatergoers, brother! The governess was taken ill," said "Beverley," as if this explained everything.

"My apologies," the newcomer said slowly. "Allow me to introduce myself. I am Samuel Roxby, the owner here."

This was the juncture at which to take control.

"My name is Mrs. Edmund Robinson, and this is my daughter," I said, unfastening the scarlet cape from around Lydia's neck and throwing it across the desk. "Our governess fainted away in the crowd but has since collected herself. We wouldn't presume to impose upon your hospitality, or your brother's, any longer."

In Mr. Samuel Roxby I had an ally. A look of understanding passed between us.

"Harry," he said, "I hope you haven't been regaling these ladies with your conversation when what they are in want of is a carriage? Go and dismiss the company for the night—they must rest for tomorrow's afternoon performance. And, Henry, lad, fetch the ladies a suitable conveyance immediately."

Lydia scowled.

"Thank you," I mouthed, surprised that "Harry Beverley" had submitted to his brother's orders and was bestowing a decidedly undramatic good-bye upon us.

His son followed him. A look of childish heartbreak passed between Lydia and the boy as he shuffled to the door, glancing back over his shoulder.

This was the end, then, of our brief flirtation with the theater. I would miss Mr. Brontë and our conversations, but Lydia must be taught a lesson about how to behave and how she should not. She'd have a piece of my mind once we were home. If that girl thought I would countenance another concert, party, or play in our last two weeks in Scarborough, she was in for an unpleasant surprise.

As for Miss Brontë, she was lucky her brother was such a favorite. I employed a governess to keep the girls out of trouble, not to embroil them in it.

LYDIA WAS IN DISGRACE for more than a week and banished from our holiday. But what a holiday it was! I had imagined her, alone in her room, pining after the gaiety we enjoyed and recognizing the error of her conduct, but, instead, the weather forced the rest of us to remain indoors also. Worse, we were all penned in together.

With all the predictability of an English summer, the rain dribbled down the windows of our lodgings. The heavy droplets collided and coupled, their courses meandering and irregular, almost as if they could think, protest, feel.

Old Mrs. Robinson snored by the fire. Lighting it was an extravagance Edmund wouldn't have allowed had I requested it, as our rooms were hardly cold. Bessy was studying the sporting pages from one of her father's newspapers, and Mary, a novel.

Miss Brontë was hunched over with her nose nearly touching a piece of paper, busy and pious as ever, Flossy wedged between her and the back of her chair. She was adding some final touches to a sketch of Holy Trinity, our church in Little Ouseburn, making a great show of her draftsmanship. She'd even announced, unprompted, that she was thinking of making a gift of her picture to Reverend Greenhow, the curate. I'd told her I hardly thought it appropriate for a spinster governess to make gifts to a married man. And at that she'd gone quiet.

"Oh, can't Lydia join us?" said Bessy, casting the newspaper aside as soon as she'd devoured the last words of the final column. "I'm bored."

"She cannot," I said, looking at the window and counting the beats between the irregular tremors caused by the wind.

"The post, madam," said Marshall, appearing at the door and proffering two damp envelopes on a tray.

I took them by the corners, so as not to stain my hands with the running ink. I was grateful for the distraction despite the fierce constriction in my chest that had come every time I'd received a letter since the one that had brought me word of Mother's death. Neither was addressed to me. One had a Haworth postmark. The knot released and fell to the depths of my stomach, like a stone sinking through water.

"Miss Brontë," I said, holding out the first missive without looking at her.

She scuttled over and snatched it, not even thanking me but whispering "Emily" as she made out the weeping letters. Not Charlotte, then, though I knew she'd now returned for good from Brussels to Haworth. The eccentric Emily probably wrote of storms and wildflowers, and sent snatches of poetry. She wasn't the one who'd delight in gossip from my household about the daughter who disobeyed me.

Flossy, the ungrateful pup, had rolled over to take up even more of the seat, forcing Miss Brontë to perch on the edge. She huddled over her letter, deciphering the tiny print.

The other letter I kept and examined, turning it over between my hands.

I stole a glance at the girls. Bessy had found a new occupation, in reading over Mary's shoulder. Neither of them was looking at me.

The rain had made the mistake plausible, and did I even need an excuse to read my daughter's letters when she treated me with such disrespect?

I took my right thumb and smeared the "Miss." The black ink pooled in the spiraling grooves of my skin.

Who was writing to young Lydia Robinson?

I unfolded the paper and held it half an arm's length away until it came into focus. A feminine hand—there was that, at least.

> *28th July 1843*
> *Kirby Hall*

My dear Lydia,

Your last letter struck me as unkind on two counts. First,
because it made me long that I might be with you in
Scarborough, rather than at home where everything is the
same as ever. And second, because you failed to mention the
date on which you return.

　　You mustn't forget me in favor of your new friends or enjoy
yourself too much at concerts and the theater, or all of us in the

Ouseburns will seem dull to you. Did you ever contrive to meet
the company at the playhouse? I should so like to see the world
in the wings, even though actors are an unscrupulous sort.

My sisters and I have convinced Papa that Grandmama
is dead long enough that we might have a picnic. Only after
you return, but I don't know when that is! I say my sisters
but mean only three of us. Henrietta is too confirmed a
spinster to care for such things and Mary Ann is indisposed
again, which is such a bore.

But at least that means Dr. Crosby attends us often,
bringing all manner of gossip from Great Ouseburn and
drawing Papa out of his study.

He—the doctor—is full of praise for your brother's tutor.
His name escapes me. I know you said he was too short to
be handsome but we face such a dearth of unmarried male
company. I wonder if your mama would countenance him
joining our party? Otherwise we'll have to invite the Milner
brothers and then we must invite the sisters too.

Do write, Lydia, and tell me when I may set the date.

Your most sincere friend,
Amelia Thompson

P.S. One last piece of news. The date for my brother Harry's
nuptials is set. He is to marry a Miss Croft in August, but
never fear, the wedding is in Kent and my sisters and I aren't
to go so it shouldn't interfere with our picnic. Harry doesn't
plan to bring home his bride until the winter. I hope she is
ugly. It wouldn't do for her to be beautiful and rich.

I held my mouth still while I read, afraid that my emotions would
tell on my face, which Edmund had told me once was as reactive as a
weather vane.

"It is a good thing, Lydia!" he'd protested as I pulled away, my lip quivering as if to prove his point. "Who wouldn't want a wife incapable of deception?"

He must have regretted that assessment since. Now, each time my anger threatened to overflow, I'd detect the surge deep inside me and see everything that would happen were I to give voice to it. How the waves would envelop me and break over him, the brief calm that would follow before my torrential tears, and when they were all spent, how I'd beg forgiveness crouched beside him or, on the worst occasions, outside his locked study door. That's how it had been in the early years—passionate arguments followed by fevered reconciliations, even when our disagreements were minor. But since then, petty bickering had become the stuff of daily conversation, and when it mattered, I'd learned to quash my rage and walk away. At least sometimes.

But on the inside, even silly Amelia Thompson still had an effect on me. Her letter set off a chain of emotions as varied as those I'd suffered the only time I'd joined the hunt, anticipation giving way to fear and ecstasy, triumph and disaster hanging in the air as we jumped a hedgerow, when I didn't know if we would clear the ditch. That must be why the others liked riding—Ned, Bessy, and Edmund when he was younger and fitter—but I had no need to seek out such thrills when I lived through them every day.

Lydia was a manipulative, conniving girl to be planning to meet the actors, even prior to Miss Brontë's unfortunate dizzy spell. And Mr. Brontë too short to be handsome? What did a girl know of such things?

At the postscript, my anger mingled with a strange mix of righteousness and pity. It determined my course.

"I will go and speak with her," I said, as if Bessy had made her request only seconds ago.

Quitting the room was a relief. I hadn't realized how close the fire had made the air or that my face was flushed. I paused in front of the hallway mirror, so that the color could subside. There were slight circles below my eyes, but Marshall had done better with my hair today—

not that anyone who cared would see me, unless Mr. Brontë joined us
for dinner.

I opened the door to Lydia's room without knocking. With a rustle
of skirts, she stood in front of me before I could determine how she'd
been using her solitary hours.

"Mama," she said as dully as the servants when they called me
"madam."

"I bring a letter for you, Lydia."

I didn't offer her an explanation as to why the seal was broken, and
she didn't ask when she took it from me.

Infuriating. Her hands were clasped in front of her, the letter between them. Her long-lashed eyes were downcast.

"Aren't you going to read it?" I asked, breaking the silence first.

"Very well, Mama." She sat on the end of her unmade bed.

Her beautiful face was motionless as a sculpture. Was she making
an effort to hold herself just so to elude me? Yet I could tell when she
reached the final paragraph. She let out a little gasp and her eyes met
mine before darting back to the page.

"Thank you, Mama," she said, her voice wobbling, as if she couldn't
trust herself to say more.

"Harry Thompson is to be married, then?" I asked, casually, lifting
her discarded nightdress from the floor and folding it.

"Yes." A single tear spilled out of one violet eye and tumbled down
her cheek.

"Oh, Lydia," I said, tossing the lace-edged dress aside and sitting beside her. "My love." Her hair ran like liquid silk through my fingers as I
stroked her, soothed her. "Harry Thompson is a handsome man, I know,
and heir to Kirby Hall, but there will be others."

She broke into sobs, wrenched away from me, and threw herself
prostrate on the bed.

I hovered over her, unsure what else to say.

Instead of Lydia, I seemed to see the ghost of my former self, crying just so when I'd learned that Edward Scott would marry my

cousin Catherine Bateman. I had been so sure when I was Lydia's age that I was destined for more, for someone better than Edmund, for somebody who would lift me higher. But my ascent into adulthood had been littered with disappointments, as hers would be too.

Motherhood was about offering truth, not comfort. For all it still tugged at my heartstrings to hear her cry so, Lydia needed to leave behind her childish notions. And I must be the one to disabuse her.

CHAPTER SEVEN

"Mrs. Robinson?"

I jumped. I hadn't heard Mr. Brontë knock or come in, but there he was, standing in the center of my dressing room at Thorp Green as if I'd conjured him.

How dare he? His sudden apparition took my breath away. And he could have interrupted me doing anything! But really, of course, there was nothing for me to do at all. That was why I'd been sitting in the window seat, staring across the lawn and delineating the intermittent bursts of birdsong.

Wren, blackbird, thrush.

Love, possession, warning.

"Mr. Brontë." I stood.

Our eyes were level, and that made me uncomfortable. There was no way to escape Mr. Brontë's deep blue stare. With Edmund, I was accustomed to addressing his cravat, or the back of his head, or the pages of his newspaper.

Mr. Brontë would be here about Ned, but it was funny he should come to me. Edmund was the one with opinions on the correct way to educate boys, and though Ned was at a clumsy age, it was Marshall who pressed herbs on bruises and kissed scraped knees.

"Is anything the matter?" I asked when he did not speak.

"No," Mr. Brontë said, frowning, "although I might have asked you the same. You appeared pensive just now."

Such familiarity might have been acceptable in the theater, in Scarborough, but it wouldn't do here.

"It is considered impolite, Mr. Brontë, to enter without knocking," I said, staring back at him. I wouldn't be the first to blink.

"My apologies." He didn't play my game but bowed.

Disappointing. I felt something slacken, like when Marshall became distracted while tightening my corset, but this time it was on the inside.

"I came to ask a favor," he said.

"A favor?" I repeated.

"Yes. But then the door was ajar. I saw you sitting there and you struck me as so mournful, like a painting—or Tennyson's Mariana in her grange. Forgive me."

Mariana? I *was* weary, to my very bones. But she'd had someone and something to look for, wait for. I had nobody and nothing.

"What was your favor, Mr. Brontë?" I asked.

Perhaps he could paint me and reveal the youthful fire I felt inside. Maybe on canvas Edmund would be able to see me clearly. But then Mr. Brontë had failed as an artist; that's why he was a tutor, after all.

"I hoped I might be permitted to use the library," he said. "After lessons and on Sundays, when Ned is with his sisters."

A practical request, then. He'd come to me only to avoid disturbing Edmund.

"The ceilings are low in the Monk's House and the windows let in little light," he said. "Now summer is drawing to a close, it would be a great joy to me to have somewhere else to write. Though even at the Monk's House I have more space than back home, where the four of us sit around one table, squabbling over ink."

This interested me in spite of myself. "What is it you are writing?" I asked. "More poetry?"

"When I can." At this limited show of encouragement, Mr. Brontë strode past me and deposited himself at the window where I'd been sitting.

I gaped at him.

"Although Charlotte talks from time to time of the novel as the 'literary pinnacle of our age.'"

"Do you agree with her?" I asked.

Surprising that this female intellect who loomed large behind Mr. Brontë thought highly of novels! I'd always assumed my taste for them was confirmation of my feminine frivolity. Edmund, and all other gentlemen, he assured me, preferred "facts."

With each new detail I learned of her, Charlotte grew more fascinating to me. She was surprising, multifaceted, not a caricature like romantic Emily or colorless Anne. I took my place on the window seat beside Mr. Brontë, very close to the edge so there was at least a foot between us.

He nodded. "The thing about Charlotte is that she is very often right, for all it pains me to say it." He was gazing at me, the rosy hue of the late-summer sky shining through his hair. "But to write a novel, one must have a tale to tell—the tragedy, the great love story—and I have not found mine. Not yet."

I couldn't assure him he would do so. To prophesy tragedy was morbid and love unthinkable. So I looked away, not trusting myself not to get lost in him if I met his eye. "I read a fair number of novels," I said at last, fixing my gaze on the French clock, although I wanted nothing less than for Mr. Brontë to go. The birds would be poor company after our conversation. "I go through a box a month from the circulating library."

Mr. Brontë saw and took his opportunity. "Perhaps you might join me in the library?" he said. "In those quiet hours between lessons and dinner when the children are racing out to the fields? I could write. You could read."

He paused, but I said nothing. I'd become aware of every sensation in my body: the weight on my head from my hair, how the lace irritated my wrists at the cuffs, the strange dip in the cushion below me now there was a heavier companion at my side.

"Unless of course you have other affairs to attend to."

He had me there. "No," I said slowly.

"I thought you might be practicing at the piano. You are a born musician."

"I only play after dinner," I said. "Edmund doesn't like to hear me in the day. He says it's 'tedious' and 'distracting.'"

Mr. Brontë raised one russet eyebrow, his face the picture of Miss Brontë's at her most judgmental. But here *his* verdict pleased me.

"Yes, perhaps we might join you—Marshall and I," I said. "On occasion."

"ON OCCASION" BECAME OFTEN.

Did Edmund think it strange that the time I spent in the library increased even as the number of novels I ordered from Mr. Bellerby's circulating library dwindled? Had he even noticed as he jotted down the amounts that autumn in his treasured leather accounting book?

I *was* still reading but now also had Mr. Brontë's scribblings to work my way through—fantastic tales of a country called Angria, which he and Charlotte had dreamed up and peopled with hundreds of characters, and poems he signed "Northangerland." In the late afternoon, after Ned's lessons, Mr. Brontë would delight me again with the story of Angria's inception or turn the force of his pedagogy on me and try to convert me from novels to his favorite poetry. There were volumes of Wordsworth and Byron, marked with his annotations, which we took turns reading aloud from. He'd written a letter to Mr. Wordsworth once, but never received a reply. Mr. Brontë told me I had a natural ear, that I felt the music in the verses that others missed.

I tried to live up to his estimation, although often I'd tease him, chastising him for his flattery, while Marshall did her needlework, head bent low, seeing and hearing nothing.

But she wasn't here today. We were on the cusp of winter, struggling through a day as gray and dreary as all the others, but today, somehow, Mr. Brontë and I had found ourselves alone.

"So Charlotte dubbed hers Lord Wellington, Emily's was Parry," said Mr. Brontë, who was talking again of the toy soldiers he and his sisters had played with when they were younger, which served as inspiration for many of his stories even now. "Anne's soldier, Ross, was a queer little thing like herself, and I must needs make mine Bonaparte." He laughed, looking not at me but several yards away toward the cheval screen and the oak sofa table, as if he could see those wooden toys made flesh before him.

Mr. Brontë was a curious specimen. A grown man who retained a passion for playing with dolls. Another living, breathing person with an inner life as varied, complex, and tumultuous as my own, but one who cared nothing for the concerns that dogged me and consumed my waking and dreaming hours.

What others thought of him was of little importance to Mr. Brontë, I'd found in the course of our many talks like this one. It made me wonder if Charlotte was the same. "She doesn't spend much time on her appearance," Mr. Brontë had told me once. "She is neat but, I'm afraid, rather plain. Yet, on closer acquaintance, men often find her fascinating. Her conversation. Her opinions. She is truly unique among women."

The contrast with Charlotte caused me some embarrassment about my vanity and predictability, but Mr. Brontë never accused me of either. He listened to my confidences when Edmund would have lectured, reacted with sympathy when my husband would have schooled me to be better.

I'd liked that at the beginning—how Edmund challenged me and how he had a steady confidence that belied his true age (he was, in fact, a year my junior). But his critiques took on a sharper edge when they were no longer followed by caresses, when they came to outnumber his compliments and I could do nothing right.

"We all had childhood games, Mr. Brontë," I said, tracing my finger along the ridged equator of one of the globes that stood near the paneled window. "But most of us outgrow them."

"A tragedy, Mrs. Robinson!" Mr. Brontë cried, his humor matching mine. He caught on to the other side of the globe, halting its slow rotation and leaning toward me.

We must have looked as if we were carving up the world between us.

"What is the object of our existence unless creation?" he said with that intensity of his that was at odds with our age's ever-fashionable nonchalance. "And while many of us create—I will not say replicas—but only pale imitations of ourselves, how much more incredible is it to craft a world, another reality that you can share and invite others into, as Charlotte and I have with Angria and Emily and Anne have with their Gondal? Another country, just around the corner, wherever you are and however you are trapped. Imagination is the only passport required for entry there."

"Hence why you call yourself 'Northangerland,'" I said, pulling back, away from his face and away from the window, although it was like moving through treacle.

"Yes," he said, his excitement subsiding and a new hollowness entering his voice as if, in removing myself, I had reminded him of the realities between us, the fact that our very presence here, alone, was an insurrection. "Northangerland is the dark hero of Angria, a man led by his passions, who acts ever on ambition. I envy him, Lydia."

A shiver passed through me. Was it at hearing him say my first name or merely at the sound of it being used with affection and not as a reprimand?

"What do you en—?" I could not complete the question. My breathy voice trailed into nothingness as I retreated. I came in contact with one of the fitted, glass-doored bookcases, solid, immovable, clearing me of all responsibility were he to come closer.

"He is free," Mr. Brontë said, his confidence growing as he stepped forward, narrowing the gap between us. "Free to do what he wants, take what he wants." He stopped, raised his hand, and ran his thumb down the spine of a book to the right of my cheek.

"And what do you want?" I asked, pausing between each word, unsure if I wanted an answer, terrified that the magic would be ruined by one false move on his part. We couldn't sustain this bizarre, romantic, almost spiritual communion were our words and actions to descend into baseness.

"A lock of your hair, Lydia," he whispered. "Something to remember you by."

Perfect. Intimate but still deferential, physical without fording the Rubicon, venturing to the place from which there could be no return.

I nodded.

Mr. Brontë drew a small knife from his waistcoat pocket with one hand and, with the other, tugged at the silver comb that secured my hair. The teeth scraped against my scalp. The trinket clattered to the floor. My mass of curls hovered for a second, unsecured, before tumbling over my shoulders.

Just as well I had never required hairpieces.

Now his fingers were running through the thick, real, loosened tresses and skirting up my neck and I couldn't think of hairpieces anymore, could I? Or how my hair would look when he was finished? I wasn't meant to be thinking of such trivial things when my life, my marriage, my virtue were hanging in the balance.

"Take the lock, Mr. Brontë," I said, struggling not to gasp as his fingertips moved across my face, tracing their way to my lips.

Too much.

Too far.

The interview was careening out of my control.

"Branwell," he said, correcting me and gazing at my bottom lip, which his thumb was toying with, his expression hungry.

"Go," I said, closing my eyes, not to drink it in but because I could no longer bear to see him.

My scalp tautened.

A low, rough sawing sound.

Release.

Branwell drew back, but I kept my eyes closed.

"Go," I repeated.

A click of the door and he did.

I walked to the fireplace.

My face stared at me in the looking glass above the mantel just the same.

It was like the morning after my wedding night, when I had been alone, shivering in my shift, before a maid had come to dress me.

"No one can see it, Lydia," I'd whispered to myself, giddy and sore and angry at being lied to. "It is not such a change. You are just the same."

But, now, on closer examination, there *was* a difference. One of the curls that framed my face was shorter than the other. How arrogant, how like a man, to go for a strand that was so visible. Marshall would fix it, without a word of reproof. And only she would have noticed anyway.

I stooped to retrieve the comb and inhaled hard.

A momentary aberration only. I was still mistress here.

"You are too kind, Doctor," I said.

I wasn't looking at Dr. Crosby but beyond him at my own reflection in one of the full-length mirrors that lined the passage to the ballroom at Kirby Hall. Thanks to their matriarch's long illness and subsequent demise, it had been some months since we'd been in the Thompsons' Palladian mansion, the finest house in the area, grander even than ours.

Edmund had been talking to Reverend Lascelles only moments ago. Yet, infuriating as ever, he'd proven missing at the very moment we'd all been summoned from the anterooms to enjoy Harry Thompson's long-anticipated wedding feast. Just as well the doctor had stepped up in his absence.

Dr. Crosby was the perfect partner. He complimented me on my appearance as we made our way up the corridor, slowed by trailing dresses and a strict adherence to etiquette, and entertained me with a flurry of gossip from Great Ouseburn, a ten-minute stroll from Little Ouseburn yet a separate parish, which meant it might as well have been a world away.

I did look beautiful tonight. I'd ordered a new dress from Miss Harvey in York. Black, of course, but with gold trim at the cuffs and along the scooping neckline. I'd thought that Mr. Brontë and Ned might come to wave us off and that the tutor would admire me with his words or his eyes. But there had only been Miss Brontë, her expression alternating between intrigued, disinterested, and judgmental; Marshall, happy and proud, eyes glittering at what she had helped create; and Mary, tearing up that she, unlike the other girls, was excluded.

I stole a glance at my eldest daughters and smiled. Bessy was on Will Milner's arm. They were a good match, although it was unclear who was guiding whom. I wondered if the boy had sent her any more notes since Valentine's Day. He was an awkward young man, whose hands and feet still looked too big for him, and he held himself stiff and unspeaking. Bessy was silent and had turned the color of her dress, which had formerly been Lydia's and was far too pink for her florid complexion.

Lydia, meanwhile, was paired with the youngest girl of the house, Amelia. I'd placated her and overspent on a new periwinkle gown that brought out her eyes, but her face was as downcast as it had been the day she'd first heard of Harry Thompson's marriage.

"What a deficit of young men we have, Mrs. Robinson!" said the doctor, tracking the direction of my gaze and thoughts. "When a daughter of a beauty such as yourself goes unaccompanied."

I gave his arm a squeeze. How good of him to dwell on my looks rather than hers.

"But—" He paused and leaned in so close I could see the silvering hair on the side of his dark head. "But it's somehow appropriate, isn't it?"

"How so, Dr. Crosby?" I asked, keeping up the whispering and hoping others thought us in on secrets of the party that they were not.

"I mean that this is a house of unmarried women. What is it? Six in all? A house that's hungered for a wedding for years and then, not only does the son wed first, but Mr. Harry must go and marry elsewhere."

I stifled a giggle. It was true that this was largely a gathering of spinsters. There were the Thompsons, from Henrietta, a fast-fading beauty who must have been five and thirty, all the way to Amelia, who was already too old to be bosom friends with a teenager like my Lydia. Five of the seven Milner girls were also here tonight, imagine! But no, my girls would never suffer their fate.

Whatever my governess had written of my showiness, I would ensure my daughters married, and married well. I knew what it took. Beauty, reputation, accomplishments. Another year had all but slipped by, but soon I would take action and defend them from a woman's worst fate—to be extraneous and unneeded. Or no, that was not quite the worst—the worst was to be forced to make your own living, like the Miss Brontës.

Dr. Crosby pulled back my chair, which was toward the upper end of the leftmost of three long, glittering tables.

At the head of the central table was the man of the hour, Harry Thompson. He was handsome, well dressed, and roaring with laughter at something Reverend Lascelles had said. This was strange, as the Reverend wasn't known for his humor, but the Thompson heir was one of those men who lived for pleasure, unracked by spiritual or artistic dilemmas, never looking any deeper, just the opposite of Bran—Mr. Brontë.

Beside the cackling bridegroom was, presumably, his bride. I'd already forgotten her name. She was small and unassuming, and her complexion was a little green. She was probably pregnant already, poor thing. That was the way of things once men decided the time had come to secure their inheritance.

"Any money on old Thompson spending half his speech talking of his mother?" Dr. Crosby muttered, as the tables filled with a flock of brightly colored dresses, occasionally broken by a pillar of black.

"You are terrible, Doctor, as is your wager." I laughed and hit him with my fan, but with a slight delay. I was fretting that Frederick, the younger, plainer, and more stuttering Thompson son, was trapped between two Miss Milners, while my Lydia languished like an unplucked lily between Mary Ann and Amelia Thompson.

There was still no sign of Edmund.

"Mr. Brontë is quite the specimen, my dear Mrs. Robinson," Dr. Crosby said.

I jumped at the sudden change of topic. It must have been at that.

"Just what one would want in their son's tutor," I replied, trying to mimic his dry, sardonic tone.

"Ha!"

A servant leaned in with a silver platter of steaming vegetables, dividing us for a second.

"I, for once, am being serious," he said, reappearing through the fog. "What we need around here are new ideas. However did you conjure up such a novelty?"

"I have my ways, Dr. Crosby," I said, inhaling my champagne too hard and before anyone had thought to give a toast.

"You do indeed." The doctor clinked his glass with mine as I struggled not to cough. "All of us at the Lodge thank you."

"Oh, the Lodge." I'd recovered my composure and was back on steady ground. "I wonder what you men think to speak of there without the fairer, and wittier, sex to entertain you."

So Branwell was a Freemason. No wonder he and Dr. Crosby had struck up such a fast rapport. Men often joined the order when they shared their home with a gaggle of women. My husband was also a member, although he hardly ever attended the meetings now. The ride to York was exhausting and the Lodge (in truth, a room above an inn) too smoky and crowded. That was Edmund's excuse, anyway. He avoided company more and more and had nearly entirely withdrawn from the circle of friends we'd once reigned over.

"Ah, I thought you were a worldlier woman than that, Mrs. Robinson." The doctor twinkled at me, looking more like an indulgent and eccentric uncle than a man my own age. "In the most respectful sense, I assure you. But you should know that it is when you are absent that gentlemen most wish to speak of you."

The blood flew to my face as it hadn't since I was a girl. Had Branwell really spoken about me? Could he have been so indiscreet? My hand reached, before I could stop it, to touch the curl he had stolen two weeks before.

But before I could open my mouth to speak, our host had risen to his feet. "Ladies—I say, ladies and gentlemen!"

A hundred conversations were cut off mid-sentence, mid-thought, even mid-word, as Richard Thompson tottered to his feet. A host of family portraits, including his own, were to serve as backdrop to his soliloquy and we as the unwilling crowd.

"There are many, my own dear mother included, who would have longed to be here on such a joyous occasion."

Dr. Crosby elbowed me in the side. I gave him an appreciative nod.

"My darling mother was taken from us, too soon, this April." Old Mr. Thompson wiped away a tear, but then, with age, eyes were prone to watering.

I snorted, and the bubbles raced up my nose. Too soon? He was on the edge of the grave himself. For his mother to have lived as long as she had was ridiculous.

But his lip was tremoring, his grief was real, and my own mother's face flashed before me. I drank long so that she might fade, and no sooner had I replaced the glass on the thick ivory tablecloth than it was refilled as if by magic.

"But now we welcome Elizabeth—"

Ah yes, another Elizabeth. I couldn't stand the name, as it was Edmund's mother's name. That's why our Bessy was "Bessy."

"—into our family and into our home. In some months Harry—where is my Harry?—will carry her off to Moat Hall, but for now she is ours."

There was a smattering of applause. I drank again, doing another scan for Edmund. He hadn't reappeared.

"Moat Hall? That rundown old place?" Dr. Crosby hissed in my ear, clapping loudly and with obvious relish. "Couldn't they have put the old maids out to pasture there?"

"Give them time," I said darkly.

Was Moat Hall really such a step down in the world? The property was a little too close to the village, it was true, but it must have been the same size as Thorp Green Hall.

"So eat, drink, be merry!" With every word, Mr. Thompson forestalled our enjoyment. "And join me in toasting to Mr. and Mrs. Henry Thompson!"

"To Mr. and Mrs. Henry Thompson!"

My glass was nearly empty when I raised it, but I drained the dregs anyway.

A clatter. The guests set upon their meals like animals.

There was gravy on Bessy's chin, but she was leagues away from me, and besides, young Milner was too afraid to look at or talk to her.

The room was rotating a little before me, but only by an inch or so. It halted when I watched it too closely, like the music box I'd had when I was a child. The dancer always did one final pirouette if you looked away from her, and the last doleful note never sang out in tempo.

I couldn't eat much. My corset was laced too tight. But I'd had enough food to bring me back to myself if I remembered to stop reaching, reaching for another sip and another.

The party was diving into dessert, and Dr. Crosby and I were laughing at how the new Mrs. Thompson's head was obscured by a decorative pineapple, when there was a tap on my shoulder.

I turned. Edmund. He was pale, almost gray.

"Wherever have you been? Are you ill?" I asked, trying to stand, although the space was tight and my gown was cumbersome.

"You needn't worry yourself, Lydia." His fingers rested on my bare upper arm as he forced me into my seat and a faint, incongruous thrill rippled through me, exacerbated by drink. "I came for the doctor. I'll send William Allison and the carriage back for you and the girls. Enjoy the party."

Dr. Crosby nodded and dabbed his mouth with his napkin, preparing to leave.

"But how can I enjoy myself if you're ill?" I asked.

"I'm sure you'll find a way," Edmund said, withdrawing his hand and then turning to my companion.

They exchanged a few hushed, indistinguishable words and then left me—stranded, unable to converse with those on my right whom I had ignored for so long.

And what was there to look forward to? Only dancing, or rather, standing at the edge of the room, watching Bessy and Will Milner stumbling into each other, while Lydia sulked at my side. Whereas, with Dr. Crosby, we could have spoken further of "Mr. Brontë."

FOR ONCE, WE'D ALL retired to the anteroom together after dinner. It was warmest in here. Besides, the rest of the Hall felt curiously empty since many of the servants had departed for the holidays. The Brontës were in Haworth, the Sewells Durham, and even Marshall had abandoned me for two days to visit her sister in Aldborough.

"I've eaten so much I could burst," said Ned, lying in front of the hearth like a pig volunteering to be roasted.

"That's hardly something to be proud of, Ned," said Lydia, with a sniff, from the window seat.

"It don't matter for boys!" cried Ned, rolling onto his rounded stomach and propping his chin on his hands. "Only girls like Bessy need to eat less."

Bessy, cross-legged in front of Mary, who was braiding her hair, stuck out her tongue at her brother but didn't otherwise retaliate. The children were always on their best behavior when Edmund was there. And so he never understood the trouble I had with them.

"'Doesn't' matter. Not 'don't,'" I said, mildly, pulling the curtain across the window unblocked by Lydia. Better to do it myself than wait for Ellis, who'd been fulfilling all the female servants' duties with a sour face and varying levels of incompetence.

"Could you read to us, Papa?" ventured Mary, nearly dropping Bessy's hair mid–intricate knot as she twisted toward Edmund's chair.

I wasn't even sure he was awake. Our Yuletide festivities, tame though they'd been, had been enough to exhaust him. He was sitting in one of the shell-back chairs, with his eyes closed, moving now and then to change the crossing of his ankles.

"Hmm?" he grunted by way of reply. "I'm tired, Bessy dear."

"I'm Mary," said Mary, pivoting again.

"Ouch," called Bessy. "You're pulling my hair."

"Lydia, will you play something?" Edmund said, through a yawn.

"I won't," said Lydia, staring out at the black.

"No, not you." He waved his hand. "Your mama."

I did as he asked, nearly falling over the chess table in my haste to reach the pianoforte. My fingers sought out the ivories even as I slipped onto the stool in front of it.

Edmund hadn't asked me to play in so long, although there'd been a time when he'd delighted in hearing me. The Robinsons weren't in general a musical race, but Edmund had appreciated my talents and turned the pages for me at countless gatherings, before and after our betrothal. It was too bad that the children had inherited his ear. Lydia was a fair player at best. And Bessy and Mary had no conception of rhythm.

I tinkered until I found the chords of a carol—one of Wesley's, I think—but I'd had more than enough Christmas for one year and soon strayed into singing popular ballads, enjoying how the room fell quiet, even if the audience wasn't as admiring as in my youth.

My heart ached for Kathleen Mavourneen as I sang the good-byes of her departing lover and for the girl in "The Old Arm-Chair," although I'd never understood how she could give up her man to another without so much as a word of protest.

With Branwell away for a few weeks, all of it—our whispered conversations, the lock of hair he had stolen from me, the way my stomach dropped at the sound of his name—seemed very foolish. He was young, yes; attractive and attentive, certainly. But he was a boy compared to my husband, and sometimes I couldn't tell where my interest in him ended and my fascination with his family—with Charlotte—began.

Besides, it was a woman's nature to be constant. Maybe there was still a way to bring Edmund back to me. Maybe he was watching, each note adding a drop to the shallow cup of affection my husband could offer me, and convincing him that, twenty years and five children later, I was still his Lydia.

I started to play snatches of a tune from memory before realizing it was a duet. The soprano line sounded lonely without the accompanying bass but I persisted, imagining Edmund's voice mingling with mine.

"*The last link is broken that bound me to thee, and the words thou hast spoken have rendered me free,*" I sang.

Bessy and Ned struck up a whispered argument.

I increased my volume, drowning them out. I closed my eyes and lost myself in the music and in the unfairness of it all. How was it that love—not a girlish love, but a love that was true and deep—could be one-sided?

"*I have not loved lightly, I'll think on thee yet, I'll pray for thee nightly till life's sun is set—*"

"Lydia—" Edmund said, cutting across my reverie.

"*The heart thou hast broken once doted on—*"

"Lydia."

My hands clunked down on the keys. "Yes?"

He was still lounging back, not looking at me. "A little quieter," he said, patting the air with his hand.

A shock of tears overwhelmed me, raining down in torrents. I rested my elbows on the piano with a clash and leaned my head against the cool, hard wood.

"Lydia!" and "Mama!" cried Edmund and Mary at once.

"Oh, please," said Lydia. Her skirts swished as she, presumably, quit the room.

"Ned, Bessy, Mary—follow your sister. To bed," said Edmund, his voice matter-of-fact. His chair made a creak as he stood. "Run along with you."

The door closed behind them.

I wanted him to wrap me in his arms, but of course he kept his distance. He'd never reward me for such a display.

"You should learn to better regulate your emotions, Lydia," he said, without much inflection. "Does Dr. Crosby need to prescribe a sedative?"

"Dr. Crosby?" I said, incredulous, starting up and not caring in that moment that my face was puffy and red. It didn't matter how I looked. There'd been a time when Edmund had told me every morning that I was beautiful, from my crusted eyes to my ever-expanding or deflating belly. But he never wanted me anymore, even when I was at my most alluring. "I don't need Dr. Crosby."

"Then what do you need?" He jerked the curtain across the window where Lydia had been sitting.

Why was he doing that now? He must be worried that someone could see us.

"You, Edmund. I need you." I rushed toward him, but he rebuffed me, gripping both my wrists in one hand and keeping me at arm's length.

"I am your husband, Lydia. Isn't that enough?"

"No," I whispered, the thought inflaming me. I didn't want the conventional, the everyday. I wanted the excitement that even a boy as inexperienced as Branwell could choreograph. "No, it is *not* enough. I want you to need me—to kiss me and hold me." I went up on the tips of my toes and pressed my wet face against his dry one, but his mouth was impenetrable.

"Lydia, you are unwell," he said, guiding me toward a chair, where I collapsed, defeated by his coldness.

I shook my head.

"And your behavior is unladylike. I don't say you mean anything by it—you were always naive—but you spend too much time with the tutor. You look to your own pleasure, keep up flirtations, when you should be setting an example to our daughters and our son."

"It is you who are unwell," I countered. He had not even given Branwell the dignity of a name. But he had noticed. And that meant jealousy could still seep, if not course, through him. That meant he still cared. "You are always tired. Your complexion is unhealthy and—" I didn't know how to word this but I wanted to provoke him. "And, at night, in our bed, you neglect your wife. How can you still think yourself a man when you fail in a husband's duties?"

He did not engage. He was moving away from me. "Good night, Lydia," he said.

"Wait!" I cried, in one last-ditch attempt to keep him. There was still one source of power that wasn't lost to me. "Edmund, please. Give me another child."

This had worked before, with Georgiana. Her birth had brought my husband back to me. Though perhaps her death had lost him to me forever.

"Another child?" he repeated, slowly, looking down at me with distaste. "Is that really what you want?"

"It is, it is," I said, although the thought had not come to me until a moment ago. But wouldn't that be magical? Months of my body blossoming with the surest sign of my youth and my husband's love for me, and then another unspoiled, loving child, one who, like Georgiana, would gaze up at me as onto a god. "Please, Edmund. For me." A nail in the floorboards was digging through the carpet and into my knee. A draft was flooding into the room from underneath the door, sending a shiver through me.

"Lydia, you are too old," Edmund said, a softer note entering his voice.

"No," I mouthed, shaking my head. "Edmund, please. I can't bear it." I had to force the tears from my eyes now. The real ones had stemmed as soon as he'd turned back to talk to me. "Without Georgie—"

This was a misstep. We never spoke of her.

A bolt of amber passed through Edmund's deep brown eyes. "Do not talk of Georgiana. Do not say another word."

I stayed on the floor that night, unmoving but unsleeping for a long time as the candles burned low, and staring into the heart of the ceiling rose. And I woke to a clatter and an exclamation of surprise as Ann Ellis dropped the coal scuttle on seeing me there the next morning.

5th March 1844
Allestree Hall

My dearest Lydia,

I am just this hour returned from Staffordshire. And it is with
a heavy heart that I must relate the sad condition I found
Father in there.

Oh, Lyddy, I fear he is much changed since you saw him
last.

Our brothers had written to me—and to you, I'm sure—
indicating that there was no cause for alarm and that Father
was taking Mother's death as was to be expected. But I found
his mood melancholy and his behavior erratic.

At times he seemed hardly to know me and once he spoke
to me in such language, that I, a married woman, blushed. I
confess I was quite shocked.

I spoke to faithful Rowley and gave him express
instructions to write to us should his master change again for
the worse.

As for myself, I returned to an empty house when I arrived
home in Derbyshire. Like you, William is in Yorkshire. He is
there to meet with another family in the paper mill business.
Their name is "Clapham" and they live in the neighborhood
of Keighley. Doesn't your governess come from a town near
there? I wonder if she knows of them. My darling Thomas
accompanied his father and Allestree Hall feels quite desolate
without them.

How lucky you are to have four children and that you
have years still when at least some of them will be near you.
But you are a young woman, Lyddy, at least when compared

to me. I tell my Thomas any time he'll listen that I ache for grandchildren, but he resists matrimony for now. I'll have William join my crusade on their return.

Kiss my nieces, and kiss my darling nephew twice, for me. And do let me know how Edmund likes your plan of forgoing Scarborough for Derbyshire this summer. Your mother-in-law has you near her the rest of the year, there is plenty of space at Allestree, and we would all so love to see you.

I remain, your most affectionate sister,
Mary Evans

How should I address you? Sweet forest nymph, ever out of reach? Cruel queen, banishing your most faithful servant from your sight? Lydia Gisborne, your true name restored to you once more? I cannot now refer to you by any other.

Why do you torture me with your coldness these last few weeks? We both know it will take more than walls to divide us. Absence will not diminish the intensity of my passion, nor closing your eyes detract from the perfect symmetry of our souls.

The kiss we have never shared hangs over us like Damocles's sword, inescapable, inevitable.

You claim the sanctity of your marriage vows.

I say we are subject only to the cues of our nature.

You are wasting away before me, my love. You are the very picture of grief. Your eyes reproach me, whether I come close or stay away. I wander through the gardens each night, the cold eating at my hands and face, as I study the solitary light in your window. Yet I am hot— with desire, yes—but also with hatred for the man who neglects you, the husband in name only whom you are true to even yet.

Unfair! Unequal! You will burn this paper, although it is a piece of my heart, while I worship the very ground on which you walk.

Lydia, the power is all yours. Summon me, any time and anywhere, and I swear I will come to you. No task is too small or too great, no hour too late, no service too insignificant.

I yearn for the freedom of the summer months, which must throw us into closer proximity.

Ever at your service and hopeful that Love must triumph,
I sign myself,
"Northangerland"

Lydia,

What is this nonsense I hear about you and Edmund not visiting Scarborough this summer? It is too ridiculous. I tried to be forgiving when you did not come to my luncheon on Easter Sunday last week. Why, your husband himself has called it a "highlight of the season"! You claimed indisposition and I chose to believe you, although your "illness" robbed me of a chance to see my grandchildren and my only son.

But to disrupt my holiday plans!? And talk of going to Allestree Hall to your sister and that political husband of hers (I mean it in the worst possible sense)? Lydia, what is the use of Derbyshire? The waters at the spa in Scarborough are the very thing to settle your nerves or cure whatever it is that is wrong with you. Your capriciousness is too much for an old woman to bear.

I write to Edmund by the same post telling him that this just won't do.

The Reverend Eade has already promised to join us this year (dear John, the only reminder I have of my dead daughter, Jane). You must not think to pass up on such edifying company. Spiritual succor is as necessary to your health as adequate medical supervision, something I doubt that upstart gossip John Crosby is providing.

I also include information regarding two alternative and well-regarded physicians, a Dr. Simpson and a Dr. Ryott, whom I've been suggesting Edmund consult on his own behalf. Dr. Simpson is a York man. Fancy, he was even

*president of the Medical Society for a time. And Dr. Ryott
comes with the highest recommendations. If they cannot
"cure" you, only G-d can.*

*How is it that I, who was born a Metcalfe, a woman still in
possession of all her faculties at five and seventy, is connected to
such a family of invalids, I don't know, but I cannot have you go
on so on my watch.*

*It is high time you thought of getting those girls married (I
said the same thing to my daughter Mary of the Thorp girls).
Lydia will be nineteen before long and we both know her
looks will decline from then. She has a pretty face, yes, but
unfortunately she has inherited her figure from you and a larger
bosom does have a tendency to sag with age. Bessy is as wild today
as she was at ten, and Mary—well, at least that girl is biddable.*

*I will visit Thorp Green Hall next week to put things to
rights. Do see to it that I don't have to converse with the insolent
tutor or his plain and pious sister, and that you keep that ugly
lady's maid of yours out of my way.*

I remain your caring and long-suffering mother-in-law,
Elizabeth Robinson

CHAPTER EIGHT

IT WAS HOT OUTSIDE, and some of the poorer worshippers had failed to
secure a pew, so busy was church on a sunny Sunday in Scarborough.
But the building, with its imposing tower, was cavernous enough that
the air still circulated.

We were a strange party.

John Eade, who was on my left, was in fine form. He had an innate
distrust of hymns, deeming singing too Catholic, and perhaps even too
pagan, a practice to introduce it into the religious services that he himself conducted. But when he was in the congregation? That was another matter. He'd been blessed with a rich baritone and was chanting
the familiar encomium about the "wondrous cross" as my mother-in-
law nodded across me, making her displeasure at my silence known.

Edmund, who was beside his mother, had that glazed look in his
eyes that haunted him often now, as if he were staring without seeing.
But I could feel other eyes on me from behind—Branwell's, Miss
Brontë's, the children's—even if my husband ignored me. They were
witnesses to my humiliation. I had fought hard for a chance to summer
with my sister at Allestree Hall, or at the very least to travel to Yoxall to
see my father, with words and tears and week-long silences, and yet

here we were in Scarborough at my mother-in-law's behest, playing out the roles required of us.

The motley choir reached the final bars, though the organ, which the inhabitants of Little Ouseburn would have thought a wonder, droned on for at least half a minute. The overconfident singers, John Eade amongst them, held the final "aaa" for as long as they could, if not a second longer, before spitting out the last consonant. The rest of us had already slumped back, anticipating a sleepy sermon.

John Eade and the rest of them, did they really believe that there was some all-powerful being who cared about the choices we made and the pain we felt, even if He made no effort to relieve it?

This was something Branwell and I had talked about more recently. When we were together, which was nearly every day now, he never gave full force to the passion that burst through the floodgates in the letters he sent by Marshall. Perhaps because he didn't have "Northangerland" to hide behind, or perhaps because he knew I would reject him. Instead he railed against convention, society, religion, talking about us but not about us, redirecting his fire toward the legal and spiritual strictures that kept us apart.

He said I understood in a way that others, even Charlotte, did not, and so I joined him, dancing closer and closer to the precipice and uncovering aspects of my nature I'd never thought to expose to the light, delighting in our shared, secret, impotent rage.

Branwell's anger, though, was fiercer. I had never believed in God as he had in those years before his eldest sister, Maria, the girl who had taught him to think and dream and pray, had died. Or at least I had never had his fervor. When I was a child, being a Christian had only ever been an act I had rehearsed and refined, like smiling sweetly at the grown-up visitors, eating without setting my elbows on the table, and crossing my ankles when I sat. And now I was too surrounded by clergy to take them or their doctrine seriously. There was John Eade, prating, Reverend Lascelles, dull, the curate Greenhow, meek. And then of course there was Edmund, who was ordained himself, although he rarely practiced. He'd preached at each of our children's baptisms, but refused to preside over Georgiana's funeral.

"What then are we to do with the woman taken in adultery?" the Scarborough minister asked, the sudden increase in his volume jolting me back to myself. "We have heard that we are not to stone her, that we must first ponder our own sins, our failings, our manifold faults. But—" He paused.

Here it came—the stone throwing.

Edmund ran his hand over his forehead.

John Eade bit his bottom lip.

Old Mrs. Robinson leaned forward, her breath bated.

"But a woman who commits adultery is committing a sin that drags many down to Hell. Not only herself or the man whom she has tempted away from the path of virtue. She infects her husband, her house, all who come near her, with her wanton deception. She sacrifices her home for a fleeting pleasure, and the best that can be said of her is to question her sanity."

I brought my handkerchief to my mouth to stifle my angry laugh with a cough.

And what if her husband is the one infecting them? I wanted to ask. *Or, worse yet, what if their house was rotten from the very start?*

But the thing was that ours hadn't been. The change had been creeping, almost imperceptible, and my realization that it had all gone wrong had been too. There hadn't been one day when Edmund's kisses had stopped or when we no longer had anything to say to each other. I hadn't treasured the last time he slipped in beside me as I slept, just to dream away the night together, or the last look of understanding that had passed between us over the children's fair heads. All that had simply faded and wasted away. Maybe because I was older, or he was, or we both were. Maybe because we had been wrong to think what we had to be love at all.

Yet there *had* been a moment when the nail was hammered in and the case closed, when our happiness had evaporated forever.

Georgiana had come into the world on one of those days when workmen down tools to lie back in the long grass and boys from the twin villages swim naked in the Ouse, whooping to each other. Her delivery had been easier than with the others. Dr. Crosby was tending to me, as he had done with Ned, his eyes full of kindness.

Agony, release, a first triumphant cry.

He'd placed my darling in my arms and said, "What a beautiful, healthy girl, made for midsummer."

I basked in my absolute happiness, in the radiating love that had been tinged with sadness and weighed down by expectation before. "Georgiana," I whispered. "You will be the sunshine of our lives."

For the next few years she was.

I didn't wish to employ a wet nurse as I had with the others, but instead fed her myself. I could interpret her every expression and movement, from the curlings of her fists to the unfurlings of her toes. As soon as she could walk, she ran, hurtling along hallways, chasing her older siblings, racing to "Papa," who met her invasions of his study with a smile. Unlike her older sisters, she was musical. She clapped her little hands in time to songs. She joyed to see mine skid across the keys.

I don't remember any winters in the years we had her with us. So it's fitting that the day that changed everything—a Monday in March—was unseasonably warm.

Flowers had bloomed too early, the birds were all a-chatter. Yet I'd felt ice cold, though my robe was drenched with sweat and sticking between my shoulder blades. In the weeks she'd been ill, I'd thought my love alone could protect her. Now I wasn't so sure. I'd raised my eyes to heaven and tried to pray. *Save her. Save her. Take me instead.* But the words wouldn't come.

Just then Georgiana had gasped, coughed up a newer, blacker, more pungent blood, and gone limp.

"She has left us," Marshall said, resting her hand on my shoulder. "God has taken her."

And I fell to my knees, holding my baby and bellowing like a milk cow divided from her calf, pleading with my Georgie, trying to shake the life back into her.

Dr. Crosby—there at the end as at the beginning—had wrested her from me, closed my daughter's eyes in one deft, practiced motion, and carried the news to Edmund, as if the whole house wasn't already shaking with my cries.

It was up to Miss Brontë, dry-eyed but quivering, to tell the other children, whom I would not see. They looked too like my darling. What if my all-enveloping grief confirmed to them that their sister had been my favorite? And even if they did in time prove a comfort to me, what was to stop this cruel world snatching them from me too? I stayed away.

Dr. Crosby left the house, leaving me to keep vigil by Georgiana's body alone. My husband did not soothe me. Instead, after thanking the doctor for his efforts, he locked his study door.

"Suffer little children to come unto me": those were the words he'd had carved on my Georgiana's gravestone. She might be at peace, but God didn't seem to care for the suffering He left behind.

"A powerful sermon today, I thought, Lydia. Don't you agree?" said my mother-in-law, gripping my arm so hard she left marks as we walked down the aisle.

The poor were waiting for those in the front pews to file past them. A seagull peered its curious head around the left of the open double doors.

"Yes, Mrs. Robinson," I said.

"A reminder to us of our wifely duties. Be sure you remember how lucky you are to have those. My daughter, Mary, why, the devotion she shows to Charles Thorp is an example to all! My poor Jane dead—what?—four years now? The good Reverend Eade will never marry again for grief. And my own husband departed this world more than forty years ago. I loved him, for all I stooped to marry him. I was a Metcalfe before."

I nodded. It was her usual monologue. I dropped my gaze to study

the intricate geometric tiles. I'd done this before. The maze was ines-
capable. And yet I followed each twist and turn as if the next tile, or the
next, would break the pattern.

God, how I hated her. How I'd triumphed when Edmund had at last
sent her away from Thorp Green Hall, although it had taken until my
third pregnancy and a threat that I would set fire to the house or throw
myself from the roof before he'd told her she could no longer live with
us.

"For your husband's family must always come first, Lydia," Elizabeth
Robinson continued. Her nails dug into my flesh. "Edmund says you
harangue him about visiting your father in Staffordshire or your sister
in Derbyshire, and that you'd gad about the North of England unaccompanied if you had your way. And that is no way for a wife, or any
woman, to act."

"My sister, Mary, writes that my father is ill," I said, as we left the
church. I pulled away from her to free my arm and shield my face from
the direct sunlight. "I wouldn't wish to go to Yoxall Lodge too late, as I
did with Mother."

Old Mrs. Robinson nearly took my eye out as she opened her parasol. "And what use would you be, my dear?" she asked, already waving
to an acquaintance, as worship turned to gossip in the crowded churchyard. "You've never been a natural nurse."

THE SCARBOROUGH SEASON WAS in full swing. Over the next few days,
there was hardly an hour when invitations did not arrive for Lydia,
Bessy, and me, asking us to join dinners, dances, entertainments, and
card parties. Bessy must have known that she and I had only her sister's
face to thank for the courtesy. We weren't invited on our own accounts,
and that was just the same as not being invited at all.

I let Miss Brontë play chaperone as often as I could avoid attending
any of these diversions myself. It gave me some pleasure to imagine her
making small talk with the more fashionable companions and govern-

esses ranged around the edges of whichever room "society" was over-running today. What would she speak to them about? The folly of parties and the edifying nature of solitude? I'm sure she criticized every family in Scarborough in her notes to Emily and Charlotte.

Yet the natural, and equally unattractive, alternative to these evenings was engaging in the interminable games of whist that my mother-in-law, Edmund, and John Eade delighted in. I could hardly fan my hand wide enough to obscure my yawns.

Tonight I had conjured up an excuse to forgo both activities. I'd take Mary and Ned—still deemed "children" and so in need of some attention—to the concert at the Spa Saloon. I'd bid Branwell join us in an hour or so. It was safer that way, for if Edmund didn't see the tutor leave with us, there'd be no reason for him to question the children or me about our behavior later.

We set off late. A letter from Dr. Crosby had distracted me. He wrote that Harry Thompson had been sorely disappointed. Instead of his expected heir, his wife had brought forth a girl. And just when we'd been about to leave, I'd caught sight of my reflection and had Marshall set upon the forest of grays along my parting.

By the time we entered the concert hall, the performance had begun, the place was packed, and there was no hope of fighting our way to our seats.

We were a sorry trio. Me, twisting toward the entrance to check for Branwell, Mary on her tiptoes but still failing to see the stage, and Ned falling back against me as if he were a boy half his size and age.

"Ned, you are too heavy for that." At a pause in the music, I pushed him off me, shifting my weight from one foot to the other and trying and failing to find a stance that was more comfortable for my back.

Another pair of suited and sweating men had materialized onstage. Their bald heads bobbed above the crowd, disappearing between bows. The hall had erupted into a cacophony of coughing and chatter be-tween performers, and the silence was not absolute when the first man raised his flute to his mouth and played. It must hurt, the disinterest.

Or maybe this musician, like the mediocre players who had preceded him, was here only for his meager pay.

Where was Branwell? Shouldn't he be here by now?

But the second player brought his instrument to his lips and my chest swelled with the lower, richer note, long and mournful below the bright birdsong of the melody. In spite of myself, I leaned forward, craning my neck as if by making out the man's features, I could understand.

Around me, gentlemen still cleared their throats, Mary frowned, and Ned fidgeted, but I was spiraling above them, pulled in by the flutist, whose pace increased and notes quavered higher, weaving above and below his partner's tune, like the pied piper dancing round the bend in the road, ever out of sight. The concert was no longer just an escape and a pretense. Here was passion, here was music.

I dropped my chin, closed my eyes, and focused on my breathing, drinking in the beautiful confusion now that it was impossible to know whose was the first line and whose the second. Would they—could they—reach the end of the piece and divide? Shake hands at the close of the concert and walk home alone? Or would that be an insult, a denial of what they had shared, as it was each time I dismissed Branwell Brontë, ignoring, as he would put it, the "cues of our nature"?

A tug on my hand, a tether binding me to earth, lest I floated away and never came back. Branwell. His face flickered into focus between my lashes.

"Are you well?" he whispered, our closeness going unnoticed in the crush. "Lydia, are you faint?"

"Tonight," I said, smiling at his concern and clasping and unclasping his hand.

Music. This was my religion, a faith distinct from that of John Eade or Edmund's mother. The sermon on Sunday had only confirmed it. Their hell didn't hold as much fear for me as their heaven, for it was cold and sexless, sanitized and chaste.

Branwell's brow furrowed. He could not read me.

"I will come to you," I said, just under my breath, pulling him closer. "It would be a sin not to. To resist." I inhaled him.

His lips parted. He was trembling.

"Do not ask me if I am certain," I said. In his desire for affirmation, he might make me retreat.

I dropped Branwell's hand and turned toward the stage, then ran my fingers through Ned's soft hair.

The music washed over us in wave after cleansing wave. I knew—hoped—that Branwell heard in the music what I heard, that his soul was vibrating at the same frequency as mine. The thought stilled the ache in my back and left me dripping with happiness.

At the final applause, the crowd pulsated and swirled like boiling broth. Our party was among the first to emerge into the balmy air, although Mary and Ned weighed me down, clinging on to each of my arms as if they'd been years younger.

The children were tired, and I should have been too, but my feet hardly seemed to carry me. Mary whined and Ned stomped, but I floated, not glancing at Branwell but staring straight ahead. The notes inside me soared even higher, sustaining me through the slow, tedious walk home.

PARTING WITH BRANWELL DID not hurt tonight. Rather, it was a relief.

I couldn't meet his eye as we waited before the door of Number 7 at the Cliff Lodgings for the man to admit us, so stared instead at the sky. The servants had forgotten to light the lamps around the door, and there was barely a moon. But the stars shone back at me, constant, unmoved by our human dramas.

Branwell played the jester, shaking Ned's hand and making Mary an elaborate bow. He even managed to draw a giggle from her after an evening when she'd been more sullen than grateful.

"Good night, Mr. Brontë," I said.

"Good night," he repeated, flashing ten fingers.

Ten minutes.

I nodded and sailed past the footman, not glancing back.

Inside I was spinning, like a spider descending from her web. In moments, Branwell and I would be in each other's arms. We had come close before, snatching at each other, engaged in an elaborate and futile tug-of-war, without quite crossing into the territory that would damn us. But it would be different now. Tonight our actions would be slow, deliberate. We would be prostrate, exposed, vulnerable to attack.

The excitement of it dried my mouth and turned my arms to gooseflesh, but still, something inside me twisted in rebellion as the children kissed my cheek good night. I pulled Mary closer and tried to embrace her (it wasn't her fault, after all, that she was at a miserable age) but she was hard and angular. I kissed her hair, released her, and shooed her away.

Marshall brought a jug of water to my room, and I splashed my face, more to remove the lingering sensation of Ned and Mary's lips than to prepare myself for Branwell.

"Mr. Robinson and my elder daughters?" I asked, not bothering to complete the sentence, as Marshall unlaced me.

"They went to bed an hour ago, madam," she said. "Will that be all?"

"Yes, Marshall. Good night."

There was no need for any special preparation. I'd done enough of that for Edmund, arranging and plucking myself before bed like a fowl being readied for the oven.

Tonight, for the first time, I would go to a man as I was—without caring what he thought of me—and go to him as a lover rather than a wife.

I could not risk bringing a candle into the hallway, and it was difficult to navigate in the dark. How much easier would it have been at Thorp Green Hall, where I knew the outline of every piece of furniture, the pitch of every creaking floorboard. But then again, there would have been an even deeper depravity in that, in going to Branwell in the place I had entered as a triumphant bride.

My hip, unprotected by my flimsy summer nightgown, struck a table and I cursed. I froze and listened hard for any movement. I couldn't be caught sneaking out dressed like this. But there was silence. I rubbed my side so the stinging would subside, following the edges of the bone and wishing the lines of my body were softer and more curved, as they had been in my youth, pillowed by plump and malleable flesh. My body seemed alien without my crinoline. For so long its outline might as well have been the shape of me. I had become as useless as a doll or a puppet without legs.

Our plan hadn't been precise, but Branwell should have the sense to linger outside. I didn't wish to be out there alone. And then—well, we had nowhere to go. Branwell's room shared a wall with the one where William Allison and Bob Pottage were sleeping, and smuggling him into the family's apartments was unthinkable. I'd have to lie down in the stables like a dairymaid, with my shift around my waist and hay clinging to my hair.

A beam of light. The front door was open?

I smiled. Branwell. Silly, impatient. He would grab me the second I stepped outside, push me against the wall, and burrow his face in my neck and hair, not caring that the newly lit lamps by the doorway illuminated us, in plain line of sight from the other apartments. Seeing Elizabeth Robinson's horrified face pushed up against the glass, with John Eade aghast beside her, would almost be worth it.

I pushed the door and stepped into the near-blinding light.

But there was no Branwell.

A night mist was descending on our lodgings, obscuring the stars. My skin tingled, although it was not cold.

Being locked out would be disastrous. I wedged the door in place with two large stones, before stepping into the shadows and inching toward the servants' quarters.

Black.

"Branwell," I breathed every few yards, but there was nothing except the low hum of my pulse in my ears. It had been at least ten minutes, hadn't it? Where was he?

My slippers slid noiseless through the grass. Thank God it hadn't rained in weeks, and there was no mud to sketch telltale trails of green and brown across the ivory silk.

Was Branwell holding back to watch me approach through the fog, a spectral figure in white? Could he anticipate my breath and scent and the incongruous warmth of my skin?

My foot met only air, and I stumbled. I reached out to save myself and scraped my palms on the rough brick of the outbuilding. Ah yes, a manicured flower bed skirted the perimeter. It would be disordered now by a patch of trampled sunflowers.

The humming grew more insistent.

That stupid, ungrateful boy. He was late. I should go back and hide under my sheets, resolve to set aside my foolish cravings, and not condescend to speak to Branwell again. But then the weight of my loneliness would suffocate me as it had before I'd known him. I'd be buried deeper, unable to reach Georgiana although she was beside me, clod after clod of earth piled higher above me, and Edmund farther away—above—than ever.

Maybe Branwell had also thought to go to the stables and was ahead of me? Was he stacking the bales to fashion a rustic bridal bed?

I hurried in that direction, seized again by the euphoria I'd felt at the concert.

There, beyond the carriage house, a feeble light was just visible through the crack of the stable door.

Inside was comfort, salvation, love.

I flew in as fast as I could without hitting the door off the wall, ready to throw myself into Branwell's arms and tell him anything that he'd wish to hear. Even that I loved him.

A scramble, a shout, a flurry of ringlets and petticoats.

"Lydia?" I gasped. My look of horror must have mirrored my daughter's. She stood mute.

"I can explain," said a man, a boy, to my Lydia's right whom I'd hardly registered.

He was wearing an old-fashioned military jacket, unbuttoned at the front, but was otherwise clothed. Lydia was dressed only in her chemise, corset, and petticoat.

I was more naked than either of them. I drew my hands to my chest, conscious of the shape of my breasts, and glanced over my shoulder. If Branwell were to appear now—

Lydia's expression metamorphosed from terror to surprise at my silence. "Mama?" she whispered. "I am sorry. We were only talking."

I laughed and slumped onto the mounting block, my body shaken by something between mirth and agony.

The scene, lit by a solitary candle, was ridiculous. The virgin begging forgiveness from her whorish mother, the strangely familiar boy acting the part of a cowardly soldier, and old Patroclus lifting and replacing his hooves and looking from each of us to the next, as if shaking his head in disbelief, shocked at this unprecedented disturbance to his slumber.

"Henry, say something," said Lydia, running her hands through her hair to dislodge a stalk of hay.

"Henry Roxby, Mrs. Robinson," the boy stuttered, extending his hand, although we were too far apart to touch. "A pleasure to meet you again."

Again?

A vision came to me, his face but even smoother and younger, his muscular legs hugged by tights. This was the actor Harry Beverley's boy. He was just in a different costume.

"Lydia, come!" I said, standing and holding my hand out toward her, although I kept the other clamped across my chest.

"Mrs. Robinson, I love your daughter," shouted Roxby, the words bursting out of him. "We have been writing to each other for a year, and we wish to be married."

"To be married?" I repeated, staring at Lydia to see if this struck her as absurd. "Lydia, you have not lost—?"

"Oh no, Mama." Lydia clasped my hand, tears pooling in her brilliant azurite eyes. "I would never be so foolish."

I could have slapped her. At eighteen, she had more sense than me. She knew her body wasn't to be given away, that she'd been bred only to be valued, bargained for, then bought.

"Mr. Roxby," I said, trapping Lydia's hand beneath my arm. "You will leave and never speak to my daughter, my family, or me again. Do you understand?"

"Lydia?" The boy turned to my daughter, his eyes as watery as hers. "Will you be so cruel?"

Her peony mouth opened, but no sound came out.

I held her hand tighter against me, trying to remember the grasp of her baby fist, but I hadn't tended to her then. Marshall had. I could only recall Georgiana's fading grip and the salty, sweet taste of her fingers when I'd nibbled her nails to protect her from herself in her delirium.

"Mrs. Robinson?" Branwell appeared on the threshold. He was fully clothed. Thank God. And his formal manner made me think he'd been listening to our dramatics for some time. "Is anything the matter? I stepped outside to smoke my pipe and heard voices."

"Mr. Roxby was just leaving," I said.

Henry surveyed the newcomer, weighing up his own advantage in terms of height against Branwell's broader shoulders and the fiery Irish temperament suggested by his hair.

When Branwell took a step forward, this seemed to decide the boy.

"Write to me!" Roxby called in Lydia's direction, before scurrying past all three of us. Soon he was absorbed by the mist and the dark.

"Mr. Brontë," I said, my voice cold and my expression fierce, hoping to convey the double import of my words. "Your discretion is required and appreciated. Lydia made a mistake tonight but, thankfully, not a fatal one."

Branwell looked as if he might cry too.

Just as well Lydia had not noticed. She, deceitful girl, was contrite and weeping into my shoulder.

"My husband must never, ever know what transpired tonight," I pressed on. "And, in time, we will forgive Lydia. Do you understand?"

Branwell dropped his chin to his chest. "I understand, Mrs. Robinson," he said, his voice hollow.

CHAPTER NINE

NED, THE LAST IN line for our nightly ritual, kissed my cheek and then followed his siblings and Miss Brontë from the anteroom at Thorp Green.

"Lydia," said Edmund, as the door closed behind them.

"Edmund?" I flashed back with a half laugh, trying to be flirtatious.

In the two months since we'd returned from Scarborough, I had avoided Mr. Brontë and increased the affection I showed my husband. I never pushed too hard or bothered him while he was busy, but performed small acts of service, folding his papers and tidying his study since he wouldn't let Ellis, who couldn't read, do so. And when I saw him, I would kiss his fingers, shoulder, cheek—any part of him made available to me, without expecting more.

It was a thankless task, as Edmund didn't appear to have registered my efforts. But it salved my occasional flare-ups of conscience at what I had nearly done and what I had kept from him—Lydia's indiscretion, which he would not understand.

I sidled up to him now and tried to hold his hand.

"I need to speak with you in my study." Edmund shook me off. "It's important."

"Couldn't we speak in bed?" I asked. I hadn't ventured there yet lest my affections be taken for lust. Perhaps one day things would be as they should and he would come to me.

"No."

"Very well." I quit the room and hurried up the stairs ahead of him to show willing.

It was only when I reached the top that I realized Edmund was far behind and pausing between steps, using the banister for support.

"Do you need me to help?"

"Go into my study and clear a seat for yourself, Lydia," he said. "Do not mother me so."

Despite my efforts a few days previously, his study had returned to a state of disarray. The chair opposite Edmund's was hidden under papers. Torn-out pages from sporting journals covered the desk. I didn't disturb the pile on the chair but perched on a clear corner of the table. That way Edmund and I could be closer.

He sighed when he saw me up there, my legs swinging like a girl's, but did not scold me. Instead he sat and, once he'd recovered his breath, reached with deliberation to grasp one paper. How he distinguished between them was beyond me. He drew it to him with the air of a lawyer. "Lydia, yesterday you may have noticed that I was gone for some hours—"

"Yes, you were surveying the estate with Tom Sewell and some of the laboring men in preparation for the harvest. You told me so," I said. Did he think I'd forgotten?

"No, Lydia, I was not," said Edmund, putting on his spectacles and examining the paper. Whatever it said was more interesting to him than I was.

I stilled my legs. "You were not?"

A few moments ago, I'd been full to bursting, suffering the uncomfortable tightness that accompanied the hour before Marshall removed my corset at the end of the day, but now my stomach felt empty, like it was folding back on itself, hollowing me out.

"I took advantage of the mild weather to ride to Thirsk," he said, without raising his head.

I flicked through a mental catalog of the people we knew, trying to identify whom Edmund might have visited in the town of Thirsk, but failed to find a likely candidate. It was typical for him to keep things from me, but yesterday's outright deception was something new. I'd thought him to be on the property when he was miles away and on an errand that was as yet opaque to me.

"What if something had happened to you?" I asked, because I could not voice my real objection. My voice was quavering, balanced on a knife edge between anger and tears.

"I can ride a horse, Lydia," said Edmund, looking up from the paper and raising his voice too.

We both knew that while this was true, he couldn't ride as he once had, with energy and confidence and power. That was how Ned and Bessy had developed their own love of horses, by clinging on to their father as he jumped hedge after hedge. I couldn't bear to watch back then, certain they would fall.

"I went to Thirsk to consult with a Dr. William Ryott, a physician. Dr. Crosby knows him well."

Ryott. The name stirred some memory, but I could not place it.

"But Dr. Crosby is our physician," I said, my tone flat now.

"I wanted a second opinion," Edmund said, with a shrug. "Crosby is hardly the territorial sort, and Mother had recommended Ryott especially."

"Your mother?" I interrupted him. "I might have known she was behind this."

"My mother is not part of this conversation."

"But she is, isn't she?" I said, sliding off the desk. A few pages tumbled to the floor in my wake. I didn't retrieve them. He shouldn't live in such chaos. "She always is. There is no escaping her."

"One's family is not something to be escaped, Lydia, but—" Edmund paused and studied my face as if searching for something. "But perhaps that *is* what you think?" he said slowly, as if this was a revelation to him. "You wish to be free of us? Of me?"

"No, Edmund, no," I said, anger giving way to a rush of fear that turned to tenderness. How to tell him that without a husband, without him, I'd be a leaf caught up in a storm, a ship without anchor?

"No matter." His voice was small and sad. His eyes were fixed again on the paper. "Dr. Ryott was most helpful. He listened to my history, let my blood, and recommended a tonic to improve my constitution."

"Did he tell you to prepare for . . . ?" My question trailed off.

Edmund shook his head. "No need for you to panic. He plans to visit here in the next months. To call upon me as a friend, you understand, not to treat me as his patient. I insisted. But on my ride back, it struck me that one day, you and the children must manage without me."

No need for you to panic. He was frightening me for nothing.

"Edmund, you are younger than me," I said. I rarely admitted this. "I won't entertain this morbid humor."

"You must." Edmund grabbed my arm and tried to force me to sit again. "And so, tonight, I wish to talk to you of my will."

"Your will? At eleven at night?" I was veering between annoyance and alarm.

"Lydia, be reasonable." He was almost shouting now. "For the last couple of months, you have fawned over me and dogged my every move. But tonight, when there is something I actually want from you, you protest. It is intolerable."

Edmund had noticed my efforts. He just didn't care. Dart after dart, piercing my pride. And I had thrown away Branwell, who noticed even the slightest change in me, and parsed my every sentence as if it were a line of poetry.

I nodded.

"Should the day come before Ned's majority, you must look after everything. See this little red book? Accounts. Consult it when wages are due or to pay the old servants their pensions. And use it to record your own spending. See, here in the margin, the date, the payee, and the amount, in pounds, shillings, and pence? And here, the opening and closing balance? Ensure that you note to yourself where you could be more economical."

"Edmund, I am not a fool," I said, tipping the book shut. I had my own money, after all, from a small inheritance. Had he forgotten that I kept accounts with milliners and dressmakers and had never kept them waiting for their dues? "Was this what you wished to tell me?" The only thing worse than Edmund's silence was when he insisted on speaking so far from the script I would have written for him.

"No, Lydia." He drew another paper to him. "About the will. Charles Thorp will be the executor."

His brother-in-law? An unsurprising choice, but should Edmund die before his mother did, he might as well have crowned her directly.

He handed the paper to me. I scanned it, but unless I was misunderstanding the elaborate prose, there was nothing in here that was unusual.

"I don't understand," I said. "Is there something in here that should seem strange to me?"

Edmund stood and strolled to the window. "Some husbands, Lydia, are draconian in their last wills and testaments." He paused.

Was he about to threaten me?

"But I want you to know—need you to know—that I will not be."

I nodded, although he wasn't looking at me.

"When I die, you may do as you wish. Marry whom you like."

"Marry again? I don't inten—"

"No, Lydia." He raised his hand to stop me as if he were saluting the far wall. "I would not have you tell a falsehood. We both know that should the time come, you will remarry before the grass has even cloaked my grave. You have too much life in you to be loyal to the dead. But, Lydia, today I ask you to choose wisely." He turned, his eyes as earnest as they were in prayer, and took a step toward me. "If not of me, think of our families and of the children—the example you must set for them, the chances that might be denied them if—"

"I reject the notion that I would not think of them," I said, just above a whisper.

Give up your body for years to birth them, stand quiet when they reject, deceive, abuse you, and, if you are a mother, you will still be called selfish, probably by the very man who gave your children nothing but his name.

"I see how you look at the tutor, Mr. Brontë," he said.

I flinched. Not speaking of Branwell directly had been an unspoken rule between us.

But Edmund's voice was oddly calm, as if he were reciting a psalm. "I see the stream of intelligence that flows between your eyes. You look at him as you once did me, now that I can no longer please you. You look at him as if he carried your heart in his hand."

"I . . . I," I stuttered. "Edmund, I do not."

How dare he bring it back to what did or didn't happen between our sheets at night? How dare he suggest that everything was so simple? Yes, I longed to wrap my arms round Branwell's neck and feel the warmth of his body against me at night, but not just because he was young and beautiful, broadening into a man while Edmund weakened with each passing day. Branwell had spoken to me, listened to me, made me whole again.

"You slander your wife, Edmund Robinson," I said. "I've never given you reason to doubt me."

"Lydia," he said, so softly he might have been speaking to an invalid. "I am not angry."

"But you should be angry." I was shaking. "You should drag Brontë out of bed and horsewhip him outside the Monk's House if you think he is taking your money and eating your food, while all the time attempting to seduce your wife."

"Mr. Brontë seduce you?" Edmund laughed. "I should think it's the other way around. The boy is a painter, a poet, an innocent. I doubt the thought has even occurred to him. You are much older than him, after all. He is practically the same age as our children."

I couldn't speak.

"Do not be ashamed, Lydia. God is merciful." Edmund was close now. He stroked my arm, his touch alien. "But should my time come soon, do not marry one so far beneath you."

"Marry?" I thrust his hand aside. "You think I would marry into his family of sickly paupers?"

"You are impulsive."

He was slicing me apart with a blunt knife, or lacing the strings around me even tighter, cleaving me in two. And I could only lash back at him, like the crushed bee who stings with his final breath.

"I married a man who was not worthy of me once before," I said. "Believe me, I will not make the same mistake again."

I PRESSED THE GRAVEL into my hand as I trudged the path to the Monk's House, but however hard I tried, I could not break my skin.

It didn't matter that Edmund had heard me leave the house, after I'd paused, panting, in the hallway for some minutes, testing to see if he would follow me. Why not go to Branwell if my husband already suspected us? Or, rather, suspected me of ruining the "innocent" boy, tempting him into sin?

Standing on the lawn to the left of the cottage, I went to throw the jagged and irregular stones at Branwell's window, but they clung to my sweaty palm. I tried again, but I was unskilled at throwing. The gravel didn't reach, not even close, but rained around me onto the grass, like early hailstones.

"Branwell," I hissed, but there was no way he could hear me, and if I spoke louder, I was sure to wake Tom Sewell.

I sank down on a fallen tree trunk and contemplated summoning the energy to cry, but it was harder when I was by myself. What was the point if Edmund saw only the swollen, ugly aftermath or if nobody saw me at all?

Maybe I should go inside. I didn't even have a shawl, and in the Hall, there were fires and blankets. Marshall could even undress me if she wasn't already in bed.

Just then, Branwell's window swung open, and there he was, the kind of hero Byron would have created—his arms bare to the elbows, his hair tousled and falling over his eyes. He leaned on the sill and puffed on his pipe.

"Mr. Brontë!" I nearly fell as I stood. "Branwell!"

He straightened up so quickly that he struck his head.

"Be careful," I said, but he had already disappeared, without bothering to close the window.

Before I'd had time to worry about Tom Sewell hearing him, Branwell was beside me, pipeless and dressed only in a long nightshirt.

"Oh Lydia," he said, tracing his fingers down the sides of my face. "Did he, your husband, upset you?"

I nodded.

"That brute."

"We mustn't be seen," I said, eying Sewell's darkened bedroom window. "Follow me. I know where we can go."

I pulled him by the hand away from the lawn and into "the woods," my body singing when his skin met mine. We walked along what had once been a path but was now only a channel of slightly sparser brush, snaking between the trees. It was too dark to see, but I knew the way.

I'd come to this building in those early years, when I'd been treasured and loved, and yet—I'd forgotten why now—still yearned for moments alone. There was no door, but the night felt milder now that I had company. Branwell procured a stub of candle, as if by magic, and lit it, making us feel even warmer.

"What is this place?" he asked as the light danced, illuminating only a few of the hundreds of nooks that lined the curving stone walls.

"A dovecote," I said.

It had been years since it had been used as such. When I'd discovered it, not long after my honeymoon, there'd been a handful of pigeons that still haunted it, slaves to their homing instincts, although the servants no longer tended to them and gave them food. Over the next months and years, they had all disappeared—died, I guessed—until only one, a dirty, limping, silent bird, had remained.

He and I were the only creatures to come here for a time, but one morning, I'd found his body bent at angles on the ground. I'd picked him up, felt, even through my glove, that his body was cold and his tiny heart was still, and thrown him aside into the shrubs.

I must have been pregnant with Georgiana then and unable to comprehend death. It was impossible to do so when new life was pulsing into being inside me. So I stopped walking here altogether and tried to be satisfied with the sterile and picturesque nature surrounding the artificial pond and the company of the children. Oh, how Lydia had tortured me with her never-ending questions! I loved to be with her and Bessy and Ned for an hour or so. But they always demanded more of me. I never had any time to myself. Years had gone by, and I hadn't even commissioned that water feature I'd wanted.

Branwell ran his hand along the wall. Didn't he desire me?

I stared, desperate with sadness and longing, urging him to come back.

When he saw my eyes, he understood. Branwell leaned toward me, paused to see if I would pull back, and when I did not, he kissed me—strong, selfish, and deep.

It was a good kiss, breath-stealing, knee-trembling, but I didn't respond as I should.

I wanted to cry—for Georgiana, the pigeon, Edmund. To mourn the vows I was breaking. Yet I had no intention of stopping the inevitable.

Branwell kissed me again, and this second time I gave in to the feeling, the waves of pleasure that ran through me, drowning out all else.

Branwell was rushing and already fumbling with the fastenings of my dress.

I'd imagined it so many times, how he would unfurl me, like a corpse being freed from her shroud. The air would bite at me, but his kisses—

reverent, methodical—would dispel the cold and beat back the encroach-ing minutes, hours, and seasons. He would marvel at each inch of me, like the tenant who has purchased a poor scrap of land, to turn and till as he has for years, but now—miracle of miracles!—every square inch of it is his.

But Branwell did not delay.

He tore my bodice, half freeing my breasts. He hitched my skirts up around my waist. His hands were everywhere, probing at me, as if he were searching a servant who'd made off with her lady's rings.

I made some noise of protest but this only inflamed him further.

He lowered me onto the cold, filthy, feather-strewn ground, clawed at me, nibbled my nipples, sucked on my neck.

At other moments I might have been horrified, but the danger elec-trified me. Still, he mustn't leave a mark.

"Branwell—" I ventured. The shape of his name was strange in my mouth. "Be careful."

He seemed far away, even as he burrowed into the hollow between my breasts, ran his hand up, around, and up my thigh again.

Instead there was Edmund, the only man who had ever seen me like this. He'd been patient on our wedding night and even more scared than me. "Can you take any more?" my new husband had asked, his tone almost coy. And his eyes had grown wide when I'd pulled him deeper, when I'd gasped at how close we were, and rocked him like the babies we dreamed we'd make.

Panic rose inside me. I'd gone too far to turn back.

Yet wasn't this what I'd wanted? I needed to escape my own head, to enjoy the sensations of Branwell's skin against mine, marvel in the feel-ing of being wanted.

I turned my mouth aside to avoid Branwell's almost medicinal breath and—I hadn't noticed him pull his shirt off, but—there he was, ready and naked, the hair bearding his crotch as fiery as the strands on his head and even more unruly.

This was enough to shock me back to myself. My body responded to the cue. Oh, it had been so long, and even before our love had cooled,

Edmund had grown too familiar and too changed by age. From my navel down, I had turned to water.

Branwell cried like a girl when he pushed inside me, arching his back and turning his face to the domed roof as if he were saluting the hidden moon.

My dress, bunched up as it was, acted as a sort of pillow beneath me but the ground was still hard. Each thrust slammed the small of my back into the stone.

"Lydia, you're an angel, a goddess, a—" Branwell's stream of incoherent compliments was torrential, making up for my silence. "Oh, God, oh, God!" he called, screwing up his face like a prisoner praying at the scaffold.

"There now," I soothed. "There."

But Branwell was alone, riding the waves of his ecstasy, thrashing so far out that I had no hope of reaching him.

"Lydia, I love you," he breathed with the final shock. He rolled off me, his expression as blissful as if we'd been lying on a cloud-soft bed. "One day, my darling, I swear we'll be together."

Wetness seeped out of me and pooled in a puddle between my legs.

CHAPTER TEN

"MISS BRONTË, MADAM. SHE insisted," said Miss Sewell with a sniff from the doorway. She must have thought such introductions beneath her.

I'd been sequestered in my rooms for a week since my argument with Edmund and what had followed. For once, I hadn't even claimed indisposition but instead simply issued an edict that all of them stay away. All of them except Marshall, my steady, unobtrusive companion. She didn't remark on my chin—red and flaking, scratched raw by Branwell's whiskers—or the bruises that dotted both sides of my neck. She brought me tray upon tray of food, emptied my chamber pot without complaint, and sat for hours at a time holding my hand as I watched summer decay into autumn through the ornate bars of my dressing room window.

"I hope—" began Miss Brontë, stopping just inside the threshold.

I raised an eyebrow in the direction of Miss Sewell, who was still standing beside her. She withdrew with a saccharine smile, shutting the door too hard.

"I hope you'll forgive the intrusion, Mrs. Robinson." Miss Brontë stepped forward and halted again. "But I can stand aside no longer. I simply must speak with you."

Anxiety suited her. It brought a little color into her pallid, almost corpse-like face.

"Indeed," I said, pushing my half-finished letter to my sister, Mary, to the edge of my desk and dismissing Marshall, who'd been darning at the window seat, with a wave of my hand.

Could Branwell have told Anne? Anything was possible in his strange family. Branwell seemed closer to his sisters than any grown man I knew, although his deepest secrets he shared only with Charlotte. If I were to beg Miss Brontë's forgiveness, fall on my knees before her and plead weakness, could she understand? I imagined Miss Brontë's wheezing breaths made even shallower, her eyes rolling back in delicious agony as Branwell's had.

"Won't you sit, Miss Brontë—Anne? And stop fraying your cuff. You are testing my nerves."

She jumped when I said her forename as if I'd pinched her, but Miss Brontë did as I'd asked. The chair opposite me—the chair Branwell had sat in during our first tête-à-tête—seemed to swallow her whole. She was clutching a letter in her left hand.

Could she be Branwell's go-between? I strained to see the script and signature, the distinctive loops of the name "Northangerland," but my sight, as ever, failed me.

"Go on," I said.

"Mrs. Robinson, it has come to my attention that—"

If only she would spit it out.

"That a correspondence of an illicit nature has been conducted from this house."

Sweat gathered between the sleeves and bodice of my gown. The silk was a dark green, so at least it wouldn't stain. Perhaps Branwell's letter spoke only of his own infatuation, sparing me from blame. I started to frame an excuse.

"Bessy came to me—" There were tears in Miss Brontë's eyes.

"Bessy?" I repeated. Vicious Lydia, yes, or Mary and Ned in their naivety, but Bessy?

"She was in great distress, Mrs. Robinson. She is only a child and, what is more, she chose to confess. Do not be harsh on her." Miss Brontë dropped the letter onto her lap and clasped her hands together as if in prayer.

My shoulders slackened, my panic subsided. She wasn't here to talk of Branwell at all.

"Miss Brontë, I must ask that you be direct," I told her, recovering my poise and examining the half-moons and the flecks of white in my fingernails.

She gulped air and launched into the longest speech I had ever heard from her.

"Bessy came to me last night—late, it must have been after midnight—and insisted on slipping into bed beside me. When she appeared at my door, my heart nearly stopped, for she looked like a ghost in her nightgown. And it took some time before I could glean from her what on earth was the matter. She wept but would not speak until I mentioned rousing other members of the household and fetching Dr. Crosby. Then she told me the truth, in fits and bursts, and through more tears.

"It appears she, for some years, has been exchanging letters with Will Milner of Nun Monkton. Their early missives were innocent enough. They talked of hunts and horses, anticipated the Thompsons' picnics, and, I'm afraid, mocked the good Reverend Lascelles's sermons. The stablehand, Joey Dickinson, acted as their messenger. Do not blame him either, Mrs. Robinson. He is a child too. He cannot read and is simple about the ways of the world!

"But, of late, Will Milner would talk of marriage and the like, and Bessy did not know how to answer him. She deferred to her sister—I mean Lydia—who fed her lines from novels and encouraged her to write all species of nonsense. I blushed when I heard what the girls had written. I am sure Bessy, at least, did not understand the import of the words.

"And now Bessy says she is not sure she wishes to marry Will Milner after all, and thinks of him as she does Ned rather than as a husband. The young man, Mr. Milner, plans to petition Mr. Robinson for her hand and asks Bessy to name a date. Oh, and Lydia is angry too. She threatened her sister with exposure should she even think of marrying first, despite being the younger. And so poor Bessy came to me. Take pity on her, Mrs. Robinson, do. And, believe me, I knew nothing of this—had not seen a sign—until last night."

A pretty monologue, but I saw now why she quaked. Miss Brontë was afraid lest I choose to dismiss her. That was a governess's primary purpose, after all—not to impart knowledge into heads pretty enough to be petted and docile enough to be yoked, but to protect her charges' flimsy, if incontrovertible, virginities. And she had failed.

Learned Miss Brontë might be—although not half as clever as her sister Charlotte—but two of her pupils had erred at the first feeble overtures men had made them. Plain women held themselves so high, but given the chance, she, and maybe Charlotte too, would crumple.

"Miss Brontë, I must say I am disappointed," I said, the power I had felt seep out of me in the hours after my encounter with Branwell returning full force when faced by her timidity.

"Be kind to Bessy, madam!" she cried.

"No, Miss Brontë, I am disappointed in you."

She didn't flinch this time but raised her eyes to heaven, as collected as a queen waiting for the guillotine to fall.

But we could never be rid of each other now. She did not know it, but she was protected by the very crimes she abhorred. Bessy's indiscretions were but a pale imitation of Branwell's and my own. What were a few harmless letters to what he and I had done?

"A match between the Robinsons and the Milners is most desirable," I said, relishing each syllable and stressing the "most" as if I'd been gossiping at a party and striking John Crosby with my fan. "I cannot approve of the execution, of course, or of the secrecy surrounding it, but it seems to me that a correspondence between Mr. Milner and our Bessy is not so terrible a thing."

"Not so terrible—" Miss Brontë let her mouth hang open.

I suppressed my desire to slam it shut from under her chin.

"Miss Brontë, I know your life has been somewhat sheltered, but I'm sure it can't have escaped your attention that Bessy, in addition to being a second daughter, isn't the most eligible of girls. She is boisterous and ill-mannered and spends most of her time talking of dogs and horses, despite the money my husband and I have invested in her education."

"I think Bessy is a fine girl," Miss Brontë whispered, ignoring the references to her salary and ineffective teaching.

"Oh, it is all very well for you to say so. To be forgiving and kind, to never say a cross word." I could contain myself no longer and stood, my yearning for the exercise that I'd avoided for days returning. "But, Miss Brontë, you are not their mother. It is not a mother's job to coo and coddle, to flatter with falsehoods or coat with sugar. There is one way for a woman to flourish, or, for that matter, to survive at all in this world, and that is to marry, and marry well."

My own mother had told me so when she'd explained what it was that husbands took from you. She'd counseled me to be "ever on my guard," to act "always above suspicion" as a maiden and once I was a wife. And what had I done with her advice? The least I could do was protect my daughters' interests, as she had mine.

Miss Brontë flinched at the invocation of my motherhood, a trump card in every argument. Branwell had told me Anne had no memories of their poor mother. She, Charlotte, and Emily had suffered from the absence of a seasoned, pragmatic woman like me. So this was a moment to teach her, not to scold.

"I pity you, Miss Brontë," I said, holding both hands out toward her. "You might not believe me, but I do. You never had your chance. You never had a mother to show you the way. And, now, look at the life you are forced to lead—you and your sisters. You must choose between being a drudge or a burden, and suffer for years with the knowledge that with death, you will slide into an only marginally more acute obscurity."

But Miss Brontë did not take this as an olive branch. She stood too, ignoring my outstretched hands. "Bessy does not wish to marry Will Milner, Mrs. Robinson. And she should not part with her hand and heart without reason. She will have other chances."

"She will have none as good as this." I snatched the letter from where she had left it on the chair and walked past her to the door.

"Mrs. Robin—"

I was already halfway down the landing, making for the schoolroom. And Miss Brontë hadn't followed me.

"Lydia, you have rejoined the world of the living." There was Edmund, pausing on the final step on his way upstairs. His cheeks were blotchy from the strain of climbing, and his eyes weren't so difficult to meet, for all I'd thought I could never face him again after what had happened with Branwell.

"Not now, Edmund." I surprised myself with my surety. "I am needed in the schoolroom."

I opened the door. The three of them were arranged as in a painting—Lydia reading a novel, Bessy staring out the window, Mary petting Flossy by the fire. They did not look like girls, but little women who'd outgrown the furniture around them and that childish way of wearing their long, loose hair. But they were my girls just the same.

"Lydia, Bessy, Mary," I said.

Looks of confusion and fear passed between them at my entrance.

"This morning Miss Brontë brought me a letter—"

"She wouldn't!" gasped Bessy.

"I told you she would," said Lydia.

"What letter?" asked Mary, studying each of our faces in turn.

"And it seemed to me we should talk," I said. "Do not cry, Bessy! Come."

I tapped the Pembroke table where they'd learned their French, geography, history, and motioned them to sit.

Mary levered Flossy off her lap and came to me first. Lydia and Bessy followed. The terrier rolled even closer to the grate, its head thrown back at a near-impossible angle.

"It is time for us to speak of our family and what is expected of you," I began. "And to discuss the behavior that is, and is not, acceptable when being wooed by a young man."

Lydia rolled her eyes.

"Lydia," I said sharply. "Don't you wish to be married?"

"I do, Mama," she said, chastised.

I took her by the hand.

"But Mama," said Bessy, her eyes downcast, "I'm no longer so certain that I do—"

"Do not be a fool, Bessy." I took hers too. "To be married is a wonderful thing."

I should have said merely that being married was better than *not* being married, but I hadn't my mother's strength to be so truthful.

The taste of Branwell's sweat came back to me. And the sound of his panting, the waves of his back muscles rippling under my hand. Silly boy. He'd just been too eager, too hasty. That was all. At its worst, lying with a man was but a few moments of discomfort, a small price for my daughters to pay for a better life. And at its best—well, I would school Branwell to please me better next time.

"Marriage is what you should all aspire to, my darlings," I said, squeezing the girls' hands harder. "For once you are married, you may do anything you wish."

I HAD RARELY BEEN in Dr. Crosby's home since the call Edmund and I had paid when he'd first moved there. He was a stalwart at local social functions, wherever they were held, and, in a household our size, there was always some reason to summon the doctor, so it seemed ridiculous to upset the order of the world and visit him myself.

His house was small compared to Thorp Green Hall, but large

when seen beside the cottages that lined the only street in Great Ouseburn. It was just a decade old (it had been built to the doctor's specifications), and so the bricks were a rich red and not blackened by smoke or bordered by lichen. A carpenter had fashioned neoclassical columns in relief around the front door, and the maidservant ushered me through here, rather than down the passageway to my right, which led to the rear of the property and Dr. Crosby's surgery. The parlor was the first room on the left, with a view of the street.

"I would not have come to you alone, Dr. Crosby, unless it was to consult with you on something serious," I said, as soon as the fuss of tea was over and we were at last alone.

The good doctor nodded.

His furnishings were tasteful. The creams and pinks that made up the color scheme reminded me of my dressing room. But I was not here to exchange observations, compliments, and small talk.

"I can rely on your discretion?" I asked.

"But of course, Mrs. Robinson." John Crosby replaced his teacup in its saucer and set it on the low table with the steady precision of a surgeon, although the only operations he conducted in the area around the Ouseburns were resetting the broken and dislocated bones of farmers and laboring men and pulling the occasional rotten tooth.

How to begin? I clasped my cup with both hands. The milky brown puddle splashed, threatening to cascade into my lap, and I held on tighter, imagining how it would scald and slice if the shards of porcelain shattered between my fingers.

"Dr. Crosby." I swallowed. "It is a sad fact of life, of our society, I think, that a girl—a woman—can at times, through, perhaps, little fault of her own, find herself in trouble."

"A sad tale but a common one, Mrs. Robinson," he said, his brow furrowing. He leaned forward from the low-slung sofa, his elbows propped on top of his knees.

"And—forgive me, Dr. Crosby, I am no doctor—but, in such cases, I believe, there are things that can be done, procedures that can take matters out of God's hands?"

John Crosby nodded slowly, as if reasoning out a complex argument, and took another gulp of tea, draining the dainty cup in one and setting it down before he replied. "That may well be the case, Mrs. Robinson. But wouldn't it be easier, and safer, to send the unfortunate girl away? With some small sum of money, of course, to support her through her trials?"

I winced. "No, no, you misunderstand me," I said, covering my face and peering at him through the latticework of my fingers. "I am not speaking of a servant."

"Oh. One of your daughters." He stood and leaned past my shoulder to fold over the wooden blinds. That was kind of him. It was true I didn't wish to be watched. "The oldest Milner son, perhaps, or—? But no, I won't inquire. In that case, Mrs. Robinson, I say, if he won't marry her, the young man is a rogue." He sat again and reached out his hands toward me. "But I can help you and do what needs to be done."

Even he knew about Bessy and Will Milner, then? But there was no imminent danger there. Edmund had been planning a visit to Nun Monkton to delay any proposal. We'd determined that Bessy was young and skittish, like the fillies she spent hours brushing. It wouldn't hurt for the boy to wait a few years. But then word had come that Nathaniel Milner, Will's father, was ailing and wasn't expected to last until Christmas. That would put a stop to his son's romantic attentions for now.

Dr. Crosby threw and caught a small, unevenly embroidered cushion that some poor girl—a niece of his, maybe—must have worked on for months. There were flecks of blood caught under his fingernails. Of course. I'd called him away from his surgery, without a thought for the injured farmhands or colicky infants he might have been examining.

I shut my eyes tight and pressed the heels of my hands against my eyelids, sick at the sight of what I had longed to see for the last month or more, streaking my linens, floating in clots on the frothing surface of my chamber pot, racing down the silver-white paths that had traversed my thighs since my pregnancies. It hadn't come, but I hadn't panicked. Not at first. For I didn't feel quite as I had with the girls, or Ned, or Georgie. Or maybe I'd simply forgotten.

"But what if, Dr. Crosby—John—what if I wasn't asking about my daughters either?"

I considered him a friend, my ally against Edmund when he tried to medicate me, my eyes and ears at the Freemasons' meetings in York, my dependable and favorite card partner. But I'd never plumbed the depths of our friendship before. My heart and stomach were giddy as dancers who'd overindulged at a ball, spiraling harder and harder until they flew apart, eating, drinking, laughing until the only release was to belch and purge.

The cushion thudded to the floor. Dr. Crosby did not speak for at least a minute.

"Then I would say that congratulations were in order?" he ventured, making a question out of what should not have been one.

"But what if—" My voice dropped to a whisper. "What if my husband— What if such a thing were impossible?"

No way out now. Branwell Brontë had seen my naked flesh and I had not felt so exposed, but before Dr. Crosby, I was Diana, trying to shield herself from the hunter with only her hands for protection.

"Then, Lydia," he said, mirroring my use of his forename and crouching beside me, "you have my utmost sympathy and compassion." He took my hand between his.

"Thank you," I whispered, my eyes welling up.

Another beat. A tear dropped.

"Mr. Brontë is a fascinating, if troubled, man," he said.

I couldn't react to that so held myself very still.

"And I know how hard it is to be spurned," he went on. "To lie alone at night with only your own thoughts between you and oblivion."

"You do?" I asked, confusion coaxing my chin from my chest.

His expression was uncharacteristically sincere. His breathing had quickened, but I did not withdraw my hand for there was not even a hint of lust in his eyes.

"But—" I cast around for the right words. "You might have married again. Chosen from any number of ladies."

He paused. "Any number of *ladies*, Lydia, yes. But I am afraid the truth is that it is not women who hold delight for me."

No wonder the discourse between us had always been so natural and easy, devoid of insidious competition or ulterior motive.

He retreated and sat on his ankles. Now he was the penitent, and I the—what?—confessor? Ridiculous. I laughed, laughed until my tears flowed with undiluted joy, and at last he joined me.

Oh, we were as vulnerable to each other now as the lovers we would never be. Ever the gentleman, Dr. Crosby had divulged his secret as a security against mine. And his admission, which might have disgusted and alarmed me before, now seemed little compared to my own baseness. It was as if he had drawn back the veil that had divided us and cast over all our past interactions a warm and unmuddied light.

I did not need him in the end. My courses came in the carriage on the way home. Not in a flood but, rather, spluttering in protest like a leaking tap that had been twisted shut.

"It is the beginning of the end of a chapter," Dr. Crosby said when he visited me later that week. "You'll bear no more children."

And he didn't ask me why my response was not relief, but passed me a handkerchief when my tears sprang up again, wrenching my heart this time, shed for the woman I had been, the girl I had lost, and the babe whom I would have murdered.

9th April 1845
Allestree Hall

My darling sister Lyddy,

I write today with somber news. Our cousin, Lady Scott, has suffered a sad misfortune. Her son, William Douglas, always a sickly child but a boy I thought out of danger since he was now sixteen, has died. Do see to it that you send your condolences to her and Sir Edward at Great Barr Hall.

Do you remember how, when you were young, you used to say you would marry Edward Scott and be a Lady? You were always an ambitious child. At times, you quite dominated me, although I was so many years older. And now look at us, Lyddy! Ah well, the remembrance of you wearing your bedsheets as a veil brought laughter to my lips even after receiving such news.

Do come and visit us in Derbyshire before long. And send word if you hear anything from Father, or his man Rowley.

I remain your ever loving and faithful sister,
Mary Evans

P.S. I was ever so surprised by your last letter. To think that the Reverend Eade is married again! Do the Thorps take it well? How irate old Mrs. Robinson must be that "dear John" is no longer loyal to the memory of Edmund's darling sister Jane! The man may be a bore, but he has certainly gone up in my estimation.

And how sad the plight of your neighbor Mrs. Milner! I can't imagine how terrible it must be for the poor woman to be widowed and with so many daughters to marry off.

This time, in truth, good-bye,
Mary

My dear Lady Scott,

It is with sadness that I write to console you on the loss of your son, William Douglas.

All of us at Thorp Green Hall were very shocked.

I know, from experience, that to lose a young child is as painful as it is expected, but to lose a boy on the cusp of manhood must be intolerable.

I hope that your own health has not worsened and that your other sons take after Sir Edward with regards to their constitution.

Send my regards and regrets to him likewise.

Ever your devoted cousin,
Yours very truly,
Lydia Robinson

CHAPTER ELEVEN

"I KNEW YOU'D COME to me, my darling." Branwell's mouth was hot against mine. His breath tasted sweet, without a hint of the liquor that had overwhelmed me the first time.

In the months since then, we'd discovered a shared rhythm when we kissed that was uniquely ours. When we paused to speak, which was rarely, we'd take it in turns to pick up the beat again. Sometimes we marveled that we'd once agonized over what felt so easy. Often we giggled together, imagining the straitlaced matrons whom we saw at church pecking their portly husbands good night with their mouths closed, never experiencing the joys that were ours for now.

"You knew nothing of the sort, Mr. Brontë." I made a play of pushing him away. "What was so important that you summoned me?"

The May Day sun streamed through the gaping holes in the thatch, illuminating George Walker's hovel. I closed my eyes to bask in it. The old man had been unwell for some weeks, with Miss Brontë making the journey each day to tend to him. But he'd at last succumbed to his family's petitions, permitting his daughter-in-law, Eliza, to nurse him at her home in Little Ouseburn instead.

"He looks frail, but in truth, he's as strong as an ox. I doubt it'll prove fatal, even yet," Dr. Crosby had told me as the congregation milled about in groups outside Holy Trinity last Sunday, enlivened by the temperate weather. The doctor usually attended services at St. Mary's in Great Ouseburn but had come to Holy Trinity especially to see me. "Yet I should think his cottage will lie empty for some weeks." He'd added this casually, without caring that Mary and Miss Brontë stood beside me. But there was a glint in his eye that made me wonder if he was delighting in the romance of helping us. I hadn't confided in him further since that day in his parlor, for all that his attentions had been decorous and constant. Yet perhaps Branwell too had turned to the doctor with our dark secret, bound as the pair was by their Masonic brotherhood.

I opened my eyes.

"You taste of blackberries and sugarplums and claret." Branwell kissed me again, with the confidence I had taught him—not too fast and not too soft, exploring but not invading me.

When I pulled back this time, it was with a smile that lingered on my lips. "You abuse your privileges, sir. You were to send for me only in the case of an event that might be deemed exceptional."

Joey Dickinson, in his slow, uncomprehending way, had delivered the coded message as I strolled around the perimeter of the stew pond half an hour before. "Mr. Brontë says, missus, there's a fox about," he'd said. "He'll tell Mr. Pottage."

Branwell stroked my cheek with the back of his hand. "I did deem it exceptional, miraculous even, until I saw your face," he said. "But now all else pales in comparison."

"Enough." I laughed.

He swept me up in his arms with ease, although my dress was heavy and our heights were equal, and deposited me on the low and narrow bed. It still smelled of age and decay, although Branwell had spread fresh blankets over the straw. But it was better than the dovecote, or the carriage house, or the granary, or the stables. Much better than those months when our desire for warmth and desire for human heat had fought against each other, when we'd writhed against the back wall of the Monk's House, our fingers so numb they'd felt like strangers'.

With the spring and with practice, our lovemaking had become more luxurious. Branwell no longer tore at me or ripped off my buttons. I'd have him watch me undress layer by layer, the breeze light against my skin, feeling his eyes touch every part of me, before his hands. Or we'd play a game where I'd struggle as if to get away until he held me close and wrestled me, laughing, to the ground. Our meetings were like musical variations. Whichever note we began on and whichever trills we added, we'd return at last to a familiar theme.

Branwell snaked his mouth along my collarbone and tugged gently upon my ear.

"Tell me, I command you," I whispered, focusing on the patches of pink scalp I could see through his thick curls.

"What would you say if I told you I had at last received news from the *Gazette?*" he asked.

"No!" I clasped my arms tight around him.

"Yes." He laughed and rolled over to lie in my lap, his blue eyes gazing up at me. In this pose, he bore a remarkable resemblance to Flossy, Miss Brontë's lapdog.

"Well, what did Mr. Bellerby say?" I asked. "Do not tease me so. Did he think the verses fine?"

A month or more ago, Branwell had been in one of his brooding humors, bewailing the lack of recognition the world had shown for his genius thus far and the sad want of poetic souls in the Ouseburns, ourselves excepted.

It was in these moods of his that the difference in age between us most showed. I relished Branwell's immoderate passion and his vitality, the energy with which he swept me off my feet, pinned me against walls, flung me across the bed. But other aspects of his youthfulness were less appealing. He sulked when we argued. He complained about writing more than he wrote. And he often gave in to fits of paranoia that Charlotte would publish a novel before he did.

Trusting that, as with Ned, exercise would do Branwell the world of good, I'd suggested that day that he ride to York with William Allison. Our coachman exchanged a box full of novels for us there each month, providing the perfect opportunity for Branwell to speak with Mr. Bellerby, the bookseller and newspaper owner. Maybe that was what he needed—something to write *for*. To my surprise, Branwell had agreed. The Freemasons would be meeting there that night, and he enjoyed any excuse to drink with them.

"Fine? Well, Bellerby didn't say so," said Branwell, pain entering his eyes for a second. "But he writes that they are to print two of the sonnets on the tenth of this month."

"Sonnets?" My heart beat faster.

"Not *those* sonnets, Lydia." Branwell reached up his hand and cupped my face.

I kissed his hand. Were I to die, would Marshall take those incriminating poems, fit only for my eyes, from their secret place—the drawer in the back of my jewelry box—and destroy them?

"'Black Comb' and the sheepdog sonnet—two the *Bradford Herald* published years ago." His hand dropped as he sighed. "But it is something."

My pulse slackened. There was no danger in these.

"It is more than something," I said, running my fingers through his hair and staring up at the cobwebs.

It would be too risky, but much as I feared his more recent poems' publication, there would be something beautiful in it. In having Branwell's love for me printed there in indelible ink right in front of Edmund at the breakfast table. But then the name "Northangerland" would mean nothing to him, and poetry, if anything, even less. When he discarded the paper, clumsy, illiterate Ann Ellis would crumple it up to act as kindling for the fire, and all would be as before.

"It is more than something," I repeated, thinking how frequently Branwell had been disappointed—in painting, the railway, his writing most of all. "But was that all?"

"Was that all?" Branwell echoed, springing up and dragging me down the bed. "No, it was not, Miss Gisborne."

I laughed my most girlish laugh, in keeping with my childhood name.

He pulled up my skirts, mock-smothering me, and dived below them so I could no longer see him. His lips left a trail of kisses along my upper thigh, sending a shiver through me.

The sun shone warmer through the graying straw, bathing my face in light. A baptism of sorts and without an ounce of guilt now. Not this time, or any time since I had trained and guided him and since our encounters had become less about him and more for me.

Sometimes I had him pleasure me and then didn't let him inside me at all. Sometimes we came to the brink, before I bid him leave me. And loyal subject that he was, he always did as I said. The power was intoxicating. This must be how a husband felt when first seeing his bride below him, her naked body his to own, demand, explore, tonight and every night until death or indifference.

Branwell pulled away.

I flinched with disappointment.

"Lydia—" he said, his voice quaking with emotion. I still couldn't see his face, but I recognized the tone.

"Don't mention 'love.' Not a word of it. Do you understand me?" I said.

He did that when impassioned sometimes, making this all too real and dampening my desire.

I found the back of his neck and pulled him down where I wanted him. His baby hairs were just long enough to hold onto.

Yes. No. Higher. A little lower. There.

"Don't stop," I breathed. "Faster, softer. Still faster. Yes."

I arched, twisted, struggled, but he knew by now to keep going.

If only I could hold on to this moment, feel this joy flooding through me forever.

WHEN I CAME DOWNSTAIRS to the breakfast room on the tenth and saw the folded *Gazette* in front of Edmund's place, that was something else entirely. I did not dare touch it. I'd smear the print with my moist fingertips and be unable to replicate the folds, as tight and crisp as those Ellis made at the corners of our many beds each morning.

Somewhere amongst those pages lurked the name "Northangerland." And even if the name didn't underscore the real poems, those guilty poems, it proved that Branwell had a mind, pen, voice of his own, much as he had deferred to me and to my wishes until now. A wrong word from him, whether spoken or written, in passion or in malice, could destroy me.

"No sign of your master, Miss Sewell?" I asked. Edmund was normally here before I was.

"I believe he is unwell, madam," she answered, not taking her eyes from Ellis, who was pouring tea under her supervision.

"But now there is no room for cream!" cried Lydia, pushing the cup away from her.

She and Bessy, freed from the travails of the morning lessons that had called Mary and Ned away, were still here—Lydia reading, Bessy eating more than her fair share.

Ann Ellis bobbed in apology and started to pour a new cup.

Miss Sewell rolled her eyes and plucked the newspaper from the table.

"Leave it," I said, my vehemence surprising me. It wasn't as if Edmund were likely to peruse the literary section.

Bessy paused mid-bite into her toast and glanced at her sister.

"I thought Mr. Robinson might like to read in bed." The paper hovered in midair in Miss Sewell's hand as she chose whether to indulge my caprice. "But you know best, madam." She threw it down rather than setting it, so that the borders no longer ran parallel to the table edge. Her skirts rustled as she left the room, like leaves detecting the first stirrings of a storm.

"Any news from the village, Ellis?" I asked. Of my three companions, she was sure to be the most agreeable.

A look of panic spread across her small, irregular features. "The Reverend's wife had her baby, madam. A son," she said at last, her relief palpable at having settled on a suitable subject.

"Reverend Lascelles must be delighted," I said without an ounce of joy. I imagined him holding up his son, enraptured, as his poor wife languished in her distant bedchamber, his daughters banished to the nursery, and the prayers of thanksgiving we'd all be forced to endure for the next rash of Sundays.

"Indeed, ma'am," she said.

"Well, are you going to clear the table?" I asked, my desire for conversation evaporating. "Bessy, you have had enough." I slapped her hand away from the butter. "Run on, now."

Lydia and Bessy swung their legs round in unison and linked arms before exiting the room. They were hurrying off somewhere to complain about me, no doubt. I was the evil witch, without whom they'd be glutting themselves to their hearts' content, penning scandalous notes to the neighbors, and rolling around with actors in the stables. Give them twenty years, until they had their own daughters to worry about. Then they'd understand.

Ellis struggled under a tower of crockery, weaving her unsteady way to the door—anything so that she didn't have to return to me.

Was Edmund really ill, or was he too avoiding me? Was it possible that he had sensed the change in me? The sleepy, not-quite-happiness that settled over me in the days after my more recent encounters with Branwell? It wasn't the happiness I'd had once with Edmund. Not the steady, sure warmth you feel when you slip to sleep beside a man who loves you and wake to his breath, his arms, his half-remembered dreams come dawn. With Branwell, things were never safe and rarely so simple. His flights of fancy were unappetizing as often as they were enticing. The more poetry I read, the more I concluded that his verses *didn't* have the power of Wordsworth's or Southey's. Perhaps he'd overstated his skill as a painter too and given too flattering an account of his dismissal from the railway.

Sometimes after our passion was over and I lay alone, not suffering Branwell to touch me, I was reminded of how Edmund had described those youthful encounters of his, with women in Cambridge, before we were married. He'd "confessed" these to me in an Italian inn, with his head in my lap, contrasting his weakness with my purity. A few moments of mania, he'd said, after too much wine and at the urging of friends. And then shame and disgust—at her, the room, the damp and dirty bed—unclouding his judgment and calling him home. Was Branwell the same—an object of lust only if you dimmed the lights and trusted the make-believe of powder and rouge?

"Mrs. Robinson."

I blinked. Not only had Miss Sewell reentered the room, but, unbidden, she had taken the seat opposite me. Her hands were stacked before her on the table.

"Miss Sewell," I said, trying to sound more horrified than shocked.

She thought too highly of herself, although in truth she was doing well, with a housekeeper's salary at her age, along with an indulgent and unattached older brother to spoil her. Her dress was modest but cut in the latest style, and her sandy hair was coiffed and curled. It was her hands that gave her away. Red and coarse, with close-clipped nails, they weren't the hands of a lady.

"You know perhaps there is a gentleman farmer sometimes brings news from Great Ouseburn, madam?" she asked. "And that he always makes it his business to speak with me?"

"I do not, Miss Sewell, make a practice of observing my servants' social habits," I said, fixating on her nails and trying to catch the drift of her questioning.

"Funny that." She let out a sharp, shrill laugh. "We observe yours."

I stiffened. "Miss Sewell?" I met her glittering black eyes and willed my breath to stay even.

"Well, my Robert—his name is Robert, madam—would like to call on me, walk me to church sometimes, take me to dances and the like in his gig, if you'd be so good as to give us your blessing, madam." From her condescending smile, you'd have thought that I was the one petitioning her.

But if she had observed me, us, if she knew— I stood. It was impossible to sit. "I don't know what has come over you, Miss Sewell," I said, pushing in my chair. "You'll do well not to mention this again. I know you are young, but to have gentlemen come courting our housekeeper? What kind of example is that for you to set to Ellis and the others?"

"I look to my betters for an example, Mrs. Robinson," she said, the left-hand corner of her upper lip curling further.

How dare she remain sitting while I stood?

"And I know my brother, Tom, does too," she continued. "Such strange comings and goings he sees out there at the Monk's House, madam. Mr. Brontë is always ranging the grounds, walking here, there, and everywhere, and talking when he's in the drink, which is on most nights. I don't say my brother's not partial to the whiskey as well, madam, but he takes one only on occasion. With such a pattern to follow, whom are we to look to for our examples, if I might be so bold?"

"Hold your tongue." The table was between us, or I would have struck her.

"Then there is the matter of my pay." Her confidence was growing. She started to flex her wrists, roll her shoulders, and relax. "All it would take is a word from you, and Mr. Robinson'd be sure to reward my brother and me for our continued service. And, of course, for our discretion."

I tried to speak but only a splutter came out.

Miss Sewell's eyes were roaming all over me, as if taking an inventory of my dress, rings, the locket around my neck, and all she would try to sweat from me. "Maybe you need a few weeks to think on it, madam?" she said, hopping to her feet. "I'm a reasonable woman. Did Ellis take the newspaper? The master asked for it in particular."

CHAPTER TWELVE

WEEKS OF WHISPERING BEHIND doorways, pacing my dressing room at night, pressing coins every other day into the scheming housekeeper's hands.

And yet life went on as ever. Nobody knew. Edmund haunted his study. The servants' gossip was benign, self-centered, mundane. And the children wished away their lives in anticipation of summer. They gazed like augurs to discern snatches of blue sky between the rainstorms. Lydia spoke only of Scarborough.

In public, I treated Miss Sewell with condescension, perhaps more harshly than before. I disguised my new expenses as brooches and shawls in Edmund's account book. It wasn't like he noticed what I wore anyway. But still the upstart woman asked for more, threatening dire consequences if I didn't indulge her.

"What, Miss Sewell?" I'd said, trying to regain the upper hand. "You'd have me think you'd tell my husband? Cut off your supply of pocket money?"

"Oh no, madam," she answered. "Something much worse than that."

I didn't tell Branwell much, only that we had best be more careful. Our meetings became less frequent. Once a week, or thereabouts, we followed our routine, like dancers tracing familiar steps. Otherwise we were strangers. It was torture for Branwell, or so he claimed during our rendezvous, although he made no other attempts to see me. But I was unchained, freed from the tyranny of his emotions. His frenzy when the words came to him fast and easy, even without the ready lubrication of wine. His abject misery when the page was blank or, worse, a distorting mirror, failing to reflect his self-professed genius. But I couldn't give him up, not entirely, not yet. How could I turn away from his words and the reassuring warmth of his body, lose again that part of me I'd thought already in my grave?

At last, after weeks of false hope, summer. The sun shone golden, bringing out the red in the Hall's brick walls. The planting around the pond, which Bob Pottage had slaved over in the drizzle only a few weeks ago, had issued forth a crush of copper marigolds, fighting against each other to drink in the light. Our little world was undergoing a glorious renaissance. It was hard to imagine that it wouldn't extend to the rest of us.

"In the center." I pointed past the halo of flowers to the middle of the pond.

Bob Pottage noted something down on the sketch that I'd given him and grunted. It was surprising that he, a mere gardener, could write at all.

"We'd have to run it by the master," said Tom Sewell, who was hovering, unhelpfully, to my right.

"Would you?" I countered.

"I mean just the cost, madam. I'm sure everything else is in order." Sewell exchanged a glance with his fellow servant.

Did it really require two of them to understand such simple instructions? I'd wanted that fountain for twenty years, but I'd waited just as long before taking matters into my own hands. I didn't wish to broker any further delay.

"Beggin' yer pardon, Mr. Sewell, Mr. Pottage." Joey Dickinson appeared before us. He was still at least a head shorter than they were, although his upper lip now sported a downy mustache.

"Joseph, what do you mean by interrupting us?" said Tom Sewell, whose seniority meant the task of disciplining the boy fell to him. "And with the lady of the house here too."

"But Mr. Sewell, sir, I've a message. And it's for the missus." Joey had made himself even shorter. He was hunched over as if he expected a strike.

The men's heads swiveled in my direction.

There was only one reason he would have a message for me.

"Very good, Joey. You can run along now," I said, locking my eyes with his, willing him to have some sense and remain silent.

"But I ain't given you the message yet, ma'am," said Joey, nearly crossing his eyes as he frowned.

"Well, out with it, lad!" said Pottage. "He's that gormless you'd think he was daft in t' head."

Joey lowered his brow even further, as if struggling to remember. "It's about the fox, missus—"

"Fox!" the gardener cried. "What fox?"

"That's to say there's another one, ma'am," Joey concluded. "I was to tell you."

I flushed. Was there any scenario in which such a public summons from Branwell would be justified?

"More than one fox?" said Pottage. "And I've heard nowt of neither. I'll get my shotgun." He thrust the sketch at Sewell and strode toward the outbuildings.

Tom Sewell looked from me to Joey.

I held my breath, waiting for his comment or question, but he shrugged and started to study my design for the pond's centerpiece. He tapped his pocketknife against the bowl the proud goddess held aloft, water cascading over the sides.

"Thank you, Joey," I said, through a forced smile.

The boy scuttled away without bowing.

"Excuse me, Mr. Sewell," I said and turned toward the house. I'd skirt the perimeter and take the long road in the direction of Little Ouseburn, George Walker's cottage, and Branwell.

"What about the fountain, madam?" Sewell called after me.

"We shall speak of it tomorrow!" I threw back.

I SHOULD HAVE LEFT my shawl behind. The sun, which had warmed me when we stood at the pool's edge, was sweltering, sticking my dress to the small of my back and the hollows beneath my arms. If only I could abandon layer upon layer of clothing on the hedgerows, which were resplendent, green, skirted with late-flowering yellow cowslips. I'd take Branwell's hand and race with him across the sodden fields so fast we wouldn't sink, throw us both into the swollen river Ouse and steal our breath away, resurface laughing, splashing, grasping for a branch or root along the bank. That was if I weren't so angry with him.

He was standing just inside the door of George Walker's cottage when I reached him, staring through a crack in the floorboards as if he'd dropped something.

"Have you lost your mind?" I asked, pushing him farther inside and trying to recover my breath.

He recoiled, offended. It was the exaggerated gesture of a drunk.

"We have to be careful," I said. "And send messages only in a crisis. I was with Sewell and Pottage, but then Joey—"

"But I don't understand," Branwell said. "*You* summoned *me*."

"Have you drunk so much you've forgotten yourself?" I rounded on him. "I mean for God's sake, it's hardly noon."

He shrugged.

"On a Wednesday."

I don't know why this made it worse, but it did. I dropped onto George Walker's stinking, uncovered bed and let the tears I had fought against for what seemed like years wash over me.

Branwell stood a few feet away, mouth open but otherwise too shocked to react. "Sorry," he stuttered at last. "Maybe I did send for you. I can't remember. Lydia?" He was beside me, prying apart my fingers to interweave them with his.

The straw mattress buckled under our combined weight.

"The words would not come," he said. "And Tom Sewell offered me a dram. I thought it might act as a sort of medicine."

"You cannot say that you drink to aid your writing, Branwell. That you think of your poetry first." I wanted to shake him, but at least my growing anger stemmed my tears. "Every night you tell me you will write the next day, but each time you turn instead to the bottle. How long before your employment at Thorp Green goes the same way as your painting or your job at the railway? Before you lose your position— and me—to this insatiable thirst?"

He retracted his hand and ran it over his face as if he would have wiped the slate clean. "You are right," he said. "I haven't written anything of any worth in a long time, if I ever have. I disappoint them all— my father, my sisters. Charlotte is writing again—I know it, although she no longer shares her tales with me. Maybe Emily too. I even saw Anne writing what looked like a story the other day. I was their hope, their light, but I have wrecked my talent, left that early promise in ruins, and now look forward only to my own extinction."

Miraculous. He did not heed my practical warnings, but fixated instead on his self-pity. I'd thought him so sympathetic, but he was envious of the sisters who'd done nothing but support him. He no longer cared for my tears, but had dissolved into his own. Branwell rocked backwards and forwards, lost in himself, not moved by my unhappiness.

A surge of jealousy flooded through me. He should try being a woman for a day. I'd never enjoyed the luxury of drinking alone. I'd only ever delighted in wine that appeared at its appointed time, matched to each course and spirited away just as soon, excluded as I was from the room when the men pored over their brandies or eyed the dining table and the world through the golden haze of their cognac glasses. Men had liquor, tobacco, horses, and whores. But there was no poison I was permitted to administer to myself. Instead I relied on Branwell for the release he found for himself in drink.

Still, whoever had summoned whom, and whatever force had drawn us there, there was a vacuum in my heart, an ache that could be quieted but never silenced. My body was calling out for distraction and for him, however briefly, to make me whole again.

"Branwell." I kissed his forehead and his eyebrows, avoiding the salt of his tears and the stench of his breath. His arms were sure and strong through his shirtsleeves, proffering protection and certainty. I need only stroke faster, breathe harder, and he would respond as surely as the ivories under my practiced fingertips.

"Mhmm." He smiled, although dewdrop tears still clung to his lashes. Whiskey, with that edge that makes your eyes sting and your throat burn, surrounded him like a halo, a fog of eau de toilette.

I slipped off my pelisse and threw it to the side with my shawl. Freedom. Air.

I pulled one of Branwell's hands to my breast.

His other found my face.

I jerked away, positioning my head so he could only kiss my neck. Move. No, don't press so hard.

Muddled as his mind was, he still used my smiles and winces as a barometer. The promise of me—velvet, dark, deep—sobered him, even if the world still spun around him.

"Oh." A gasp, not from Branwell, not from me, but from somewhere behind us, followed by a lung-rattling cough.

I leapt from Branwell's embrace and from the bed and twisted toward the door.

There was Miss Brontë, blocking the light in the doorway, a slender silhouette against the sky. She seemed taller than she was and held herself as rigid as St. Joan at the stake.

"Miss Sewell told me George Walker had returned and needed me," she said, more to the room than to me or to her brother. Then, with a moan of almost-pain, she added, "Oh, Branwell."

"Anne," he said, but he was slurring again, now that there was another witness to his drunkenness. "Lydia, help me rise."

I didn't. I let him flounder there before us—the chaste sister and the bad wife—as he struggled to his feet to go to her, to make things right.

"Please, Anne," I said, her name sticking in my throat.

The plea shook Miss Brontë from her reverie. She turned, left, fled.

"Lydia—" Branwell called after me as I began to follow her, but he was a broken wreck of a man, and there was nothing here to keep me.

Miss Sewell had raised the stakes and made good her threat, hoping to sap still more from me. She'd used Joey and her brother (still ignorant, surely?) to catch me in her trap. But I had fight in me yet.

I scooped up my discarded clothes and ran from the cottage, after Miss Brontë, my hair streaming in the wind, as fleet as if I had been on horseback, bare-armed like a savage, desperate and true as the bitch tracking the bloodied hare.

I GAVE UP ONCE I'd lost sight of Miss Brontë, which was soon, despite the coughing that usually overwhelmed her at even the slightest of exertions. It was best to stop and fix myself. I'd give credence to her tale if I returned to Thorp Green undressed. Where would she go? To Edmund? The girls?

But when I entered my rooms, she was waiting for me.

She was standing with her back to the door, gazing out across the driveway as I had the day when I first saw her brother. My old gray muslin, fraying at the hem, hung loose around her childlike frame, so that she looked for all the world like my emaciated ghost come back to haunt me with the things that I had done or thought, and those I had not—the things I was not woman or wife or mother enough to feel.

My entrance did not startle her and it was several seconds before she turned to face me, her expression calm, her breathing steady, excepting that little catch in her throat that had always irritated me.

"Mrs. Robinson," she said, clasping her hands in front of her waist, "I have come to tender my resignation."

"Your resig—? No, Miss Brontë—Anne—you mustn't." I took a step toward her, but she recoiled, hitting her calf against the window seat in her haste to get away from me.

I would rather she had slapped me.

"I don't know what you saw, or thought you saw—" I paused but she gave me nothing. "But it isn't as you think. You are young and inexperienced, and know nothing of the world or of men, but you must understand how persuasive your brother can be, how easy it is to be caught up, swept away to the kingdoms and castles he builds in thin air."

No one believes in me as my sisters do, Branwell had told me time and again. This was the line I would take to try to win Miss Brontë over.

"There is nothing you can tell me of my brother, Mrs. Robinson." Miss Brontë's voice was flat, expressionless. "I know him as I know my sisters. Better than I know myself. You must step aside. I can no longer work here."

"Nonsense," I said, dropping my skirts, which I'd been holding since climbing the stairs, and relaxing my hands, seeking to reassure her that I was not afraid. "Your family needs you to work. And you simply do not know—cannot appreciate, I think—Branwell's genius."

No response. She might have been a woman made of stone, silent and stubborn, as impossible as Edmund. I needed to draw a reaction, any reaction, from her.

"Ask Charlotte," I went on. "She has some understanding of what Branwell is and of the great writer he could become. Your brother tells me she has his spirit, a twin flame burning red inside her. That same light he saw smoldering in me."

Miss Brontë raised one eyebrow. How dare she stand in judgment over me? I had a mind and a soul as much as the Miss Brontës. What had any of them ever achieved to hold themselves so high?

I lashed out. "But you don't have it in you. That is why you will always be in your siblings' shadows."

Was that a tear, hovering in her eye? If it was, she willed it not to fall. Miss Brontë held every muscle in her body tense as if steeling herself for a physical blow.

"Strength of passion should not be judged by its outward manifestations, Mrs. Robinson," she said, as if delivering a lesson in the schoolroom or a sermon from a pulpit. "Just as a quiet, steady faith is as precious as martyrdom to Him, who watches over us all. And while it is true my experience of men may be limited, I can tell you that affections are felt no less deeply when they remain unspoken. You think perhaps you love him?"

If this was a question, she gave me no chance to reply.

"To love, Mrs. Robinson, is to treasure your beloved's soul and protect it even above your own. But you! You have corrupted a soul too gentle for this world and unsuited to its harshness."

Gentle? Branwell as I had seen him on that Easter night more than two years ago flashed before me, his eyes roving independently of each other, vomit on his shirt, the discarded bottles rolling across his bedroom floor.

"A gentle soul?" I laughed. "Anne, please! You are being naïve. You are mistaken in what you think you saw. I take some small, patronizing interest in my son's tutor. That is all. Your brother is emotional. A writer. I wouldn't expect you to understand."

Her face folded into a small, sad smile. I couldn't imagine why.

"You can't tell me you know nothing of illicit passion," I pressed on. "I see the way you look at the curate Greenhow when he preaches. I know how wounded you were when he married another."

I couldn't tell if my shot had been true. As I spoke, she didn't move, her expression didn't change. "Good-bye, Mrs. Robinson," she said, walking past me toward the door.

"Wait!" I called.

She did.

"The girls. They will miss you," I said in one final attempt to keep her.

Lydia without a governess was a daunting prospect, for all that Miss Brontë had utterly failed to police her thus far.

"And I will them," she said. Her hand was on the doorknob.

"My husband?" I could barely frame the question.

Would she tell him? Or was she too loyal to Branwell even now? It had come to this, then. To me, acting as Miss Brontë's supplicant. Indignity after indignity, eating me from the inside.

"Pass on my apologies and thanks to Mr. Robinson," she said, as she left the room. "He has been very kind to me."

Mercy comes easily when you believe that condemnation is inescapable, although no doubt Miss Brontë thought herself very virtuous.

I stood for at least a minute, hearing her coughing her way down the landing and staring at the patch of carpet where she had stood. Then I reached out my hand to pull the bell cord.

Seconds later, Ellis quaked before me.

"Did you call, madam?" she asked.

"Tell Mr. Allison to prepare the carriage, Ellis. Miss Brontë is leaving us."

"Very good, ma'am." Her face didn't betray a response. "I'm to tell you, madam," she went on, "that Miss Sewell wishes to have an audience with you."

"You may inform Miss Sewell that I am indisposed."

A nod, a tremble, and a hasty retreat.

"And, Ellis?"

She tripped over herself, twisting back toward me. "Yes'm?"

"Ensure Miss Brontë leaves those old gowns of mine she wears. You are welcome to them."

"Thank you, madam. You are too good, you—" She tried to wring my hand.

"Do not touch me, Ellis." If anyone showed me tenderness now, even her, I would buckle. "Only leave me."

As it was, Miss Brontë did not leave that day, or the next, or the next, although she kept to her room and to the schoolroom, out of my sight. She was to depart with Branwell, as planned previously, for their usual summer trip. But this time, after five years of service at Thorp Green, she would not return from Haworth. She would instead quit our lives forever.

I waited until the girls' wailing good-byes were done and the carriage door had slammed before peeking around the curtain, resting my knee on the dressing room window seat and trying to stay out of view. I couldn't see Miss Brontë, or Branwell for that matter, only Flossy's furry face pressed against the carriage window, as if the little mutt was doing her best to make Mary's misery complete.

The three girls were holding on to each other. For all the world, you would have thought they were penniless orphans, huddling against the cold. Even Ned looked dejected, staring at an unmoving whirligig between his feet as he sat on the steps of the Hall.

William Allison said something in a jovial tone, but none of the children laughed in response. A crack of his whip, a loud "That's a boy, Pat," invoking his favored moniker for Patroclus, and the Brontës were on their way, the carriage lurching down the driveway.

Relief flooded through me, stemmed only by the thought that in one short week, Branwell would return. And days after that, we'd all be in Scarborough where the holiday spirit and our close quarters would make enforcing distance even harder.

I'd avoided Branwell for the last few days as Anne had me, without incident so far, but he wouldn't give up that easily. He wouldn't have the sense of an older man to know when love—or something like it—had run its course, and was best treasured only as a memory for those nights when the moonlight makes romantics, and loneliness fools, of us.

"Lydia." The door opened as Edmund said my name. He stepped inside and closed it.

"Ed—"

"No." He raised his hand and walked toward me. "Do not speak." There was something new in his eyes. Was it anger or the passion I could scarcely remember?

"It has been a taxing week," he said. "First, our daughters' governess quits her post with little by way of warning or explanation. And today I have the pleasure of receiving a visit from another disgruntled servant, the housekeeper, Miss Sewell." He took another stride.

Miss Sewell, the shadow at my steps and the constant rap-a-tap-tap at my door. In the last few days, she'd become more insistent, even once forcing herself into my presence and naming a lump sum in addition to her previous requests. I'd been unable to parry her thrusts, had placated her with weak promises that mustn't have been enough.

"That woman—" I started now.

"No," said Edmund.

"But—"

He grabbed me by the throat and pushed me against the wall.

The power of his body knocked the breath out of me, as did the control he was exerting over me more than the strength of his grip, which was loose (he was, after all, still unwell). In it was the promise that he could squeeze with ease were he to want to, were I deserving of his hatred, and were he the bully I had painted him to Branwell.

I pressed the pads of my fingers against the embossed wallpaper in a halfhearted attempt to free myself.

"Miss Sewell came to my study," he continued, softening his grip but not moving away. "It appears our housekeeper is suffering under some"—here he paused—"misconceptions regarding your relationship with the tutor, Mr. Brontë."

He released my neck, and I gave an exaggerated gasp. Would it mark? If it did, I would wear the bruise like a medallion, proof that somewhere, deep down, my husband still cared.

"I have, of course, corrected her," Edmund said, staring at the intricate pattern in the Indian rug rather than at me. "And I gave her some money to thank her for her concern. But it is necessary—no, crucial—that you never give our staff cause for speculation again."

"Then send Mr. Brontë away!" I cried, the opportunity opening like a gate before me. I lurched for Edmund's hand but caught only his wrist. Maybe he would overpower me, strike me, force himself on me. Maybe, at last, I would goad him into acting like a man. "We could be rid of both of them—the Brontës," I said. "We need only send the tutor's things after them to Haworth."

In the moments since they'd left, I'd grown more certain: I had to make an end of things with Branwell. Affairs had careened too far out of my control.

"And what would be said of us then? Of you?" Edmund drew back, his passion evaporating, and shook me off like a fly. "No, Lydia, you must learn self-control and to curb your natural—" He could not complete the sentence. "Dr. Crosby could prescribe you something."

I laughed and turned to press my palms into the wall, as if I were in labor and doubling over with the pain of it.

"Edmund." I was not sure what to say, but hoped that by speaking his name I could convey the warmth that still spread through me at the thought of our early years, when we'd slept in each other's arms every night in a space only wide enough for one, the closeness that comes when you know the contours of another's mind and body as intimately as you know your own, the pattern of the hours, days, decades we'd spent together since.

"Enough!" he cried. "I am your husband, Lydia, and I command you to act in accordance with your station." The door slammed hard behind him.

My dear Mrs. Robinson,

I have given some thought these last days to the conundrum you confided in me during our last consultation. I mean, of course, how to dispose of Mr. Brontë.

I must, in a professional capacity, beg for a report on your nerves before I go any further. Are you still confined to bed? Do send me word by the illiterate boy who bears this letter from Great Ouseburn. For appearances' sake, yes, but also due to my very real concern for you.

I have thought, as I said, on the difficulty before you, and a solution may, at a most opportune time, have presented itself.

You will have heard, I know, that a date is set at last for the opening of the new railway line, between York and Scarborough. On the 7th of next month, that is to say in ten days, when you and your family have already arrived in Scarborough, a celebration is to be held in York in honor of the momentous occasion.

The committee has planned a great breakfast, which will be attended by many gentlemen connected to the railway. They'll talk mechanics and dynamite, quaff champagne, and toast to the success of their investments, before waving off the train on her maiden voyage into previously uncharted waters.

A veritable bore, but it appears I must go and so, I say, should Mr. Brontë.

What could be more natural? Most of us from the Lodge will be there. What's more, Branwell is a former railway man and is sure to see some old acquaintances. That engineer friend of his, Gooch, for one, is sure to attend.

And you? Why not indulge your tutor's hobbyist interest in locomotives and bid him stay at Thorp Green Hall once he returns to you? With no governess for the girls, give Master Ned a holiday from his studies likewise and enjoy Scarborough with a smaller party than in previous years.

I will watch Brontë and ensure he doesn't overdo it at the breakfast. It wouldn't do for him to give in to his natural exuberance, which he's given rein to a little too liberally in our recent meetings. And I will attempt to impress upon him, subtly at first, that if he cares for you, he must resign before you return from Scarborough and put an end to all close communication between you.

I have never been of the belief that absence makes the heart grow fonder. A separation of a month is just what the boy needs to see reason. I will school him to make the right choice.

Send me word of how you like my plan.

I remain your humble servant,
Dr. John Crosby

27th June 1845
Thorp Green Hall

Dear John,

I am as well as can be expected and better for receiving your
letter. It is the very thing. Thank you from the bottom of my
heart for your friendship and assistance. It is a kindness to us
both. Yes, to Mr. Brontë too. For he needs constant supervision
to keep him from the drink. It is best that he go home to
Haworth where his father and sisters may care for him.

Yours very truly, with gratitude,
Lydia

CHAPTER THIRTEEN

"YOU HAVE TO COME with me, ma'am. Now." Panic was written across Marshall's wan face.

"What is it? It is not—? Is *he here*?"

She nodded, and I gripped her arm tight.

"Lydia, must you whisper with the servants?" my mother-in-law called across the front room of our Scarborough lodgings. She was lying on the chaise with her eyes, mercifully, closed, fatigued from "too much sunlight."

"I'm not whispering. Maybe you're going deaf?" I called out as loudly as I could without shouting.

I steered Marshall through the door, down the hallway, and into the garden.

"Well?" I rounded on her.

"You dismissed me for an hour or so, ma'am, and so I went with the others to see the new train come in from York."

"The others?" I squeezed tighter.

"Just some of the Scarborough servants, ma'am. Nobody as knows Mr. Brontë."

"Go on, go on." A lump was rising in my throat as it had when I was a girl and one of my brothers had run to Father, saying I'd struck him. And I had. But I'd had right on my side, and if anyone else had had such a provoking brother, they would have done the same, and even if they wouldn't have, well, that was my mother and father's fault too, wasn't it? For where was I to learn except from them?

Marshall looked at her arm, and I released her.

She spoke on. "It was such a to-do. Hundreds of folks had gathered, with the children and women waving flags and handkerchiefs, and street sellers racing their model engines. I never seen nothing like it. Then the train was here with a confusion of noise and smoke. A lady fainted away at the sound of the whistle. It rounded the corner so fast I must say it took my breath away. Gentlemen spilled out of all the carriages, brandishing their top hats, their faces red from the thrill of it, and the wine I daresay."

"Never mind all that, Marshall. Mr. Brontë was there?"

So much for John Crosby's promises: *I will watch Brontë and ensure he doesn't overdo it.* It was always the same when men got together, away from the critical eyes of their womenfolk.

"I was about to turn back when I saw him emerge," said Marshall. "He was one of the last. I couldn't believe my two eyes, but it was him, all right. On the platform and swaying so much I feared he would fall onto the tracks. I sent the others away, said he was a cousin of mine, for I was afraid what he might say of you. When I reached him, he was talking of the railway, how they'd ill treated him once and had now done so again."

"But did he come with you without protest?"

"Oh, yes, ma'am. He recognized me all right, though he said once or twice you might have greeted him yourself. How he thought you knew he'd be on the train, I don't know. Kept talking about souls, he did. Connections, messages that can be sent through the air. At first, I thought he was talking of the telegraph, but I reckon it was some sort of magic. Love that defies the laws of nature and even God, madam. That's what he said. There was no reasoning with him, so I put my efforts into helping him walk straight. He's safe now. And I fetched him some water."

The wind stirred, buffeting the grass and forcing the sunflowers into graceful and sweeping bows.

"Oh, Ann Marshall," I said, overflowing with a sudden rush of tenderness toward her. "You are the best servant that a lady could ask for."

Her cratered face flushed crimson in patches, but her expression registered only alarm. Servants hate nothing more than when their masters act out of character. "But whatever's to be done with Mr. Brontë, madam?" she asked. "Will you see him?"

My heart was tied to a spiraling anchor. "I suppose I must," I said.

She led the way past the buildings that made up the holidaymakers' homes, around the stable where I'd found Lydia with the acting boy—was that only a year ago?—and along a path that snaked down the side of the Cliff itself, a path I'd chided Ned for using once. It was rocky and steep with no railing. One misstep and you'd tumble like an acrobat to the crowded beach below.

"Where on earth are we going?" I called after Marshall, struggling to keep my footing for the third or fourth time. My ankles were weak. On terrain like this, it was tricky to keep to my pattern. Left, right; left, right. I didn't like to stop on an uneven number.

"We servants call it 'the boathouse,' madam." She turned to face me so her voice wouldn't fly from us on the wind. Strands of her hair had come loose from her exertions in the last hour. They streamed around her like a mousy gray mane.

"A boathouse? Up here?"

I didn't think she could hear me, but she understood the sentiment. "It's more of a shed, ma'am. You'll see."

Clinging to the promontory was a shack, scarcely six feet high and only a little broader, with an ill-fitting door and holes in the roof. No one would think to lug a boat up here unless it was in pieces.

Marshall fought with the door to hold it open for me. Mr. Brontë didn't come to her aid. There was just a gaping void where light and warmth would have welcomed me had this been a home. Had the tutor been capable of giving one to me.

"Go!" I cried to Marshall, when we were at last opposite each other, the door threatening to whack into me were she to lose her grip. "Leave me!"

"But—" At least I thought she called "but," but the wind was even louder now and pelting sand at us, as if for ignoring its angry roar.

"Go!" I screamed again.

This time she obeyed.

I'd just fallen inside when the door closed behind me, shaking the building to its seams.

Darkness and dust, the distinctive tang of men's urine and the taste of tobacco.

"Branwell?" I ventured, with the same softness I'd adopted for Ned after nightmares. "Branwell, it is me. Don't be frightened."

"There, there, she's come for me. I told you!" I made out Branwell, delirious, crouched in a corner, talking to the walls of the dingy hut. He looked bad, even worse than that day long ago in the Monk's House. His face was pale, his shirt was untucked, and he seemed to have misplaced his coat.

"Branwell." I dropped to my knees beside him, entangling my skirts in the cobwebs. What would Edmund's mother say were she to see me now? "Branwell," I said again. "Why are you here?"

"Why am I—?" he repeated, but the sentence trailed off. His pupils were so wide that his eyes had lost their blue. Had he only been drinking or had he tasted something stronger? "Why, to save you, Lydia. Crosby—"

"What of Dr. Crosby?"

"He delivered the death blow. Is it true, Lydia?" He grabbed my arms and shook me. "Am I to be banished forever from your sight?"

"Things cannot go on as they are," I said, slow and measured, wishing I'd bidden Marshall stay so that I had a protector here beside me. "You need to go home. To your father. To Emily and Anne. And to Charlotte."

"But, Lydia, I love you."

Branwell had told me that a thousand times, but this one hit me, strong and true as an arrow with a poisoned tip. I nearly called out in surprise at how it conjured Edmund before me, young and shy at confessing the mundane secret of his heart to mine for the first time. We'd been in the library of Yoxall Lodge, while our elders, who'd seen it all before, waited a few rooms away, hushed and mock-reverent as you are with children, counting the interminable days and hours until Christmas.

But Branwell was young, behind. He did not know. He felt each cut as if it were the first. I had been subject to vivisection upon vivisection, in public and in private, had had men peer at my most private parts, examine my soul with judging eyes, prescribe me drugs and rest and prayer to fix me.

"I am sorry," I said, kissing his crown. My tenderness surprised me. By God, I missed Georgiana, the smell of her, the soft wisps of her newly curling hair.

I felt hope stir in Branwell at this act of compassion on my part, but for me, the end was definite. There was no way back now that he was not just a boy but an infant to me, bare of armor, yesterday's fool.

A cough.

The far wall moved.

And—

No, it wasn't a wall at all. The gardener, Bob Pottage, appeared through the gloom. He'd been here the whole time. He'd seen everything. His eyes were wide, transfixed at the scene before him, and he was deathly white.

"Bob—Mr. Pottage—" I started.

It was not one of the Sewells, at least, or William Allison, who'd always thought so well of me. Just soulless, stupid Bob Pottage, who spent his days thinking about cabbages and rosebushes, who understood that steady, predictable propagation, not the intricate irregularities of the human heart.

"I didn't believe it, madam," Pottage stuttered. "Though Mr. Sewell and his sister said—I didn't believe it, e'en when Mr. Brontë spoke of you so." He pointed an accusing finger at Branwell. "I just came in here for a smoke. The other missus, the master's mother, hates the smell of it about the garden and stables. But I found him layin' here. The way he spoke of you! I'd have gi'en him a good braying had he been himself and not in the drink."

Clumsy, stammering man. And now he held my heart like a quavering nestling in his rough, unready hand.

"Bob!" I crawled forward and grabbed him by the ankle. Lydia had done that to me at two or three years old when she'd screeched so loud I thought the house would fall around us. "Keep our secret, my secret. I'll do anything."

"I'm an honest family man, madam. I've got six bairns." Pottage jerked his foot away from me, disgusted.

I hadn't meant what he thought. But give yourself to one man, and they'll all think you'd just as easily give yourself to them, or, perhaps, that you have nothing else to offer.

"You have to help me." My tears fell unheeded to the damp and uneven stone. "At the very least, take him away." I gestured toward Branwell, who was hiccupping beside me.

"*That*, ma'am, I can do," Pottage said. He grasped Branwell's collar between his calloused workman's hands and hauled him toward the door.

FOR NINE DAYS I waited, breathless, for the death knell. The railway between Scarborough and York had opened a dangerous portal between my world and Branwell's, a gaping wound that cut through fields and hills, obliterating paths trodden by peasants for centuries, revealing England's murky insides, perhaps even disrupting time itself.

Still Branwell's expected letter of resignation did not come. Only several notes of apology from Dr. Crosby, which I ignored. I was petrified, unable to dismiss Branwell myself, for Ned's education was Edmund's domain, or to beg my husband to do so, given his anger the day the Brontës had left for Haworth.

There was fear in Marshall's eyes when I asked for the post five times a day. I slept late in the morning but could not still my mind at night. At dusk, when the other ladies had all retreated to their bathhouses, I paddled and dreamed of wading out farther and farther. I longed for the sea to embrace me like a watery quilt, as if my body wouldn't fight and swim and rage against the surf's dominion, unwilling, even now, to submit.

It was just as well dying was not easy. If it were, women and men would choose it oh so often, in each blinding rush of fresh pain. Instead we soldier through, thralls to that irrational master who bids us "live," clinging to the hope of waking to a brighter dawn.

Once a day, Bob Pottage made some small pretense to talk to me. And his question when he found me was always the same: "Has Mr. Brontë written to the master yet, madam?" he'd ask. "He must resign. This can't go on so."

Yet he was wrong. The world carried on regardless.

We attended parties so numerous that even Lydia bored of them, preferring, oddly, solitary walks. And then there were the picnics and card games and concerts and Ned reciting poetry, eager to impress Mr. Brontë on our return to Thorp Green.

"Could we stay in Scarborough a little longer?" I asked Edmund on a night when he suffered me to sit at the base of his bed and massage his ugly, mannish feet. "What is it that calls us home?"

"What has come into you, Lydia?" He laughed. "Are you actually asking to spend *more* time with my mother? You must be unwell. But no, you have never looked better."

An exaggeration, perhaps, but this was not entirely untrue. It was as if I were operating under some species of mania, which brought blood to my face and energy to my once listless limbs. I outdanced our boisterous Bessy at a gathering in the Scarborough assembly rooms and flirted as Edmund liked me to, with a lightness of touch that could cause no misinterpretation. I was the calculated, social creature whom he had married, alive enough for the both of us, an antidote to his constant fatigue and dull conversation.

"We should go home," Edmund said. "Nathaniel Milner's widow writes, at last, about the necessity of discussing a union between her son Will and our Bessy. It is high time one of our girls was married."

Strange. I felt for Lydia when he said that. Bessy's union would be hard for her. A girl's vanity is a fragile thing, her worth determined solely by a market run by men. That was why, when my cousin Catherine had married Edward Scott, who would be a baronet, I'd been inconsolable for days.

Nine days and still no letter from Branwell. When I woke that morning I asked at once—although the sun was so high it might already have been noon.

"No letter, ma'am," Marshall said, tightening my corset, her voice low and serious. "But Mr. Robinson is asking for you."

This was it, then. Bob Pottage had broken, had told him.

Did Anne Boleyn, kneeling for her execution, feel as I did, walking the hallway to Edmund's room? I pictured her, chin raised and snowy throat unfettered by her jewels, which were too precious to fall alongside the droplets of her ruby red blood.

But no, Edmund wouldn't strike me. He wouldn't force me against the wall. I'd committed the ultimate sin by bringing disgrace upon us, and so lost forever the honor of his touch.

What I didn't guess was that *she* would be there. Although Edmund had turned to her at the beginning, when our arguments were rare, I wouldn't have thought it possible. Yet when I entered Edmund's room, his mother had been restored to her "rightful place" at his side. She was stroking his hair, with the authority of one who had loved him longer, had thrilled over his every breath and heartbeat.

"Lydia, the tutor Brontë is dismissed," she said, once I'd closed the door. "Edmund just dispatched the letter." Her fingers sharpened into points, clawing at his scalp. Edmund's eyes rolled back in pleasure.

"It is just as well that your mother isn't here to see your shame," she added. "And that your father is too senile to know it."

How Mother had hated her. She'd cautioned me the day Edmund proposed about the consequences of marrying "that woman's" son. She would have flown at her throat for these insults.

But I no longer had a mother. Nobody loved me now.

I was mute, pleading wordlessly with Edmund, who looked through me as if I were a stranger.

"I always knew she would muddy our Metcalfe blood." A thickness entered Mrs. Robinson's voice as she turned and addressed her son. Could it be that she would cry? "But all is not lost. My grandchildren still have half of you in them." She nodded hard, as if trying to convince herself. "Your servants sneer at you, but at least your neighbors—our neighbors—back home know nothing. And you, Lydia. You can still behave with honor."

"Edmund?" I ventured, ignoring her. "Say something."

His mother gave his shoulder a squeeze and walked toward me. "Take to your bed, Mrs. Robinson," she said, her lip twitching at the mockery I had made of our name. "You are ill." Her withered face was only inches from mine.

"Ill?" I echoed.

"So ill, so broken, you cannot have your children near you."

"Is that how it's to be?" I asked, searching behind her, desperate for it to be Edmund's voice that sounded the sentence and banished me to the shadows.

"That is how it's to be," she said. She brought the back of her bejeweled hand across my face in a decisive, stinging slap, branding me with the fortune I had sold myself for.

18th July 1845
The Cliff, Scarborough

My dear Dr. Crosby,

My husband dismissed Mr. Brontë two days ago.

Your apologies are unnecessary, but should you wish to help me, perhaps you might advance him some cash (I will repay you) and ensure that he in truth leaves for Haworth? He must not be at Thorp Green Hall on our return.

I am terrified too about what he might say to the other Freemasons at the Lodge. See to it that any rumors there are quashed.

Once we are home, Edmund will summon you to attend on me in a professional capacity. I have had a shock and illness keeps me to my rooms. My nerves, you know, are capricious.

I remain, dear sir, your most unhappy friend,
Yours very truly,
Lydia Robinson

Lydia,

Divided in the flesh, my love, but still one, inseverable soul,
made of whatever it is that souls are made of.

Write to me! Command me! I am yours.

I am in Haworth, stealing moments to write to you when
Charlotte is gone from my side. But, in my imagination, I
am standing at the base of the tower in which they have
encased you, hovering by your window when the flame is long-
extinguished, dreaming of the day when you are free of that
man, or, rather, eunuch, that long-promised day when we are
one.

I send this by Crosby, our Cupid, who tells me to stay away
for now for love of you,

Branwell

My dearest, sweetest Lydia,

Why don't you answer me? I write again by our friend, Dr.
Crosby, true friend to me, or, indeed, to us, in this our darkest
hour of need.

I am in self-imposed exile in Liverpool, distant from my
sisters' love as well as yours, and no longer smarting under the
censure of Charlotte's judgmental gaze.

Fresh cruelty to find that my favorite sister is a hypocrite!
For, though she condemns me for my adoration of you, I have
discovered that she also yearns for a forbidden love. A married
man. She sends that Belgian schoolmaster of hers countless letters,
although days, weeks, months go by without reply. She roams
the moors in the day and, at night, paces through the graveyard
that surrounds our home, a bitter reminder of the myriad losses
we have suffered. Who is she to stand in judgment? Who are my
father, Anne, any of them to say that I must not drink?

My rooms in the city are bare and my rations meager. The
money you gave me, alas, did not last long here—but I care
not for these comforts. I seek the spiritual succor, talisman
against the crushing loneliness of the world, which only you
can bestow upon me.

And what of you, my love? Crosby says you keep to your
rooms, but that there is no need for alarm. Doctor though he
is, I say he cannot watch you with a lover's care. Were I to
think you in true danger, I would rush to your side. I would
turn back to God and pray on my knees, for all you and
Crosby have cautioned me to keep away.

Write to me. Instruct me. I am your slave, your prince, and your bard. I enclose a poem I wrote this week, speaking of my agonies. I will send it to Mr. Bellerby along with the others so that they might trumpet our love to the world! They are the best work I have completed in years, though born of my sorrows.

Write, my beautiful and afflicted one,
Your Northangerland forever,
Branwell Brontë

"Cannot my soul depart
Where will it fly?"
Asks my tormented heart,
Willing to die.
When will this restlessness,
Tossing in sleeplessness—
Stranger to happiness—
Slumbering lie?

Cannot I chase away
Life in my tomb,
Rather than pass away
Lifetime in gloom,
With sorrows employing
Their arts in destroying
The powers of enjoying
The comforts of home?

Home, it is not with me
Bright as of yore
Joys are forgot with me
Taught to deplore.
My home has ta'en its rest
In an afflicted breast
That I have often pressed
But—may no more.

P.S. If you can send me more money, dearest, do

4th August 1845
Thorp Green Hall

My dear Mr. Bellerby,

It has come to my attention that your esteemed publication, the Yorkshire Gazette, has been publishing poems signed "Northangerland," penned by a tutor previously under my husband's employ.

Without shocking you with the unsavory details, I must let you know that all ties have been severed with this person, whose conduct was not only unsatisfactory for a gentleman in his position, but outrageous by all standards of moral decency.

I hope we—by which I mean not only my husband but all the great families in the vicinity of the Ouseburns, from the Milners of Nun Monkton to the Thompsons of Kirby Hall—can rely on you to do likewise and to refrain from publishing any libels that reach you from his hand.

Looking forward to many more years of reading your publications and patronizing your circulating library,

I remain, dear sir, yours very truly,
Lydia Robinson

CHAPTER FOURTEEN

OUR JOURNEY HOME FROM Scarborough was as painful as it was bizarre. The children were scared, sensing something had shifted. Edmund and his mother pretended all was as before. And I, weak and pale, closed my eyes to avoid them all, resting on Marshall's bony shoulder for support.

And then, my rooms. Solitude. I stayed in there as summer turned to autumn.

The days were long, punctuated only by Dr. Crosby's visits and the letters they brought, peepholes into Branwell Brontë's mind, as deranged as before, or, perhaps, even more obsessive now that Mr. Bellerby had reneged on his word.

"The world is conspiring against us, Lydia," he would write. "But, do not fear, it was ever thus for destined lovers. It is human nature to be jealous of the absolute happiness we find in each other."

I didn't answer him. But I dreamed often of Charlotte, my twin in pain, my distorted mirror image. Despite the differences in age and looks and station, Branwell had said we were alike. And now she suffered from an unrequited love, just as I suffered from an unrequited longing for something more.

My head lolled, my limbs ached with stiffness. The light that fought its way through the crack between my curtains shone less brilliantly than it had just days ago, abandoning me to the dark.

And yet even though Marshall said his mother had left the house, still Edmund did not come. He'd sent Ned away to be tutored by his uncle John Eade, in Aycliffe, and cared for by that gentleman's new, young wife. And I would not have the girls visit me on the rare occasions that they asked, so I saw only Marshall.

With her, I was testy, spiteful even, complaining at the bitterness of the soup I had no appetite to eat and fussing over the arrangement of my pillows. At times I felt a flash of guilt at the toll it took on her; she was growing even thinner than before.

"Mrs. Robinson?" she called to me one morning from near the door. It might even have been afternoon. Her voice was soft but with a note of panic in it, a fear that went beyond her usual nervousness at waking me.

"If you're addressing me, come closer, Marshall," I said, angry to be thought asleep, although I'd bobbed about on the sea of semiconsciousness for some hours.

She did so.

"Well, what is it?" I asked, hauling myself up. The sheet was damp and uneven below me, soaked with sweat and sprinkled with crumbs from yesterday's meals.

"It is Miss Robinson, madam. Miss Lydia. She is missing." She coughed.

"Missing?" I repeated, thinking for a second that I had misheard due to her hoarseness. I rubbed the hardened drool from around my mouth and licked my cracked lips. "I am sure you will find her soon. She is always going about her own affairs without asking permission. She spent most of this summer ranging around Scarborough like an unpenned chicken."

"No, madam, she—" Marshall came even closer. "Miss Lydia said she was feeling unwell last night and so took to her bed early. Now her room is empty. Nobody has seen her since. And just now, Miss Bessy found a letter from her."

"A letter? For whom?" My eyes adjusted.

Marshall was holding a silver tray toward me. "Why, for *you*, madam."

There was the letter, small, sealed, and addressed to "Mrs. Robinson." I took it from her and gestured for Marshall to open the curtains. She twitched them apart just wide enough for a faint beam of sunlight to stream across the bed.

Mama,

Do not blame me. You know I was always willful and, no doubt, always shall be. I wanted to marry Henry as much as he did me and so here I am, on my way to Gretna Green and soon no longer "Lydia Robinson" at all, but "Lydia Roxby" henceforth and forever.

Other girls might find the change strange, but not I. My name has never seemed my own. You are welcome to it.

I am sorry that you hadn't the chance to see me decked out looking fine. I promise I look very pretty, although you won't be with me to pin the orange blossom in my hair or wonder at how your oldest child has grown a woman and so no longer needs you.

Please see that Papa isn't angry. I couldn't bear that.

To run away was the only choice I had open to me. The more I thought of it, the more I realized I wouldn't choose to live as you have and marry a man I hardly knew. Henry loves me and always shall. It won't matter if we're poor, although why should we be? If Papa will be kind, we shall want for nothing. And besides, Henry is so clever at his acting, he is sure to be the next Macready!

Does it make you blush to think that the coming night will
be my wedding night? Other girls quake at the thought, even
with their mothers by their sides, but not I. I have waited but I
am ready. You taught me better than you knew.

Ever loving, though no longer yours,
Lydia

"Where is she?" Marshall asked with unaccustomed directness.
She'd returned to stand by the side of the bed and was still holding the
tray, calm and dutiful, although a slight tremor, throwing glances of
light from the silver, betrayed her emotion.

"She is—" I let the letter fall to my lap. "She has gone."

"Gone?" Marshall moved her hand as if she would have taken the
letter from me, but she remembered herself and instead set the tray on
top of the washstand. "Should I tell Mr. Robinson?"

"No," I said. In spite of everything, he should still hear this from me.

When she was a child, Lydia would increase the pitch of her screech
semitone by semitone until it provoked a scream from me, or kick me
harder and harder until I had to leave the room so I wouldn't strike her.
Yet she'd always smiled like a cherub at the footsteps of her father,
basked in the warmth of his admiring love, and cast me into the shadows. Tonight, would she laugh over her wedding dinner, with that handsome actor beside her, her teeth flashing bright as the crystal decanters,
at the thought of me lying dejected in the dark?

"Dress me," I said.

"Oh, madam, it is so good to see—" Marshall broke off again,
coughing.

"Ann Marshall!" I threw the blankets from the bed for the first time
in weeks and pulled the cap from my limp and lifeless hair.

I was not ill. Or old. Or dying. I would not have her pity me.

"Dress me." I swung my legs out of bed and brought my feet to the floor. "And ask Miss Robinson and Miss Mary to wait for me in the schoolroom while I speak with their father in his study."

"Miss Robinson?" she repeated, her forehead creasing in confusion.

"Miss Bessy is Miss Robinson now," I said.

I KNOCKED ON THE study door. My mother's brooch was pinned at my breast. I was wearing that shade of green that made men judge my eyes handsome.

Edmund called out in answer.

I rested my hand on the knob for only a fraction of a second longer than I should have before walking in.

Months of fearing to face him and yet Edmund's expression was, as ever, neutral, excepting one raised, inquiring eyebrow. He would have looked at me the same way had I tumbled in in my stained nightgown, fallen on my knees, and howled for forgiveness.

"Yes?" he said, when I did not speak.

I scanned his study, as if by just looking around the room I could gauge his mood during my seclusion. Messy, as usual, but nothing out of the ordinary.

News has a terrible power when you hold on to it. My secret was itching to be spoken.

"Your daughter has eloped with an actor," I said as he inhaled to question me again.

The eyebrow fell. He blinked.

"Which daughter?" he asked, dropping his eyes and pulling a copy of the *Times* toward him.

"Which daughter?" I cried. For over twenty years I had been this man's wife, and still, each time I tried to predict his responses, my husband found fresh ways to infuriate me. "Why, the one who has been a flirt since her days in the cradle. The one you would not reprimand but indulged in every whim, every fickle fancy."

"Lydia." I wasn't sure if he was answering his own question or commanding my silence. Emotions scared him, his own most of all.

"It is not my fault!" I called out, losing the ability to moderate my responses despite all the promises I had made myself. "Do not think this due to me alone. She is ours. She was ours. Oh, how we loved the very dream of her."

It was only a few months after our wedding. He had been sitting there at his desk, just so, but back then, I had treasured every hair of him, wanted to kiss every pore. I'd perched on the edge of the desk and whispered it to him, once I was sure but before I'd summoned our doctor (not Dr. Crosby then). Edmund had pushed away his pen, cast aside his papers, rested his head against me, and promised me I would make the most wonderful mother. I'd been scared he was wrong but had held him there below my heart, caring more for him than for her who was growing inside me.

"Lydia, this is a difficult blow," Edmund said, running his hand through his hair, which was grayer than when I'd combed my fingers through it back then and thinner than it had been even a few months ago in Scarborough. "And you must steel yourself for another."

Could he, would he, divorce me? No.

But perhaps he would send me away.

Or was my father released from his pain at last, or had something happened to Ned? Of course, those Eades would be careless. He was not their son, their treasure. I shouldn't have let him, Lydia, Georgie, any of them, out of my sight.

"I am dying," Edmund said, his voice unwavering.

"What?" I caught onto the back of a nearby easy chair.

I wanted to fly to him as I had every time he'd returned home in those early months, when I devoured tales of his day like the latest novel, knew his opinions on every issue, however dry, and absorbed them as my own. But now, when I took a step toward him, he raised his hand, bidding me stay back.

"Dr. Crosby didn't tell—" I began, fastening on to anger as the only response that made sense to me.

"Dr. Crosby doesn't know. I've been consulting with Dr. Simpson and Dr. Ryott."

"And they—?"

"They are quite sure. 'Riddled' was the word they used. My innards, my gut." He pulled some paperwork to him. "There is nothing to be done about Lydia now, but you must care for Ned, Bessy, and Mary in my . . . absence. See that both girls marry well and that Ned goes to St. John's. Look after the property until his majority. Young Milner is a fine match for our Bessy. You judged wisely there."

Edmund did look frailer. I could see the hollows where his smile had once been, as bewitching as our Lydia's in those now rare moments when his mood took a turn away from the serious.

"How long?" I whispered.

The memory of our youth and love hadn't been enough for me. I had blighted all that we'd had with my desire for more. I was just like our Lydia, sustained by praise, starved if a day went by without attention and affection.

"A few months," he tried to tell me, but his body was wracked by a wrenching cough halfway through, giving me enough time to rush over and crouch beside him, touching his chair with the tenderness I wished I could have shown him.

"Will you let me nurse you?" I asked, once the spasm had subsided. We both knew I meant, "Will you let me love you?"

Edmund stood and pulled the bell cord. "I will need your assistance in making all ready, Lydia. I will teach you what you must do with the house, the farms, and with Ned."

I would not be a nurse, then, but a secretary, a bookkeeper, anything that would keep me by his elbow until the end.

"That way, all will be in order should you choose to remarry."

"No!" I interjected.

Never, never. He still thought I would install Branwell, a mere boy, in the house where we had lived, for better and, oh yes, for worse, as man and wife? Where we had loved, had hurt, had seen our dear Georgiana die?

"I will not—" I grabbed his cold and unresponsive hand. "Edmund, I never wished to marry him."

"Very well," he said, as if we had been discussing the removal of the furniture. "No matter. As I told you, my will makes provisions for you, regardless of the future on which you decide."

He was too good. Better than I deserved.

"Edmund—" I started, but there was a tap on the door.

"Come in," he called.

Our interview was over.

THE BRIDAL PAIR WAS to go to Edmund first, for a consultation. He and I had agreed. Would Lydia notice the mortal shadow that hung over her father and the house? Bessy and Mary had, I was sure of it, although for the last month, we'd taken care to close all doors and speak in whispers.

The crunch of the gravel and thump of the carriage door. Lydia's laugh floated to me, but I didn't go to the window. Was it my imagination, or was there a forced note in there? Her laughter was the flirt's, the liar's, the gambler's show of carefree gaiety.

"Very good, William," she said.

The front door was open, or I wouldn't have heard her. The chill dusk air flooded under the library door. Ellis was letting a draft in.

"Thank you kindly," said William Allison. "But you mustn't, miss. I mean 'madam.'"

Foolish girl. She was trying to force money on my servants when she had hardly a penny to her name. Lydia should be grateful I'd sent the carriage to pick her and her actor husband up from the station in York at all, and that William Allison had been happy to go.

I'd been thankful when his face hadn't registered surprise at the request. "Collect Mr. and Mrs. Roxby from the new station? Very good, ma'am," he'd said, giving me a small, encouraging smile.

The voices crescendoed but then faded as Lydia and her husband took the stairs to Edmund's study. I stared at the pages of my book as if into a crystal ball, picturing how the scene would play out between them. At times in my vision, Lydia was contrite. At others, she was defiant. She dropped to her knees, lamenting her father's poor health, or she gazed, distracted, at her own reflection in the mirror, not noticing the change. She hid behind her husband's protective arm, or she shrank from him like a dog that understands only a kick.

When the grandfather clock in the hallway chimed the quarter hour, I rose and ascended to the schoolroom, where our girls—our two *other* girls—spent their idle days together now, without studying and with only Marshall as their lax custodian.

Today, though, they were quiet, reverent, almost scared, as children are when Death is in the house.

"Come," I said. "Your sister has arrived."

Mary took my arm and Bessy followed behind. Their stiff new dresses rustled.

"Mama!" Never one for awkwardness or reserve, Lydia fluttered over to me as soon as we entered the dining room, planting a kiss on my cheek and moving on to her sisters before I'd had time to react. She was dressed in her favorite shade of powder blue, and although I scanned her belly for those symptoms of being a young wife, she was still slight as ever, maybe even smaller.

"Have you missed me terribly?" she asked nobody in particular. "Oh, don't pout so, Bessy. I know you have! Henry, Henry, aren't they all just as I said they were?"

The acting boy—Henry Roxby—bowed in my direction with a sheepish smile and tried to say something, but Lydia was already rattling on. "They're not a bit like me, are they? Well, *some* say Mary's hair and mine are a similar shade, but hers isn't so brilliant and simply refuses to hold a curl. Why, Bessy, I swear you've grown even taller! Tell me, how does Ned get on with those dreadful Eades? And what is the news in Little Ouseburn? I heard that Harry Thompson's wife has given him his son at last!"

"Shall we?" said Edmund, who was standing at the head of the table, holding on to his chair.

"Oh, I will sit at your right hand, Papa, as a married lady now! Move down, Bessy." Lydia was everywhere, arranging us all. "Henry, you may take Mama."

I had anticipated silence, but there wasn't a moment to think between Lydia's descriptions of the theater in Manchester, the city where they'd apparently rented a set of rooms ("magical"), Scotland ("Fancy it, just like England!"), and married life ("Really, Bessy, you must marry Will Milner now the oldest is wed. Surely he has grieved the death of his father long enough by now"). An absence of taste, a total lack of refinement.

Mary's eyes grew wider and wider. Bessy looked as if she might slap her older sister. And when I glanced toward Edmund for help, all I found written across his face was pain. The very effort of raising his fork to his mouth overwhelmed him. At intervals, he clutched his side and grimaced. And our firstborn didn't bat one well-combed eyelash, but gossiped on about musicians, players, and ne'er-do-wells.

"Lydia," I said, interrupting her at last. "I think we're all eager to hear more from your husband. About your family, perhaps, Mr. Roxby?"

The boy's face turned vermillion. "I—I—" he stuttered.

"Oh, the Roxbys are all so talented!" cried Lydia. "The theater is much maligned, I think. I say it is the highest art form of our age."

"Well, I don't know about that, Lydia, dear," Henry Roxby said, head twisting between her and me in turn. "But you could say that the theater is in the Roxby blood. You met my father and my uncle once before, I remember, Mrs. Robinson?"

"You did?" I hadn't thought he'd been listening, but Edmund turned to me, his question descending like a dark gauze between us.

"No. That is, yes. You see, Miss—" But I didn't wish to speak the name "Brontë." I paused in indecision. "They were actors, I think?" I asked, addressing Roxby again.

"Harry Beverley, my new father, isn't just an actor. He's a star! And his brother, Henry's uncle, is the manager of the Scarborough theater," Lydia corrected me. "Really, Mama, I'm surprised by you."

And I of you, Lydia, I would have said, but she was gushing over the kindness of "Mrs. Beverley," who I hoped was the father's wife, and bragging about the accomplishments of another "new uncle," some paltry scene painter.

Lydia and her husband left two days later, in the same frantic flurry in which they'd arrived.

"I will change my will. Ensure she gets nothing," said Edmund, as we stood in the doorway, watching Allison guide the horses down the drive.

Our shared contempt for Roxby and his ilk had brought us closer together. It was bad enough for Lydia to marry without our blessing, worse still for her to put on such a show of heedless vulgarity.

"Not a penny," he added, shutting his eyes to stem the pain. "Do you understand me?"

"Yes," I whispered. Ironic that now, after all this time, we understood each other.

14th February 1846
The Parsonage, Haworth

My darling Lydia,

The feast of St. Valentine is upon us, my love, and you are still far from my side. Crosby writes that your husband (God, how I hate to write the word) is ill. Forgive me but my wicked heart rejoices at the news.

As he bids farewell to his life, so must you feel yours teeming back into existence.

At the word of your release I will journey to Thorp Green Hall without delay, choosing to ignore your cruel silence.

Months and no letter, weeks and no money (I value this, of course, only for what it means: your remembrance!). Send me some sign, some token, my dear one. Yet even if you do not, cannot, your love will still fly to me on the wind and whisper to me as I sleep.

Dr. Crosby's missives, with their glimpses of you as a patient ministering angel at that brute's bedside, sustain me. Charlotte tries to hide them from me, but Emily and Anne are not so fierce.

Ever yours, although weak,
nourished as I am by your love alone,
Your Northangerland

25th March 1846
Yoxall Lodge

Mrs. Robinson,

It is with sadness that I write to tell you, and Mrs. Evans by
the same post, that your father and my master, Mr. Gisborne,
died gently last night in his sleep. I found him in his bed.

Pray forgive me for not writing sooner, madam. Mr.
Gisborne hadn't been himself these three years but there had
been no recent symptoms to cause particular alarm. Indeed,
no doctor had visited Yoxall Lodge for some days.

I have written also to your brothers and am preparing
the Lodge to receive visitors. I have heard, ma'am, that Mr.
Robinson is also unwell. I'll be sure to keep him, and you too,
in my prayers if his indisposition precludes you from attending
the service for your father.

Yours humbly, with respect,
W. Rowley

24th May 1846
Thorp Green Hall

My dear daughter Lydia,

Your father's health is failing fast. If you wish to see him before
the end, you should come at once. Ned arrived today from
Aycliffe. The doctors tell me there is little hope.

Very truly, your ever-forgiving mother,
Lydia Robinson

CHAPTER FIFTEEN

"HUSH NOW, HUSH, MY love," I said, kneeling by the bed and kneading Edmund's hand.

His breathing had grown more labored in the space of the last hour. The fight was fruitless. It was time for him to go.

Ned's eyes were red from crying. Mary was sobbing into Bessy's arms. Edmund's mother was sleeping fitfully in an armchair closer to the door, one of his nightshirts across her knee.

Only Lydia had not joined us. What might have been a baby had come too soon, and she was confined to bed, according to her husband's latest letter.

The velvet bed curtain fell against me, brushing my cheek. I gasped. It was almost a caress. How many nights had Edmund and I shared here? Each of our children had been made here. I lowered my forehead to his knuckles and prayed—half-whispering and half-willing him to hear the words I could not say.

If you hold on, your hands will be burned by the rope that ties you to the world and to me. If you fight your way to the surface, another wave will strike you, with more force than before, and another and another.

"Mama?" said Ned, his voice wobbling. "Mama." He dropped down beside me. I wrapped my other arm around him and he nuzzled into my neck.

But if you slip away, it will be as if into a slow and steady slumber, ex-cepting those jolts of remembrance. You'll start back from the precipice, but be still now. All is well, my love. We are here.

My heart was on fire with all the words that Edmund and I should have said to each other, with the poetry that had been ours, more real than anything Branwell and I had shared.

We are here. We have fought with you, but now you must leave us.

"Mama," Ned said again, more panicked now.

Mary's sobs stopped.

I raised my head as Edmund's hand slipped from mine.

"God, God, no," I heard myself say. "It is over. He is gone."

"THEY ARE HERE!" I flew from Marshall, who had been trying to make me decent for the first time in a week and teasing the stubborn, minuscule buttons through the stiff hoops of thread to strangle me to my throat.

New mourning. This time we'd had a chance to prepare.

William Allison was hastening to greet the carriage when I emerged into the sun.

I hadn't been outside for a long time—not since before—and the daylight was blinding, hot.

Allison tipped his hat to his fellow coachman, eyeing the younger man with wary politeness.

The Evanses' carriage was grander than ours, with a crest on its side, two horses, not one, and a groom who sat to the rear, whistling and spitting to the road behind them no doubt all the way since Derbyshire.

Allison ignored him, speaking instead to the coachman. When had the horses last had food and water? How was traffic on the road?

"Mary," I whispered, tempted to fling the door of the carriage open myself, as the servants dawdled.

It had been two days since Edmund had died and a yet-unmeasured portion of myself with him. Two days when only the thought of my sister had sustained me. We were both orphans now, deprived of mother and father, but I was also something still stranger: a widow. And only she, who, after all, had known me longest now our parents were both gone, could bring me back to myself.

Metal was cold to my touch, light unbearable. Bessy, Ned, and Mary raised their voices too loud; even the loss of their father couldn't put a pause to their bickering. The very hours seemed to have passed more slowly since Ellis had stilled the grandfather clock in the hall, the minute hand pointing neatly to the hour. Edmund had never before been so punctual.

His mother, robbed now of a second child and so more pitiable than me, had conducted all. She told us when to eat and where to sit. She was the one who'd set the date for my husband's interment.

The Hall's innards had been exposed to a parade of visitors, stabbing me anew. Richard Thompson, our grand neighbor, condescended to set foot in Thorp Green Hall for the first time in our long acquaintance, even though he had lost a daughter recently—the sickly one, Mary Ann. The Reverend Lascelles haunted us every day, urging me to pray. Mrs. Milner turned up uninvited, claiming kinship in our shared widowhood. And my brother-in-law, Charles Thorp, assumed his role as Edmund's executor with all the pomp and circumstance of an archbishop presiding over a coronation.

I'd feared for my Lydia's life in the days after Edmund's death—each tragedy makes the next less unthinkable—but Roxby had written that she was out of danger now. I would be the one to suffer when she heard that her father had left them nothing in his will.

Allison opened the carriage door with a bow. "Welcome to Thorp Green Hall, sir. I'll have Joey see to your bags," he said.

William Evans, my sister Mary's husband, nodded toward him, but did not take his hand to quit the carriage. William was a large man and one who hardly knew his own strength. With a jump, he crunched onto the gravel and closed the door himself.

She wasn't here.

"Mary?" I repeated, questioning this time. I walked toward my sister's husband with my hands outstretched, still staring at the empty carriage behind him.

"Lydia, you don't look well." He took me by the shoulder, his grip powerful, sure.

"She isn't here?" I asked, blankly, hating him for not being her.

"No," he said kindly, weaving his arm through mine. "I'm afraid my wife is convalescent with a cold. It has, after all, been a busy few weeks."

"Busy?" I echoed.

I'd endured months of the sickroom and doctors, of servants complaining about overdue wages. At night, Edmund had sweated and moaned as I watched over him, but he still struggled to lord over his account book, propped up against his pillows, in the day. It had been months of fear—fear that I would prove unworthy of the task that falls to half the married, as I had been deficient in all my other duties as a wife; fear that everyone would find me out and know that I was just an ignorant child, hiding behind an older woman's face and a married woman's name; fear that the money and Dr. Crosby's letters would not be enough to keep Branwell Brontë away.

And yet my sister, Mary, was the one who was busy? Too busy to come to me?

"Our son Thomas was just married," William Evans said, talking to me slowly as if I were a child.

"Yes, yes." I shook my head to unfog my mind.

"Your dress." He gestured to the exposed skin at my neck. "Perhaps you had better go to your rooms, to your maid?"

"Yes. No. That is, then, what will you do?" I said, grasping his arm, overcome with the panic that I was failing as a hostess somehow, that Edmund or his mother or somebody would be angry if I left him outside in the driveway.

But Charles Thorp, a man who towered over even William Evans, had appeared on the front steps, his greeting booming out toward us.

"Charles!" William Evans said, untangling his arm from mine. "It has been too long."

"Quite, quite. Terrible circumstance, of course," said Thorp, jerking his head in my direction. I wasn't sure if the tragedy he referred to was Edmund's death or the sorry state it had reduced me to. "A lot to tell you. Edmund made me his executor, you know. But first, a brandy?"

William Evans strode away from me and up the steps, then followed Charles Thorp through my front door.

The breeze was biting for all that the day was mild. I attempted to close the fastenings of my dress, but my fingers wouldn't work. My body shook with something between a hiccup and a sob.

"Madam," William Allison said softly, placing his rough hand with infinite gentleness where William Evans's had been.

"Yes, William?" I said, looking him square in his rosy and wind-worn face.

"We are all so sorry, madam, about the master. If there's anything I can do to help, you tell me. Anything, ma'am. I'd do it without question."

"Would you, William?" I grasped his other hand in mine. "There might be something. Wait here."

CHARLES THORP AND WILLIAM Evans's voices emanated from the library, cut off now and then by my mother-in-law's strained questions. Hopefully, there would be enough time to go to the study and do what needed to be done before the men went back to deciphering the paperwork, totaling up what I, and my remaining children, had to live on.

Edmund's study was as quiet as a mausoleum. It had been months since he'd last spent time here.

I'd been a little in awe of the place when he'd first taken to his bed. I would only enter for practical reasons, such as issuing the servants' salaries or recording the collected rents. I hadn't followed Edmund's notes blindly, at least where the servants were concerned, but had made adjustments. A little less for that upstart Miss Sewell and the hapless Ellis, a little more for Marshall and Allison.

When Bob Pottage stood before me, cap in his hands and eyes downcast, I could tell he was expecting the worst. "I've six bairns, ma'am," he muttered, as if I didn't remember him telling me that before, in Scarborough. Then he added, raising his chin, "And I'm a good worker."

"I know you are, Mr. Pottage," I said, dignifying him with a "Mr." and opening my own coin purse. "Which is why I'd like to give you this." I pressed a ten-pound note into his hand.

His eyes grew wide as serving plates. It was doubtful he'd possessed such a sum before. "Ma'am," he said, more as an exhale than with his voice.

"I think the time has come for you to leave us," I said, retying the bag. Pottage nodded.

"Is there somewhere—at some remove from here, perhaps—that you can go?"

"We've some family in Dringhouses, ma'am," he said after a pause.

I suppressed a smile. Dringhouses wasn't much above ten miles away, but that was far beyond the limit of our servants' worlds.

"That should do nicely. You'll depart tomorrow, shall we say?" I made a point of glancing toward the door. "You may go."

After that encounter, I'd come into the study more regularly and often for no reason at all. I would creep into the room in the middle of the bitter winter nights, when my shift in the sickroom was done, just to sit opposite Edmund's empty chair and watch my breath in the light of a candle. Once I'd even smoked one of his cigars, gagging at the smell and choking on the smoke, but struggling through to the end.

Charles Thorp had been working his way through the papers methodically, judging from the piles of yellowing manuscript spread across the desk. It had never looked as organized as this in Edmund's day. But I didn't care to look at these. I sat in the desk chair, opened three drawers before I found clean writing paper, and then wet the discarded nib pen.

Mr. Brontë, I wrote.

I crossed it out and began again on a new page.

Branwell,

I send this letter by William Allison. See to it that he has beer and vict-uals after his journey and, if you can, keep him from Anne so that no one in Haworth will know whence he hails.

There is no need for you to send a reply. I would rather indeed that you did not.

I write only to say—

I balled the discarded paper in my left hand, crumpling the well-formed letters of *Brontë* between my fingers and fighting back tears.

My head swam with memories of Edmund signing his correspon-dence with a flourish, as sure of his convictions and decisions as I was uncertain, unshaken in his authority, while I was like that poplar beyond his window, still standing but swayed by the slightest breeze.

I write only to say that my husband is dead.

I had never sat in his chair before.

And that, when it comes to you and me, all connection must be sev-ered between us.

My hand juddered, making the full stop into more of a comma.

Would I could have ended the letter there, but a vision of Branwell's baby face seemed to beseech me, his tears hanging like ripening fruit on his lashes, even thicker than Georgiana's. Branwell had not yet ac-cepted life's capricious cruelties. For him, every pain demanded an ex-planation. But what could I write? Could I tell him that at Thorp Green, he'd been my distraction, just as, when a boy, he'd been in Charlotte's shadow?

No. I could raise the knife but not deliver the final blow. So I libeled the man whose house I had sullied with shame, whose ring I still wore on my finger, whose corpse lay quiet in the anteroom below.

My husband's will precludes our union.

That was what Edmund had said, wasn't it? That some men wouldn't surrender their monopoly over their wives' bodies, even in death? They were the husbands who would wed you to the grave.

Choose you and I must relinquish all—the home I have created, the friends I have around me, and, worst of all, my children. I must choose and, Branwell, I choose my fortune and the world it represents, a world in which a man like you could never be my equal.

I pictured him, his face falling at every word, his hand running through his frizzing curls.

I needed to give him something, some small kindness to hold on to.

But know, I wrote on, *that I will always be your princess in Angria. You will never know me as I am now—an old and unloved widow. There I will ever be young and always beautiful, accepting your arm at the Duke's grand balls, running hand in hand with you, Northangerland, amongst the bluebells.*

I reread my words and shuddered. They were designed only for effect, as transparent as a child's first lie. And I had believed Branwell's flatteries when he'd sworn he saw a musician and a poet in me, Charlotte's equal, fighting against my chains and screaming at the very walls around me.

My convulsion turned to a retch. Nausea swept through me like the sickness I had suffered with Ned. My body's rebellion, which, the doctor had told me, meant that this time, at last, I was growing a boy inside me. But there would be no more babies now.

I should go.

The paroxysm passed. I signed and sealed the letter.

Marshall was waiting for me when I reached my rooms. She didn't look well herself. She was thin and wan from her exertions in the sickroom. But after taking one look at my face, she guided me to my bed.

"Marshall, you are very good to me," I told her, slumping back. "I know that caring for me is not always easy." I stroked the rough wool of her dress, a decades-old indigo thing of mine that she was trying to pass for mourning.

She unwound my fingers and wove them between hers, her grip light yet sure as a sparrow's on a twig.

"Send William Allison to me when you go," I said.

She nodded, with a furtive glance at the letter I still clutched in one hand.

"Only, do not leave me yet," I whispered.

Her other arm slipped around me and I let her rock me, just as she had the children in their infancy. Once or twice she coughed, shaking me from near-sleep, but then she'd still and soothe me.

"Quiet now, madam," she whispered. Her breasts were warm and soft for all that her hands were clammy and the rest of her was bony. "It is all over now."

1st June 1846
Manchester

Mama, is it true? Has Papa left Henry and me with nothing, abandoning his eldest daughter at this time of my direst need?

He would not have done so without you at his ear.

You have always hated me. How could you? How could you, my mother, have despised me so when my heart aches with love for the child I might have held, although he never even had a chance to draw breath?

I loved him before I felt him kick. I loved him, or the thought of him and his siblings, from the day I first met my Henry's eye. In the theater, in Scarborough, do you remember? Our eyes locked across the crowd and that was it. The course of my life was determined.

God punish you, even as He holds close my father's soul.

Your daughter no more,
Lydia Roxby

2nd June 1846
The Parsonage, Haworth

My one, my only Lydia,

Your letter affected me so deeply that I was incapacitated for some days. Charlotte says they feared for my life. Oh, that unfeeling fiend, who once had the honor of calling you his wife! Lydia, must I abandon all hope? I penned the following poem when I recovered my powers of speech and thought to title it "Lydia Gisborne" in anticipation of the day when you will cast off the shackles of your husband's name and tyrannous last will and testament.

Yours, even in the face of cruel rejection,
Branwell Brontë

LYDIA GISBORNE

On Ouse's grassy banks—last Whitsuntide,
I sat, with fears and pleasures, in my soul
Commingled, as "it roamed without control,"
O'er present hours and through a future wide
Where love, me thought, should keep, my heart beside
Her, whose own prison home I looked upon:
But, as I looked, descended summer's sun,
And did not its descent my hopes deride?
The sky though blue was soon to change to grey—
I, on that day, next year must own no smile—
And as those waves, to Humber far away,
Were gliding—so, though that hour might beguile
My Hopes, they too, to woe's far deeper sea,
Rolled past the shores of Joy's now dim and distant isle.

8th June 1846
Manchester

Mama,

I was too hasty in my last letter, forgive me. What could you have known of Papa's will? Men do, I am learning now, often keep us in the dark.

Henry had told me all was well and that we were making ends meet, but he admitted tonight that, in attending to my doctor's fees, we have missed several rent payments. If we cannot find the means to pay we will be evicted in one week.

Send money if you can, Mother, do.

Ever your darling daughter,
Lydia

11th June 1846
Great Barr Hall

My dear Mrs. Robinson,

I write to express my condolences on the death of your husband. I did not hear of it until after his interment last week, or else I would have written sooner.

Edmund Robinson was a good man and news of his untimely departure must, I think, affect all who hear of it.

My wife, Catherine, would also have written, but sadly her poor health does not allow for such exertions. She does bid me send you word of her cousinly affection.

I do not know what your future plans may hold. Do you intend to give up the house? Do not hesitate to write to me if there is any service, however small or large, I can render. And do know that you are always welcome at Great Barr Hall. Perhaps Catherine's health will have improved by the time you grace us with a visit.

Yours, with regret,
Edward Scott

CHAPTER SIXTEEN

Do you intend to *give up the house?* The question haunted me over
the next few months, lingering on the tips of my interlocutors'
tongues, although few voiced it as directly as Sir Edward Scott, that
old hero of my girlish heart, had in the only letter he had ever written
to me.

Edmund was gone. The carriage bearing his body had crunched
over the gravel in our driveway, carrying him from his home one last
time, and trundled down Thorp Green Lane, with all of us—Ned, as
was to be expected, but also, breaking with convention, Bessy, Mary,
and me—walking behind.

Reverend Lascelles had sprinkled the earth over him.

Old Mrs. Robinson had stayed in our pew in the chancery of the
church, staring up at the plaque dedicated to her daughter, Jane, too
overcome to stand at the open graveside.

And, one by one, on that day and over the months since, the other
mourners had melted away, making my isolation complete.

"Another one of our men gave notice today," I said as Edmund's
mother and I sat next to each other in my dressing room.

She was sewing with a steady rhythm in spite of the swelling in her bejeweled, arthritic hands, in the last of the day's feeble light. Winter was coming, and the nights were starting to draw in.

My own work sat in my lap, forgotten. I couldn't embroider when the weight of our futures was upon me. By Edmund's own calculations, which Charles Thorp had found in a stark addendum to the official accounting book, we were in trouble. Even with the land I'd let this summer on the advice of my brothers-in-law, the children and I would be in dire straits within a twelvemonth. No more small sums sent to Lydia in response to her pitiful letters, no dowries for the girls, no Cambridge for Ned, and for me? Who could I turn to with father and husband gone? Must the burden, which neither of them had schooled me for, fall on me?

"Hmm?" said old Mrs. Robinson. Her eyes looked tired and less fierce than usual.

I'd nearly forgotten what I'd said to her.

"One of the laboring men," I continued, when the thought came back to me. "He married a dairy maid and is to go to Eshelby's farm."

"Loyalty. No servant knows the meaning of the word nowadays," she started to complain, but I could tell her heart wasn't in it. She looked exhausted, weak. Maybe now was my chance to tell her.

"Mother," I said stiffly. She'd asked me some months ago to call her that.

"Yes, Lydia?" There was a hint of wariness in her voice when she heard me obey her.

"With the farmland leased and more and more servants leaving, I have been thinking. It may be prudent for us to go too." I managed to hold her gaze.

"Go, Lydia?" She placed her hoop on the side table. "Whatever do you mean?"

"Dismiss most of the servants, shut up the Hall. Or, better yet, let it. The girls I could send to relatives while I deal with the house, and then we could all three go visiting. Perhaps we will join my sister, Mary

Evans, at Allestree Hall in Derbyshire. Ned could live with a tutor. And you could—"

"And I could what?"

"Well, you could go home."

She drew herself up tall, ready to tear into me, but the truth had streamed across me like a beam of light. She could no longer turn Edmund against me, secure in her prior claim. And that meant there was nothing she could threaten me with.

"You seem to forget, Lydia, that Thorp Green Hall was *my* home, long before it was yours."

I nearly laughed. How could I forget it? She had reminded me that I was a stranger in my own house, not a Metcalfe, or even a real Robinson, not "one of them," since the day Edmund and I had returned from our honeymoon.

"No." I stood. "It is no more your home than it is mine. It was *your husband's* home. After that, it was *my* husband's. And now it is my son's. I have a duty to protect it, and the rest of his inheritance, until he reaches his majority."

"And you would have me believe that your affairs are as bad as all that?" She also stood.

I nodded. It had taken me time to believe it too. At first I couldn't fathom the truth, how the amounts Edmund had placed on horses had grown even as our investments diminished, how he hadn't told me that affairs were bad, even when he was dying.

"When my son—" Her voice cracked. "When my son was the best son a mother could ask for, a prudent father whose only fault was being too kind, a loving husband whose weakness was being too forgiving. He spent all day in his study caring for the estate, keeping his books—"

"Loving?" I spoke over her. "My husband had a shallow pool of love. After that was spent, he passed his life locked away from us, and now he has left us with next to nothing. He failed us." Yes. And I had never known it. I had thought him perfect. For, after all, how was I to know that he was as poor a husband as I was a wife?

"You, you." The old woman clenched and unclenched her hands, rage radiating from her. "What have you done, Lydia? Have you frittered away all his money, sent it to your whorish daughter and to your lover?" She threw the word at me, showering me with spit.

I blushed. It was true I was still sending Branwell money from my monthly stipend and receiving a flood of poems—some intelligible, some much less so—in return. The checks were a salve to my conscience through my many sleepless nights, as well as a feeble insurance to keep him away. But what was the pittance I had given Branwell compared to what Edmund had lost?

And this had not been the only way in which her precious son had neglected me. Without Edmund here, without the hurt in his eyes, it didn't seem so wrong at all that I had gone to Branwell's bed. After all, Edmund had refused to make love to me. And I had not been ready to live only on memories.

"You must leave the Hall at once if you speak to me so," I told her, very matter-of-fact, wiping the wetness from my cheek. "The children leave in two days. There is nothing to keep you here."

"Will you send Ned back to John Eade?" she asked.

My calm seemed to have mollified her. If only I'd learned not to match fire with fire long ago.

"No," I said. "To another tutor, a man in Somerset. It is all settled."

"You would take my grandchildren away from me?" This was a different tactic. She was pathetic, reaching out her cupped hand to caress my face.

I flinched. "Why don't you go to your real daughter? To the godly Thorps?" I couldn't resist this last barb. "I hear their children are angels, at least compared to mine."

EVEN WITH MRS. ELIZABETH Robinson turfed out, it still took some time to extricate us. We were part of the fabric of the Ouseburns. I hadn't quite comprehended that before. The Robinsons, like the Thompsons, weren't just employers or almsgivers. We were a symbol, a source of pride, a surety against the changing world beyond. I resented my superiors, or at least coveted what I had not—a title, a house in London, a chance to see the world. But the peasants here delighted in their betters' triumphs and grieved our misfortunes as their own.

"All is settled, then?" Dr. Crosby reappeared around the side of the Thompson mausoleum, the grandest resting place in the graveyard surrounding the Holy Trinity, the Little Ouseburn church. He'd been running his hand across the columns that ornamented the building.

This was the hardest of my many good-byes.

"Yes," I said, drawing my shawl a little tighter as the wind picked up. "Bessy and Mary return from visiting relations next week, and soon after, we will all decamp to Allestree Hall, to my sister."

"Is there anything I can do? Any preparations, perhaps, for the new lodgers?" The doctor strode down the bank to walk beside me, toward the church where we'd be less exposed. His boots flattened the browning grass, which was fighting hard for survival through the winter.

"Oh no, my agent will see to all that," I said. How bizarre the word felt—not "our" or "my husband's" but "my" agent. "The Sewells, Ellis, Joey—they will all stay on at Thorp Green Hall for now. And Marshall of course must come with me. My only concern is for William Allison. It will hardly be necessary for us to keep our own carriage and coachman in addition to the Evanses'. But I will think of something there." I said it breezily, though the thought had kept me up at night. Allison, discreet though he'd proved himself to be until now, had, after all, been my emissary to Haworth. He knew so much and had always been kind. For that, I owed him something.

I paused as we neared the church. Over there lay Edmund, just feet away from our pew. Yet the stone wall of the building divided him from us when the girls and I trooped in for Sunday service. The patch where the ground had been disturbed was still just about discernible, but, come spring, flowers would obscure my husband's grave. And I wouldn't be here to see them.

My throat tightened.

I couldn't look anymore, so glanced instead toward Fish Pond Bridge and the winding road to Great Ouseburn beyond.

It wouldn't do for me to be so morbid when I wouldn't see the doctor for who knew how many months. I opened my mouth to ask him some question about the gossip in the larger village but realized he was pensive too, staring back toward the domed mausoleum, with a fixed and faraway expression in his eyes.

"Is something the matter, Doctor? John?" I asked.

"Well, for one, I will miss you, Lydia," he said. "The Ouseburns won't be the same for me when you are gone. You are, after all, the only one who understands my—"

"Enough." I cut him off. He'd shared the shameful secrets of his heart once, but that didn't mean they required repetition. I started back toward the Thompsons' vault, hearing the squelch of the doctor's steps behind me. "I will write. I promise."

"But that is the thing, Lydia. Didn't you promise Mr. Brontë that too?"

The squelching stopped, and I turned.

"I fear you will not," he went on. "That you will leave my letters unanswered like Branwell's when you are with your grander friends."

"Is that what he said—that I promised him?" I demanded.

For the last month, Dr. Crosby had been returning Mr. Brontë's letters unopened, on my instruction, although they still arrived with almost the same regularity as the checks I made out to him were deposited.

"You did not?" asked Dr. Crosby, head bowed.

He had never questioned me before.

"I did not," I echoed.

"Then I apologize. Only—"

"Only what?" I snapped.

Raindrops were misting the air between us.

"Forgive me," he said. "Only, when one has gone so long without love, it seems to me it would be impossible to turn it away."

There was a time when I would have thought that too.

The rain was falling harder, so I ran up the bank and into the unlocked mausoleum. There was just about room for my dress and me to fit into one of the eight marble alcoves. The doctor perched in the one beside me.

"There was a time when I longed only to be loved, ideally to madness," I said, a low laugh creeping into my voice. "And, for a while, the adoration, the idolatry—for that is what it is—was enough. But then—"

"Then?"

"Then the loneliness returned, only more acute. I want more than to be loved, John. Any handsome woman can win a fool into loving her. I want to be seen clearly and loved for what another soul sees there. I want love to be a perfect mirror that reflects me, flaws and all, and still meets me with a smile."

"Lydia, I see you," John Crosby said.

My heart nearly burst with it. I reached out, took his hand, and gave it a short, sharp squeeze. "And I see you, Doctor," I said.

"Do you know, Lydia, what the villagers think?" he asked after we'd sat in silence for some minutes.

"What's that?"

"When they see me visiting the Hall each week? Attending church at Holy Trinity, rather than St. Mary's, just in order to be near you? Giving you my arm on our walks? Well, they whisper that I am in love with you." The doctor smiled.

I laughed loud and true this time and imagined old Mary Thompson, in the crypt below us, seething in her coffin at our disrespect.

"Ah, Dr. John Crosby, another naive man enraptured by the dazzling Mrs. Robinson," I cried. The rain drummed harder on the lead roof. "It makes for a fine story, it's true. If only they knew the truth. That would be much more scandalous."

BUOYED BY THE KINSHIP I had found in Dr. Crosby and the revelation that love was sometimes sweeter for being platonic, I practically ran home once the rain lightened.

I would quit Thorp Green Hall within weeks, although it had never been so dear to me as in the last months. But at least Marshall, that second loyal friend, would be with me wherever we went, always present, ever patient, and making each grand house we visited feel like home.

Thorp Green now ran to my rhythms. Breakfast was when I rose, dinner whenever I was hungry. I had even torn down those awful faded floral curtains in my dressing room, although I wouldn't enjoy for long the heavy dark velvet I'd chosen to replace them, an almost indefensible extravagance given our current situation.

I'd missed the children on occasion since the girls had gone visiting, but it was in that fleeting way, where I hoped Ned and Mary were eating enough and Bessy not too much, otherwise enjoying the silence. Or enjoying that I was the only one who could interrupt it.

Today, although my boots were wet and my hair was ruined, I rushed straight to the anteroom when I entered the Hall, lobbing my sodden shawl at Miss Sewell en route.

I threw back the lid of the pianoforte and struck a chord, rich, harmonious, and unapologetically loud. I could play what I liked, without trying and failing to please Edmund. There was something magical in the way my body remembered, in how my fingers flew just as fast over the keys as they had in my girlhood, and in how the music thrilled me, just the same. It was as if the melodies wove a fine, taut, invisible thread between my earlier self and me, as if I could give voice to what I felt inside without the necessary translation and obfuscation of speech.

"Madam?" By the time I heard her, she was so close I jumped, so maybe Marshall had been calling to me for some time.

I swiveled to face her, although I knew her from her voice. "Yes?"

"May I— I should like to talk with you," she said.

"You are talking to me now," I replied, my earlier affection toward her evaporating at her unexpected, almost insolent, interruption.

She began to answer but broke into a cough. It was too shallow at first, and it took her several attempts before she was able to break through the phlegm. She struck her chest with the heel of one hand as if the gesture would clear it, raising the other to me in apology.

"Honestly, Marshall, it is as bad as having Miss Brontë here again," I said, closing the piano.

I'd done it. I'd said the name "Brontë" and without so much as hesitating.

"I am sorry, madam," she said, weakly. "Do you mind if I sit down?"

It was unlike her to ask for anything for herself.

"Not at all," I said, taken aback. "Please do."

She sank onto the sofa. It was strange to see her there.

"Are you unwell?" I asked, rising from the piano stool and moving instead to the armchair, closer to her but not so close that I'd risk catching her cold. I couldn't bring sickness into the Evanses' house. A widow, two daughters, and a servant were already enough of an imposition on my sister and her husband.

"Yes, madam, I am," said Marshall, her voice low and steady. "I am sorry to say it, but I will not be well enough to accompany you to Derbyshire."

"Nonsense!" I had the urge to stand up again but instead began plucking at a loose thread in the upholstery. My fingers weren't strong enough to break it. "A cold is unlikely to last more than two weeks, and we can always delay our departure, although that is less than desirable."

I couldn't go to my sister, Mary, in such a sorry state, without even a maid to dress me. I wanted to cause a stir in society there, to be thought a sophisticated and fascinating widow, not a poor relation down on her luck.

"But, madam, Mrs. Robinson, I am not suffering from a cold." Marshall studied my face like she would a baby's when he is on the verge of tears.

"Not a cold? Then what?"

"Consumption, madam. I've known for some time."

"No."

"Yes." She said that very sharply.

Marshall had never been one for melodramatics. I could not doubt her.

"The blood, it comes more frequently. The fits, they last longer. I cannot serve you as I should."

I waved her objections aside. "But you are welcome—" I struggled to find the words. "You can stay with us—with me—until the end, like you did with—"

How many nights had she dabbed Edmund's and Georgiana's brows, how often had she reasoned them out of their fevered delusions?

"I wish to go to my sister, Mrs. Robinson." Ann Marshall stood.

This was it, then, all she would give me by way of good-bye. It was her sister she wanted. Not me.

"Of course," I said.

Had I been wrong? Had there never been anything more than the relationship between a lady and her maid between us? But it had felt that way when she rocked and caressed me, when I grabbed her hand to kiss it, when, during my weekly bath, she had sponged my back and tickled my neck with a steady stream of water, through those months and years when Edmund wouldn't touch me at all.

Who would nurse me to my end when it came? I had no mother to hold me, no husband to mourn me. By then, perhaps, *all* my children would have faded away.

Marshall held out her hand and I pressed it, unable to rail at her for abandoning me, unwilling, even now, to admit that I needed her.

"You will come to the study later, so I can settle your pension and the pay that we owe you?" I asked.

She nodded.

Her bones poked through her papery skin under my too-tight grip. If only I need never release her. My Marshall, dying. How was it I hadn't noticed before?

15th February 1847
Thorp Green Hall

My dear Sir Edward,

Some months ago, you bid me write if you could render any
assistance to me. Now I do so, remembering the generosity of
that offer.

The months since my husband Edmund's death have been
a sore trial for me, and I have taken on much beyond the small
realm of a woman's knowledge. I have secured the services of
an agent, and Thorp Green Hall is now let. I have managed
sales of oak wood and farming stock and learned all manner of
agricultural terms.

My daughters and I are to travel to Allestree Hall, home of
my brother-in-law, William Evans, MP, in Derbyshire, within
the fortnight.

Yet one difficulty remains, which I have been unable to
surmount: the fate of our coachman. William Allison, for
that is the fellow's name, has been a most loyal servant to
my husband and to me, but I, a widow, can hardly think of
maintaining a carriage or expect my sister and her husband
to harbor my horse in addition to myself and my unmarried
daughters.

I have, as you know, never been to Great Barr Hall, but,
having heard of the size of your estate and fame of your
stables, thought I would inquire whether you were in need of
a man?

Allison is decent, hardworking, and honest. He has a
family who rely on him.

If you can't offer him a place, perhaps you have an acquaintance who could?

> *Ever grateful for your kindness and sending my familial love to my dear cousin Catherine, I remain, yours very truly,*
> *Lydia Robinson*

19th February 1847
Great Barr Hall

My dear Mrs. Robinson,

What a joy it is to bring comfort and help to a friend in need when to do so is to lose nothing oneself!

I must tell you I am deeply touched by your compassion for your inferiors, even in this time of your own grief.

Your man William Allison would, of course, be a most welcome addition to our household. Bid him come to Great Barr Hall as soon as it is convenient for you to part with him. If all goes well and I find him to my satisfaction, his family should follow him shortly after.

Looking forward to a time when we will meet again (how I desire to hear your lectures on agriculture!).

I remain your most sincere admirer,
Edward Scott

CHAPTER SEVENTEEN

"LYDIA!" MY SISTER, MARY, threw her arms around me. I submitted gratefully.

It had been kind of her and her husband to send their carriage for me. Patroclus and our other horses I had sold and William Allison had already decamped to Great Barr Hall. A part of me couldn't help but envy him. Yet the journey here, while comfortable, had been lonely. The girls wouldn't arrive in Derbyshire for a few more days, and the latest novel from Mr. Bellerby's circulating library wouldn't hold my attention. So I'd stared out the window, trying not to think, and when the country-side was too monotonous or the hedgerows too high, read and reread Sir Edward's letter, delighting to have such a lofty and considerate friend.

"It is so wonderful to see you, Lyddy." Mary hugged me tighter, al-though her servants, a few of whom were lined up to greet me, must be staring at us. She was shorter than me, and her hair, which had grayed since the last time I'd seen her, at Mother's funeral, was coarse against my neck.

I breathed deeper. Nobody had touched any part of me other than my hand since the day Marshall had left us for Aldborough, and now I would never feel her calming caress again.

"Welcome, welcome to Allestree Hall." My sister released me.

I turned to learn the servants' names, but they hadn't been lining up to greet me at all and were already scuttling off with my many trunks and boxes. Of course, I was only a guest here. Introductions were hardly necessary.

"William is at the mill, one of our mills. He is always working," Mary said as she ushered me toward the house.

Allestree Hall was larger than Thorp Green, although not so charming. The building was three stories high with unflinchingly symmetrical windows, and the exterior was a gray ashlar, which was unwelcoming compared to our warm red brick. The only flights of fancy were some Romanesque entablatures and columns (Ionic, if my half-remembered history lessons served me well) and an ornate central porch, which my sister had rhapsodized about when she was first married. *William's father added it, you know.* I thought it out of place.

"Your bedroom is to the rear, overlooking the grounds," she told me as we entered the hallway. "It's a little small, but the view is considered rather beautiful. Tea in my parlor, Jane, at once, and see that Cook doesn't overboil the mutton." Mary switched between addressing me and addressing her servants without pausing, every inch the older sister. "Would you like to change? But of course you have no maid, and mine is busy running errands. No matter. Perhaps she'll have time to attend to you later."

Changing wasn't necessary, I assured her with a smile. After all, I now lived in a wardrobe of black, black, and more black.

We climbed the grand main staircase, double the width of ours, with stone steps and an ornate metal balustrade.

Being here, seeing Mary, was strange. It was like visiting my parents' friends' houses when I was a child and unsure what I could touch and where I might go. Mary had always been with the grown-ups then, while I'd been banished to the foreign nurseries on the occasions I'd accompanied my family on such visits at all. The dark, maze-like houses were only slightly less terrible than our hosts' children—

unfriendly and annoyed to find I was invading their territories. Once some boy, no doubt a peer of the realm or respectable clergyman by now, had bitten me.

I followed my sister, as lost as I had been then, until she turned into a room on our left. "There, isn't it perfect?" She surveyed her parlor with satisfaction.

We sat as yet another maid smoothed a lace tablecloth over the round table between us.

"Go on. Tell me everything," said Mary.

"I—" I cast around for the easy gossip that came to me when I wrote her letters, but it was difficult to reconcile the silver-haired and plump woman who sat before me with the slender girl, with hair as raven as mine even if she had never been so handsome, whom I'd written to throughout the years. "Well, the Thompsons hired a painter," I said.

Mary's brow creased.

"To paint the family's portraits," I clarified.

"A painter?"

"Yes. 'Say'—that's his surname. Francis Say, or was it Frederick?" I said, as if more details would make this more interesting. What was it I had said to confuse her?

"Lyddy!" Mary laughed, reaching out her hand toward me across the table. "I mean tell me everything about *you*."

This I had not expected. Mary had never been privy to my personal dramas even before we were both married. And now? I doubted whether I'd even told her Ned's tutor's name.

"Why, you first, Mary," I said. "After all, I am the one occupying your home, and besides, I am rather fatigued from my journey."

This was a good way out of my difficulty. Soon she was rattling on about improvements to the gardens and some insolent groundskeeper who had a penchant for uprooting the wrong shrubs, gesturing so wildly that she nearly knocked over the rose-printed teapot the maid had set down between us.

I hardly listened, judging the room instead. It could have been my dressing room at Thorp Green Hall. Mary too had neat piles of letters, half-finished embroidery projects, and a near-identical stack of novels. But the color scheme here was a blue bordering on teal, not pink, and the country visible through the window was unlike ours. Thorp Green rose organically, if unexpectedly, from the fertile Yorkshire landscape, surrounded as it was by trees, but Allestree Hall subjugated its surroundings. A luscious, well-manicured, impossible lawn rolled from the house toward distant and uniform trees. It was all a blur of green and brown to me, but Mary had said something about silver birch and fine English elm.

"And what's more," Mary added, pausing to breathe or for dramatic relief, "nothing is certain yet, but I hope soon to become a grandmother."

This revelation revived me. "Oh," I said, delighted to have found something, anything, in common. "Why, my Lydia's first baby should also arrive before the summer."

"With the actor?" Mary asked, dropping her voice and righting the teapot mid-pour. "Is that cause for celebration?"

I stiffened. "Yes, with her husband," I said. "Surely I couldn't hope for anything else?"

We were silent for a beat, except for the sound of the brew tinkling into her cup. Mary's smile looked as painted as the teapot. "And what of my other nieces?" she asked at last, stirring until the silver spoon sang against the china. "Bessy and my dear little namesake? Have they any prospects?"

"Mary is too young. And Bessy? We had hopes, for a time, of her and the Milners' eldest son, but the deaths of both their fathers delayed anything definitive being done about that."

Perhaps I ought to have bid the tedious Mrs. Milner a farewell visit and sought an excuse to leave her son and Bessy alone. But I had not been active here. Part of me did not want to lose another daughter, for all that Bessy and Mary were poor company. And part of me found it hard to comprehend that my Bessy was twenty and, for all her faults, undeniably a woman now.

"Mary is hardly too young," my sister said, draining her tea in two gulps. "But let us talk of that later. I must go to the kitchens and see what headway Cook is making with dinner." She stood. "I only hope you will have something to do with yourself, Lyddy. I can't imagine how I should spend my time without a house to run."

FOR THE NEXT TWO weeks we—all three of us, once the girls arrived—were my sister's "project" and subject to her near-constant commentary.

My hair was unnaturally dark for my age. Was I sure I didn't dye it? Young Mary was too shy. Bessy's table manners left a lot to be desired. Such a pity that I hadn't taken time to bestow my musical talents on the girls. Gentlemen did find dueting such a pleasant pastime.

I braced myself, laughed when my sister's advice could be taken as a poor attempt at humor, and inclined my head in agreement when it could not.

At times I'd glance toward my children, hopeful that one of them would feel as I did and share a look of understanding with me, as my Lydia would have, a fleeting rebellion against our shared shackles. But Bessy and Mary's senses were too blunt to feel their aunt's jibes, and besides, the pair of them flourished when being clipped, corrected, and pruned. They'd been too long without an instructor.

"That was a beautiful rendition," my sister told her "little namesake" once the latter had recited the final lines of some verses by Mr. Wordsworth one night after dinner. "Wherever did you learn it?"

"Miss Brontë taught us," said my daughter Mary. "She is very fond of poetry."

"The governess?" asked our hostess, with an eye on the door.

There was no sign of William or Thomas, the Evanses' son, who had joined us for dinner and, unprompted, educated us about the operation of paper mills throughout the entire meal. The men must, thankfully, still be sitting over their port.

"Yes," I said, answering for the girls. If only there was some way to change the subject, but we'd exhausted all topics of conversation some days before.

"I miss Miss Brontë," said Bessy, who was constructing a pyramid from a set of playing cards. She'd been terribly fidgety since her aunt had scared her out of gnawing on her fingernails.

"So do I," said her sister. "And Flossy too. Flossy was the best dog in the world," she added to her aunt by way of explanation.

The girls hadn't mentioned Miss Brontë in a long time, not since those weeks between Branwell's dismissal and Lydia's elopement, those weeks when I'd wished for death and thrust the children from me, relying instead only on Marshall. My poor Marshall.

"Mightn't we write to her, Mama? Could we?" young Mary asked in a rush, glancing at Bessy.

Was it possible my daughters had planned this? Chosen to ask me in front of my sister when my power was at its lowest ebb?

"No," I said, so firmly that Bessy's tower of cards came tumbling down. "If Miss Brontë missed you, she would have written herself, as I've told you before. And if she'd cared about you at all, for that matter, she would not have resigned. Nobody made her do so."

"But now she won't know *where* to write to us," Bessy ventured. "What if we miss her letter?"

"Enough." I clicked my fingers before her face. "Enough from both of you, do you hear me?"

My sister had been twisting her head this way and that, as if following a game of tennis. "These Brontës live near Keighley in Yorkshire, I think?" she asked.

These Brontës? We hadn't been speaking of them in the plural.

"Yes."

"No, in Haworth."

"The towns are close to each other, silly."

The girls argued back and forth. There was such a roaring in my ears that I didn't register who was saying what.

"We—William and I—have connections in the area," my sister said.

"Their name is Clapham. They are another family in the paper business. Perhaps, girls, the next time your uncle William travels there, he can bring you with him? That way you can visit your dear Miss Brontë. And see Flossy too."

No. Not now.

"He could?"

"Oh, would he?"

Little Mary bobbed up and down in her seat. Bessy let the cards rain down on the table in celebration.

"Mary!" I said, jumping to my feet.

My younger daughter flinched, but I hadn't been addressing her.

"My daughters will *not* be visiting the Brontës," I said, staring down at my sister and conquering my desire to scream. "Do you hear me?"

This time it was the girls' heads that turned. How would their aunt react to this challenge?

"Sit down, Lyddy," my sister said, half suppressing a yawn.

I did not.

Hadn't Edmund's mother told me the same that Easter night? The first night that sent me running to the Monk's House and to Branwell?

"I hardly think your daughters need suffer for your mistakes," she added. My sister's eyes had turned as icy as my blood ran now.

What did she know, and how? Nobody knew about Mr. Brontë except—not Marshall, no. And Bob Pottage was long gone. William Allison owed me for his recent good fortune. But surely Dr. Crosby, the only friend I had left, would never have betrayed me?

From ice to fire, ravaging my veins and daring me to rage against this latest injustice. But my sister was our hostess, and we had no home. And thanks to Edmund, we had little money.

"My head begins to ache a little. Excuse me if I retire," I said, my voice wobbling.

My sister nodded.

I left the three of them to their evening of poetry reading and card games, crept from the room, and ran up the stairs.

234   *Finola Austin*

By the light of the solitary candle in my room I wrote a desperate letter, unable to soothe myself without appealing to the affections of another. Sir Edward was my only hope, the only one who could now save me.

Oh, if only Marshall were holding me here in the dark. If only my love alone could bring the flesh back to her bones and the light back to her eyes, swell her lungs with sweet, refreshing air.

My dear Sir Edward,

When glancing at the postmark of this letter, you must have
assumed I was asking you for another favor, but fear not. I
ask for nothing except your indulgence in reading the next few
sorry lines. If they are foolish, you may throw the pages into
the flames of the fire. Even if they are not, it is best you forget
them.

I write because I find myself in sore need of a friend and
your last letters brought me such comfort. A widow is like a
rudderless ship, and, as a sort of cousin to me, I hoped you
could give me some advice and direction.

My younger daughters and I are all very comfortable at
Allestree Hall. My sister and her husband are, as you know,
good Christian people. I want for nothing physically and yet—
there is an expression when a man suffers defeat. He feels he
is "unmanned." Well, I, Sir Edward, if you can believe it, feel
"unwomaned" by the loss of my home, my servants, and my
husband.

If my life was idle before, now it is no life at all. I choose
nothing for myself. Food is selected for me, certain rooms are
forbidden to me, my bedtime is set. I stalk the corridors of
Allestree Hall like a shadow and watch over my daughters like
a ghost. For if I had died alongside their father, wouldn't they
be here just the same? And my sister would be, as she is now,
mothering them in my place.

Is such a feeling inevitable? Should I school myself to be

grateful only and to deny those parts of me which are self-interested and self-serving, as ridiculous in a widow as they are undesirable in a maid?

I remain, dear sir, yours very truly,
Lydia Robinson

20th March 1847
Allestree Hall

My dear Sir Edward,

Please disregard the letter I sent by yesterday's post—unread if
you have yet to break the seal. I dispatched it in error.

I remain yours very truly and ever grateful,
Lydia Robinson

CHAPTER EIGHTEEN

ALLESTREE PARK WAS A fine piece of land. There was no denying that.

Today the April air had been crisp and cool, but the sun warmed you when you stood unshaded for long enough. And now, in the gathering twilight, the swaying trees were as graceful as the chorus at the ballet. A falcon circled overhead, seeking its last meal of the day. Rabbits hopped over the great expanse of grass, careless of the danger above them, their scuts bobbing as they ran and leapt and played.

I had taken to walking alone a lot in the past few weeks—to escape the house, clear my head, and stretch my languid limbs. And it had worked. Out here, my wounds didn't sting as sharply. In nature, I could breathe.

Sir Edward still hadn't written, but, perhaps, as instructed, he'd simply thrown my first, melodramatic letter away. That was the best interpretation of his silence, anyway.

There'd been no more talk of Keighley or the Brontës, and on reflection, my sister, Mary, could have meant anything by what she had said. A letter had arrived from Dr. Crosby a handful of days after the "incident," which had assured me of his friendship. I should have more faith and measure my responses, learn to curb my adolescent temper. Edmund would have said so had he been here.

Strange. As I drew nearer to the Hall from the side, a carriage parked before the main entrance came into view. It wasn't the Evanses'; I could tell that even from this distance. And for an intense, wild, beautiful moment, I was convinced it was Sir Edward's and that he had come like an errant knight to spirit me away.

Yet once I reached the set of semicircular stone steps leading to the house from the lawn, I could see that the conveyance wasn't nearly grand enough to carry Sir Edward Scott, baronet, of Great Barr Hall. William and Mary must have an unexpected visitor.

I diverted my path regardless, intending to satisfy my curiosity by entering through the front door. The guest, no doubt some ghastly businessman, must already be inside.

I stepped into the hallway.

Empty.

Yet here was something else to rescue me from the monotony. Perched on the occasional table was a letter, addressed to me and (this I saw only when I lifted it) bearing the Scott seal. My face reddened with a fresh rush of shame at the diatribe I had written and to whom.

"No, William!" cried Bessy from somewhere upstairs, before I could open the letter. Her voice was shrill and anguished. "You cannot leave me so!"

William? She had never addressed her uncle by his forename alone.

There was the pounding of heavy boots on sandstone. A young man hurtled into view above me. He was large and, dare I say it, fat, even. And he must have been wearing riding boots, from the terrible clanging his shoes' metal heels made against the steps. The banister rattled as he raced down the stairs.

I stepped into his path to slow him.

"Will Milner?" I ventured, hardly believing that he was here and that he had grown still more since that sad, sorry dance I'd last seen him at—the celebration of Harry Thompson's marriage.

"Mrs. Robinson." Young Milner came to a staggering halt three feet from me. "Good day, ma'am." He ducked his head and went to dodge around me, but I thrust out my hand to stop him.

His shirt brushed against my forearm. It was damp with fresh sweat. "Why, you can't be leaving already?" I said, laughing and adopting the style of lighthearted flirtation that I defaulted to in moments of doubt.

"I'm afraid I must, madam," he said, not meeting my eye. "Good evening."

"William!" Bessy's face, very red, appeared above us, her dark hair hanging over the stairwell like leafy tendrils. "I am sorry. Do not blame me."

Will Milner didn't look up at her, but blinked, pushed my arm aside, and marched from the house.

Bessy had disappeared, but I hurried up the stairs anyway, with my precious letter pressed against my chest.

How dare she send that poor boy away? Didn't she know how rare it was to find a man who would chase after you? And all the way to Derbyshire? Imagine.

But it was my sister, Mary, who met me when I reached the landing. "This way," she said, her voice curt.

She steered me into her parlor. Nonplussed, I let her guide me. Could she be interfering *again*? I didn't need her help in scolding Bessy. This was my lecture to deliver.

Bessy wasn't in her aunt's parlor. Instead, William Evans was waiting for us by the window, with his back to the door, gazing out across his grounds. The trees were only just visible now through the gloom.

"Bessy has just rejected an offer of marriage from Mr. Milner," said my sister, still hanging on to my arm as if she were afraid to free me.

The pair of them would have me in handcuffs next.

"She was always a silly, unthinking girl," I said, but I didn't pull away. I would show them both that I could be calm, that I still had it in me to be rational. "Will Milner shouldn't mind what she says."

"And she did so on my advice," William Evans said, turning.

"On your advice? But I—" It was better to invoke my dead husband's name than to try to convince my brother-in-law with my own opinions. "Edmund thought an alliance with the Milners most suitable."

I escaped my sister's grip. My arm had stiffened, held viselike by hers. I shook it hard to dispel the numbness.

"Your horizons are limited, Lydia," said William, ignoring the reference to Edmund. "Bessy can do better."

"Better?" I repeated. "Why, how many young men do you think my daughter knows? And have you seen how she conducts herself? She'd be lucky to have another such offer."

"We can help you there, Lyddy." My sister nodded with her eyes stretched wide, as if she were afraid to blink. "William has so many connections in politics and in business. The Jessops, for instance, have a son."

"I don't know any Jessops."

"They own an ironworks," said William. "It does a fine trade."

"And they are very well regarded socially," Mary said, as if in contradiction to this first statement, although she still started her sentence with an "and."

How dare they? We'd been here barely a month, and here they were auctioning off my daughter to the most convenient bidder, using her for their own mercantile and political ends.

"It was not your place to advise my daughter, William," I said, ignoring my sister and holding his gaze. "I am grateful, of course, for all you have given us. But this. There is precious little else I can do for her—for them—now. For God's sake give me this."

I was shaking, although I didn't know why. It had always been difficult for me to distinguish between anger and sadness. The man was unbearable. How had I come to be the one beseeching, rather than admonishing, him?

"Lydia, your judgment is impaired." William Evans strode back to the window and tugged the curtains shut, hemming us in.

"Impaired by what?"

He didn't reply.

"And what do you two know of raising girls or marrying them off?" I pressed on.

Mary flinched beside me. She'd always wanted a daughter but had only had the one son, Thomas, in the end. And birthing him had almost killed her.

"Edmund wanted Bessy to—" I started.

"Edmund asked me to use my discretion when it came to his children," said my brother-in-law. "He knew that you could not be trusted."

"Please, William!" Mary interjected. There was fear in her voice. She didn't want him to say whatever it was that was coming next.

"Go on," I said, not shying away from him. "And why exactly did he say I could not be trusted?"

"You know why," he said, without inflection. His eyes roamed across the letter I held, but my fingers obscured the seal.

"I have no idea—" I started.

"Oh, Lyddy, William, please," Mary cried. She rang the tasseled bell cord as if tea would fix this, or at least as if the presence of another person would delay the fatal blow.

"Edmund left a letter for us," William said. His wife's protests wouldn't halt him now.

"Us?" It was as if I yearned for the pain of hearing the explanation.

"A letter addressed to Charles Thorp and to me."

The pounding of my heart was too loud, drowning out my thoughts. But I held a weapon neither of them knew: a letter from a great, powerful, and titled man. There was still a chance. Maybe, just maybe, Sir Edward Scott was going to save me.

"I didn't believe what he wrote at first," William Evans said. "A tutor? The man was practically your servant and young enough to be your son. But I questioned your staff, and that woman Sewell confirmed it. You have lost all right to be your daughters' compass. You should be grateful we let you set foot in our home. I only did so for Mary and for my nieces' sake."

"Lyddy, no!" Mary called out as I retreated to the door (I could no longer face them). "William only lost his temper. He didn't mean it."

"Oh, but he did, Mary," I said, holding up my hand to signal that she should not touch me. "And he is right. We won't stay longer than a few more days. Only let me make alternative arrangements. Once we are gone, I have no intention of coming back to this Godforsaken place again."

I strode out of her rooms and slammed the door.

"Mama, are you angry?" Bessy had emerged onto the landing.

"Not now, Bessy," I said.

I had to open Sir Edward's letter. It was our only hope.

"Oh, but Mama, I couldn't marry Will Milner." My daughter took a tentative step toward me—her dimpled arm outstretched. "I didn't love him as I should."

"Loving your husband is overrated."

I inched my finger under the crisp corner of the page. My body was craving an answer, his answer; the wax was melting under my nail. But I couldn't open it in front of my daughter. I couldn't have her see my agony if Sir Edward too rebuffed me.

"You think it's enough, then? That Will Milner loves me even if I don't him?" Doubt had crept back into Bessy's voice. Her eyes flitted toward the stairwell.

Yes. I would have said "yes" before—before Branwell, before I'd felt the cracks that marble your body when you're daubed in plaster and set upon a shaking pedestal.

I didn't reply.

"Only I want both, Mama," Bessy said. "I want a love that is even, as Lydia has with Henry—"

"Your sister will die a pauper, and now you may well too."

Bessy's face crumpled. She flew into the room where the girls had been sleeping to sob out her heart on her younger sister's shoulder.

Still no noise from the parlor behind me. Maybe my sister didn't need words to converse with her husband. Maybe she enjoyed what I'd only ever dreamed of—the perfectly matched duet, like those flutists in Scarborough, albeit one that was born of shared smugness and superiority. Maybe that, or perhaps they were both silent, listening for what I would do.

I pulled myself along by the banister and sat on the cold top step. There was dust in the corner where the stair met the wall. I would never have allowed that in my house.

My fingers were shaking so much that in my speed, I tore the paper as I opened it. The ragged scar ran right through Sir Edward's letter.

8th April 1847
Great Barr Hall

My dear Mrs. Robinson (or may I address you as "Cousin Lydia"?),

Pray forgive me for ignoring the instructions in your second letter and for my slow reply to your first. Business kept me from Great Barr Hall for some days.

If you will allow me to make such a presumptive statement, your present situation appears to be intolerable. And I should very much like to provide a solution to your dilemma.

In the strongest terms, I beg you and your daughters to come and visit us, for as long as is convenient for you. My wife shares my wishes, although she is confined to the sickroom. You need only name the day of your arrival.

Come, cousin. We will not "unwoman" you (a curious turn of phrase but a good one, I think).

Yours truly,
Edward Scott

Freedom and with it the sweet salve of flirtation. For that was there, wasn't it, imbuing each word Sir Edward had written with the fizz of a newly lit match?

I would be magnanimous with my sister once we'd been catapulted into a world above hers. I would write her letters, just as before, trading gossip and pleasantries, but without the pretense that there was anything of that childish love left in our hearts. The girls and I would go from Allestree to Great Barr Hall.

And when I arrived there—

But no. Flirtation was one thing but, what with Edmund and Branwell, I might as well have lived through a hundred loves, each more painful than the last. Sir Edward might be saving me, but I would not abdicate my power. I could not allow myself to make the same mistakes again.

NOTHING COULD HAVE BEEN a greater contrast to our arrival at Allestree Hall than our departure. Sir Edward had sent (imagine it!) his very own carriage to collect us. Maids peeked from behind curtains to stare at the livery. The Evanses' grooms inspected every inch of the horses, nodding to each other.

I floated from the house and bid my sister and her husband goodbye with only a perfunctory kiss on her cheek and a pat of his shoulder. "I will do what I can to win you an invitation to Great Barr Hall," I told them. "But I wouldn't want to petition such dear, generous friends so soon."

"Don't trouble yourself," said William Evans, turning to go back inside.

My sister held her jaw so rigid she could not speak.

"I will miss you, Auntie!"

"We will write."

The girls clung to Aunt Mary and said their good-byes with a predictable show of cloying emotion. They had been complaining and weeping for days at the prospect of leaving "Auntie and Uncle."

Yet all that stopped when they saw the plush seats and sheer size of the carriage's interior.

"Sir Edward must be so rich," said Bessy with the low whistle she had learned from her years frequenting the stables.

Little Mary even blushed when William Allison, a man she had known since her infancy, handed her up.

It was easy to be taken aback by the coachman's transformation. His hair was combed, and he wore a fine uniform now he was in the Scotts' employ. He'd given up his wooden pipe for one that might even have been ivory, and his gold buttons winked in the sun as he closed the door behind us.

The amazement on my daughters' faces, as they sat opposite me, acted as a mirror to my own. I, a woman of forty-six, indulged in the daydreams of a girl of sixteen as we sped through the undulating English countryside. This was my pumpkin coach. I was being whisked away to the ball. But when midnight fell, the dream *wouldn't* evaporate. I would have another day and another and another to enjoy this luxury. This must be the delicious freedom men feel when they enter adulthood.

And Great Barr Hall? At the sight of it, my spirit soared even higher. It was everything I had dreamed about when I was a child, acting as my cousin's bridesmaid, and more. It didn't appear to be a house so much as a castle, complete with turrets and lancet windows. The Gothic, sanitized; the romantic, made practical. The estate would be the perfect setting for my happy ending, which felt so close now. Except, of course, for the wife upstairs.

OUR ROOMS WERE LARGE and well appointed, and scores of servants bobbed to me at every turn. Within a week, Sir Edward hosted a dinner so rich it put to shame all other meals I had tasted for years—a dinner held in honor of our arrival.

"You have the appearance of a woman who is looking for something, cousin." Sir Edward brought his cigar to his mouth and puffed. "I hope we don't disappoint you."

He and the other gentlemen, a handful of middle-aged local digni-taries, had just rejoined us in the drawing room. The ladies were few—Bessy, Mary, and me, along with one of the men's wives, who was snoozing in an armchair.

"We?" I laughed but stopped mid-peal. Sir Edward might consider me rude and think I was referring to his wife's conspicuous absence, when she was the only pretense for kinship between us.

I had not seen Lady Scott, the mysterious wife in the attic, in the few days we'd been at Great Barr Hall. The army of servants was always talking about her in whispers, as if they were in a library or crypt, and carrying heaped trays of food to her room before toting them, just as full, back downstairs a few hours later.

"I couldn't think of being disappointed," I said, hiding behind my fan. "Being here at Great Barr Hall, this welcome, all of it. It is wonder-ful. I am so grateful to you—to both of you. My daughters and I owe you so much."

Sir Edward smiled at my earnest expression of gratitude. Could he guess that he'd always been at the center of my rendition of an age-old fantasy? That his name had been writ large on the pages of my youth-ful imagination and folded into the very fabric of my being?

He tapped ash into the bowl on the side table between us. It was Irish crystal and cast stunted rainbows on the dark wood tabletop. "Can I tell you a secret, cousin?" he asked, leaning closer.

My eyes stung at the smell of smoke, the unapologetic masculinity of it.

"Of course." I lowered my fan so he wouldn't see it shaking.

"Great Barr is a bore," he said. "There. I've said it."

"No!" I cried, thinking he was joking and trying to make the merri-ment dance in my eyes, as Lydia would have had she been here in place of her moping sisters.

"Look around you," he said.

A retired lieutenant colonel was pontificating on politics to the re-maining gentleman. The only other lady was still asleep, her chins resting on her lace collar. And Bessy was thumping away at the pianoforte as Mary turned the pages, often at the wrong moment.

I laughed, but pulled myself up when I saw his face. He was serious.

"This isn't living." He extinguished his cigar and glanced toward Bessy as she struck another false note. "My sons are away. My wife is ill, as she has been these God knows how many years."

"My husband was also unwell for some time." My gaze dropped to the fan on my lap.

"Oh?"

I looked up and caught the slight raise of Sir Edward's eyebrows.

"I thought Edmund Robinson's illness was sudden?" he said.

"Yes." I paused, feeling as if he'd caught me in a lie. "That is, for a time, to the outside world he appeared himself, but I knew otherwise. After all, I was his wife."

And am his wife yet.

I became aware of my wedding ring, as warm as my skin. I had worn it so long it might as well have been a part of me.

Sir Edward scanned my face, seemed to come to some conclusion, and smiled. "Perhaps, Cousin Lydia, you can bring some life to this place, you and your daughters?" he said, his voice soft. The darkness that had come into his eyes had ebbed away. "Although I hope you don't mind my saying that Miss Bessy's playing leaves something to be desired."

"Say no more." I jumped up, desperate to please him. "I will displace her."

The rest of the evening wasn't long. How could it be with such tiresome company? But for me, it was intoxicating. I played as I hadn't for a long time, basking in Sir Edward's admiration, even if, for politeness's sake, he couldn't devote himself absolutely to listening to me but had to enter into conversation with his dull guests.

At Thorp Green Hall in those months after Edmund's burial, I'd played out only my soul's misery but here there was something else, something bright and hopeful. And as the music ran through me, Lady Scott retreated to where she had always been: in the shadowy recesses. She was an obstacle only as substantial as the thoughts you gave to it.

I was still humming the final tune—a waltz—by the time I was in my rooms. I dismissed my cousin Catherine's maid—a real French maid who braided my hair with dexterity and skill, even if she didn't stroke my forehead and caress my shoulders as Marshall had—as soon as I was in my nightgown. And I went through the rest of those mechanical steps that precede slumber alone. I tugged at my ring and set it on the dressing table. It teetered and rattled like a spinning top.

What was this? A letter? I hadn't noticed it before, perched between my perfume bottles. The hand was unfamiliar and, from the postmark, I could see that the missive had been redirected from Allestree Hall. I opened it, trying to remember the scent of Sir Edward's cigars, deeper, richer, than Edmund's.

16th April 1847
Aldborough

Mrs. Robinson,

My sister, Ann, went to God this morning. She spoke of you to the last.

Sending my gratitude for your kind treatment of her,
Jane Atkinson

I could have screamed. Marshall, my Marshall. And just when I'd felt the first stirrings of joy inside me at last. Was this mercy? Was this God's love, which Reverend Lascelles had promised me? If He existed, it seemed God was determined never to allow me another day's happiness.

8th June 1847
Manchester

Dear Mrs. Robinson,

My wife was delivered of a healthy boy yesterday, 7th June 1847, weighing a round eight pounds. Her labor was mercifully short and mother and baby are both well and resting. Lydia bids me send you, and her sisters, her love.

We plan to christen our son "Henry Edmund," uniting my name with your late husband's. It is our hope that, harsh as Mr. Robinson's treatment was toward his daughter on account of our union, soon our families may come closer together in honor of his memory.

Any token you can send for the benefit of your grandchild would be appreciated by both of us. We are behind on rent by some weeks.

Ever your devoted son-in-law,
Henry Roxby

23rd August 1847
Great Barr Hall

My dear daughter Lydia,

How is little Henry Edmund, my grandson? Is he still suffering
with colic? I do wish to see him and judge for myself if he has
the look of your father about him.

But for you and your husband to come to Great Barr
Hall is, I hope you know, for the time, impossible. Sir
Edward is kindness itself; so accommodating and attentive, a
consummate gentleman. But I cannot countenance inviting an
infant and an actor into his well-ordered home.

Enclosed instead is a check. Use it well and do not think
that the frequency of my gifts to you over the last few months
is set to continue.

Be wise, Lydia. Drag your husband up with all your might,
if you have to. And, above all, avoid the expense of having
another child. You owe it to your sweet boy.

Bessy wishes to add a postscript. I will turn the page to
have her write there.

Lydia,

A piece of gossip from back home, for the Ouseburns are
our home and Mary and I miss them. Great Barr Hall may
be very grand but we have no friends here and are beyond
bored. Well, to the news.

Remember Henrietta Thompson, the confirmed
spinster? Would you believe she is a spinster no more? She
married that painter who came to Kirby Hall to do the

family's portraits! And back in April, too. Fancy that we
only heard of it now! I presumed you would not know of
it either. It is not likely Amelia would have kept up her
correspondence with you, all things considered.

With love, your sister,
Bessy

Lydia, do not heed your sister's complaints. She was always
prone to sulking. Great Barr Hall is as good a home as any of
us could wish for.

Your mother,
Lydia Robinson

CHAPTER NINETEEN

"THERE IS SOMETHING ON your mind today, Lydia," said Sir Edward as we took our accustomed turn about the grounds.

He had given up the "Cousin" months before. We were something else—something better though less certain—to each other now.

"Yes. Edmund's mother," I said. "She has written."

The sky was the color of amber, and with the sun playing peekaboo above the horizon, I had to shield my eyes to look at him. The occasional browned leaf had already fallen, plotting our course across the grass (there were no paths here) like litter from an old parade.

"And what does she say?" Sir Edward asked. I could feel his confusion that I hadn't volunteered this information sooner.

Usually during our walks, I played the role of entertainer. I'd retell the plots of novels he didn't have the time or inclination to read, teach him about music (he had a good ear but had never studied with a master), and ask for explanations of the latest speeches in the Lords and Commons. These I read to him from the newspaper each morning in his study. By the time this ritual was finished, it was sometimes past noon.

"Where have you been, Mama? Reading to Sir Edward all this time?" Bessy would ask, her expression skeptical.

She was getting impertinent, as was Mary, for that matter.

It was true that Sir Edward did wish to have me near him more and more. But perhaps that was because he missed his wife rather than because he found me charming. I tried not to hope, imagine, dream, that he or the house or any of it could be mine, and fixed my mind instead on the image of Lady Scott as she had been the one time that I had seen her.

She'd been pale, yes, with yellowed cheeks and palsy in her hands, but she was still heartier and more solid than most invalids I'd seen in my time. She didn't have the look of one standing at death's threshold. And it horrified me that I wished she did.

Sometimes I dreamed that she stood beside my bed, glaring down at me and angry at my secret desires. Once she was joined by another figure—short, shadowy, and slight. I understood, although we had never met, that this was Charlotte Brontë. The figures flanked my bed on either side. Each grabbed one of my hands so I could not escape. And then, with a smirk, Charlotte touched a flickering candle to the curtain of my bed, enveloping me with fire. I awoke screaming and screaming that they'd come to kill me, but Great Barr Hall was large and no one heard my cries. That was probably just as well.

I hadn't yet risked much with Sir Edward. I hadn't shown him anything of my true self or spoken with him on those subjects that mattered most. And neither had I, as I had over the course of months with Branwell, talked of nothing at all, luxuriating in discussions that begged no firm conclusion. It was tiring, always calculating how I might appear best, but what other options were open to me? If I had to tie myself to a mast—and I had to—it might as well be to the one on the grandest, proudest ship.

"Edmund's mother says she misses her granddaughters," I answered. This was part of the truth, at least. "She accuses me of keeping them from her."

Sir Edward's brow furrowed. A strong, steady, principled man like him couldn't resist coming to the aid of the mistreated or weak. "Was Edmund's family unfair to you?" he asked at last.

We had stopped. He took a step closer to me.

I shrugged one shoulder and dropped my chin to my chest, but I couldn't even summon a single tear. Had the stream run dry? Had I shed them all? For Marshall, Edmund, Father, Mother, Georgie?

"Lydia?" He was used to having his own way.

"There are many wives who have been happier," I said, after a pause. I mustn't overstate my case, overplay my hand. Sir Edward was such a solid, unemotional man that in doing so, I might lose him.

"Because," he spoke on, "if you are fond of her and she so wishes to see the children, you know Edmund's mother would be more than welcome here."

"No!" I cried.

That startled him.

"No," I repeated more softly, correcting myself. "She cannot. Please."

My vehemence had taken him by surprise. His face had a hardness about it I hadn't seen before. There was a small bead of doubt glimmering in his eye. "Show me," he said.

"Show you what?" I asked. But I knew what he wanted. I took a step away from him.

"Show me her letter," he said, holding out his hand.

I twisted over my shoulder toward Great Barr Hall, whose turreted towers were gleaming in the final fiery flood of light.

Could I say I had left it in my room? No, I had been with Sir Edward since the afternoon post had arrived, and we'd each read our respective correspondence in silence. He would know I was being untruthful.

"Lydia," he said. From his tone, he might have been my father, although he wasn't that much older than me.

I could refuse, but then all intimacy between us would be over. He would not trust my word again.

I retrieved the paper from inside my pelisse and nearly dropped it as I handed it to him.

That witch and her bitter accusations. It was just like that woman to blight my last chance of happiness, even from leagues away.

Sir Edward read and reread the letter for a long time, and I studied him for as long, but his face was unmoving, like the bust of an inscrutable Roman senator. "Lydia," he said at last. "What does Mrs. Robinson mean by this?"

He held the page toward me, but I could not see without my reading glasses, which I'd left in his study.

"I cannot—" I stuttered. "What does she say?"

He pivoted into the last of the light.

"She talks of 'Bessy and Mary learning from your shameful behavior' and says—" He swallowed. "She says 'you are running after a married man now, as you did a serving man before'?" He turned this last charge into a question. His proud face was the color of the reddening sky behind him.

"I am not running after you," I said quickly.

Worst of all accusations! It was the place of a woman to be pursued, hunted, felled, not to throw herself at any man, especially not her host as his wife lay dying.

"Never mind that." He flapped the page for emphasis. "A servant? A—" He took a step toward me. His voice dropped in pitch. "Not the coachman, Allison? Don't tell me I've played the part of an unwitting fool in keeping the two of you together."

"William Allison?" I repeated, horrified, before he finished his sentence. "No, Edward, no."

I hadn't called him just Edward before. My hand was on his shoulder.

He glanced at it as if he might cast me off.

"May I explain?" I asked.

"Yes." He broke from me and massaged his forehead as he walked away. "I thought— Please explain."

His distress was confirmation of what I had only hoped before. My performance had been virtuosic and my arrows had found their mark. Sir Edward would believe me no matter what story I concocted and would accept any explanation that preserved the place I had held in his thoughts before now. And this meant that I would be acting always—not just until Catherine died, until Sir Edward confessed his love, until we were married. I wouldn't be a woman at all but a mannequin, forever holding a convoluted pose in the tableau of his home, his castle.

"Ned was not always away from us," I said. "Before Edmund died—I mentioned the girls' governess, I know. But there was a tutor too. Her brother."

Sir Edward ground a weed into the lawn with the toe of his shoe but remained silent.

"And this tutor, he—" *He saved me and destroyed me all at once, taught me I could still feel so I could discover that I needed more than him.* "He was a drunkard."

The word had a harsh sound to it. But I had to follow the pattern I had set for myself and sew Sir Edward a new story, the canonical tapestry of our shared life from this point forward, were my life to be tied to his.

I went on. "He was a drunkard, a failure, brought up in an industrial town on the edges of the bleak moors by a doting father along with a pack of unmarriageable sisters—Anne placid, Emily tormented, Charlotte stern. He'd been dismissed by the railway, was unskilled in painting, and deluded about the poetry he composed when he should have been giving lessons."

No reaction.

"I did not, of course, know all this at the beginning," I added, with a touch more desperation. Maybe I had painted Branwell too darkly. "Edmund managed the man's appointment, and I, of course, deferred to my husband."

"How could he?" asked Sir Edward, his reaction cued as an audience's at a pantomime. "How could Edmund have let such a man around his wife and children, into his house?"

I took these questions as rhetorical. "At first, I admit, I showed some kindness to Mr. Brontë—that was the tutor's name. And, more so, to the governess, his sister. She was a sickly, quiet girl, with little to recommend her. But I took to her as if she'd been my own."

"Of course." He nodded. "Quite so."

"The pair of them dined with us on occasion. I gave her my old clothes and the bookish brother run of our library. They even had a holiday of sorts in the summers when they accompanied us to Scarborough."

"You were too kind, Lydia," said Sir Edward. Somehow he was beside me again. "People like that never know their place."

I nodded. "So I found out, to my horror. Mr. Brontë, he— I can hardly say it."

"He fell in love with you." Sir Edward caught my gloved hand in his.

I didn't disagree. "He dogged my steps, wrote me poems, and even published some, under a nom de plume, in the local newspaper. And when I went to Edmund, later perhaps than I should have—"

"He didn't believe you," said Sir Edward, squeezing my hand harder.

"Worse. He accused me of encouraging Mr. Brontë, and believed the slanders of his jealous mother over me."

"Lydia, my darling, how could they?" Sir Edward pulled me close and planted a kiss on my temple.

"And now she has poisoned you against me too." I sprang from him, nearly tripping on a tree root that had been hiding in the grass. "You, a married man, take me in your arms and kiss me. You must think I am a— Or too weak to resist you."

"No! No! Lydia, it is I who am weak, not you." Sir Edward was pacing and looking at intervals toward the upper windows of the Hall.

Inside Catherine was waiting for him. He always went to her around sunset, although the hours he spent each evening at her bedside had dwindled soon after I had arrived.

"God, what are we to do?" he said. "You have no home, nowhere else to go. And besides, you have grown so *necessary* to me." He stopped himself from touching me this time, but the impulse was there. I could tell.

Winning the admiration of such a man—a baronet—was meant to be difficult. This was the prize I had coveted since girlhood, so how had I won it so easily?

"I will be strong for us," I said. "Make sure we don't give in." What I felt inside was far from lust. It was hard to believe that I had been the woman on the dovecote floor or in George Walker's bed with Branwell. "I have held steadfast before, Sir Edward. In the face of my husband's distrust, his mother's cruelty, and Mr. Brontë's infatuation. I can do so again."

"Oh, Lydia, marry me!" he cried.

Why, with some men, was a woman's indifference so appealing?

My hand was in his once more, and he was kneeling on the grass, gazing up on me as at an altar.

"Rise, Sir Edward, please." I tried to drag him up but was not strong enough. "It is too early for that. You still have a wife. Would you compromise my position and force me into leaving?"

"No," he said, scrambling to his feet. "No, I would not. Lydia, please forgive me."

"MAMA?"

Odd. The girls knew never to interrupt my toilette. Yet both of them had entered my room just when I was waiting for Lady Scott's maid to prepare me for tonight's dinner, the first in a series of festive entertainments in the weeks before Christmas.

"You aren't wearing that," I said.

Bessy's dress was torn at the hem. And Mary had been wearing the same gown for days. At this rate, they would make us look every inch the poor relations when Sir Edward's guests arrived.

My new gown lay on the bed in preparation for its debut. The beading around the neckline glinted at me in the candlelight.

Maybe that was it? Were Bessy and Mary jealous I hadn't ordered anything for them? But they would be out of mourning soon, unlike me, and getting not just one new gown but many. This had been my first extravagance in months. I'd had a dressmaker travel from Birmingham to take my measurements, although I hadn't gained or lost an inch in years.

"We're not coming to the dinner," Bessy said.

Mary nodded, her eyes downcast.

"Nonsense. I might even have something of mine for you to wear," I said, trying to be consolatory. I rose from the dressing table and gestured toward the open armoire.

The girls had to be there tonight. It wouldn't do for me to be the only lady. Great Barr Hall was a destination, I'd found, for widowers and escapee husbands. Here, with Lady Scott safely out of sight and Sir Edward's wine cellar open for business, they could fly, for a night at least, on the wings of a second bachelorhood.

"It is not about our clothes, Mama," said Bessy. "We"—she gulped— "we don't wish to witness you making a spectacle of yourself."

"Making a spectacle of myself?" I repeated. "Mary, what is your sister saying?" I rounded on the weaker half of their partnership.

"I am saying that you are behaving disgracefully, Mother," said Bessy, answering for her sister. "And that Sir Edward is too."

"What exactly is it that you say we are doing?" I asked, walking past them to secure the door.

I couldn't have the lady's maid overhear us, for all that her English was limited.

"Why, flirting," said Bessy, haltingly.

"And what do you know of flirting?" I laughed. "Oh, yes, you wrote a few foolish letters to Will Milner once. I hope he's burned them. Did you bid him do so when you sent him away at Allestree?"

She lit up like a lantern.

"Oh, Mama," said Mary, taking Bessy's confusion as her opportunity to try a different tactic. *"Mightn't we go home to Thorp Green?"*

God knows how she thought we'd afford that.

"Or, if not home," she added, following up quickly, "back to Allestree, to Auntie and Uncle? There is nothing for us here."

Nothing here? There was nothing at Allestree Hall, except fading into the wallpaper as my sister and her husband used the girls as pawns in their scheming games.

"Enough," I said. There was no time to disillusion the pair of them about the Evanses now. I had to look dazzling. My hair was too flat, my complexion dull. "If you wish for a change of scene, the pair of you may have one. Your grandmother has given up Green Hammerton, but I'm sure Christmas at her new apartments in York will be just as entertaining as Easter used to be at the Hall."

"Send us to Grandmama?" said Bessy, recovering. "You wouldn't."

"I will if you do not get dressed for dinner at once," I said, walking to and opening the door.

My daughters looked at each other in a fleeting conference.

"We're not coming, Mama," said Mary. "We are sorry."

The door closed behind them. I inhaled and turned back to what needed to be done.

THE MAID'S FINGERS WERE clumsy, my hair wouldn't sit right, a fastening on the new dress kept coming undone. I was late by the time I joined the gentlemen in the dining room.

"There she is," said Sir Edward as I swept in, smiling apologies. "The inimitable Mrs. Robinson!"

Some of the gentlemen had already taken their seats, but at my entrance, they all stood to greet me.

My hand was pressed, shaken, kissed, as I danced the dance of greeting with all five visitors. After a dizzying turn, I at last took my place on Sir Edward's right.

My suited companions dropped down likewise, as regimented as a battalion.

"How do you like Great Barr Hall, Mrs. Robinson?" asked the bespectacled man on the other side of me.

Innocuous as the question was, he wasn't the only one awaiting my answer. There were other snatches of conversation and other voices, Sir Edward's foremost amongst them (was he, he couldn't be, drunk?), but the energy in the room centered on me.

"How could one not like Great Barr Hall?" I said, laughing a little too hard and drinking deep of the jewel-colored wine in the glass before me.

That was what men did when alone, wasn't it? They told jokes and attempted to outwit each other in one breath, debated the future of our country in the next. I could do the former, or at least appreciate and mirror their humor. For what man doesn't enjoy the accompaniment of a woman's twinkling laugh as he jests? But as for the latter—

As pleasantries and introductions gave way to more serious topics, my supremacy over the room fell away. I drank heavily, although it was Sir Edward, with the abandon of Branwell and the authority of Edmund, who called for another bottle and another and another. I pretended to understand as the gentlemen made jibes at the expense of absent friends and each other and to listen as my interlocutor made his arguments against the necessity of another Reform Bill.

Loquacious as he was tonight, Sir Edward didn't say a word to me, so at times I had nobody to talk to at all. Then I'd crane my neck to catch the drift of the discussion opposite, leaning so low my breasts nearly skimmed the gravy in their soft black silk.

Now and then an image of the girls as they might be some years from now seemed to swim before me. There was Lydia, burdened under the weight of another pregnancy, as four poorly dressed children clung at her skirts. Bessy and Mary, married ladies now, sat with my sister, William Evans, and their immortal grandmother, all of them laughing at me, reminiscing about the time I'd thrown myself at a tutor. And the Brontë sisters were huddled together in a corner, united by a secret

I could not fathom, until William Evans invited them to join the rest of the party, lifting a glass and crying, "To Charlotte!"

Soon my exclusion became unbearable. I should tap Sir Edward on the shoulder and make a wry observation. That would prompt my readmittance to the conversation. Yet the thing was, I had nothing to say. I had no opinions on anything that mattered.

Instead, I pressed my leg against Sir Edward's. Hard. It had to be hard for me to feel him at all through my voluminous skirts. He didn't react, in kind or otherwise. I pressed again. Could I risk moving my hand to his knee, telling him to acknowledge me in a gesture that was half reprimand and half caress?

At last, after an out-of-turn laugh of mine prompted a frown from an older gentleman opposite, I risked it. Sir Edward's knee was bony and cool. He wasn't burning up like I was.

A second later, his hand touched mine, but not to stroke it. He lifted my fist and deposited it back in my lap, without so much as breaking the flow of his political argument.

I went to drink again but found my glass was empty. I twisted for the footman. No sign of him. In the last few minutes, without me even noticing, our dessert plates had melted away. But everyone else still had wine. In my urge to keep up with them had I been drinking too quickly?

"Lydia," whispered Sir Edward, just when I had given up hope that he would remember me and begun to curse him inwardly, laying that terrible charge against him that he was "just like Edmund."

"Yes?" I smiled, but then covered my mouth with my napkin. Had the wine stained my lips and teeth?

"Don't you think it is time for you to leave us?" he asked, softly.

He was trying to save me embarrassment, but the eyes of the other men were on me again. Of course. Why would it be any different because I was the *only* woman? I was no longer wanted here.

"Oh. Yes." I scraped back my chair too violently. It screeched across the flagstone floor, putting an end to the remaining fragments of conversation. "Gentlemen," I said, rising. "I will retire, I think, to the draw-ing room."

My eyes swept around the table, alighting last on Sir Edward. He was shaking his head. "No. There is no need for you to wait up for us, Lydia," he said.

What was he thinking, using my Christian name before them? I flushed.

"Or perhaps, to bed," I added to the company, fighting to smile. "Good night."

I had to battle my way back to the door, returning handshakes and acknowledging kisses planted on my knuckles, even one bestowed on my cheek. But that particular gentleman had spent years on the Conti-nent, hadn't he? That was the custom there. He didn't mean any of-fense by it. Or had that been his friend?

The corridor was cold and dark, save for the sliver of warm light be-neath the door behind me. Male voices rose and fell behind it.

This was their world, not mine. And in their world, I could only ever be on the peripheries, setting the stage and ornamenting the room, be-fore slipping away like a servant or a shadow. That was a fact as ines-capable as church on Sundays. And yet I couldn't leave. Not yet. I couldn't creep upstairs through the chilly, yet somehow still close, air. I couldn't go from that animated scene to an empty bed or to Bessy, with her puppet, Mary, facing judgment from the children I had made.

I crouched by the door, brought my ear to the wood, and then lower still, to the crack below.

It took some time to distinguish between their voices as there was little variation in pitch, but after around a minute I could make them out, Sir Edward's dominating.

Funny. I could follow the train of the conversation better when I wasn't *meant* to be listening, now I was under no pressure to perform. There were even a couple of questions I would have asked my former bespectacled conversation partner had he been lecturing me.

But then Sir Edward's voice cut across the heated debate. "Gentlemen," he said. I imagined he was raising his glass (as large as those we'd had earlier but now filled with bloodstain-purple port). "You have not told me what you all think of my Mrs. Robinson."

My veins turned to ice.

"She is a very fine woman," said one. Could it be he who was too nervous before to take my hand without stuttering? "For her age," he added.

This solicited a collective laugh.

"And keen, no doubt." This surely was the European traveler. "You know what they say about widows!"

More laughter, this time accompanied by the arrhythmic drumming of several pairs of hands on the table. The splashes of red would dot the freshly laundered tablecloth.

"Are her daughters as lively?" said one. "Is her hair all hers?" asked another. But those questions went unanswered.

"What I want to know, Scott," said the nervous man, buoyed no doubt by his earlier success, "is *what is it like?*"

"What is what like?" asked Sir Edward, all mirth gone from his voice.

Was this the limit, then? Had the guest overstepped?

"Why, what it's like having *two* wives?" The man crescendoed as he delivered his punch line.

Guffawing.

"Now, now, Theodore, that's enough," said the master of the house, through a low chuckle.

I stumbled to my feet, my joints aching from my unnatural position and the cold, but not before I had heard another man compliment Sir Edward on his "veritable harem."

No good comes to those who eavesdrop, I'd told Lydia when she was a small, inquisitive child. I had only myself to blame for ignoring my own lesson today.

I didn't have a lamp or candle and so had to feel my way up the winding, uneven stairs. Great Barr Hall, of course, was Gothic to a tee, inside as well as out, and difficult to navigate in the dark. The corridors were deserted. The servants must have anticipated a night of drinking, finished their duties, and gone to bed, registering the timbre of the evening before me.

I had to breathe, resist the urge to fly back in there to berate the men or to pack my bags, write accusing letters, weep with abandon until Sir Edward came to calm me.

However good you were, there would be men who thought you a whore or spoke of you as such in your absence. But that didn't mean, as I'd thought for a time, that all men fell into both camps or that you had to prove them right. Sir Edward might speak of me like this to his friends, but he also kept a respectful distance from me, for now. He hadn't repeated his overtures from that day on the lawn. Instead he deferred to my power—the power the woman ought to hold until a couple's wedding day.

I stumbled back into my room. There now. My anger had passed.

I'd seen a sketch once, in a book of natural wonders, of a sort of lizard—a chameleon—that could melt into the foliage behind it. Yet he could also change himself to match the desert, the bark, even the sky. People like that were life's survivors. Those who, like Branwell Brontë, clung to a fixed vision, a dream, of themselves or of others, were doomed to disappointment, hoist by their own petard.

Lydia,

I swear you are trying to hound me, an old woman, to my
grave.

First, you thrust those daughters of yours on me, and just
before Christmas, when servants, without a care in the world
for their mistresses' inconvenience, insist on taking holidays.
(Bessy's table manners are appalling, by the way. However did
you raise her?)

And, next, my home is set upon by a woman who claims
to know me. An upstart young farmer's wife in a dress more
fashionable than it was warm or, for that matter, decent. She
arrived in a fury, but at last I managed to wring from her who
she was. I've already forgotten her name but that matters not.
Prior to her marriage, and its attendant frippery, she went by
"Sewell."

Sewell, I thought. It does have a familiar ring. And then
it came to me. This Harpy was once my poor lost son's
housekeeper.

No sooner had she won access to me than this woman
dissolved into unconvincing tears. She confirmed who she was,
simpering when she mentioned her marriage and holding out
her hand to show me her little brass ring. Did she expect this
to impress me?

When I advised her to state the purpose of her visit before
I had her removed, she got to it. She had come to protest the
dismissal of her "poor brother" at your hands. He'd received
your letter a few days before and was distraught, she said,

to be so ill used when he had been such a dutiful steward to my son. She evoked Edmund's memory, expressed her condolences, and begged me to petition you on her brother's behalf.

She understands nothing of my grief. She has not even carried a child inside her, let alone buried two. Yet my heart softened a little as she spoke of my Edmund and his goodness and how you, and you alone, had poisoned his home.

Listen here, Lydia. I need hardly tell you what I made of my visitor. But we can't have disgruntled servants running off to new positions throughout the county, reporting your sins to all and sundry. What were you thinking in dismissing Sewell? Have you no sense? His sister may be a piece of work, but the man is unobjectionable. Didn't I hire him myself while you were bedridden by a mere pregnancy?

I insist you write to him at once and undo his dismissal.

Ever hopeful of a change in you for the better,
I remain, your mother, in law only,
Elizabeth Robinson

29th January 1848
Great Barr Hall

Mr. Sewell,

I hereby retract my previous letter. You may keep your post as steward for as long as you like, as long as you and your insufferable sister leave my family in peace.

I remain, sir, yours very truly,
Lydia Robinson

3rd February 1848
York

Mama,

Mary and I want to come back. May we rejoin you at Great
Barr Hall?

Do write to us and say that we may.

Grandmama is dreadful, perhaps worse than before.

She quite ambushed me yesterday. I went downstairs
for breakfast and (horror of horrors!) Will Milner was in our
apartments waiting for me. She had let him in!

He held fast my hand and argued his case, although it has
been a year since I last saw him. And he would not leave until
I cried.

Once he was gone, Grandmama accused me of being a
flirt, screamed that I was "my mother's daughter," and told me
I was to go without pudding for a week.

I swear I would have gone into hysterics, were Mary not
there to comfort me.

Send for us, please. Or say we can go to Auntie and Uncle
at Allestree Hall.

Your loving daughter,
Bessy

6th February 1848
Great Barr Hall

My dear daughters,

I am sorry to report that Lady Scott's health has deteriorated. Sir Edward is quite unable to accommodate any more visitors at present.

You expressed a desire to leave me, and so I sent you to your grandmother. Now you appear to dislike your grandmother as much as you do me. I cannot deal with such capriciousness.

If you were to go to your Aunt Mary, you'd be sure to hate her too within a fortnight, as you do anyone who tries to curb you.

Life isn't always pleasant. We cannot always act in accordance with our own desires.

Bessy, if your need for change is so pressing, you could always consider accepting young Milner's persistent (if rather melodramatic) proposal. My mind on the matter remains unchanged.

With affection, I remain, very truly, your mother,
Lydia Robinson

Lydia,

Your daughters, I thought you should know, arrived at Allestree Hall around a week ago, mercifully unharmed. They traveled unaccompanied by stagecoach to escape the tyrannies of their grandmother, looking like bedraggled orphans by the time they reached our doorstep.

They are welcome here. In fact, upon hearing of your proceedings at Great Barr Hall, William and I must insist that this become, for the foreseeable future, their home. Bessy and Mary are good, honest girls, with fine futures before them. Mind you do nothing to jeopardize their prospects further.

Sending prayers for your soul and for our cousin
Catherine's recovery,
I remain, your sister,
Mary Evans

CHAPTER TWENTY

I HAD RARELY GONE into the sickroom during my time at Great Barr Hall but, as fate would have it, I was the one who was with Lady Scott at the end.

We—Sir Edward and I—had thought it best when his sons hurried home for the crisis for me to appear useful and take shifts by his wife's bedside. I was a widow who had watched my husband and daughter die. That marked me out as Death's custodian in this house full of men.

We were lounging through the dog days of summer, but it was gloomy in Catherine's chamber at night and in the day. I could see only a hint of sunshine at the edge of one of the heavy tapestried curtains. Otherwise the room was lit by candles and one solitary lamp, which was shaded by a black veil, as if it were sentient and already in mourning.

I sat as far from the bed as possible and tried not to look at her. To do so was to confront myself. The instinct of the living to avoid the dying coupled with my guilt that her liberation would be my salvation. But the poor woman's breath was a constant reminder of her presence and an unwanted accompaniment to my latest novel. When my eyes slid from the page to her, the stories that her face told horrified me.

She was scared. She was confused and angry. She didn't understand who I was.

A clock somewhere down the echoing, uncarpeted landing struck three. Another hour until the nurse came to relieve me. Sir Edward and the "boys," as he still called them, were out riding and enjoying the summer weather while I was shut up inside. For months I had lived under the rays of his near-constant attention, but now that his sons were here, the master of the house no longer needed me.

"Write some letters to while away the hours," he'd told me that morning, kissing my cheek (he did that now) and assuring me he was grateful for "my service to dear Catherine."

But whom was there to write to? I'd written to Dr. Crosby so much I feared he'd tired of me. I pictured a younger, more vivacious woman at his side, or a sandy-haired man, little more than a boy, sneaking through the side entrance of the doctor's house to visit him at night. And I hadn't heard from my son or my sister or my daughters—not for months.

"Edward."

I jumped and twisted toward the door before realizing it was Lady Scott who had spoken.

This was new.

I didn't stand but leaned toward the bed, steeling myself for blood, excrement, vomit, delirium. Anything but the unthinkable: her recovery.

"Edward," Catherine said a little louder. This time her body was thrashing.

I put down my book and went to her. Up close, I could smell her, or, rather, each day, week, month since she'd last bathed.

Her hand grasped mine. She was still wearing her wedding ring.

"He's not here," I said.

The sound of my voice quieted her. Without the creaking of the bed and the dull thump of her arm against the pillow, there it was again. Her breathing.

"Stay," she whispered, and a memory fell across me like sunlight.

"Stay," she'd whispered once before, on Valentine's Day many years ago when I'd acted as her sullen bridesmaid.

But she hadn't said it to me. Why would she? I was fifteen and foolish. I'd believed that the ceremony itself was the most important moment of the wedding day. Besides, I'd been surly, for what I'd thought then to be my heart was breaking. What was I worth if this man who would be a baronet hadn't chosen me, if I was only standing at the edges of the scene?

Yet "stay," Catherine had said to my fellow bridesmaids, and although the rest of them must have known what she meant, we all left her anyway. We'd had our own lives to live, our futures to protect, and she had her side of the bargain she'd made for herself to fulfill.

"Hush now," I said, more to reassure me than her. Catherine, the ghost of what I could have been and one day still could, would, be.

The silence became terrible, like audible darkness.

The weight of it pressed on me, but the truth took some minutes to register.

Silence meant she was no longer breathing.

Lady Scott had gone.

Two days later, finally, Sir Edward and I were alone.

Since the moment when Death had transformed Great Barr, when the nurse had found me, staring at Catherine's cooling hand in mine, he and I had had only hasty conversations. These were a reprieve for him between dealing with undertakers and clergy, comforting the "boys," and greeting relations. But they were sweet manna to me.

I'd been tied to the sickroom for so long I wasn't sure what to do with myself now I had my freedom. I practiced the piano, drifting from one tune to the next, or read a few pages of the latest novel Mr. Bellerby had sent me—*Jane Eyre* by one Currer Bell. The topic, however, the life of a governess, held little interest for me. What did a governess, barely out of the nursery herself, know of life and love?

"Oh, Lydia," Sir Edward said, closing the parlor door and walking over to me. "Tell me it gets easier."

"It gets easier," I said, mechanically.

He sat next to me on the low divan and leaned his head on my shoulder.

"Once the service is over, everyone will leave and—"

"But it does me good to have the boys here," Sir Edward said, raising his head.

"Of course. But, I mean, we will be just *us*."

He said nothing.

What if he didn't want me now all obstacles were gone? What if I never had him to myself again? Or had never had him at all, had merely acted the part of a diversion?

"How much longer need we wait?" I blurted out.

Sir Edward cocked an eyebrow. For me, asking this was the culmination of constant and many questions, but my plea had taken him by surprise.

"Mightn't you wait until Catherine is buried, at least, Lydia?" There was an edge in his voice.

I chose to ignore it. "But how much longer after that?"

"I hardly see any harm in waiting." Sir Edward slid open his initialed case and started to play with a cigar, spinning it between his hands before chewing the end. I doubted he had any intention of lighting it.

"That is easy for you to say," I whispered.

"Hmm?"

"I said, 'That is easy for you to say,'" I repeated a little louder, shocking him into replacing his cigar in the case. "But for me, my whole life has been waiting. Waiting to be asked, waiting to be visited. Human beings must have action, or they will make it themselves. When I think of myself, it is as a figure standing at the window, or poised for laughter should the gentlemen enter the drawing room, or listening for the squeak of my bedroom door hinges at night. Waiting is all there is. That's all I've had and I can't—I won't—have it anymore." I made to stand but Sir Edward caught me by the elbow and reeled me to him. The final words of my tirade were muffled against his chest.

"I know you are upset, Lydia," he said.

"But you don't know," I said, pulling away. "I have been waiting for you since I was a girl. You should have been mine, but you chose her— Catherine. And if you'd only waited a year or two, it might have been me."

My hurt was foolish when said aloud. For the first time, one of our interactions was slipping from my control. I followed the pattern of the rich red rug under my slippers to try to right myself.

Sir Edward caught my hand and kissed it. "You are a goose, Lydia. Did I really meet you back then?"

I nodded through my welling tears.

"We will marry soon," he said. "Just a few months more. I promise. I have been thinking that dear Lady Bateman might manage things. She is a sensible woman, for all she was fond of Catherine. She will know how to make this right."

My tears dried. I threw my arms around his neck and kissed his cheek.

This was it. I had won the laurel in the first negotiation in the first chapter of our marriage. So why wasn't I happy?

THERE WAS SO MUCH to arrange, even though Sir Edward and I had agreed on the wedding being a quiet and modest occasion. Lady Bateman, who'd promised to "see to everything," sent missives from Bath each day asking about flowers, guests, dainty dishes. Acquaintances of Sir Edward whose names I barely knew had their wives write notes to me. And I was obliged to answer these with thanks, although I knew what those women must say of me behind my back.

I'd had a desk set up in the parlor, so I could stare out the window across the grounds while I worked. I'd been productive today. It was easier to make headway when Sir Edward was in London on business. The sun was setting over Great Barr, bringing a hard day of harvesting to a golden end. If only there was a pond at Great Barr Hall to reflect the sky. I did miss the Thorp Green one a little. I'd never have my ornate fountain now.

A rap at the door. One of Great Barr's innumerable servants.

"I'm busy," I called.

"But, madam, your daughter is here," said the maid.

My daughter? Bessy and Mary were such a pair to me now that when she spoke in the singular, I could only think it was Lydia. But why? I had sent her and her actor husband money enough for now, hadn't I?

"Should I send her in, ma'am?" she asked, but she didn't wait for an answer.

"Mama."

I blinked. This wasn't Lydia but my little Mary, and she didn't look so little at all. She was standing taller and wearing new clothes that I certainly hadn't paid for—a deep jade riding jacket with a skirt in a red-and-green tartan.

"Are you well, Mama?" she asked. "You look unhappy."

"Unhappy? No," I said, standing and scraping back my chair. "I am surprised. How did you get here?"

She couldn't have been in another stagecoach or walked very far. Her hair was perfect, pinned high and shining almost as brightly as Lydia's for all it was that awkward middling color.

"Uncle William brought me in his carriage. But he doesn't wish to come inside," she added.

I hadn't been planning to offer.

"Why are you here?" I asked.

Mary gulped. So she was nervous too, for all her fine airs and new gown.

"Should we sit?"

She nodded.

We dropped down side by side on the divan, only our skirts touching.

"Mother," she said, with more formality than her usual "Mama." "I am going to be married. In three weeks."

"*You?*" She didn't like that so I moderated my tone. "You are very young, Mary."

"I am twenty years old."

"And what if I——?"

"Uncle William and Uncle Charles say you must not stand in my way. That you are to sign, or have your lawyer sign, whatever documents they give you."

"I see." Another daughter launching herself into the world without so much as my blessing. "Who is he, your bridegroom?"

"His name is Henry Clapham. His is the family near Keighley. They own those Yorkshire paper mills."

Ah, these stupid girls and their Henrys. But Mary was making the opposite mistake to her sister, beautiful, foolish Lydia, who had married a penniless boy for love.

"You are William Evans's chattel, then? To be traded as he sees fit?" I asked.

Mary shook. "It is too late, Mama," she said.

"Not for you." I gripped her arm. She had been such a guileless, affectionate child. Had I been the one who taught her this harsh pragmatism?

"Auntie and Uncle have been good to me since Papa died," she said. "They have looked to my prospects when, as the youngest daughter, I might have been overlooked."

"They have used you for their own ends."

Mary's expression wasn't one of sorrow or fear. She simply didn't understand. And how could she? Her whole life I had sought to sell her to the highest bidder. I had raised her and her sisters as I had been raised myself: as prize pigs, on a diet of worthless promises and useless talents. And now I scolded her for going willingly to the slaughter.

"Do you love this Henry Clapham?" I asked, stroking her arm and trying a different tack.

She shrugged. "Did you love Papa?"

"I loved the idea of him, the idea of being married, and, of course, I grew fond of him," I said, my heart opening up as it did with music. "But, my darling, *that isn't enough.* We have as much passion as men do and full as much heart. Small morsels of affection won't be enough to sustain you. Your spirit will yearn to address another, to—"

"I am not interested in what drew you to Mr. Brontë, Mama," said Mary, twisting from me.

She was wrong, of course. I'd never had that kind of communion with anyone. Branwell had loved only the dream of me, had made the same mistakes I had years—decades—before, when I hadn't seen Edmund so much for who he was but for who I wished him to be. And I'd loved Branwell for a time only for what he gave me, not for who he was. Nor would I have such mutual understanding with Sir Edward now. There were the shadows of too many secrets across us. The ghosts of Edmund and Catherine would stalk our dreams and beat against the panes of our bedroom window at night. Lady Scott's name, now my own, would mock me in every mouth and in every letter.

Mary stood and walked to the desk.

I focused on the ceiling and the tremble of the crystals in the chandelier. They were perfect, vibrating raindrops, threatening to fall.

"Mama, I brought a letter for you." She picked up Sir Edward's ivory-handled paper knife and handed it to me along with small note. A message from her future in-laws? Or my sister?

Glancing down, I nearly stabbed myself at the return address:

The Parsonage, Haworth

Why now? It had been a long time since Branwell had written. Dr. Crosby had proved a loyal friend to me, keeping him at bay, and there had been a total silence of some months when even the doctor had heard nothing, and without a single payment required. But this didn't look like Branwell's hand, though I couldn't be sure. Funny how quickly you forgot details you once treasured.

I needed to breathe. Branwell was far away, at Haworth, and even if he was not, news of his reappearance if it traveled to Sir Edward would be confirmation of the story I had fed him, the story I'd almost started to believe myself.

I sliced the letter open and set the knife beside me.

Mary paced the room.

20th September 1848
The Parsonage, Haworth

Mrs. Robinson,

I did not think we would ever write to each other again and the Lord knows it pains me to do so now. But Branwell is gravely ill—indeed, dying—and I could not live with myself were I not to tell you and give you a chance to offer him some peace. He speaks of you often in his delirium, recites snatches of poetry meant for you, and sketches your face between pictures of the ghouls that torment him. Charlotte and I bid him pray, but it is your name he calls out in the night.

If you can come to him, do. I do not ask for your money. Or your pity for myself. But have compassion for Branwell and my father and my sisters. They suffer so to see the son who was our dearest hope reduced to this.

Sincerely, I remain,
Anne Brontë

I let out a low cry.

"Is something the matter, Mama?" asked Mary. "Are you well?"

"Mr. Brontë is dying," I told her, my voice cracking.

The pacing stopped.

"Poor Miss Brontë," she said.

Mary pitied *her*? The pain inside me moved from my heart to my gut. I doubled over but would not let myself cry.

"She hadn't mentioned he was ill, though Bessy and I have been writing to her," my daughter said from somewhere far away.

I couldn't look up.

"We will visit her, of course, once I'm married and live so close to Haworth. Should you like me to carry her a message from you?"

"A message?" I repeated, managing to raise my head. "No, I have no message for Miss Brontë."

She nodded. "Then good-bye, Mama. Uncle will leave the paperwork with the butler. Bessy and I will not be at the wedding, but I wish you and Sir Edward every happiness."

With that, Mary glided to the door, the plainest of my daughters all at once the finest, ready to cast off on the adventure that I had ill prepared her for.

"William!" I cried. "William!" I tumbled into the Great Barr stables, a carpetbag in my hands, my hair coming loose from its pins.

Two grooms I did not recognize doffed their hats and glanced at each other. Seconds later, William Allison appeared between them, a horse brush in his hand. Thank God it was the other coachman who'd taken Sir Edward to London.

"Mrs. Robinson," he said, gesturing to the others that they should return to stacking the hay. "Can I be of service?"

He wasn't in his livery. His forearms were exposed and dirty, with a stark line below his elbows where tan met white. He steered me out into the sunshine as I composed myself to answer, more concerned for my reputation than I was.

"I need to go to Haworth," I told him, dispensing with all explanation and clasping one of his hands in mine. "Now."

"The master has the carriage," he said, matching my bluntness. "And it's a fair distance from here t'there."

"We'll take a smaller vehicle, the dogcart, and travel through the night. Please, William. I need you."

He nodded grimly. "It's thanks to you I have this job, ma'am. We go where you command."

"Oh, thank you," I said, dashing myself against his chest. "Thank you."

"Give me half an hour to ready the horses, ma'am," he said, patting my back. "Then we'll be on our way."

WHY WAS I FLYING to Branwell? What could I say to him? There were long, lurching hours through the night to ponder these questions between stops at inns, where the horses had water, William his pipe, I mugs of small beer.

William and I didn't speak as we sat side by side in the dogcart, knocking against each other. I slept fitfully now and then, falling onto his shoulder, but I never saw him yawn, though he must have been helping in the fields all through the day.

I'd never been so impetuous and yet, for once, it felt as if I were doing something right. I hadn't helped Lydia or Mary. Edmund and I had never learned to open our hearts to each other. But perhaps Branwell I could save and bring back to himself. And in doing so, I would prove to Anne, and to Charlotte, that I wasn't such a monster, not so wretched a woman at all.

It was Sunday morning. Several church bells were clanging as we rounded the hill that brought Haworth into sight. High smokeless chimneys, idle for the Sabbath, low, slated cottages clinging to the steep streets, a miasma of rain and something thicker clouding the atmosphere, frizzing my hair and invading my throat.

We didn't need to stop to ask the way. William had been here before.

He drew the horses to a stop beside an inn where the ground was level and pointed up the main street. "Walk to the top, then past the church on your left. You'll see the parsonage, all right, ma'am—there's nought but moor beyond."

Good William. He understood. This was something I must do alone.

It was hard to hold my handkerchief to my mouth and lift my skirts to avoid the horse dung. The incline was sharp, knocking the breath out of me, though I could roam the flat country around Thorp Green or Allestree or Great Barr for hours.

What if Branwell were better and the Brontës were all at church? Or there had been a change for the worse and the family wouldn't let me enter his sickroom?

I turned left at the church as instructed. There was the parsonage just as Branwell had described it, with a sea of gravestones to the front and a vast expanse of nothingness to the rear. I knew that was the moor, the siblings' playground, where Emily would lose herself for hours. But the clouds were so low I could see nothing but gray. This might have been the edge of the earth.

Just then, what I'd taken to be one of the gravestones—short, gray, and drab—moved.

It was a woman.

I found a gate and picked my way between the memorials—six, seven, sometimes twelve names to a stone.

The woman moved toward me, without needing to look down to find her way.

We each knew who the other was as if by magic.

"Charlotte?" I said, when we were mere feet apart.

She nodded. "Mrs. Robinson?"

I nodded too.

I stared at her, trying to compare her to the figure who'd haunted my dreams and daydreams, and detect any trace of Branwell in the woman he thought of as his twin.

Branwell wasn't a tall man, but Charlotte was tiny. She must have been less than five feet. Her brown hair was fine and parted down the middle. When she took off her glasses to wipe away the rain, I saw that her eyes were dark, beady, and rimmed with red. As his had been, the first day.

"Anne wrote," I said, nervous around her, though she was even less imposing than her youngest sister. "I came to see Branwell."

"My brother was taken from us this morning," Charlotte said, meeting my gaze steadily.

"No!" I cried. "How?"

She tilted her head to survey me. "His body and soul could struggle no longer under the ravages that he and others had caused them, and he went to our Maker."

She looked surprised when my body convulsed, still more so when I slumped onto a nearby fallen tablet. It was edged with lichen. Each letter was a rivulet of rain and mud.

"He spoke of you to the last," she said, her voice strained. "But be assured that all writings and sketches from his hand which could be said to impugn your character are destroyed. All that I could uncover, at least."

"Thank you," I muttered, wishing she were close enough that I might catch her hand. "I am sorry that we are meeting only now and that you must think so ill of me. It seemed to me sometimes, from speaking with your brother, that you and I must be alike."

Her expression hardened. "We were both loved by my brother, Mrs. Robinson. There all resemblance ends."

Branwell had told me many stories about Charlotte. There was one that came to me now. She had been a small and sickly schoolgirl, decidedly plain, dressed in hand-me-downs and already wearing the eyeglasses that I had needed too but disdained for vanity's sake. For hours she had stood on a chair as punishment, surrounded by students and teachers too scared to help her, defiant in the face of one of those injustices that stay with us always if they happen when we're young. And she hadn't flinched, she hadn't cried, she hadn't faltered. She was more the boy than her younger brother. She was always the hero, Wellington to his Bonaparte.

I wanted to reveal my soul to Charlotte, ask about her schoolmaster and force her to see the parallels between us that she rejected, but I had come to help, not to argue. I swallowed my pride. "Can I go to him?" I asked. "I would like to see him one last time."

Her eyes flashed lightning. "Anne might have bid you come when he was living, but there is no need of that now. I cannot ask you to come inside—you whom my family speaks of as his murderer."

Murderer?

"Anne, along with our other sister, Emily, is prostrate from this shock. My father is a broken man. I must be their strength. As always. There is little joy in life for me now, except that which I take in my sisters' health and happiness."

"I never meant him harm, Charlotte," I whispered.

But had I meant Branwell any good? Had I thought of him at all? Even now, part of me was longing for Charlotte, not for him. I wanted her to accept me, embrace me—Emily too and even Anne. I longed for a place at their table, beside the three of them, creating new worlds, writing their own stories, yearning for more.

"Good-bye, Mrs. Robinson." Charlotte turned and walked back to the house.

The tears I was choking on now seemed less for Branwell than for his sisters, for the fact that they would always hate me. Charlotte would stand steadfast in the grief for her brother that I would be denied. She could wear the mantle of her pain with virgin dignity, while I was shrouded with shame.

The rain soaked through my hair and beat down on me. The invisible moors were howling, telling me I should have stayed away. My teeth were chattering by the time William Allison found me and hauled me up, as easily as if I'd been one of his children.

"There, ma'am, there," he said, holding my shaking shoulders. "We have to get you dry and then home. You've been through too much to throw away your reward."

LADIES IN GAY SKIRTS promenaded down the wide streets of Bath, picture-perfect against the limestone townhouses. Invalids, wrapped in blankets to protect against the cold, juddered over the cobbles in wheeled chairs pushed by nurses. Everyone was on their daily pilgrimage to take the waters at the spa.

And I was a bride, playing at gaiety for all of a few hours, less nervous than I'd been the first time, although, in the soft light of this city, at least, as fair.

A short, brisk walk before the ceremony.

The customary vows.

Sir Edward and I didn't linger over the "Death" part. That was the only way this could end—we both knew that now—with one of us outliving the other.

Then, as if by metamorphosis, I was "Lady Scott." In a few words, I'd assumed my dead cousin's name and set aside Edmund's, with all the relief that had come with putting away my mourning.

Lady Bateman had organized a gathering of men and women I did not know. They were kind and decorous and didn't dwell on my or Sir Edward's widowed states or the manner of our meeting. But there wasn't, as there had ever been at the weddings I had been to before, that hushed veneration at the part of the ceremony that was yet to come.

I was used to the wry smiles of men patting the groom on the back, the sorrow of the father as he bids his daughter good-bye, and the at times abject and visceral fear of the bride, who clings onto her mother as if her life depends on it, as if she were being set upon by pirates intent on stealing her away.

Tonight no one seemed to feel any need to hurry. Perhaps none believed that we had really waited. Maybe they imagined that Sir Edward and I were too old and so beyond such foolishness. Or maybe that they were sparing me—a woman who might have been free from "all that" had she only been richer, but was now bearing the yoke once more, so she could wear fine dresses and throw lavish parties at Great Barr Hall.

But at last the evening was over and I was in my room—or rather, Sir Edward's room, now ours to share.

My husband, dangerous, delicious bigamy to say the word, was still bidding Lady Bateman good night on the stairs.

"Edward!" I cried as soon as he was safe within and the door had clicked closed behind him. I flew across the chamber and kissed him with every ounce of passion in me, although his lips were dry and, up close, his skin was lined and sallow.

"What are you doing?" he asked, when I at last came up for air.

"Why, kissing you!" I laughed and leaned in again.

My fingers were working at the buttons down the front of my gown, which was ivory. How Edmund's mother would have shuddered at the horror of it. The idea that I might undress Sir Edward Scott was too fresh, too new, for me to attempt it and, besides, Lady Bateman's maid had laced me so tightly that I was gasping for freedom.

"But Lydia—" This time Sir Edward pushed me off, but at least he was gentle. "There are still lights."

There were still . . . Oh.

I scurried around the room, extinguishing each candle and turning the oil lamp low. Sir Edward couldn't make out that I was smiling at his silliness in the dark.

Branwell had seen me in every light and from every angle. He'd hitched up my skirts against the wall of the Monk's House, admired my naked body under the dappled sunbeams fighting through the thatch of George Walker's dirty old hovel, felt his way to me when all was black in the dovecote, which smelled of hay, cheap gin, and piss.

When the lights were all but extinguished and the curtains were drawn, Sir Edward began to undress, not looking at me.

He was shy.

I turned away too.

So many layers. I unbuttoned my dress and draped it over a chair, unhooked my crinoline, unlaced my corset.

Once I was down to my shift, I risked another glance at him.

This time, he was watching me.

"Lie down," he said.

I went to peel off my underthings but he shook his head.

Instead I came as I was to the bed. I sat, swung my legs before me, leaned back and gazed at the dark canopy above, its pattern indistinguishable in the gloom.

A creak.

A shadow looming over me.

Sir Edward's breath was warm against my neck, but still he didn't touch me.

"Are you ready?" he asked.

"Yes," I said, trying not to sound too eager. I arched my back in an attempt to reach him.

I needed proof that I was still alive, that this part of me hadn't died along with Branwell.

Sir Edward brought his hand to my breast, the linen still between us.

I gasped.

His other hand was pulling down my drawers and creeping up my thigh, but not for my sake. For his. He was feeling out his target.

Seconds later, he pushed into me. Quick, yes, but it didn't need to be good the first time, did it? With Branwell, that first time had been frenzied. It was only later that he'd learned— But no, I mustn't think of him now. *With my body I thee worship.* I had to prove that I was all Sir Edward's.

I wrapped my arms around his neck and my legs about his back, kissed a soft spot of skin behind his ear.

"Edward," I whispered, rocking with him. "Edward."

He stopped abruptly.

I drew back my hands as a reflex, although my ankles were still crossed around him, the hairs on my legs prickling in the cold.

"What is wrong?" I breathed.

"Lydia, you are acting like a whore," he said.

My heart, poor caged thing, did a death throe inside me.

My legs fell with a thud to the mattress.

"There, it is not your fault," Edward said, softening. "But you are *my* wife now. Lie still."

He brought his hand to my face and stroked me.

I willed myself not to cry.

Seconds later he thrust into me again.

The pillow was cold against my cheek, the sheet was folded too tightly around the mattress for me to grasp it.

One strike, and another, and another.

The black awning of the bed billowed above us three more times, then fell still.

Mama,

I hope your wedding was all that you wished for.

Mary's was a fine celebration, although her subsequent letters from Keighley give me some anxiety about her happiness. The Claphams don't live as well as she had hoped, and her husband is often absent. Auntie says she must give marriage time and that brides often feel so. Is that true? Either way, I will see Mary soon. In a little over a week, I go to stay with her. We will visit Miss Brontë together, if her sister Emily's health has not worsened. They fear at Haworth she will soon join her brother.

For now, though, it is hard for me to be the only one left. I had even taken to writing to Ned, but he insists on replying in pig Latin. My spirits were already depressed and then, a few days ago, Uncle Charles arrived, looking very grave. I thought it was on business, as he spoke with Uncle William first, but then the pair of them called me into the study and told me what was the matter.

Will Milner means to sue me.

I didn't understand at first what it was he could sue me for. Uncle Charles called it a "breach of promise," but when had I promised him anything? Then they read me a passage from one of those foolish letters that Lydia helped me write years ago.

Oh, Mama, I've never been the sort to blush or to agonize over mistakes in etiquette as girls in novels are wont to do. But just then I wished that the ground would swallow me whole. I couldn't defend myself or even blame Lydia. She'd known then nearly as little as me.

When I stayed silent, my uncles made excuses for me, saying I had learned from you or "hadn't been watched by the governess, that scoundrel's sister." And I started to say that it wasn't true and that Miss Brontë was the best governess we could have wished for.

They didn't care what I thought, but sent me away and conferred again, this time with my aunt too. And when I came back, Aunt Mary took my hand and patted it. She told me that she and Uncle could pay lawyers, and even the Milners if necessary, to make those girlish letters melt away. I need only trust them to advise me and I might make myself a fine match—with the Jessops' son, perhaps, who is due to visit next week.

But I could not help thinking, Mama is Lady Scott and has money now, mightn't she help me? And, were I to owe such a debt to Uncle and Aunt, what if I found myself unhappy like Mary, married to a man of their choosing?

Mother, I am frightened. I delight in the open field and the fair chase, in having no one before me, just a straight shot to the horizon. Must I give that up? Must I be hemmed in? Aunt and Uncle are good and kind, but I'd much rather have my freedom from Will Milner delivered by your hands.

Ever your loving daughter,
Bessy

22nd November 1848
Southampton

Bessy,

I cannot abide these dramatics. A girl cannot spend her life riding horses or clinging to the freedom of her youth.

You have two choices. If you wish to marry young Milner, do so. If you wish to marry someone else, take my sister and her husband up on their offer.

You will learn, in time, that your mother cannot fix everything. What would you have me do? Change the world and your place in it?

Your letter was forwarded to me in Southampton, where Sir Edward and I are seeing to the fitting out of his yacht. We will be in London briefly but will soon leave England.

We want to get into warmer quarters for the winter, and the yacht is to meet us in Marseilles.

I will send you an address where you can write to me. I will answer when I can, but you mustn't expect to hear from me for some time.

Very truly, your mother,
Lady Scott

EPILOGUE

December 1848

IT WAS QUIET ON the deck of our yacht, save for the lapping of the waves.

Sir Edward was in the cabin below. He'd been worried I would catch a chill. "Yearning for solitude again, Lydia?" he'd asked when I told him I'd wanted to read. But then he laughed and told me it was warm enough to sit out if I wrapped a thick shawl around me and placed another across my lap.

A seagull screeched overhead. I drew the packet toward me, although I'd read the contents twice since its arrival.

I'd turned it over, perplexed, and examined it by candlelight four nights before as Sir Edward snored in our hotel room. Something had warned me to wait until he was asleep to open it. Who would send such a heavy package all the way to Marseilles? Hadn't they cared for the expense?

Inside were six books, tied together with string. A gift?

One of the works was familiar: *Jane Eyre* by Currer Bell. I'd never finished it. I'd been busy with the wedding and so set the first volume aside, where all three still languished by my bed at Great Barr Hall.

I picked up the others. "Bell" again, but this time "Ellis Bell" and "Acton Bell." I flipped to the frontispiece of one novel and a sheet of paper slipped out.

A letter. A familiar hand. My Dr. Crosby.

I bent in and drew the candle so close to the page I was afraid it would catch alight. What I read there knocked the breath out of me.

In one novel—Agnes Grey—you might discern certain
similarities to the Ouseburns and our lives there—

The authors' names—Currer, Ellis, and Acton Bell—recall a
family who share their initials—

I thought it best to write, to warn you—

There was a buzzing in my ears as I drew the volume that contained *Agnes Grey* toward me. My shadow fell across the pages. The candle was burning low. I read in a furor, not caring if Sir Edward awoke to find me there on the floor. I had to know how Anne had made a mockery of us. Of me. Unfeeling. Ungrateful. Arrogant.

A twisted distortion of Thorp Green Hall swam before me. There was the lady of the house, "handsome, dashing . . . who certainly required neither rouge nor padding to add to her charms." She was indulgent and shallow, cared only for "frequenting parties and dressing at the very top of fashion." Anne had even repeated descriptions of me she'd included in her letter to Charlotte, all those years before. One daughter was "far too big-boned and awkward ever to be called pretty." The other, a flirt, "knew all her charms, and thought them even greater than they were."

No Georgie, calling out for water. No sweet Mary, who'd loved Miss Brontë and cried for a week when she left us. Anne had excised Branwell entirely and replaced Edmund with a caricature of a straightforward country man, well humored and gregarious, who cared only for his horses.

Since then I'd read and reread her rendition incessantly, smarting at the injustice of it. And I'd read the other novels too. *Wuthering Heights*, strange and romantic as Emily herself, a work birthed on the Haworth moors, and Charlotte's *Jane Eyre*, which I owned was better, if self-centered. For hadn't Blanche Ingram suffered too? Or the first wife, the one Mr. Rochester had cast aside? Readers were so quick to lap up the sorrows of moping governesses when that was only one side of the story.

You are a poet, Branwell had told me once, although he didn't have to; he could have had me anyway. But he was dead, and unlike his sisters, he had left nothing of himself behind in ink other than a few verses signed "Northangerland" in Mr. Bellerby's newspaper and some worthless ramblings about me that Charlotte had burned.

Sir Edward's ring was on my finger, and my children were lost to me—to marriage, my sister, that world of men that Ned would soon enter and that I could never understand. As I sat there on the deck, trying to taste whether the water that splashed my face was from sky or sea, an urge rose inside me, as sudden as it was alien. It was the almost overwhelming desire to write a novel of my own. A story about me.

If the Brontë sisters could do it, why shouldn't I?

I'd sequestered paper for my belated reply to Dr. Crosby. It flapped in the breeze, so I held it fast against my knee. The inkwell was wedged between my feet. My pen was poised, dripping with what, for the pain it had cost me, might as well have been my blood. Plain, poor, and virginal, Charlotte hadn't even sampled half of it—the mewling infants, the cold marriage bed, the years of silence before death.

How had it felt that day at the beginning, when Branwell had arrived? I closed my eyes to bring the scene in the schoolroom back to me. Branwell laughing up at me through the window. Ned and the girls, young and spirited. Miss Brontë meek, beside me though she might have been a thousand miles away. Oh, and I had been a dead and shriveled thing, with one foot firmly in the grave.

I opened my eyes.

Already a widow in all but name, I wrote. *Fitting that I must, yet again, wear black.*

"What are you doing, Lydia?" asked Sir Edward. "I thought you were reading."

I jumped.

He had emerged from below and was squinting at me, haloed as I was by the dazzling sun. His face already looked ruddy against his white boating jacket.

"Nothing," I said, drawing a clean page above the first. "At least, nothing important."

The wind lifted my unpinned hair from the roots, massaging my scalp. A few black strands flew into my field of vision, as dark as they had been on my first honeymoon. I could almost believe, out here where the sea mirrored only the sky, that I was young and that it was Edmund who stood beside me, that we were only just starting out.

"Come here." Sir Edward walked to the stern and stared toward the shore.

It was early enough in our time together that I did as he said and barely even resented it.

"Isn't it beautiful?" he asked, once I was next to him.

I nodded, although the French coast was a haze to me, a dark and ragged scar across a watercolor awash with dancing whites and blues. There was a stronger gust of wind. My hair took on a will of its own, Medusa-like, and wrapped around my throat.

I struggled to free myself, and the page I had written on—my first feeble attempt at honesty—escaped my hand. Like a bird, it settled on the railing before fluttering to the water, which was darker when you looked deep into it rather than toward the horizon.

I glanced at Sir Edward. He hadn't noticed.

My words would be bleeding into the sea. But perhaps they had been foolish anyway. What had I been thinking? What could writing it all down possibly achieve?

There were women from here to England, crying over curtain fabric, scolding their children, and aching for change and love or, at least, excitement. And most, if not all, of them would be disappointed. Their fate and mine was too common to be the stuff of tragedy.

And do I even have it in me? I wondered, as Sir Edward pulled me close, smothering me against his chest.

Could I risk failure, rejection, and indifference?

Imbue our tale with dignity?

Live it over and over, line by line, and word for word?

And what fresh agony, to suffer through it all again, and find: I was not clever enough; I was not good enough; I was not Charlotte.

AUTHOR'S NOTE

I WAS ALONE IN my Brooklyn apartment when I discovered Lydia Robinson, although she wasn't named.

Elizabeth Gaskell's *The Life of Charlotte Brontë* (1857), the first great Brontë biography, had been on my bookshelf and "to read" list for an embarrassingly long time. While studying for my master's in nineteenth-century literature at the University of Oxford, I'd seen this biography cited time and again for its importance in establishing the "Brontë Myth." I'd just shipped my books across the Atlantic and made a promise to myself: It was time to read what I should have read then.

Near the end of volume 1, I found Lydia and Branwell, introduced by Gaskell with the (now very apt) sentence, "The story must be told." What followed was a cutting character assassination. The wife of Branwell's employer was described as a "wretched woman, who not only survives, but passes about in the gay circles of London society, as a vivacious, well-dressed, flourishing widow." She was "bold and hardened," a "profligate woman, who had tempted [Branwell] into the deep disgrace of deadly crime." She had even "made love" to him in the presence of her children.

What fascinated me was the gender reversal Gaskell drew readers' attention to. In this case, "the man became the victim," she wrote, equating the alcoholic, opium addict Branwell with the naive (and eventually ruined) maidens we find in many Victorian novels. Ultimately she suggested that the unnamed Lydia was responsible not only for Branwell's demise but for all the Brontë siblings' premature deaths.

I closed the book and, buzzing, turned to my laptop. My first "research" was chaotic. I found Gaskell had retracted her allegations and removed them from future editions, after being contacted by Lydia Robinson's (now Lady Scott's) lawyers. I'd been lucky that my second-hand paperback had been based on the original version. There was scholarly debate about whether the affair had happened at all. But most important, I learned that no one else had written the novel I was aching to write—no one else had even suggested that the affair *could* have happened without Lydia being the adulterous monster Gaskell made her out to be.

I had my project. I'd write a novel inspired by the themes of the work of the Brontë sisters, especially Charlotte—women's lack of choices, a feeling of being trapped, passion bubbling beneath the surface—but my novel would have a heroine that a Brontë novel hadn't seen before: older, richer, and sexually experienced, with children of her own.

So began two years of research and writing that transformed my apartment into a murder detective's bulletin board and, later, took me home to the UK to search for traces of Lydia in the country I'd left behind.

CONFESSIONS

So, what's true? I'm going to approach this a little differently with a series of confessions about what's *not*.

First, on the use of original texts. None of the letters in the novel are real. However, Branwell's poems in Chapter 3 and in the letters dated 1st

August 1845 and 2nd June 1846 are his. Anne Brontë's characterization of Lydia in the letter referenced in Chapter 1 is from her novel *Agnes Grey* (1847), which I also quote in the Epilogue. Charlotte Brontë's dialogue in Chapter 10 borrows a line ("There's little joy in life for me") from her devastating poem "On the Death of Anne Brontë" (1849), which she wrote in response to her youngest sister's death. Lydia also paraphrases one of the most famous passages in Charlotte Brontë's *Jane Eyre* (1847) in the same chapter, in her impassioned speech to her daughter Mary. Lydia says, "We have as much passion as men do and full as much heart," and Jane, "I have as much soul as you—and full as much heart!" In Chapter 19, Lydia fears that Charlotte and Sir Edward's wife will set fire to her bed, evoking Bertha Mason, the "madwoman in the attic," in Charlotte's most famous novel.

Meanwhile, Branwell's question to Lydia in Chapter 3—"Have you never felt that there is, or ought to be, something of you beyond you?"—is indebted to Cathy's famous plea to Nelly in Emily Brontë's *Wuthering Heights* (1847): "I cannot express it; but surely you and everybody have a notion that there is or should be an existence of yours beyond you." And Lydia's fear of being haunted by Edmund and Catherine in Chapter 20 mirrors the narrator Lockwood's paranormal experiences when sleeping at Wuthering Heights.

Eighteen letters written by Lydia to her business agent in 1847 and 1848 survive in the archives at the Brontë Parsonage Museum in Haworth. From these I took her sign-off, "Yours very truly," in the letters from her throughout my novel.

Second, there is no evidence the Robinson family owned a horse named Patroclus, but every other character in my novel, whether human or animal, is real. I started with secondary accounts—including biographies of the Brontës by Lynne Reed Banks, Juliet Barker, Edward Chitham, Daphne du Maurier, and more—but soon moved on to primary sources.

Digitized census records were key for understanding the Robinsons, their servants, and their neighbors and led to my solving many mysteries. I discovered, for instance, that the Sewells—assumed to be husband and wife by other Brontë enthusiasts, including Daphne du Maurier in her *The Infernal World of Branwell Brontë* (1961)—were in fact siblings. In my novel, for clarity, the sister is referred to as "Miss Sewell," although as housekeeper, she was known as "Mrs."

Supplementing the census information was an incredible and improbable resource—over sixty years of journals recording "births, marriages, deaths and sundries" in the Great and Little Ouseburn area, kept by local carpenter George Whitehead (1823–1913). These were published in 1990 as *Victorian Ouseburn: George Whitehead's Journal*, thanks to the scholarship and fund-raising efforts of the late local historian Helier Hibbs and his army of volunteers. Whitehead's blunt entries helped me establish the roles of various Thorp Green servants, not all of whom made it into the final draft of the novel (there were so many Williams and Ann[e]s). But he also at times had a flair for the dramatic. Of the younger Lydia's elopement, for instance, he wrote: "Miss Lydia Robinson made her exit with Henry Roxby (a playactor) Monday morning, Oct 20th. They went to Gretna Green and got married that night. She was a fortnight turned 20 years that day. A bad job 1845."

Third, there is no evidence the Robinsons were suffering from financial difficulties. I was lucky enough to be able to look through the account book mentioned in Chapters 9, 15, and 16 of my novel (this is also in the archives at the Brontë Parsonage Museum in Haworth), and the numbers seemed healthy, although I don't pretend to be an expert on nineteenth-century finances.

Edmund's gambling was suggested to me by his love of horses, attested by Anne Brontë's depiction of the Murray family in *Agnes Grey* (1847) and by the life of Edmund and Lydia's son, Ned. A keen hunter, Ned died at only thirty-seven years old, along with several other sportsmen, two ferrymen, and several horses, in a ferry accident at Newby Park in Yorkshire, which received attention across national and sporting press.

The family's other problems and tragedies are all real. Georgiana died. The younger Lydia eloped. Bessy *was* sued for breach of promise by a Mr. Milner. But I made an assumption about *which* Mr. Milner, choosing the oldest of a local family with sons, despite his unfortunate name—William. Bessy went on to marry another William—William Jessop—a business connection of her uncle William Evans (keeping these Williams straight?).

There is even some slight evidence that Lydia senior had to put up with a difficult mother-in-law. In one of the letters to her agent in 1848, Lydia wrote that Elizabeth Robinson, here referred to as "grand-mamma," had been "exceedingly angry" when she tried to dismiss Tom Sewell. From this seed sprouted the animosity between Lydia, the Sewells, and Edmund's mother, which fuels several subplots in the novel.

Fourth, there is no extant evidence about Dr. John Crosby's sexuality. He was well loved in Great Ouseburn, as demonstrated by the beautiful and prominent memorial to him you can still read in St. Mary's church. It concludes:

> *His universal kindness*
> *Professional ability benevolent*
> *Disposition and active usefulness*
> *During a residence here of 30 years*
> *Warmly endeared him*
> *To a large circle of friends*
> *Who deeply lament*
> *His sudden removal*

An even longer eulogy appears on the obelisk that marks his grave in the churchyard. Despite becoming a widower at age twenty-eight, he never remarried, although he appears to have had the resources to support siblings, nephews, and nieces. According to Branwell, he acted as a go-between following the end of the Brontë/Robinson affair. This has led some scholars to suggest that Dr. Crosby was a second victim of the femme fatale, Lydia. This didn't fit with my vision for the novel, and so I conceived of Dr. Crosby as Lydia's one true friend, sympathetic to her attraction to Branwell due to secrets of his own.

Branwell and Dr. Crosby were both Freemasons, suggesting a basis for their intimacy. Branwell even held office at the Lodge in Haworth. During my visit to Yorkshire, I noticed that the quote on Edmund's memorial plaque in Holy Trinity Church ("When the shore is won at last, Who will count the billows past?") was from a poem in John Keble's *The Christian Year* (1828) for St. John's Day—an important milestone in the Masonic calendar. And so I made the local Freemasons' Lodge (a room above an inn in York) the center of the educated Great and Little Ouseburn men's social lives, from which Lydia is naturally excluded.

THE AFFAIR

What, then, about the all-important question: Did Branwell and Lydia conduct an affair? Generations of Brontë academics have tried to answer this question, and I'm happy to offer a perspective.

Branwell wrote to a friend, "My mistress is damnably too fond of me," in May 1843, and by that November, he claimed to have a lock of her hair (the inspiration behind the events of Chapter 7 in my novel). *Something* caused Anne Brontë to resign on 11th June 1845 (Chapter 12) and Edmund Robinson to dismiss Branwell by letter on 17th July 1845 (Chapter 13). Following this, it seems certain that Branwell told the Brontë family that he and Lydia had an illicit relationship and likely that the coachman, William Allison, took news of Edmund Robinson's death to Haworth in 1846 (Chapter 15). We also know for sure that Edmund's will did not preclude Lydia's remarriage (you can read the document in the archives at the Brontë Parsonage Museum), although Branwell told his family that it did. The conclusion? Branwell, Lydia, or both of them lied.

Key to the debate about the affair has been tracing the movements of all parties in June and July 1845. Why was Branwell alone at Thorp Green Hall, rather than with the Robinsons, as usual, in Scarborough, or home with the Brontës in Haworth? My novel provides a tentative solution. The opening of the railway line between York and Scarborough—a huge public spectacle, with plenty of celebratory champagne—was a potential connector between the lovers in this crucial period and one that felt in keeping with my characters, given Branwell's interests in locomotives and drinking.

Brontë's Mistress is a work of fiction. I don't pretend that it records what happened between Lydia and Branwell, but given the facts at our disposal, it imagines what *could* have happened.

LOOSE ENDS

Finally, a few notes on what happened next to some of the main characters after the end of my novel.

The fates of the Brontë siblings are well known. After Branwell's death in September 1848, Emily's and Anne's followed in quick succession, on 19th December 1848 and 29th May 1849, respectively. Charlotte enjoyed literary celebrity when her identity became known and lived until March 1855, when she died in the early stages of pregnancy. The Reverend Brontë outlived all his children. He died in 1861.

Lydia and Sir Edward were married for only three years, meaning Sir Edward didn't live to hear Mrs. Gaskell's allegations against his wife. He died at Great Barr Hall on 27th December 1851, leaving Lydia (Lady Scott) a widow once more. In his will, he left her an annuity of £600 a year, a house in London, and the family diamonds. His sons inherited the rest of his property. Lydia herself died, aged fifty-nine, in London on 19th June 1859.

The younger Lydia had two sons with her actor husband, Henry Roxby. The pair moved from city to city due to his career, presumably

under somewhat straitened circumstances, given Edmund's excision
of them from his will. At some point, Lydia too was widowed, as she
married a Henry Lincoln Simpson in Islington in 1877. Her first son
was a journalist who never married. Her second immigrated to Brooklyn. He and several of his descendants are buried in Evergreens Cemetery, not far from my current apartment.

Bessy's lot seems to have been the happiest of the three sisters. She
and her husband, William Jessop, enjoyed considerable wealth and
lived in Butterley Hall in Ripley, Derbyshire. They went on to have five
children and eventually retired to the Isle of Wight, where William was
vice commodore of the Royal Victoria Yacht Club. They are buried together in Ryde Cemetery.

Mary was widowed in the seventh year of her marriage, when her
husband, Henry Clapham, was only twenty-eight. She and her one
daughter continued to live with her father-in-law until she married her
second husband, Reverend George Hume Innes Pocock, in 1862. She
had no further children and died in Florence in 1877.

Ned's early death is described above. Following this, Thorp Green
Hall was sold to the Thompson family.

ACKNOWLEDGMENTS

WHEN I BEGAN TO work on the novel that would become *Brontë's Mistress*, I had no idea I'd end up with as many people to thank as I did characters. Writing can be a lonely pastime, but writing this novel has brought me closer to so many people. I am grateful to you all.

First and foremost, thank you to my editor, Daniella Wexler, and my agent, Danielle Egan-Miller, for bringing this novel into the world with me. I couldn't have asked for better guides. Thank you too to the wider teams at Atria Books and Browne & Miller Literary Associates for transforming my manuscript into a book. Special thanks to Ellie Roth and Loan Le for fielding my many emails!

Thank you to the scholars, alive and departed, whose work was invaluable to me in researching this novel—especially to Helier Hibbs, dedicated local historian of the Ouseburn area; Juliet Barker and Edward Chitham, Brontë academics; Mick Armitage, blogger and Brontë fanatic; Richard Horton, chronicler of Yorkshire graveyards; and Daphne du Maurier, whose novels and biography of Branwell inspire me with their scholarship and humanity. Thank you too to Julian Crabb, chairman of the Poppleton History Society, and to Deborah at Poppleton Library, who furnished me with information on the poetry of the curate,

Edward Greenhow, which references Edmund Robinson, and to Neil Adams, archive assistant at the Borthwick Institute for Archives, for his investigation into the York Medical Society.

Thank you to those I met on my Yorkshire pilgrimage, including Sarah Laycock and the team at the Brontë Parsonage Museum in Haworth; Margaret and Dave Hillier, who invited me into their home to have tea in Dr. Crosby's living room; the staff at Saint Ethelburga's School, which is on the site of the former Thorp Green Hall; and the Reverend Sarah Feaster and her congregation (including Mick Lofthouse, June Sanderson, and Alison Smith).

Thank you to my prompt and thoughtful past and present beta readers—Alexandra Da Cunha, Elizabeth (Lily) Barker, Kathleen Flynn, Valerie Gatignon, Alec Macdonald, Alison Pincus, Kathryn (Katy) Moyle, Emily Rutherford, Raya Sadledein, and Henry Ward.

Thank you to my two writers' groups for critiquing this novel and others—the "Panera Collective" (Sarah Archer, Adina Bernstein, Megan Corrarino, Christina Cox, Joe Fisher, Harry Huang, Virginia Kettles, Vicki Kleinman, Sara Lord, David Marino, Alexander Milne, Lindsey Milne, G. M. Nair, Boyd Perez, Sophie Schiller, and Karen Sesterhenn) and my historical fiction group (Gro Flatebo, Barbara Lucas, Laura Schofer, and Susan Wands). And thank you to my fellow writers Kiri Blakeley and Leanne Sowul for their critiques, companionship, and advice.

Thank you to Jon Steel, John O'Keeffe, and the WPP Fellowship for launching me on a career path that expands, rather than strangles, my creativity, and to my colleagues for their encouragement and support through the years.

Lastly, thank you to my family for your love and assistance. Thank you to my father, Kevin Austin, and to my sister, Siobhán Austin (the first captive audience for my stories). Above all, thank you to my mother, Alison Austin, for being my tireless research partner on this project. You are a historian as dedicated to discovering the knowable as I am to creating from the unknowable. It will take more than the Atlantic to divide us.

ABOUT THE AUTHOR

FINOLA AUSTIN, ALSO KNOWN as the Secret Victorianist on her award-winning blog, is an England-born, Northern Ireland–raised, Brooklyn-based historical novelist and lover of the nineteenth century. By day, she works in digital advertising. Find her online at www.finolaaustin.com and www.secretvictorianist.com.

Brontë's Mistress

FINOLA AUSTIN

This reading group guide for Brontë's Mistress provides an introduction, discussion questions, ideas for enhancing your book club, and a Q&A with author Finola Austin. The suggested questions are intended to help your reading group find new and interesting angles and topics for your discussion. We hope that these ideas will enrich your conversation and increase your enjoyment of the book.

INTRODUCTION

YORKSHIRE, 1843: Lydia Robinson—mistress of Thorp Green Hall—has recently lost both her youngest daughter and her mother. Now, with her teenage girls rebelling, a hateful mother-in-law breathing down her neck, and her marriage grown cold, Lydia is a ghost in her own home, encaged in corsets and curtains. A taste of freedom arrives with her son's handsome new tutor, Branwell Brontë—brother of her daughters' governess, Anne, and of the aspiring writers Charlotte and Emily. A soulful, temperamental poet nearly half Lydia's age, Branwell is sensuous and alive one minute and miserable the next, wasting away in the shadow of his talented sisters. Soon, Branwell and Lydia find a dangerous match in each other, spinning a vortex of passion and peril that threatens to consume everything she has built.

Deliciously rendered and captivatingly told, *Brontë's Mistress* skillfully reimagines the illicit affair that has divided Brontë enthusiasts for generations, giving voice to the woman accused of destroying literature's most beloved family.

TOPICS & QUESTIONS
FOR DISCUSSION

1. On page 51, Lydia Robinson remarks, "How funny it is that men and women struggle as they die, but few of us kick or scream as we are lowered alive into our tombs." How would you describe Lydia's state of mind at the start of *Brontë's Mistress*?

2. What is Lydia's relationship with her daughters like? Why do you think that she is often critical of them? On page 80, she pens, "Motherhood was about offering truth, not comfort. For all it still tugged at my heartstrings to hear her cry so, Lydia needed to leave behind her childish notions. And I must be the one to disabuse her." Why does the elder Lydia feel that it's her duty to do so? Do you agree with her (taking into account the historical context)?

3. Lydia feels strongly about her daughters' marriage prospects and remarks on page 90, "I would take action and defend them from a woman's worst fate—to be extraneous and unneeded." Given that this is Lydia's greatest fear, how does this worry drive her actions and affect her decisions throughout the novel? Does she ever become "extraneous"? Do the Brontës?

4. Women throughout history are often cast as the temptress when they engage in sexual relationships outside of wedlock. What famous examples of this can you think of? How is this portrayed in *Brontë's Mistress*? Is more of the burden for the affair put on Lydia than it is on Branwell? Do you believe that Edmund's emotional

distance from Lydia played a role in her affair, and if so, does any of the burden fall on him?

5. A great deal of Lydia's focus revolves around what is economically safe and savvy for herself and her family. Why do you think she engages in this affair with Branwell, given all the risks to her financial well-being and societal status?

6. On page 136, Lydia says to Anne Brontë, "You never had your chance. . . . And, now, look at the life you are forced to lead—you and your sisters. You must choose between being a drudge or a burden." Do you think Lydia is being harsh or truthful here? Are we meant to sympathize with her? Did writing novels offer a third alternative path to the Brontë sisters? Do female main characters have to act a certain way for readers to sympathize with them?

7. Why do you think Lydia is so fascinated with Charlotte?

8. How would you characterize Lydia's relationship with Marshall? Compare Marshall to Lydia's own mother (as we're told) or to Lydia and her daughters' relationship. Do you think there is anything romantic and/or sexual in their connection?

9. Before Lydia travels to Allestree Hall, she says on page 245, "Sir Edward might be saving me, but I would not abdicate my power. I could not allow myself to make the same mistakes again." In what way did Lydia abdicate her power in past relationships? How does she work to change that dynamic when she's with Sir Edward? Do you think she's successful in keeping her power?

10. Women have more options today than in Victorian times. But do you think there is still undue pressure on women in romantic, sexual, or economic relationships? Do some aspects of Lydia's experience apply to women today?

11. Consider Lydia's relationship with Dr. Crosby. Why do you think he shares with her the fact that he's attracted to men? How does

their relationship grow over the course of the novel, and how is it unique from any of the other relationships in Lydia's life?

12. Lydia's affair with Branwell has been historically characterized as bringing down the entire Brontë family. Having read this novel, do you believe that to be true? Why do you think this blame has been laid at Lydia's feet?

13. Did Lydia's encounter with Charlotte go the way you expected it would? Lydia writes, "The tears I was choking on now seemed less for Branwell than for his sisters, for the fact that they would always hate me" (page 286). Why do you think Charlotte's rejection of Lydia affected her so much? Do you think she feels closer to the Brontë sisters than to Branwell by this point? Why?

14. What do you think of the ending and Lydia's "almost over-whelming desire to write a novel of my own. A story about me?" (page 296)? In what ways was her own story told for her in the past? How did her tangential relationship with the Brontë sisters inspire this? What stories of real women from the past may be lost to us?

ENHANCE YOUR BOOK CLUB

1. Read some of the Brontë sisters' famous works, such as *Jane Eyre*, *Agnes Grey*, and *Wuthering Heights*. Did you notice any references to parts of these novels in *Brontë's Mistress*? What were they? Was your opinion of the characters in *Brontë's Mistress* affected by your reading of these famous works? Conversely, if you've already read works by the Brontës, was your perspective on their family changed by reading *Brontë's Mistress*?

2. Read and reflect on other works where female figures from history or literature are cast as the main character—for example, *The Paris Wife*, *Mrs. Poe*, *Loving Frank*, and *Z: A Novel of Zelda Fitzgerald*. Consider how the retelling of their stories gives voice to women whose history and perspectives are often glossed over in a telling of history and a literary canon written almost entirely by men.

3. You can find the fully designed book club kit at finolaaustin.com/book-clubs. In it, you can read Finola Austin's travelogue of her visit to the grounds of Thorp Green Hall and see a map of the buildings mentioned in the novel.

A CONVERSATION WITH
FINOLA AUSTIN

How did you first become interested in the Brontës? What made you decide to tell Lydia Robinson's story?

I've always loved nineteenth-century literature. Charlotte Brontë and Charles Dickens were probably the first two Victorian novelists I read as a child, and in my teens, I raced through the works of all three Brontë sisters. After doing an undergraduate degree in Classics and English, I stayed on at the University of Oxford to complete a master's in Victorian literature. While my dissertation focused on sensation novelists Mary Elizabeth Braddon and Wilkie Collins, I also wrote a paper on Charlotte Brontë (particularly on romantic relationships between students and teachers in her novels).

It wasn't until 2016, though, when I was reading the first biography of Charlotte Brontë (by fellow nineteenth-century novelist Elizabeth Gaskell), that I came across Lydia Robinson's story. I was immediately fascinated—by Gaskell's assassination of Lydia's character and by what a contrast this Mrs. Robinson would be to many of Charlotte's protagonists. Brontë heroines are often poor, plain, young, and virginal. But here was a woman who was wealthy, beautiful, in her forties, and sexually experienced. I realized hers was a very different story, and one that I wanted to tell.

You've done a great deal of research in order to write this novel. Where has your research taken you, and what was the most surprising thing you discovered?

I spent a full year researching *Brontë's Mistress* before I began writing, and I went on a research trip to Yorkshire ("Brontë country") after completing my first draft. I detail a lot of my research in the Author's Note at the end of the novel, but some of the highlights for me were taking tea in Dr. Crosby's front parlor, holding Lydia's letters and Edmund's accounts book, seeing the wonderful statuette of a monk above the front door of Monk's Lodge, and, of course, visiting the Brontë Parsonage Museum.

A particular focus of the research for me was doing justice to the Thorp Green servants. I wanted to understand their roles in the house, but also who they were as people. These details really helped me to picture them as individuals with stories of their own and families at home, even when I wasn't able to include all of them.

It seems that you were drawn to a woman who was wronged by history's telling of her life. Are there any other such women in history or literature who spark your interest?

Lots! While Lydia was cast as the villain of the Brontës' story, many women have been wronged by history because their stories haven't been told at all. Women have often been confined to the domestic sphere rather than acting center stage in politics or standing on the front line of battlefields, but for me, this doesn't make their histories less important.

On page 83, Branwell says to Lydia, "Charlotte talks from time to time of the novel as the 'literary pinnacle of our age,'" and Lydia thinks to herself, "I'd always assumed my taste for them was confirmation of my feminine frivolity." How were novels regarded in the mid-nineteenth century? Did the Brontës' works cause novels to be held in higher esteem at the time, or did their fame come later?

In the nineteenth century, women were major consumers of novels, just as they are today. They read them in three volumes, borrowed from circulating libraries, or serialized chapter by chapter in their favorite publications. Perhaps because of this association with femininity, novels were often regarded as inferior to highbrow literature such as poetry.

Victorian novelist George Eliot (another woman writing under a male pseudonym, like the Brontë sisters) wrote an essay, "Silly Novels by Lady Novelists," in 1856, criticizing the formulaic genre fiction so many women wrote about and enjoyed. Her title clearly linked femininity to frivolity.

While the Brontës' works (especially Charlotte's) have always been regarded as a step above the writing of many of their contemporaries, I think even today we see a repetition of this pattern. When I've told people I'm writing about the Brontës, many respond to me by dismissing *Jane Eyre* and *Wuthering Heights* as "just romances" and "for women." While for me, Brontë's Mistress doesn't seem romantic, I don't see writing romance as lesser than other genres or writing for women as a weakness.

Why did you decide to make the dynamic between Lydia and her daughters a more distant one? Was that common for relationships between women in families at the time? What historical texts and examples did you refer to when shaping this relationship?

Attitudes toward parenting have shifted dramatically since the nineteenth century (in fact, the word *parenting* started to emerge only in the late twentieth century as theorists started to understand the formative nature of our early experiences). The Victorians engaged in many practices we typically turn away from today, including employing wet nurses to feed their infants and regularly using corporal punishment to discipline children. Lydia then might not have seemed like a "bad mother" to her contemporaries as much as today we might question her choices in the novel. With sons much more valuable to families at that time, due to women's limited options, it also made sense to me that Lydia might have a strained relationship with her daughters, believing that "tough love" was the right way to prepare them for the realities of their position as women.

I had two main literary models in mind here. First, Mrs. Bennet from Jane Austen's *Pride and Prejudice*. Mrs. Bennet and Lydia are very different in terms of temperament, but their outlook is similar: their daughters should seek to marry well, but be practical and unromantic about their prospects. The second model was a character named Mrs. Winstanley from a lesser-read Victorian novel—*Vixen*, by Mary Elizabeth Braddon. Mrs. Winstanley is a mother obsessed with her daughter Violet's size (similar to how Lydia worries about Bessy's figure in *Brontë's Mistress*). Braddon eventually reveals that Violet is five feet six inches with a 22-inch waist (she could probably fit into a US size 0 today). Braddon is clearly playing this for laughs. She's pointing out the maternal character's ridiculousness, but she strikes at a truth: when women are valued solely or largely for their physical appearance, mothers can and do become hypercritical of their daughters' looks. Even today, I know many women who can trace a direct line between their insecurities about their appearance and their mothers' own warped body image.

There are many letters throughout the book between the characters. Are these letters based on actual letters from the time? Are any of them the letters that the historical figures wrote?

None of the letters in the novel are real, though the poem Branwell includes in his letter dated August 1, 1845, is. Eighteen letters written by Lydia are extant and part of the Robinson Papers collection at the Brontë Museum Parsonage. I was lucky enough to be able to read these. They are business letters written to the agent Lydia mentions employing in my chapter 16. From these I took her distinctive sign-off, "yours very truly," and details about the honeymoon and the yacht meeting Lydia and Sir Edward in Marseilles, which shaped chapter 20 and Lydia's final letter to Bessy.

We can see from your novel that Charlotte Brontë originally published *Jane Eyre* under the pen name Currer Bell. Was it common for female authors at the time to publish under a male name? When was Charlotte revealed to be the author?

There are certainly many examples of women novelists from the nineteenth century hiding their identities by choosing to remain female but anonymous (Jane Austen's *Sense and Sensibility* was described as "by a lady" on its publication in 1811) or by adopting a male persona (the option taken by the Brontës, George Eliot, and Louisa May Alcott, who often wrote as A. M. Barnard).

What's unique about the Brontës was the huge level of public interest in discovering who the "Bells" were. Were there really three? Were they brothers? Sisters? A married couple writing together? Reviews were rife with argument and speculation about the writers' (or writer's?) gender(s).

Charlotte and Anne revealed their true identities by visiting their publisher in July 1848 (when Lydia is tending to a dying Lady Scott in my novel), but it wasn't until the publication of Charlotte's 1850 preface to a new edition of *Wuthering Heights* and *Agnes Grey* that most readers knew who the Brontës were. By then, both Emily and Anne had already died. Charlotte's characterization of her sisters formed the foundation of the so-called Brontë myth and has had a lasting impact on the family's depiction in popular culture.

The role of women and the expectations placed on them, whether by men or by society, is prevalent in your novel. Why is this a subject you wanted to explore in such depth?

I am a woman, and so, unfortunately, these roles and expectations are something that I (and more than half the population) have to face all day, every day. I feel it would be impossible to write a novel with a woman main character, whether set today or in the past, that didn't touch on any of these issues.

If it was indeed not Lydia who "brought down" the Brontë family, do you think any particular factor or factors led to their undoing?

The Brontë family's story is fascinating and tragic. The early loss of Mrs. Brontë and the two eldest sisters, Maria and Elizabeth, had a lasting impact on the Reverend Brontë and the four children who made it to adulthood—something I reference a few times through the course of my novel. There was extremely poor sanitation in Haworth, leading to many probably preventable deaths (just take a walk around the graveyard there to see the shocking gravestones with multiple names per family).

When it comes to Branwell, it is clear that he was troubled long before meeting Lydia. He'd failed in his dream of becoming a painter and had been dismissed from his job with the railway due to his excessive alcohol consumption. Blaming Lydia for what happened to Branwell (and the rest of his family) seems to me to be an archaic way of thinking. There's a clear gendered double standard in vilifying her for any sexual affair, and our understanding of the ravages of addiction is much more nuanced today.

This story is told as a first-person narrative from Lydia's point of view. What made you choose this perspective rather than, say, a third-person narrative? What do you think we gain with this access into Lydia's mind, and why is that important for the story you tell?

I always knew I was going to write *Brontë's Mistress* in first person. Charlotte Brontë's *Jane Eyre* is written in the first person, and my novel is in some ways an answer to hers. Jane is poor, plain, young, and virginal. Lydia is wealthy, beautiful, older, and sexually experienced. But both characters have limited options open to them just because of their gender.

Because Lydia has so often been blamed for Branwell Brontë's demise, I thought it was important for readers to understand her position (even if they don't always agree with her actions). Lydia can be incredibly selfish. For instance when any of her servants are ill, she thinks first of the inconvenience to her. And she can be blind to just how good her life is (e.g., she compares herself to a slave going to the galleys when forced to endure an awkward Easter luncheon!).

But many people, whether they admit it or not, spend their lives obsessing over the petty and failing to see the bigger picture. In the last chapter, Lydia says, "There were women from here to England, crying over curtain fabric." Curtain fabric isn't just curtain fabric: it's being trapped in a system where women have no property, power, or recourse to divorce and limited, superficial education. Flawed as Lydia is, I have empathy for her impossible position, and I hope others do too.

Do you have any favorite books or movies that inspired you as you were writing *Brontë's Mistress*?

I was of course inspired by the works of the Brontë sisters in writing the novel, especially Anne Brontë's *Agnes Grey*, which was based in part on her time working at Thorp Green Hall, and Charlotte Brontë's iconic *Jane Eyre*. Emma Bovary and Anna Karenina were important models for literary adulteresses. And I was also inspired by nineteenth-century American writer Charlotte Perkins Gilman's short story "The Yellow Wallpaper," and by the 2016 film *Lady Macbeth*, both of which deal with the psychological impact of women's limited choices during the Victorian period.

Do you have a next project in mind? If so, can you share anything about it?

I *am* working on a new book! It's also historical fiction, but set during a different time period and in a different country from *Brontë's Mistress*, which has been a fun challenge. In both novels, I was inspired by the true stories of real women, though in this case, my main character was an artist in her own right, unlike Lydia.